THE PARIS REVIEW BOOK

of People with Problems

Also available from Picador

The Paris Review Book for
Planes, Trains, Elevators, and Waiting Rooms

The Paris Review Book of
Heartbreak, Madness, Sex, Love, Betrayal,
Outsiders, Intoxication, War, Whimsy, Horrors, God,
Death, Dinner, Baseball, Travels, the Art of Writing,
and Everything Else in the World Since 1953

THE PARIS REVIEW BOOK

of People with Problems

⌗

By the Editors of The Paris Review

WITH AN INTRODUCTION

BY STEPHIN MERRITT

PICADOR • NEW YORK

www.picadorusa.com

Picador® is a U.S. registered trademark and is used by St. Martin's Press under
license from Pan Books Limited.

For information on Picador Reading Group Guides, as well as ordering, please
contact the Trade Marketing department at St. Martin's Press.
Phone: 1-800-221-7945 extension 763
Fax: 212-253-9627
E-mail: readinggroupguides@picadorusa.com

Library of Congress Cataloging-in-Publication Data

The Paris Review book of people with problems / by the editors of The Paris
    Review.—1st Picador pbk. ed.
        p. cm.
    ISBN 0-312-42241-5 (pbk.)
    EAN 978-0-312-42241-7
        1. Psychological fiction, American.   2.   Domestic fiction, American.
        3. Conduct of life—Fiction.   I. Title: Book of people with problems.
        II. Paris Review.

    PS648.P75P37   2005
    813'.08308—dc22   2004060249

First Edition: August 2005

10   9   8   7   6   5   4   3   2   1

Contents

꙰

A Brief Note
on Architecture and Interior Design in
The Paris Review Book of People with Problems

by Magnetic Fields
Troubadour
Stephin Merritt

The big problem, the one that keeps popping up in every story, is: missing women, or missing missing women, and in Charlie Smith's "Crystal River," even missing missing missing women. It seems everyone needs a mother, including a mother; instead, everyone has an ex. Torn from somewhere (always mother?) or somebody (always mother) we are left in the cold with a stick, some intoxicants, and maybe a fluffy animal. With never enough clothing, we have to express our bootless rage not through the second skin of fashion (it's too cold) but through the third skin of our decor.

Among this book's treasures of dreadful decor we find the contemptuous psychoanalyst's office in Joanna Scott's "A Borderline Case," a nightmarish room full of objects chosen for their symbolic weight, yoked in the service of proving the therapist's superiority to his patient. At the climax of a page-long description of this office, we learn that it is presided over by a bronze statuette of Galatea with a clock in its belly, as if the analyst means to say: You are mine, you exist only in relation to me, I will make of you what I want, as I watch time passing inside you, aging you toward death and the end of the session, when you will pay me.

The forty-dollar monthly rental on a single-wide trailer in Annie Proulx's "The Wamsutter Wolf" is more than such a room is worth to any self-respecting tenant, but if our hero had any more self-respect there would be no story. The trailer has pathetically insufficient utilities and comes furnished with sofa, table, bed, and a flimsy exercise bicycle. Everything is discolored, and tacky to begin with, and looking out on it all is an oversize elk's head. Nothing good could ever happen here, so someone has painted religious slogans on the walls "Love God, Love God, Love God," as if anyone could love anything in such an ill-decorated place.

In "The Dream-Vendor's August," Ben Okri's description of his protagonist's room is entirely negative. Ajegunle Joe has woken to find he has been robbed, so all we ever know of his room is what is missing from it: paper, ink, radio, pornography, and his favorite book, *The Ten Wonders of Africa*. For contrast we visit the dark shop of an herbalist, which is literally crawling with life, blurring the line between pets and decor: the walls are covered with snakeskins, spiderwebs, snails, and a lizard. A turtle putters around the floor. In the corner is a juju with feathers stuck to it, glistening. It is a place from which one might run screaming.

Wells Tower tells the story of a dilapidated cinderblock house in "The Brown Coast," but the story is so intertwined with the architecture that I don't want to give it away.

Julie Orringer's "When She Is Old and I Am Famous" cuts between a dreamlike Florentine villa, in which one can stretch out on a yellow chaise longue, and our heroine's own apartment, described in shorthand as never having any hot water, for anyone, ever.

The cabin described in the framing device of Rick Bass's "The Hermit's Story" is snug and cozy, warmed by fires and lanterns and dogs, filled with hope and pleasant smells, all of which makes quite a contrast with the setting of the body of the tale: a dangerous alien landscape under ice, from where there seems to be no possible escape. We have brought ourselves there by accident, and we may not all return.

James Lasdun's "Snow" is seen from the eye of a child on Christmas Eve, who concentrates on whatever glitters (silver picture frames, golden hair tangled in a silver braiding device, melting snow) and so remains unperturbed at being surrounded by terrifyingly dangerous machines, including one that conclusively demonstrates the profound unknowablity of the world.

The heroine of Malinda McCollum's "The Fifth Wall" can't even stay inside her home because the walls, ceiling, and floor are moving closer. The alternative is Sam's Tackle Box, crammed with merchandise and stinking of bait, brine, and methamphetamine.

Norman Rush sets up his "Instruments of Seduction" mostly through interior design. His female seducer sets the scene with an erotic atmosphere of death achieved through lighting, the absence of timepieces, and government-issue furniture that makes her apartment look like a bordello.

"Random things, dolls and mirrors and bridles, all waterlogged," are all the townsfolk have left after the town burns in Denis Johnson's "Train Dreams." The house becomes just a highly undesirable campground where nothing will grow, and you can't really breathe, and everyone else is dead.

The ironically named Buddy, of Mary Robison's "Likely Lake," lives in a typical suburban house except that no one else ever enters it. Those he once loved are dead or gone, his girlfriend Elise never makes it, and the Connie woman has to stay in the yard. And what good are the cats? Buddy can't even tell them apart.

Charles Baxter's bleak blue-collar Detroit suburb "Westland," named for its shopping mall, is nearly greenless, with interchangeable houses. The garage is full of junk, and there is a "play structure" in the yard that hasn't been used for years. Activity at the house consists of tearing the play structure down, and drinking a great deal of beer.

In Miranda July's "Birthmark," "there were empty rooms in the house where they had meant to put their love and they worked together to fill these rooms with high-end, consumer-grade equipment. It was a tight situation." And the only action involves shattering glass.

Richard Stern decorates the lonely Malibu house in "Audit" with a bedside telephone used for speed-dialing the broker, and on the terrace, blue bottles hung by the deceased wife to be filled with sugar water for the hummingbirds. But the house's main feature is its distance from downtown Los Angeles, an anxiety-filled hour on the freeway.

The large Victorian houses in Elizabeth Gilbert's "The Famous Torn and Restored Lit Cigarette Trick" only matter as far as they either contain or do not contain Bonnie the rabbit, who is too big to be used in magic tricks (or is she?).

Frederick Busch's miniature "Widow Water" features a house that is all basement, a house where lives a little old lady (maybe the one missing from the other stories?) with her clogged old pipes. This basement is filled with junk and old firewood, "whatever in her life she couldn't use." The view from outside is of a house all dark except for one window showing a weak yellow light. It won't be long now.

In Charlie Smith's "Crystal River," a house is made for leaving. The train track runs just across the fence. The bed is a place of awkwardness. And even food preparation takes place outside anyway, apparently facilitated by a sink on the back porch. This house might as well not be there at all, and soon, it's empty. There is no indication that anyone ever comes back.

—Stephin Merritt

THE PARIS REVIEW BOOK

of People with Problems

✠

Joanna Scott

✠

A Borderline Case

THE ANALYTIC SITUATION

This is the story of K and B, analyst and patient; specifically, this is the story of their first session together, before K had cured his patient, "dispersed" B, as he'd say, helping him to become "more B than ever before." K loved B, and if K hadn't had such a highly developed *le-moi-peau* he might have become irrevocably attached to B "by cock, in mouth and arse" (B's description of his own furtive activities). But K attached himself to his pen instead, and for thirty years, on and off, through three periods of analysis, he listened to and recorded B's anxious, obsessional narratives. Instead of admitting that he loved him, he used B, turned his life into a notable if not groundbreaking case history. K took credit for B's achievements and ultimately for his happiness. B died a contented man, thanks to K, or so K would have it. And K died without ever once making love to B, neither buggering nor buggered by—a professional to the marrow. A prince. A lay analyst who believed himself a genius.

They met in 1953, when B was far less than he could have been, less B than B. He had a high-ranking post at an embassy in London at the time and had become increasingly adept at seducing young boys. Not boys who wanted him for himself but boys who wanted B's quid, boys on their way to a better life. "Escapades," as K referred to B's encounters with admitted distaste, discouraging B from supplying any graphic details, K stifling his own "clinical curiosity" because he feared that curiosity would make him B's accomplice, "an agent to his sexual prowling and practices." Though B was a "very narcissistic borderline psychopath," he was also a survivor, and if nibbling on the foreskins of nameless youths gave him a sense of purpose, K wouldn't interfere. Just as long as B didn't talk about it. K didn't want to know. "There will be time enough to hear all that," he told B at their first meeting, and for the next thirty years he diverted B whenever he began to talk about "all that," until there was no time left—B died of heart failure in 1981, and K realized too late that his favorite patient had remained a mystery to him, on paper a sharply defined borderline case but in K's memory only the shadow of a man.

1953. K is twenty-four years old, at the start of a promising career; B is thirty-nine. K allows himself a quarter of an hour between patients so he can review his notes, pour a glass of fine Scotch whiskey, fill and light his pipe. The houseboy is responsible for meeting each patient at the front door and taking him up in the lift; the secretary escorts the patient into K's office as soon as the sideboard clock has chimed the hour. Ordinarily, a patient finds K waiting by the window, his back to the door. Not until the secretary has left does he turn to face his visitor, revolving slowly, his leather riding boots creaking, soles scratching against the wood, the sounds magnified by the vaulted ceiling. But on the day B arrives for his first consultation K is still in his chair, the letter from the referring analyst lying open on his desk.

"A homosexual who complains of a theoretical dislike of homosexuality. Prognosis: poor." So why bother? K wonders wearily, his mind so bored by the conjecture that he doesn't hear the knock. Why bother about anything? Why work, why talk, why write, why eat? In moments like these K indulges himself with the patronizing boredom that only the rich can afford, a boredom that, when flaunted, gives a bored man immeasurable control over those who bore him. K, a Punjabi Muslim, has more than enough wealth to keep himself entertained, but he values boredom, understands intuitively that boredom is as necessary as hunger, and he relishes the power gained with a well-timed yawn. He doesn't need to work and didn't choose this profession in order "to secure himself a place in the human community," every man's ambition, according to Freud. He works out of indifference—rather, works in order to channel his indifference, presides over his patients as he once presided at his father's side over Punjabi peasants.

On this sultry August day in 1953, however, K is caught off guard. From the beginning B's case annoys him: a homophobic homosexual with doubtful therapeutic potential. K hasn't even had time to pour himself a drink. He looks up as the secretary knocks again, and a drop of perspiration slides into his eye.

B's first sight of the famous prince is of a thin young man behind a sprawling mahogany desk rubbing his fist against his eye. And from his side of the room K sees a blur, a watery ghost—uncharacteristically, he wants to see more. He rises abruptly from his chair and bumps his knees against the desk drawer, recognizes then, as the sharp pain travels along the nerve up his thigh, that this man B is extremely dangerous. B, despite the verdict from the referring analyst, already has the upper hand.

Not often in K's experience will a patient prove as witty as B, as daring, as "in the world," as B will say of himself, subtly proud of the intensity of his emotions, though long ago he developed a sardonic public manner, effective self-protection for a pederast who has worked both as a diplomat and as a coal miner. K, in contrast, swings back and forth between indifference and satisfaction, each day of his week organized carefully so that he can look forward to his pleasures without concern. B has never been able to plan ahead, much less to arrange his life so that he knows what to expect. His days are full of mishaps and coincidences, with few vacant moments for reflection. In a later session with K, B will compare himself to a small child abandoned in Piccadilly Circus, a child bumped and jostled, shoved, petted, squeezed, pinched, and pushed aside, a little boy without a sense of direction but determined to hold his own. B has taught himself to hold his own. K hasn't had the experiences that would make him B's equal. But K does have one advantage over B, an unqualified advantage: B may live more intensely than K, but K is more beautiful than B.

A polished diamond looks its value—the purer the stone, the more intricately it absorbs and refracts light, its crystalline surface suggesting to the human mind a fourth dimension, even the illusion of magic, as though, if we could see into the diamond, we would see the future. Young Prince K has a similar beauty: Like a diamond he looks his value; like a mounted, expertly cut diamond he is inevitably the focus of any social gathering, startling enough to take your breath away. Even if you don't love K you will love to gaze at him. By 1953 K has reaped much from his beauty, ascended quickly into the top ranks of his profession, a mere dilettante with a parasitical intelligence but a feast for the eyes. Perhaps his wealth has made prominence easier, but his beauty has made prominence possible. No photograph can evoke the immediate lure of the man in person. K's unique beauty rests mostly in the complicated dance of light upon his skin. When they know each other better, B will describe K's skin as "a lake of eucalyptus honey."

On their first meeting, as K moves from behind his desk, the heels of his riding boots clicking, his britches rubbing softly between his thighs, B gives in to the same passion that spectators lavish on movie stars. B falls in love with K at first sight, though he knows even then that he'll never possess him. K's beauty cannot be captured either by a stranger or by a loner—he is an illusion, a projection on a screen, all surface, a voluptuous imitation.

Still, as he extends his hand, B imagines drawing his tongue along the curve where K's neck joins the shoulder, sliding down the side of his smooth skin, feeling the heat of his testicles, inhaling the residual smells of urine, semen, sweat, soap.

K the healer. Eucalyptus K. He can read B. He knows what the man is thinking, the laconic pansy, a puff out for a joy ride. Dangerous? Not as dangerous as K himself. K will make B panic, will throw him off balance, will unnerve him, since B has already tried to do the same to K. K has a theory about people like B: "Instead of transference-readiness they tend to provoke or seduce the analyst into a tantalizing relation to their material," K will write, and though years later he will regret not involving himself "transference-wise" or "interpersonally" with B, from the beginning of the treatment he is determined to defend himself against seduction, not because of professional etiquette but because he considers himself too valuable for the likes of B, too valuable for anyone—with the exception of a prima ballerina, his fiancée—in ugly London town.

The men shake hands firmly, efficiently, and K motions toward a small oak table. He talks with new patients here before he moves them to the couch, first intimidates them with a face-to-face interrogation before he lets them spin on their own. But B proves too nimble for K—he walks past the table, sits at the end of the couch, crosses his legs at the ankles, and says, "Of course, you want to know about my childhood."

Without a word K takes a seat in the rattan chair by the raised end of the couch, the least comfortable chair in the room, his "working-chair," as he calls it, preferring it precisely because this chair is so uncomfortable. An analyst owes it to his patient to stay awake and alert, an effort not as easy as it might seem, since the ambiance of the analytic situation is so conducive to sleep: voices droning on and on, words blending like musical notes until the analyst hears only the enervating melody, his eyes close, his head starts to nod, he sags and eventually topples from his chair. Such a fall would make K the laughing-stock of the British Psychoanalytic Society, despite his good looks. Note-taking helps K to fend off sleep, and the chair keeps him from relaxing. No patient has ever found cause to fault him for inattention; he always appears assiduous if not entirely captivated, always looks as though he has an opinion about the matter at hand. Suave K, sophisticated K, will never be the object of laughter. He carries himself with an elegance that equals his fiancée's, a dancer with the Royal Ballet. Just like his future wife, K is virtually incapable of awkwardness.

B, obviously to K, would prefer to spend his time lying on beds, on chaise lounges and analysts' couches, torpid and engorged, like a boa that has just swallowed a small rat. He is an American. K despises Americans, a classless, cultureless people, their civilization representing the nadir of history. Yet he finds himself drawn to them, fascinated by these reptiles that don't chew their food. Perhaps it is a coincidence that in a later session B will recount a dream in which he shed his skin "just like a snake." Or perhaps K himself in some forgotten aside makes the comparison first.

With a manicured thumb K pushes the cap off his pen and records B's leading statement. Of course K wants to hear about B's childhood. Of course. "Affectless," K scribbles in the margin of the notepad as B lifts his feet onto the couch and reclines. K writes furiously, trying to keep up with B, while B describes three important experiences from his childhood. B is K's last patient of the day, so K doesn't bother to draw the therapeutic session to its normal close. Except for one terse comment to steer B away from the subject of perversity ("There will be time enough . . ."), he lets this arrogant Yankee talk until the supply of analytically pertinent (from B's perspective) and charmingly outrageous childhood memories has been depleted.

Finally, B licks his lips, parched from over an hour's worth of monologue, and falls silent. K exploits the silence, extends it, keeps B waiting for a response. A breeze ripples the edge of the window drape, the silky maroon color appearing almost fluorescent in the light. The flat spans the entire fifth floor, and by late afternoon the front room smells of exhaust from idling traffic on the busy street below. But this main room of the flat, the treatment room, faces the back, and the rich scent of the summer's second bloom of roses fills the air: Amber Queen roses, Pacemaker and Harriny roses—K can name them all because he himself ordered them. K leaves nothing to chance, designs his world as if it were a stage set. Horses, Scotch, and Muslim piety: These are the main elements, and everything else is filigree.

He breathes softly, and B begins to shift on the couch, bending his legs, holding up one arm and letting the wrist go slack, clenching his fingers, opening them, grinding his palms together. Then all at once he looks up with an expression less smug than before, eyes narrowed, corners of his lips turned down in a kind of pout, as though he is about to beg K to do something, to say something, above all to cure him. For the last hour and a half B has been trying to seduce K with his unconvincing attempt at free association, secretly inviting the young prince to test his patient's virility; K, however, will make it perfectly clear that B shall never earn a place on his list of pleasures. He keeps B waiting, pretends to be deep in thought while privately he gloats, enjoying his privileges as jury and judge. Only when B exhales loudly and swings his feet to the floor does K finally say: "What else have you rehearsed for me?"

It should end here. But right then B looks with such pathetic surprise, the look of a man who has been hurt time and time again but still doesn't believe in cruelty, that K can't help it—he reaches out and touches his patient on the shoulder to console him. Immediately he regrets it. With his hand resting on B, the muscles taut beneath his fingers, K is as helpless as B was a moment ago, unable to pull away, unable to convince himself that such contact has no lasting significance. *What else have you rehearsed?* The impact of his ill-timed comment has been lost; he is stuck to B's surface, on the verge of complete annihilation. In the few seconds before he is swallowed whole, K begins to discover the true meaning of panic for himself.

B TAKES IN HIS SURROUNDINGS

Among the many images in K's office B notices: a 4 by 6 inch etching of the Bridge of Sighs, a Cubist painting of a cityscape, a Giacometti-style female figurine on a side table, a diploma from the University of Lahore, a certificate from the British Psychoanalytic Society, a shelf with six ribbed tumblers and a decanter, a coke fireplace, a white polo cap on the hook attached to the door, a marble polo-ball paperweight on the desk, a felt blotter, an ornamental ink stand and fountain pen, three photographs—one of K as a teenager standing between a white man (his tutor, B assumes) and his horse, one of K with his father, one of K alone in front of what B recognizes as the main bazaar in Lahore (B has been to Lahore twice on diplomatic missions)—a stack of empty file folders, a desk chair on wheels, a small Persian rug, a sea chest, four oak dining chairs upholstered in red leather, an oak sideboard, a telephone, a bronze nude Galatea with arms outstretched and a clockface in her belly, a small table beside the couch, a box of tissues on the table.

IN WHICH B BOLDLY IMAGINES A CONVERSATION BETWEEN K AND HIS TUTOR

"Are there not Western nations, I might ask—excuse me for a moment, sir, I must give my Anarkali a sugar cube. Every afternoon I bring her a sugar cube. One day I forgot, you know, and I hadn't been astride her for two minutes before she threw me. Would you like to ride her? She's particular, my Anarkali, you have to win her approval. Here, you feed her the sugar. You're not a horseman, I can tell. Hold your hand flat, like this. You see, I'm supposed to learn from you, but maybe you shall learn something from me, too. They say I'm precocious. Do you want to hear the truth, sir? My father prefers me to my brothers and sisters. This is why I'll be your only pupil. And this is why Anarkali belongs to me now. She used to belong to our neighbor, an Englishman like you, but much richer—he owns the fields that you saw to the left of the road as we came from the station. We own the fields to the right. I wanted to ride Anarkali, but Mr. Brooks wouldn't let me near her—he thought her too high-strung and was worried that I would be injured. So my father bought her from him. Perhaps it disturbs you that my father has more than one wife? Perhaps you would prefer to travel in a taxi instead of in our tonga?

"Now, as I was saying, are there not Western nations more backwards than ours? Are there not Western nations, your own, for instance, where one religion is the state religion? And was not your Anglican faith founded by a monarch who himself had many wives? My father says that Christians and Muslims are cousins, much closer in kind to each other than either is to the Jews. The Jews don't revere Jesus, but we do. My father says as well that your country today is full of gentlemen farmers and gouty politicians who don't know—how did he put it? What a spade is called?

"When to call a spade a spade, that's right, thank you, sir. Your country doesn't understand humility. And yet you are needy people, my father says, and needy people are doomed. Look at the beetle there on my shadow. Simple creature. It doesn't know that it should be afraid. It thinks its shiny carapace will protect it. Your country is like this beetle, sir, a beetle on Allah's shadow. You fancy yourself invulnerable. Not you, I don't mean you. Your people. There is a difference, surely. Just as there's a difference between my brothers and me. My oldest brother, Jamsheed, you know how he would spend his time if he could decide for himself? Making pots and sharing a *huqqa* with other potters. He wanted to ride Anarkali, so I gave him the reins and stood aside and watched. Jamsheed mounted and dug in his heels, but she wouldn't move for him, so he beat her with a stick, and still Anarkali stood there as proud as the most beautiful mare in the Punjab has a right to be, and Jamsheed, he looked like a madman atop a statue. I had a good laugh that day, let me tell you. And I swear my Anarkali laughed too, after Jamsheed had dismounted and skulked away. She flattened her ears, she flicked her tail, and she started to whinny, like this—believe it or not, sir, she was laughing. What do you think of my Anarkali, by the way? You haven't told me. Do you want to ride her? You're not afraid, are you? Have you served your time in the military?

"I ask too many questions, yes, I know, it annoys my mother. Do you have a girl back in England? Maybe you will like my sisters. They're not as particular as Anarkali. It is a funny name for a horse, isn't it? Anarkali. I named her after the concubine of Akbar, who was buried alive because she smiled at a prince. I will take you to see her tomb, if you'd like. And then you will take me to London. Don't tell my mother. She believes what the mullahs say—that all vices come from the West. Not my father—he thinks you people are too stupid to be corrupt. So why are you here, you must be wondering? Why has my father brought an Englishman into his home to teach his son if he has no regard for your institutions? But it's not the institutions he holds in contempt, not your laws or libraries or hospitals or banks. He understands the importance of these in the same way that he understands the importance of a moneylender's gold. You are here to give us your gold, sir. You know, we put cream on our currant buns, we speak your language, we read your books. Yet we haven't grown careless. Look what happens when I flip this beetle onto its back. This is what is happening to you. To your people, I mean. My father says that the West is committing suicide with its own dagger. My mother says that Allah's foot is descending and England will be ground to dust. Like this.

"I hope I see London before there's no London left. Tell me about the taverns, sir, tell me what I should order for my supper. *Cold beef and a pint or two of ale, please.* Is this what I should say? Do I sound like an Englishman? Do you carry a snuffbox? Tell me the truth—do they really tie little girls onto the backs of circus ponies? Does the Lord Mayor eat curried cat's meat for breakfast? Have you ever seen a drowned man floating in the Thames? I don't want to go to London if I can't bring my Anarkali with me. I'll wear a surtout and Bucher boots and I'll ride Anarkali along the Serpentine Lake—you see, I know more than I pretend to know. I'll have an audience with the Queen, I expect. Will you teach me to play cricket?

"To be frank, sir, I don't entirely share my father's contempt. He has raised me to be one of you, and already I am a stranger to my own family. England is my proper home, though I've never been there. Someday I shall live in London, if the city survives the war. My father wants me to go. He wants me to go and after three years he expects me to return home. But when I go I shall never come back, I know in my heart that I shall never come back. I am as much a foreigner here as you are, and London is my only true home. Please don't tell my father this—if he heard of my intentions he would take Anarkali away from me.

"You may smile, but without her I would have no reason to live. I know I speak passionately, but that's how it is. Take Anarkali from me, and I will wither and die, just as our fields would if you shut off the headworks of the canals. So now you know why I fear my father. He demands much from all his children, though it's obvious that he prefers me to the others. Still, I have to prove myself worthy. He wants me to study economics, but I would rather be a poet. Maybe you would read my poems and tell me what you think? I compose my poems in my head when I am riding, and I write them down at night, after everyone has gone to sleep. I'm not interested in the science of money. A man who enjoys delicate food doesn't need to train to be a chef, so why should a wealthy man be his own accountant? My father says that after he is gone the bankers will try to take advantage of me. But I am too clever for them. Do you think I am clever?

"My governess—she was Irish, the daughter of a widower who worked as a groom, or who was supposed to work. Mostly he drank beer while his daughter took care of the horses. She taught me to ride. She said I was too handsome to be clever, that boys as beautiful as me are always dull. I don't think she meant it. She was fond of me and liked especially to comb my hair. Violet. That was her name. She taught me everything I know about horses. After she left us she went to live in Amsterdam, and for seven years she sent me packages of black licorice on my birthday. Last year no package arrived, not even a card. I wonder what has become of her. Someday when I'm a famous poet she'll find me in London, and she'll admit that she'd been wrong about handsome boys. She had so many freckles—she let me count them once, seventy-five altogether. She said that's how old she'll live to be: seventy-five. No one could handle horses better than Violet. She broke my arm—did I tell you that? So my father sent her away. Really, he dismissed her because I had grown too old to have a governess, and he didn't think her a proper influence for my younger sisters. She hadn't intended to break my arm. It was a game we used to play. She'd hold me by a wrist and ankle and turn as fast as she could while I flew around her above the ground. One day she lost her grip and dropped me. The bone came through the skin here, you can see the scar. She didn't mean to hurt me. I wonder if she has a husband. The morning she left us I asked her to marry me. Hah, now I consider myself lucky! What if she'd accepted? I would have been obliged to honor my proposal. Maybe you will marry one of my sisters and settle among us. But you Englishmen never settle here. You do your job, you hoard the profit, and as soon as possible you retire to your distant island. I don't mind, though, since I plan to accompany you when you go.

"All this that I tell you is secret, please, at least while we live under my father's roof. But many years from now, when someone asks you to describe your time here, you may report this conversation word for word, as well as you can remember it. You will remember accurately, won't you? Or do all imperialists have an imperialist memory? Will you represent me fairly? Because I think, sir, that in the future someone shall want to hear about me. I am a prince, after all, and you are a prince's tutor."

B's Proposition

There is a tavern, unmarked but not unknown, on the outskirts of Rye. Except for the tile roof rising above the tangle of holly, the tavern, a gray brick structure with stucco molding, can't be seen from the road. B wouldn't know how to give directions to the tavern to someone approaching by car. He prefers to walk there. Usually, he walks alone.

He begins at the railway station, walks across the tracks, past the jackdaws pecking at the gravel, and follows a raised path leading to a farmhouse. In front of the farmhouse he climbs over a stile and walks up a grassy slope dotted with sheep droppings. At the top of the hill he climbs over another stile. On the other side of Leesam Lane he follows a track that leads past an abandoned farm and the charred frame of a barn to a stream. He crosses the stream and continues through a small clump of trees and along the edges of several fields. Few people traverse this path, so it is up to B to keep the way clear. He carries a hunting knife whenever he walks to the tavern. In the early summer the journey takes him two hours instead of one, and his calves burn from nettles for the rest of the day.

At the end of the last field he goes through a gate and hurries past Flint Cottage, always with his hat pulled low over his forehead. He knows the owners, was on occasion their dinner guest, until he made one of his typical social gaffes, something about the hostess's hair, he can't remember exactly what he said but he does remember the glowering eyes of the woman. He hasn't been invited back.

In the meadow behind All Saints' Church in Iden Park B rests and takes refreshment. In summer he brings only a pint of strawberries. By the time he reaches the church the brown paper is always stained red, the strawberries inside warm and partly mashed. He lies in the grass, holds a large, misshapen strawberry by its green tuft, and lowers it into his mouth with his eyes closed. He eats all the strawberries this way, one by one, relishing the luxurious surprise as the seeded skin touches his tongue.

After he finishes eating he dozes for a few minutes in the sun. His large body always feels boyish and light when he wakes, like a feather on the enormous bed of grass. He has read somewhere that, according to the ancients, beyond the Pillars of Hercules the air is full of feathers. How close they were to the truth: Beyond the Pillars of Hercules lies America, a continent full of feathers. B, an American by birth but a stranger wherever he goes, is a feather, blown about, from time to time picked up and used to decorate a hat but soon discarded. Though he claims to be an expert seducer he rarely takes the initiative. Even now, he waits passively for some young boy to come along. What boy wouldn't pick up a handsome feather lying in the grass? B spends most of his life waiting. An expert seducer? As seductive as any ornament—and as useless.

After he leaves Iden Park, B follows the road toward Houghton Green and Appledore, then turns onto the footpath that leads through the holly into the tavern yard. Inside the tavern he sits at a round table covered with green felt and drinks gin. Despite its secluded location, the tavern is never empty—carpenters, lorry drivers, gardeners, and housewives stop in during the day for a pint and a game of dominoes, and the proprietor's children are always chasing one another through the room. On one visit a little red-haired nymph had met B at the door of the tavern. He'd bent down to kiss her on the cheek, but she had lifted a cane, tucked the curled handle under her arm, pointed the stick at B, and chortled to imitate a machine gun's rattle before she ran away.

Ordinarily, B stays aloof in the tavern. He enjoys drinking by himself in public places. At social gatherings, conversation dilutes the alcohol, and a man can't appreciate his intoxication. Alone, B can feel the gin taking effect, can enjoy the gradual increase of buoyancy until after an hour his body feels light again, not like a feather on the grass but like a feather floating on the choppy surface of a lake. Floating. B will drink until the midafternoon closing time, and then he'll make the long journey through the fields back to Rye.

"There is a secluded tavern on the outskirts of Rye," B says to K. "I'd like to take you there, someday." And K, eucalyptus K, finally frees his hand and draws back with an indignant jerk as though he has burnt his elegant, tender, noble fingers on B's shoulder.

THE CHALLENGE

K: "How come you are in such a mess?"

B: "Take me on as a patient and find out."

K: "For my own sake? No thank you, I have little curiosity about others."

B: "You are not going to refuse me?"

K: "First let us see whether we are the sort of persons who can work together."

B: "Then I'd better warn you—I have no unconscious. Now you're going to refuse me."

K: "I am not going to refuse you. Not yet, at least. First I am going to offer you a drink. And then we shall see what we shall see."

TEMPERATURE OF EQUILIBRIUM

K doesn't know yet, not after this first meeting, that B was a prisoner of war in Japan. K doesn't know that in 1936 B left the school where he was studying toward a law degree and went to work in a coal mine for a year. K doesn't know that in B's spare time, when he has no diplomatic obligations and isn't pursuing young boys, he is carrying out experiments on guinea pigs in a makeshift laboratory in his Marylebone flat. His purpose: to accumulate data on animal procreation. K would never have suspected that B has any scientific interest whatsoever. But over the next thirty years K will hear at length about B's significant secrets, his past addictions and his latest obsessions, as B continues to live with the same intensity that is so passionate and so destructive.

B will fall in and out of love, will be convicted of pederasty and spend fourteen months in solitary confinement, will lose his job at the embassy and devote himself to scientific research, will publish, and eventually will accept a teaching post at a major American university. He will dream, and K will interpret his dreams. He will confide in K, and K will give him advice, will help B to become more B than B until there is no portion of B's psyche untouched by K. B will become K's arabesque, the patterns delightfully intricate and always symmetrical. B will die without ever regretting K's influence or trying to tamper with the design. B lacks the power, if not the will, to design his own life, and he will give himself up to K. But after his death B will dominate K ("Nothing which has once been formed can perish," Freud wrote), will live on like a parasite, feeding off his host and eventually devouring him. Only after his patient is gone will K admit to himself that from the very first moment of physical contact he was obsessed.

It is the intimacy that makes this initial analytic session more important than any other, forcing K to make a commitment. Yes, he will work with B. He will work upon B. At the end of the session K announces that B does have therapeutic potential, that B might prove to be a valuable patient. They will toast to their new relationship.

K pours two drinks, holds his tumbler up to the light, gently tips the glass so the generous measure of Scotch coats the ice cubes. "Ice," he murmurs. "A luxury." Most Americans take ice for granted, but K, raised in the Punjab, land of fire and water, still considers ice something of a miracle. Ice is water in its purest state, especially ice taken from the tray of K's office freezer. K drinks only the finest Scotch and so insists upon the finest ice made with bottled Alpine water, snow water without traces of chloride, sulfates, nitrates, or ammonia, without traces of human sewage or industrial waste. Pure ice with milky threads at the center of each cube, pure Scotch the color of butterscotch. Luxurious purity. He raises his glass and motions to B, who does the same.

The ice cubes rattle in the glasses. It is important to drink Scotch chilled but not diluted, to finish the drink before the bulk of ice has melted. B drinks with admirable alacrity—not piggishly but with the quick, dainty sips of someone trying both to extend and appreciate a rare pleasure. As B and K drink, from time to time savoring the smell of the liquor, they discuss the artwork in K's office. B learns that the dancer on the pedestal is an original Giacometti. And the pastel cityscape is a Braque. During pauses in the conversation the men swallow in virtual unison, though B, the larger man, takes in more with each sip and finishes before K. He sets his glass on the oak table without thinking about the ring the condensing moisture will leave in the wood. K likes this about B. His nonchalance. B is no aristocrat, but K detects the vestiges of an aristocratic sensibility.

After they have scheduled a second session and agreed upon a fee, after K has escorted B to the lift and returned alone to his office, shutting the door behind him with such force that the polo cap falls to the floor, K feels unusually optimistic, despite himself. Yes, he'd made a mistake in touching B—his hand feels dirty, as though contaminated by B's perversity. He would have to redefine "the correct psychic distance" at their next meeting. But perhaps something had been gained from the brief contact. Perhaps K has established the foundations for a successful transference.

A borderline case. And borderline cases are the most challenging, K knows. How dreadfully easy it is to tip the patient over the edge, especially in the early, blundering phases of the analysis. He must be careful with B, must initially withhold interpretation. Let B do the work. Let B work for him. There is potential here, it's clear to K that there is potential. He stares at B's glass, recalling, without the help of his process notes, B's lengthy narrative, sinks so deeply into revery that he doesn't hear the six chimes of the Galatea clock and doesn't start preparing himself for the photo session with his fiancée. There is nothing further from his mind than his fiancée right now. He wants to savor this moment. As the nuggets of ice melt into the puddle of lemon-tinted liquid, K's elation grows.

Annie Proulx

❈

The Wamsutter Wolf

Buddy Millar was the kind of driver who avoided traveling on a main road with other cars. This distaste for sharing the highway often took him rough-wheeling across the prairie or into a labyrinth of faded gravel tracks. Some of these roads were shortcuts but most were long, and a few were serious bad dirt.

He had grown up thirty miles from Greybull in a hamlet without traffic lights and learned to drive at age eight on the perimeter roads of his parents' sugar-beet farm.

An hour after his high-school graduation Buddy's father handed him a beer and said, "Well, what's it goin a be—college or a job?"

"Job," Buddy said.

The shining light in the family was his cousin Zane, a wildlife biologist assigned to Denali National Park. He came back to Wyoming every year at Thanksgiving to see family. At thirty-eight he was still single, and Buddy, who didn't like him, thought he might be queer. He kept looking for telltale signs but Zane was a good actor. His "area of specialty," as he called it in a supercilious tone, was wolves, although earlier he had worked with tropical fruit bats. He subjected the family to lectures on wolf behavior, wolf physiology, crimes against wolves. At Christmas he sent cards featuring wolves leaping through the snow. Buddy's mother, during one of Zane's visits, had said something about how wonderful it was that Zane was helping preserve the balance of nature, and Zane had made a face and said the balance of nature was a dead dodo.

"Nothing is really balanced. Try to think of it as an ongoing poker game, say five-card draw, but everything constantly changes—the money, the card suits, the players, even the table, and every ante is affected by the weather, and you're playing in a room where the house around you is being demolished."

Buddy and his father, in sympathy for once, exchanged glances.

"Truth is," said Zane, "most of the time we don't know what we're doing. Just tinkering, is one view, another view—"

"Quit while you're ahead," said Buddy's father and silence fell on the table.

At first Buddy worked for his father but the old man had a temper and the son had a way of saying the wrong thing. When the methane-gas boom opened up he hired on as a roughneck with a crew in the Powder River Basin. After a few months he gave the tool-pusher some lip and was fired. He went to Denver, where he picked up an indoor job as a grouter helper. When he got laid off he took a job that Latinas usually did—making dice from precut nitric-celluloid cubes, but the volatile solvents gave him bad headaches and the tedium of drilling and painting little spots sent him back to construction.

He blamed the city for his increasing depression. He could not get used to so many people and Denver, especially Sixteenth Street, was a freak parade of half-boiled Indians in stacked jeans, women the hundred colors from charcoal to cheese. Street people swarmed everywhere and a handful of water dipped out of Cherry Creek could not lighten the tan that went with being down and out at high altitude. There were tourists asking each other for directions. When all they found were fast food and sleazy T-shirt shops and, down near Market Street, a demented sculpture project of metal buffaloes with human knees, they got a look on their faces that said, "why did I come here?" To this he added his own dislikes—mulletheads in suits and skinheads in waddle-shorts, waiters out on the street for a smoke break, a lesbian couple sharing a caramel apple, a black man sweating in a mink coat in the September heat, caps emblazoned *Avalanches, Rockies, Broncos,* people cruising, hanging out, waiting for whatever came next, all cranking along against the western flash of mountains. And there was his boss who, when he gave an order and wanted to be sure he was understood, said, "You lookin at me?" For a year Buddy endured, then, after a scuffle with a trench trimmer, said the hell with it and headed north seeking out back roads.

Within a mile or two of crossing the Wyoming line it began to snow—sparse, dry flakes. The map showed a gravel road cutting west in the vicinity of Tie Siding and he watched for it. He thought he must have missed it, pulled into a ranch road to turn around and then saw it was the one he wanted. He could see it snaking west, the distant Medicine Bows, where the snow was falling heavily, almost obscured.

The road was rough with stiff ruts left by hunters' trucks, but passable. Despite the snow the surface was dry and his Jeep raised a pillar of chill yellow dust that mixed with the flakes and hung in the air for minutes.

His parents pretended to be glad to see him but let him know in little ways that he was wrecking things for them. The sugar-beet harvest had been good and they had set up a vacation. Now, out of the blue, here he was, Mr. Monkey Wrench.

"You want a take a cruise? Take a cruise," he said. "I'll look out for the house, cook for myself. I'll house-sit while I look for a job. Got enough money, I'll buy my own groceries."

"Oh Lord, I can see it when we come back, dirty dishes, mud, dust—" his mother moaned. "And I really don't want a go on a cruise. It's your father's idea. I don't care about icebergs."

But he had convinced them and they left. It was wonderful at first, having the house to himself, and he made a big effort to keep it clean. He slid into the silence of his childhood, slept like a stone at the bottom of a lake.

About ten days after they left someone broke into the house and cleaned it out while he was down at the bar—took the two television sets, the kitchen appliances, including the dishwasher, his father's golf clubs, his mother's fur coat, which he had promised to put in cold storage for her, his father's coin collection. He remembered telling his mother she should bring the fur coat, that it would be cold among the icebergs, but she took her sea-green anorak with the wolf-fur trim that always brought approving chuckles from ranchers.

"It zips," she said. "The coat does not zip."

It had been late, after two A.M., when he lurched in and found every-thing tipped over or missing. He had called the police but they seemed to think he had done it himself, disposing of the stolen goods through some seedy receiver, and they changed their minds only when the mixer and the golf clubs turned up in a Casper pawnshop and the pawnshop woman shook her head at his photograph.

"The one brought the stuff in was a little guy, sort of dark-complected but not a—not a colored man. I don't know, maybe Mexi-can, maybe part Indian. Maybe a Arab."

That made them sit up, the idea of an Arab creeping around Wyoming, breaking into houses.

Then the coin collection and one of the television sets were found at another pawnshop in Cheyenne and the cops told him that was an indication the robbers were heading for Lincoln or Denver. Probably Denver. Denver, they said, was better for burglars; Lincoln was for bank robbers. The fur coat, the rice cooker, the dishwasher, and the other television set did not reappear and he dreaded his par-ents' return.

It was as bad as he thought it would be, shouting and accusations, his hot-voiced promises to pay them back, his father shaking his head in I-told-you-so disgust.

"People just don't *do* that here," his mother said, all memory of the icebergs and the shipboard buffets crushed by the disaster. "I knew we shouldn't have gone," and there was a flick of triumph in her voice as she glanced at her husband. Buddy put down his head and pre-pared to weather the storm.

"They think maybe it was Iraqis," he lied. He made the mistake then of faulting his father for not carrying insurance that would have covered the loss, and the paternal volcano erupted. After an hour of shouting, his father demanding how he could possibly pay them back when he didn't even have a job, he slammed out of the house.

He drove around, cooling down, taking turns onto roads he knew too well, wishing for new territory. It had been a big mistake to come back. Things were worse than they had ever been. He couldn't stay there. He'd find another place, get some lousy job and send them like, fifty dollars a week or whatever. He'd move, he thought, to some almost-gone town like Gebo, Ulm, or Merna. Remote and difficult. A new set of bad dirt roads to explore. He would not have a telephone. They wanted distance, they would get distance. But in the end it was Wamsutter, the town enjoying a methane-gas boom that promised to equal the happy oil years of the thirties and seventies. The only problem was that he had arranged for his last paycheck and the balance of his savings account to be sent to his parents' address. His mother promised to forward the money to him as soon as he had a mailing address.

Wamsutter was a desperate place, a hairline away from I-80. The first street was a strip of gas stations and convenience stores. Butted against this strip like the teeth of a comb were five or six short streets crowded with hundreds of trailers and a few houses. Fading into the desert was a second cluster of trailered streets. The entire town, he saw, was a huge trailer park, pickup trucks in front of every mobile home, license plates from Texas, Oklahoma, Louisiana, Nebraska, California, identifying the migrant gypsies of the gas and oil fields who followed the energy booms. This, he thought, was the real Wyoming—full of poor, hardworking transients, tough as nails and restless, going where the dollars grew.

The single-wide he looked at was five miles out of town, in the Red Desert, at the end of a lumpy hog-rock track. It had been advertised as "furnished" at forty dollars a month. He hated it at first sight, the scarred brown exterior, the clumsily painted sign over the door that read *King Kong*, the stained sofa in the living room with its design of sea anemones and broken nutshells, the crusty carpet which he could see someone had tried to vacuum by the flattened paths crisscrossing it. An enormous elk head took up most of the space above the sofa. He thought it would probably kill someone if it fell. In front of the sofa was a homemade coffee table with splayed legs; on it two china kittens romped beside a stamped metal ashtray dark with cigarette burns.

"See, all set to go," said the owner's daughter, Cootie, a fat woman in grimy sweatpants, flicking the wall switch. She turned on the faucet in the miniature sink and a yellow dribble appeared. The doll-sized gas range produced a tiny blue flame. The wall behind the range was covered with ill-matched pieces of aluminum foil, discolored and crinkled. The bed was close beside the kitchen range, separated from it only by a food-stained wooden box. Handy, he thought, if he wanted to fry eggs without getting out of bed.

The walls were trimmed with red, white, and blue bands painted around the doorways and windows. Along the top of the kitchen wall were the painted words *Love God* repeated several times. Partially blocking the bathroom door was a cheap bicycle exercise machine that looked like an ironing board with pedals and mini-handlebars. In the bathroom he noticed a tiny hot water heater with a five-gallon capacity. He'd have to be quick in the shower.

On the way out Cootie mentioned the stove again. "The other burners don't work, but you can only use one at a time anyway, right?"

He wanted to say "Wrong," but did not. Between them lay the unspoken sentence: What do you expect for forty dollars a month?

"I'll take it," he said. He would only be using it to sleep in once he found a job.

That night, rolled up in his sleeping bag, he heard the nearby yip and yodel of coyotes, but near morning, the five A.M. light milky in the windows, he heard deeper howling. Someone's dog, he supposed, and got up to start the day. He had a hundred things to do in Rawlins, the nearest town with real stores.

There was another trailer near the turnoff, obviously occupied as there was a truck in front, clothes flapping on the line. Around this structure was a moat of automotive junk, horse trailers, oil barrels, and a fiberglass boat with a hole in one side. A pile of fence posts lay half in the driveway and tire marks veering around them showed they had been there for a long time. Pink-stemmed halogeton weeds choked the background. The owners had dogs and he supposed they were the source of the predawn howling.

After a few days he realized there was a third single-wide about a mile farther out in the desert. He walked to it one day, passing the hulk of an ancient truck with solid tires, faded lettering on the door that read *J. O. Sheep Co.* In the distance he could hear a drill rig.

The trailer was in ruins, broken-backed because its west end had slipped off the cinderblock supports. All the windows had been shot out. He went inside. The floor groaned and moved and something ratlike whisked into a hole near the floor. Sand-filled rags and a tiny sneaker lay under a table. No chairs. Small heaps of dried grass and hundreds of scat pellets lay everywhere. He sneezed at the strong musky smell.

"Packrats," he said aloud. He opened cupboard doors. In the tiny bedroom a yellowed newspaper story dated 1973 was tacked to the wall. It told of several urban families who had bought land south of Wamsutter from a fly-by-night development company. In the story one of the buyers was quoted as saying, "This is our dream come true, to own our own ranch. We're the new pioneers." This passage had been underlined with red crayon, a line that went into the margin and attached to the words *Dad says* in the same red crayon. But, the story reported, townspeople said the "pioneers" would never make it through a single winter and no crops would grow in the desert. The accompanying photograph showed a girl about six sitting on the steps of a trailer. After a hard look Buddy thought it might be the trailer he was renting.

But it was the next-door trailer that became the focus of his attention. On his first weekend, cleaning trash out from under his place, something bit him and his arm swelled to the size of a telephone pole. At the Rawlins emergency room they thought it might have been a rattlesnake and, after antivenin and tetanus shots, ordered a week's rest and no activity, no reaching under dark trailers or beds. He felt plenty sick. Recuperating, he watched his neighbors.

On sunny days a small boy play-fought with a plastic gun in the driveway while a woman in a striped shirt (the same shirt day after day) sat on the steps and smoked cigarettes. A baby crawled in the dirt. The wind blew the woman's long orange hair. She looked a little familiar, as did all fat, fair women, perhaps because that was his mother's physical type. He dubbed her "Fat Wife." During weekdays there was no vehicle in the yard until evening. In the mornings the rumble of a diesel woke him before daylight. The neighbor worked hard and long at something. On the weekends a very old Power Wagon arrived and the driver, a huge bearded lug dressed in sagging jeans, a deerskin shirt with fringe and a wrecked hat, disappeared inside the trailer for hours. This man (he thought of him as "Big Boy") seemed to be a bow hunter as sometimes in the afternoons he and the hardworking father of the children (this was "Old Dad") would come out and shoot arrows at a hay bale transformed into prey when they tied on a plastic deer's head. Old Dad looked familiar, too, but he couldn't say how or why. He guessed Big Boy was Old Dad's pal or maybe brother-in-law. After the shooting matches Old Dad fired up the barbecue and Big Boy cooked something on the grill. Buddy could see him turning meat with his hunting knife.

So far, so good, but then their dogs began coming around. He had a trash bag of garbage in the Jeep to drop at the dump on his next trip to town, but was disagreeably surprised one morning to see a dog leap out of the vehicle with a slice of moldy bread in its jaws. Trash, coffee grounds, bacon grease, plastic wrappers were all over the Jeep and it took him a long time to clean the vehicle. When he was done he walked over to their trailer.

Old Dad had built a plywood entryway with three steps and a handrail. Next to the entryway was a scrap-wood lean-to with a basketball hoop on the center post, milk crates of automotive parts lined up on the ground.

Fat Wife opened the door. The smell of cigarette smoke came with her.

"Yeah?" she said, lighting another.

"Hi. I'm your neighbor—Buddy Millar. Uh—I'm having a little problem with your dogs. Dog. The brown one." Two were black and one was brown, all of indeterminate breed.

"Buddy Millar! I *knew* there was something. I told Rase you looked real familiar."

He stared at her. The frizzled red hair showed dark at the roots and the long ends straggled across her shoulders like damp raffia, the finer strands caught in the fleece fabric of the grimy anorak she wore. Her face was so oily it seemed metaled. Behind her he could see a brown chair, the floor littered with clothing and toys.

"I'm Cheri. Cheri Bise back in high school. Cheri Wham now. Me and Rase Wham got married."

Slowly it came to him, the high-school bully, Rase Wham, had dropped out in tenth grade. Wham had been a vicious sociopath. Cheri Bise, the overweight slut whose insecurity made her an easy sexual conquest, had disappeared around the same time.

"Come on in, have a cup a coffee." There was a highway of festering pimples alongside her nose. She cleared a path in the debris by kicking toys left and right. Reluctantly he went inside. It stank of cigarettes, garbage, and feces. The television set stuttered colors.

"What are you doing down here?" he asked, taking shallow breaths.

"Rase is workin for Halliburton now. He used a work for a drillin outfit but the well froze and there was a blowout and it kind a hurt him. He had a concussion. Last year. And I work Fridays in the school cafeteria."

He understood from the tone in her voice that she considered the cafeteria job a career.

"Barbette's in school, second grade, and that's Vernon Clarence—" she pointed at the dull-faced boy of four or five holding a box of Cracker Jack. "And that's the baby, Lye." The diaper-clad baby was crawling toward them, his sticky fingers furred with lint and clutching a tiny red car that Buddy recognized as an Aston Martin. The kid, clinging to Buddy's knee, clawed himself upright and thrust the toy at him.

"Caw!" said the child.

"Yes, it's a nice car," said Buddy. In the room beyond he could see a bed heaped with grimy blankets.

"Caw!"

Cheri reheated stale coffee in a saucepan, poured the pungent liquid into mugs emblazoned *Go Pokes*, set one before him. She did not proffer milk or sugar. She sat down at the table and blew on her coffee.

"And we're expectin the next one in December, week before Christmas. It's hard on a kid, have a birthday that close a Christmas, but you sure don't think a that when you're doin it." She had a spit-frilled way of talking.

The baby was staring at Buddy with savage intensity as though he were going to utter a great scientific truth never before known. His face reddened and the vein in his forehead stood out. He grunted and with an explosive burst filled his diaper.

While Cheri changed him on the kitchen table less than eighteen inches from Buddy's coffee cup, he looked around to avoid watching her mop at Lye's besmeared buttocks and scrotum. On the floor several feathers were stuck in a coagulated blob. Wads of trodden gum appeared as archipelagoes in a mud-colored sea while bits of popcorn, string ends, torn paper, a crushed McDonald's cup and candy wrappers made up the flotsam. An electric wall heater stuck out into the room. On top of it were three coffee mugs, two beer cans, several brimming ashtrays, a tiny plastic fox and a prescription bottle. Through the amber plastic of the bottle he could see the dark forms of capsules.

There was a sudden plop as Cheri threw the loaded diaper into an open pail already seething with banana peels, coffee grounds, and prehistoric diapers.

The older child, Vernon Clarence, edged along the sofa toward the wall heater. His small hands grasped a beer can and shook it. He dropped it on the floor and tried the other, which responded with a promising slosh. He drank the dregs, warm beer running down his chin and soaking his pajama top. Buddy wondered if he should mention to Cheri that the kid was drinking beer, decided against it. The freshly emptied can rolled under the sofa.

Cheri suddenly got up, lunged for the cupboard and retrieved a package. She shook several small bright pink cakes bristling with shredded coconut onto a chipped saucer.

"Go on! Take one!" She held the saucer in front of his face as Lye had held the toy car.

He took one. A coconut point stuck into his finger like a staple. He put the cake on the table. Lye seized it and mumbled, "Caw!" as he gummed the confection. From across the room Vernon Clarence started to bawl, pointing eloquently at Lye, whose face was crowded by the pink mass.

"Here you go! Catch!" shouted Cheri, hurling a cake at the child. It hit an ashtray on the coffee table and sent butts and ash flying.

"I've got a get goin," said Buddy, rising. "I just wanted a mention about the dogs—dog. And introduce myself."

"Well, I'm thrilled," said Cheri. "I always had a big crush on you in school. All the girls thought you was cute. Rase will just about pass out when I tell him who our new neighbor is." She snapped a cigarette from the package on the table.

"Say hello to him for me," said Buddy, struggling with the door latch, which was some devious childproof design. He glanced around the room as he backed out. The fastidious Vernon Clarence was picking a cigarette butt from his confectionary prize.

Buddy's trailer seemed a cozy haven in contrast with the Whams' and he quickly made his bed and washed the dishes lest he become like them.

On Saturday, unseasonably warm, he felt better than he had in a week and went into town for groceries—chocolate bars, pork chops, frozen French fries, frozen waffles, two bakery pies, and no vegetables. At the liquor store he bought a bottle of bourbon. As he drove past the Whams' trailer he saw them all outside, leaning over the back of Big Boy's truck, where several rigid animal legs indicated a successful hunt. Old Dad—he had to start thinking of him as Rase Wham—was wielding a bloody knife. There were two six-packs on the roof of the truck cab. Cheri, also with a knife, waved at him and he waved back.

He put his groceries away, eating one of the pies as he did so, wishing the refrigerator's freezer compartment was bigger. He had bought a newspaper and settled down with a cup of coffee to read the want ads. Truck driver, heavy equipment operator, motel clerk, framing carpenter—there was very little that suited him. He had just started on the gas-field ads when someone knocked on the door.

"Come in," he said, expecting to see one of the Whams. It was Barbette, an overweight seven year old with sly, fox-colored eyes, her pale brown hair pulled into a ponytail. She wore jeans and a pink shirt which had traces of blood on it.

"Dad says come over for the barbecue. Graig shot some antelopes and we're goin a have a barbecue. Mama's makin the sauce with ketchup and sugar. Dad says don't bring no beer, he got plenty." Without waiting for an answer she turned and ran back.

"Okay," said Buddy to the door. But he would not go empty-handed. He lit the tiny oven and heated up the French fries, slipped the bourbon bottle into his jacket pocket.

The adults were half drunk when he went over and he thought Vernon Clarence was drunk as well, for the child was staggering around, sucking at a beer can. This time Buddy did mention it to Cheri, but she laughed.

"Oh, Rase lets him do it. Figures if he starts young he won't be a bad drunk when he gets up in size. It's your late starters are the bad ones. He says."

Amazing, thought Buddy. He and Rase were the same age, but Rase had made all these kids and one of them was an alcoholic even before hitting kindergarten.

Rase came slouching over, stuck out a blood-crusted hand. There was the familiar shaved bullet-head, the wide neck, and great swollen mounds of muscle. Rase Wham's face was scarred and there were tattoos of barbed wire, fanged snakes, and an AK-47 spitting red bullets on his arms. His smile showed a set of broken yellow teeth.

"How the shit are ya? How'd you end up in this fuckin dump? This here's my asshole buddy, Graig, Graig Deshler. Mountain Man

Deshler. He's the real thing, sleeps on the ground, tracks lions, cooks cowboy coffee."

Graig Deshler glowered at Buddy. "Fuckin bullshit," he said, but the glower was for show. He bore the traces of acne so severe that his sallow skin resembled sand drilled by a fast-moving cloud-burst. But he had an air of surety that Buddy liked, and his shrewd, twinkling eyes took in everything. After he had a good swallow of the bourbon he began telling Buddy how it was.

"See, everbody tells me I was born a hundred years too late. Hundred-fifty, more like it. I should a been a mountain man, they tell me. I'm a throwback and proud of it. I live by my wits, see? Trap, hunt, got me a little cabin, no electricity, get water from the crick. Done it all my life. Trap, hunt, got me that little cabin. Only thing different between me and the old-time mountain man is I ain't got no squaw woman. I been on the lookout for one but hell, they are all too civilized for me, just like the rest a the population, got a have that deodorant and perfume, fancy clothes and go see the hairdresser six times a week. I wouldn't touch one a them. I got a friend, he's a Northern Cheyenne, he makes these art pieces for tourists. Needs eagle feathers and hawks, fur. I keep him supplied. It's unlawful they say. They can kiss my butt. I never had a huntin license. Game and Fish knows better than mess with me. They give me plenty a room." His voice went on and on, rising and falling like the outboard motor of a boat circling a lake.

"So this friend a mine, the Cheyenne, I ask him once, 'You got any sisters?' Christ, he got mad. Sore as hell, he's still all fired up. All I did was ask a simple question but you might a thought I was askin him to suck my dick. I *never* paid no taxes. The U.S. government, and that goes for the Game and Fish, can kiss my butt. Old Claude Dallas had the right idea. They come messin around your camp, shoot em. I don't pay taxes, I don't need their stinkin pensions or social security or that Medicare shit. Cut my own hair, never shaved since I were a colt but I keep my beard trimmed up. Never liked a see a woodsy man with big bushy whiskers. Catches in the willers. I was goin a run for governor last election."

He released a prolonged blast of wind and a stench of burning tires surrounded them. Buddy wondered what in the name of the revered outlaw Claude Dallas the man had eaten—raw skunk? Graig seemed not to notice and stuck out his calloused hand for the bourbon bottle.

"Now that's good stuff. I made moonshine and all kind a homemade whiskey but I can't get it to be no good in the taste. You got a have a good whiskey barrel and all I had was a goddamn old pickle barrel. That's the one concession I make to civilization—liquor. It's hard a make and I have to say it is worth all they ask for it."

Buddy, glancing at the muddy Power Wagon, the rifle in the back window, the mountain man's stainless-steel wristwatch, thought Graig made a few other concessions to civilization, and excused himself, saying he had to bring his French fries in to Cheri.

In the trailer Cheri was mixing the barbecue sauce. She had dumped a large bottle of ketchup into a bowl and was stirring in brown sugar and Tabasco sauce.

"What I really need," she said, "is whiskey. About a tablespoon a whiskey makes it real smooth. But I tell you what is almost as good is cough syrup." She rummaged in the cupboard and brought out a small bottle whose contents went into the red sauce.

"And some salt. There." She dropped the raw slabs of antelope meat into the bowl and laid a newspaper across the top.

"Just let her set for half a hour or so and then Graig can cook it. He does all the cookin when he visits. He won't let nobody else even try. He's out there at that grill long as anybody wants some meat. He's a sweetheart." She lit a cigarette and got two beers from the refrigerator, passed one to him. "Let's go join the party," she said, pulling on a huge green sweater.

Cheri and Graig were talkative and half-flirting, Graig explaining what his platform would be if he ran for governor again.

"First thing I'd do is make the wolf the state animal, put the wolf on the license plate, get rid a that damn buckin bronco. People say them big Canadian grays they brought into Wyomin is not the native wolf."

Rase interrupted, spoke very loudly. "What *I'd* do," he said, "is open up Yellowstone Park for huntin. Clean the place out and get the oil and minin interests in. Could be like Alaska used a be—pay each resident a couple thousand dollars just for livin here." He let out a huge gobbling laugh, then fell silent again. His eyes wandered and he was jumpy.

Graig continued. "Anyway, they say the native wolf, the Rocky Mountain wolf, was smaller than those Canadian grays. Little bit bigger than coyotes and they didn't use to run in no packs. Solitary. It's a lot a hot air. Same animal. Everbody in the state got a opinion about wolves, mostly wrong."

"Wuf!" said Lye, rubbing the nipple of his baby bottle in the dirt.

"But if I was to be a animal that's what I'd want a be—a big gray Canadian-Wyomin wolf. I look at a wolf, I look at myself. *Owooooh!*"

"Oooow," said Lye softly.

Rase Wham sat on the picnic table jiggling his leg impatiently. When Buddy, trying to make conversation, asked him a question about his job, he only grunted. After about ten minutes he suddenly shouted at Graig: "When the hell are you goin a cook that meat?" Little Vernon Clarence, on the steps with the barrel of his toy revolver in his mouth, gave a startled jump and began to cry. Rase turned on the child.

"Shut that fuckin mouth or I'll kill you," he screamed.

"Take it easy, Rase baby," said Graig, getting up and going to the grill to see if the coals were ready. He tried for a light tone. "Don't never rile a mountain man or you'll have your hands full. Old Mountain Man Vernon Clarence there will tie you in a pretzel." He winked at the drunk and bawling child.

"You don't want a cry so loud," Graig said to him. "Them wolves'll come and eat you up. That's what they do, they eat up cryin boys, crunch their bones." Vernon Clarence cried harder.

"I'll get the meat," said Cheri and she ran up the steps and into the trailer, hauling Vernon Clarence with her.

"Everthing I ever done," said Graig to Buddy as though all were calm, "I done because I wanted a do it. Nobody made me do nothin and nobody ever give me a medal for doin what I done. No matter what I never heard a fuckin word of appreciation from nobody. And I don't care. That's how the ball bounces, that's how the wind blows. I come over here with two nice pronghorns, cook the meat, and I *will* make the coffee. When we are ready. Cheri can't make decent coffee if you was to give her a hundred dollars a cup. I'll make it. No matter what you do, no matter who you help, they'll step all over you, wipe their boots on you if they get the chance. But they don't affect me. I'm used a shitty people. Hell, I even like em."

"Goddamn," shouted Rase, "work all week like a dog, have to sit and starve on the weekend? Listen to a lot a hot air about wolves? Where the hell are my smokes? *Cheri!*"

"What!" she shouted from inside.

"You got my cigarettes? And bring that meat out here so Graig can get cookin!" Buddy could see the cigarette package under the picnic table. He picked it up and handed it to Rase.

"What the fuck are *you* doin with em?"

"They were under the picnic table."

"Yeah? I bet they were."

As Rase's face bunched up into a deformed squash shape Cheri opened the door at the top of the trailer steps holding the bowl of meat and sauce, edging out, trying to keep the spring-loaded door from slamming on her heels. Partway down the steps her sweater sleeve caught on a protruding nail. The slight jerk cut a notch in her balance and she dropped the bowl, which hit the bottom step and broke into several large pieces. Sauce splattered and the meat fell in the dirt under the steps.

"This fuckin lousy mean old trailer!" she howled. "If I ever get me some money I will buy a real house somewheres, not some fuckin trailer in the sand." She turned and kicked at the door, sat on the top step and began to cry, plump hands over her face. Behind her Vernon Clarence's tear-smeared face appeared and he too set up a fresh howl.

Graig picked up the largest piece of the broken bowl, almost a complete half, and began piling the dirt-crusted meat into it.

"Shit," he said, "this's no biggie. Quit bawlin, Cheri. We'll just rinse this here meat off with a little beer—that will give it flavor, throw these steaks on the fire and the cookin will fix everthing. You won't never know they'd fell. You come huntin with me one day, and you'll see I carve my supper meat up out in the field and it got plenty dirt and leaves and hair on, but all that stuff cooks off. It is not important. The old-time mountain men knew that. Anyways, don't it say in the Bible somewheres you got a eat a peck a dirt before you die?" He shook a piece of meat, laid it in the broken crockery. "Now, Vernon Clarence, remember what I told you about them wolves that eat crybabies? You better hush that noise or they'll hear you. Them wolves just gobble crybabies like they was peppermint sticks. And they can find you easy because they can hear you cryin."

Cheri pointed at Rase. "It's important a *me*. This is just the worse place I ever lived." She glared at him and he fired up.

"Worse place? How about that dump you was brought up in? And I'd like to see how you save up enough money for a house in town by passin out hot dogs at a school cafeteria one day a week. You think you got it bad, but this is *the best I can do*. I been workin since I was seventeen, supportin this family. You're dissatisfied with everthing, but you ever think a that, ever think I might a want a go into a different line a work than what I do? I wanted a be a high-school coach, but you got a go to college for that and I been hustlin miserable jobs for *years* so I could afford a buy this goddamn trailer you piss on, support you and all these goddamn *kids*. You don't *get it* that the bad comes with the good. You don't take notice that there's a lot a guys would a walked, you bein so fuckin fat and always knocked up."

"You don't like your kids you shouldn't a made so many a them. Use a rubber once in a while and you'd have the money—and no family."

"Whyn't you get on the pill? You take the fuckin housekeepin money and buy them goddamn dumb magazines you always get. You could get birth-control pills instead and not jump on *me* about kids."

At this point Buddy decided to go back to his own place and said good-bye to Graig. Rase heard him and spun around hotly.

"What the hell you doin here anyway? Come for the free dinner?" he sneered. "The dinner in the dirt? Come to mess with that fat bitch I married? Come to complain about my dogs? You keep garbage in a open vehicle you deserve dogs. You deserve a punchout, complain about it. Go get your fightin clothes on and I'll show you what you get."

"I thought you invited me. But I'll sure as hell go." And he turned and started walking back to his trailer. He heard footsteps behind him. It was Graig.

"Shit, Buddy, don't go off mad. I am about to cook them steaks and they *will* be good. Beer'll clean them off good."

He stopped and looked at the self-described mountain man. "It's not that. I lost my appetite. Some other time when Rase isn't so hot for a fight."

"Hell, he just flares up ever now and then. Ten minutes from now he'll be in a good mood, laugh and hug old Cheri. He just likes a little bit of a fight—gives him a appetite."

"There's some fights you don't take. I had my fight with Rase about ten years ago."

He had been fourteen, a strong-enough kid, sturdied up by chores, but Rase already had a man's construction, big muscled shoulders, hard arms, and hands like a stonemason's. What started as a shoving scuffle became a snorting, choking fight that ended with Rase repeatedly slamming Buddy's face onto the cement sidewalk. That night, after one look at his damaged features, his father had taken him to Doc String, who said he had a broken nose and broken cheekbone. The bones in both hands were broken as well. His father wanted to call the sheriff but Buddy pleaded nasally against this as he knew Rase would follow up with a fresh assault.

Graig was still walking beside him. "I didn't know you knowed him that long."

"We was in grade school." Buddy didn't want to talk about the Rase Wham of yesteryear.

There was a distant howl and then another from a different direction. Graig snatched at his sleeve and breathed heavily—bourbon, beer, and bad teeth. His face was golden in the late light.

"You hear that?" said Graig, "That, my friend, was a *wolf*. And it weren't so goddamn far away, neither. I never knew them to be down this far but I sure as hell know one when I hear one. There's wolves in the Red Desert, gettin a bead on Wamsutter. We just heard the livin proof."

Buddy doubted that.

Back in his trailer he realized he had left the precious bottle of bourbon on the Whams' picnic table. There was nothing he wanted more at the moment than to get stinking drunk and pass out in his bed. Cursing, he decided to drive into town and get another, and because he didn't want to pass the Whams' trailer, where billowing clouds of smoke now rose from the barbecue, he decided to cut cross-lots over the desert, past the old packrat trailer. He planned to circle around, pick up the new methane gas road that shot in a straight line to the county road. He figured it was about three miles cross-country to the gas road. It could be a little tricky, but he was full of adrenalin, and welcomed the difficulty. There was still enough light to see what he needed to see.

Driving unknown desert terrain was dangerous, even in daylight, and with twilight close he might have trouble. Chains, a shovel, several planks, a come-along and assorted tools, including his .30-06, were already in the back of the Jeep. He threw his heavy jacket, a gallon of water, the second pie, a package of pork chops onto the backseat. In the glove compartment were matches and candles. If he got stranded he'd be all right. He might just park out in the desert and do his drinking there.

A few hundred yards beyond the ruined packrat trailer he was surprised to find the faintest of trails, the barest suggestion of narrow-set wheel ruts. He thought he might be on part of the old Overland Trail or one of its many side shoots. It was almost full dusk but his headlights picked out the ghostly ruts and for now they headed in the direction he wanted. But after half a mile the ephemeral track disappeared into a deep and brushy draw and he turned north, looking for level ground. By the time he cleared the draw it was dark but a hundred yards away he could see the lights of a truck on the gas road.

In ten minutes he was in Wamsutter. Coming into the town he realized he was ravenous. He skipped the liquor store and went to a place on the strip he had not noticed before, the Wild Horse Café, part restaurant, part bar. He ordered a bourbon and the pork chop dinner special without looking up.

The Whams' trailer was dark when he drove past it but he caught a glimpse of Graig's Power Wagon. Climbing the steps of his own place he yawned hugely, opened the door. He knew instantly something was different. There was a certain faint smell, and then a child's low whimper. He switched on the light. Vernon Clarence lay on one end of the sofa, and a blanketed lump he assumed was Lye on the other end, and on the floor, wrapped in the blankets from his bed, lay Cheri and Barbette.

"Cheri? What the hell is going on?" he said.

The woman sat up, her red hair mashed flat on one side.

"It's Rase. He got real drunk and mean like he does sometime. He hit Vernon Clarence pretty bad. I think his little arm might be broke. So Graig said he would quiet Rase down, we should come over here and wait for you. I took the blankets off your bed but you can have em back now."

"Jesus," said Buddy, sitting in a chair. He looked at his watch. Eleven forty-five. Hours to go before daylight. "You want a take Vernon Clarence to the emergency room in Rawlins? Have him looked at?"

"I don't know. He's asleep now, but he been cryin bad and he won't let me touch his arm. It does look kind a funny the way he holds it. He just cried his little self to sleep."

As if in confirmation the child whimpered again and turned his head from the light. Buddy looked at him. The boy's nose was swollen and he could see dried blood on his upper lip. He could not see the arm because the child was covered by one of his jackets. It was cold in the trailer and Cheri had helped herself to whatever coverings she could find. He lifted the jacket slowly and the child woke, screaming. Vernon Clarence's lower left arm seemed to have an extra elbow.

"Okay," he said. "This is not good. I'm goin a drive you to Rawlins and while they take care a the kid I'll get you all a motel room. He's hurt and this is not a good place for you to be. Rase could come over here easy and start up again. And as soon as Graig leaves I bet you that's what happens. Come on, Cheri, let's go, get the kid to a doctor." He wished now he had a cell phone.

The trip to the hospital was a nightmare, all three children crying, Cheri chain-smoking, his head ringing with bourbon and fatigue. Barbette had sat on the package of pork chops and the cold, wet meat had set her off.

At the hospital Vernon Clarence was carried into a curtained cubicle by a tall, foreign-looking nurse. He heard Cheri tell her that Vernon Clarence had fallen down the trailer steps. There was a lot going on in the emergency room and every cubicle was full, people rushing back and forth. There were deputies and troopers leaning over people. He understood there had been a major accident on I-80. Cheri came out and while she sat in the crowded waiting room under the pitiless glare of lights, surrounded by signs that said NO SMOKING, he went to find a motel room that could accommodate the four Whams.

At the first motel he got the details. East of Rawlins a semi had jack-knifed and caused a chain reaction involving more than thirty vehicles on the interstate. The highway was closed and every room in town was occupied. There was nothing left, and people were knocking on residents' doors asking for shelter. He would have to take Cheri and her kids back out to his trailer. He was involved in something ugly and made up his mind to move to Alaska as soon as he could get out of it.

Back at the hospital he found Cheri standing outside the doors, smoking.

"They're not done with him. Been some kind a accident on the interstate so everthing is takin forever. They got a lot a hurt people here. Lye's fell asleep on that couch thing and Barbette too. It could be a while."

"I got bad news, too. There's no motel rooms because of the accident so I guess I will have to take you back to my place. You better be thinkin what you want a do in the mornin—I can take you to a shelter if they got that kind a thing here."

"Oh, I don't need a do that. Rase will be okay in the morning. He gets bad sometimes when he's drinkin, but you'll see, Graig will talk him out a the meanness and he'll be just as sweet as pie in the morning, all sorry and nice."

"Cheri, I don't want a tell you how to run your life but you got a think about the kids. He could really hurt them. Hell, he could kill them. He could kill you. He's a strong guy and drunk strong guys are dangerous."

"I guess I know Rase pretty good, better'n you, anyway. He'll be okay. It's happened before. And Graig can handle him. He's probly got him calmed down right now."

"Jesus," he said. "So do you want me to take you back to your place?" He had the worst headache of his life and it wasn't all from bourbon.

A nurse's aide came out the door and said "Mrs. Wham? The doctor wants to talk to you."

"I'll wait here," said Buddy as Cheri threw her cigarette down and went inside.

She came out pulling her big sweater around her breasts.

"They are goin a keep him tonight. They are writin up a report says it was a possible child abuse. The cops are goin a pick Rase up and question him. I had a tell them he hit Vernon Clarence. They didn't believe he fell down the steps. Rase will be real, real mad. So I can't go back there tonight."

"When are the cops goin a pick Rase up?"

"Right away, maybe. Or in the mornin. They got a lot happenin right now."

He looked at his watch. It was past one and by the time they got back to his place it would be pushing three. It looked like he was in for it.

. . .

There was only Rase's truck and Graig's old wagon in the Whams' yard.

They put Lye and Barbette on the couch. He gave Cheri his own bed, rolled up in his sleeping bag near the door and was asleep in minutes. He was dreaming of a waitress at the café, dreaming that she flashed different colors from a kaleidoscope of whirling cop car lights, and that she was stroking his penis, her enameled nails just tickling his pubic hair, when he felt the stroking was real and could smell Cheri, a mixture of burned meat, baby shit, and sweat. She pulled him on top of her. He wanted desperately to stop, and tried, but it had been too long, the dream was strong and his traitorous body went for the jackpot.

The sharp wind wedging under the door and some slight noise woke him. He was shivering, his face pressed against the door and for a moment did not recognize where he was until he rolled over and saw Barbette on the sofa staring at him. He sat up, the terrible night returning in big indigestible lumps.

"Mama can't find the Sugar Puffs," the child said.

"Don't have Sugar Puffs," he croaked. His head was swimming.

"*Mama, he don't have no Sugar Puffs!*" the outraged girl shouted, kicking the sofa and rousing Lye, who began to cry.

He saw Cheri then, fiddling with his coffeemaker, stymied by the unfamiliar gadget. He got up, conscious of his stained, bagging underwear which seemed made of transparent plastic wrap, seized his jeans and shirt from the floor and went into the bathroom. As he passed her he told Cheri to leave the coffee alone, that he would make it in a minute.

The shower was a sometime thing, but he had to get the smell of the night's horrors off and was grateful for the sputtering trickle, even when the water went cold and left him gasping and shaking. He urinated in the drain.

Dressed, he went straight to the coffeemaker. Cheri was sitting at the table smoking a cigarette and drinking a soda she had found in the refrigerator.

He looked out the tiny window. There was a tumbled mass of indigo and salmon cloud in the East. The faded rabbitbrush lashed in the blustery wind and a streak of color showed where the sun would soon rise. There was no sign that the police were coming for Rase. Graig's old Power Wagon stood in its usual place. The first flakes of snow shot through the fierce air. The coffeepot quit mumbling and he poured himself a cup of strong black, then another for Cheri. He wanted to get her moving.

"Thanks, Honey," she said in an artificially sweet voice that he interpreted to mean she thought she now had some claim on him.

"Cheri," he said, "look, last night was nothin. It was a mistake. Tell the truth, you kind of raped me. Sooner you get goin the better."

She pouted for a minute, then said, "but we got a go get Vernon Clarence. They said he could be picked up any time after nine."

"Yeah? Well I suggest you go get Rase's truck and drive up to Rawlins yourself. And I sure don't see any cruisers comin for Rase."

Cheri slurped at her coffee and looked at him from under her eyelashes as though measuring. "I just said that about them pickin him up. I knew you wanted a do it with me and I did too so I just said it."

"But you told me they didn't believe you about Vernon Clarence falling down the stairs."

"Yeah, they did. They just said they'd keep him overnight and us come pick him up this mornin."

"Cheri, let's get something straight. I *didn't* want a do it with you. It was against my will." Yet he knew there had been a measure of vigorous participation motivated by vengeance against Rase.

"Could a fooled me," she said, and gave him a horrible smile.

He was beginning to guess that she might be picking him to replace Rase. He literally felt his neck hair bristle.

"I want Sugar Puffs," whined Barbette.

"Then why the hell don't you go on home and get some," he snapped.

"Can I Mama?"

"Sure. Go on over."

The child was out the door, slamming it behind her, but the catch failed and the door began to boom and swing in the wind. He got up and closed it, poured himself another cup of coffee. Out the window he could see Barbette scampering up the Wham steps just as Graig came to the door, fumbling at his crotch. The girl disappeared inside and the mountain man pissed on the ground, turned and went back into the trailer. He was replaced by Rase, who apparently preferred fresh air to his own diaper-flavored bathroom.

"They're up over there. I think you better go home and get things back on track."

She leaned back in her chair and shot a stream of cigarette smoke at the ceiling. "He ain't goin a like it that you fucked me."

"He's not the only one don't like it," said Buddy. "Besides, you'd be dumb to say anything about that. He's got a temper—which you know. Think a your kid with the busted arm. Could be you next time. Probly will be you." He wanted nothing so much as to throw his gear in the back of the Jeep and take off for Alaska. The problem there was that his mother had not forwarded his checks amounting to several thousands and he had less than fifty dollars in his wallet and a credit card close to its maximum. He was in a bind. It was Sunday but he would drive to town, call his mother and see what was holding up the checks. First, he had to get Cheri out of here and on her way back to Rase.

"Well, you got to go back over there. You picked him, he's your husband, father a your kids. Go on over and fix things up. Get right with Mr. Wham. If you are smart keep your mouth shut about what happened. And he got any idea a comin over here to make trouble I got my .30-06 ready for him. You just let him know that. And you keep your ass over there, too. What happened last night was a big mistake and it will never happen again. I tried a help you with the hurt kid but that's where it stops. Get out a my life."

She gave a snort through her nose. "You sure don't get it about Rase. I bet he'll kill you. He won't be scared a no .30-06 in the hands somebody don't shoot much."

He knew she was right, and it made him furious. "Get out. *Now.* Get out."

She got up, leaving her still full coffee cup, and uttered the ultimate Wham riposte. "Fuck you."

She stuffed Lye under her arm, made a big deal of dropping the wetted blanket on the floor, and left, kicking the door closed with her nimble foot. As soon as she was around the corner he went out to the Jeep and got his rifle, brought it inside and loaded it.

He watched their trailer through the scope, expecting to see Rase Wham leap down the stairs in a blind fury, coming for him. But nothing happened and he supposed Cheri had kept her mouth shut for the moment, that they were all pigging out on Sugar Puffs, even the mountain man. He stripped his bed and shoved every soiled garment and sheet and pillow slip he could find into the laundry bag ready to go into town and spend the morning at the local laundry. He'd call his mother and find out about his checks, get his cousin Zane's telephone number.

Before he could leave he saw Graig and Cheri get in the Power Wagon and drive away. He guessed they were going to pick up Vernon Clarence, who probably had quite a hangover. That left Rase alone in the trailer with Barbette and Lye. If he was going to make a move, now would probably be the time.

He rushed out to his Jeep, threw the laundry in and took the back way past the packrat trailer across the sand and sage rather than drive past Rase's place where the aggrieved husband could pick him off from a window.

His own tires had left distinct tracks from the night before, and he followed them easily, but drove across the shallow end of the wash rather than going completely around it. The incline was steep but not impossible. Still, a bad place to get stuck.

While his clothes were washing he called his parents' house.

"Buddy, where in the world are you?"

"Didn't you get the letter I sent with the address?"

"No. Quite a lot a mail *for* you, but nothing from you."

"Ma, I got a ask you for a favor. I need my paycheck and savins account check real bad. Kind of a difficult situation has developed here. I decided I'm probly goin a Alaska, maybe contact Zane, stay there a few days if it's all right with him, get a job on one a the fishin boats. So I need Zane's address and telephone number. So I can call him. Like

I don't know if he's on the coast or what, but most of all I need those checks. Can you send them express mail? Or I suppose I could drive up there and get them if Dad's not still mad."

"Denali is in the middle, not on the coast. And Dad *is* still mad and as a matter a fact he's got all your mail in a big envelope out in his truck."

"Oh God." His father was capable of forging Buddy's signature and cashing the checks, taking the money against the value of the stolen goods. "But I need those checks. Can you talk to him, tell him I'm kind a desperate? Call you back tomorrow?"

"I'll try, Buddy. And I'll dig up Zane's number and address. Some place like 'Banana.' I keep it up in the attic with the Christmas card boxes."

"Okay, Ma, I'll call you tomorrow around noon."

He spent an uneasy night, the rifle in bed with him, half expecting to hear Rase Wham kick in the barricaded door. Hadn't Rase said he had an AK-47? Mr. Kalashnikov's little invention could shoot through the trailer as if it were made of rotten muslin. But Monday morning came, and with it the receding rumble of Rase's truck as he drove to work in the near dark.

At noon Buddy went to town to call his mother. His father answered.

"Yes, your checks are here. I got them out in the truck. Your mother told me you were havin a problem. What kind a problem?"

There was no point trying to hide anything from his father. He told him that Rase Wham had erupted in his life again, that something had happened with the wife, that he was worried that Rase might shoot him.

"Jesus, Buddy, not *him* again. You got a real talent for trouble. Listen, you better get out a there. He could do it and maybe get away with it. His old man is Apollo Wham—Polly Wham—in the legislature now, knows everbody. He could pull strings and sweep dirt under the rug. Just come on home right now. Don't waste time talkin on the phone, don't go pack your bags, just get in your Jeep and get here. Say it will take you five hours—get your ass home. *Now.* We'll discuss the ramifications when you get here."

It was a relief to know that his father thought the situation was serious. He was right—get out now while Rase was at work. But he didn't want to leave his clothes, the arrowhead he'd found, and the .30-06 still in the trailer. At some point he would have to go back for them. At home he spent hours with his father driving around and talking. He told him everything, about the mountain man, about Rase's kids, Vernon Clarence's broken arm, the drive to the hospital and about Cheri's successful assault.

He called Zane in Nenana, Alaska.

"Buddy, that's great! I've been trying for years to get some of the family to come on out here and look at the finest piece of real estate on the globe. I got a couple friends know some guys that fish and I'll ask around, see if there's any jobs. Even if you don't get on a boat there's some work. When do you think you'll be out?"

"Pretty soon. I got a go back to Wamsutter and get my stuff and I got a do it before the storms come. There's already been some snow. You got snow there?"

"Do birds have four toes?"

The next day, a Thursday, cold, cloudy and packing a strong wind, he drove back to Wamsutter and took the bad dirt track out to the trailer, sliding down into the wash and clawing his way up the other side. Although he'd been gone only three days there were two more drill rigs in sight. The weather report said possible snow showers. As he parked at the trailer a few flakes of snow fell and he could smell a storm closing in, not showers but a mean storm. Once again the weather report was wrong.

Nothing inside the trailer was disturbed. He went first to the little kitchen window and looked out.

There were no vehicles at the Wham trailer.

"Nobody home," he said to himself. He gathered his clothes, blankets and sheets, and his rifle, still in the bed, packed them in the Jeep. He would call Cootie and tell her that one month of trailer life in the Red Desert had been enough for him.

· · ·

In Wamsutter he parked in front of the post office and, mindful of the rifle in the back, was locking the Jeep when he heard a child's voice.

"Buddy!" It was Barbette, a half-eaten apple in her hand.

"Well, well, it's the Sugar Puff girl. How are you, Barbette?"

"I'm not the Sugar Puff girl anymore. Graig says Sugar Puffs aren't no good for you. But apples and bananas and grapes are."

He looked around nervously but did not see Rase's truck. He did see Graig's old Power Wagon, and walking toward it were Cheri, holding Lye, and Graig. Vernon Clarence skipped along, singing some small song and gripping Graig's shirt fringe with his good hand.

"Mama! Graig, *Look it!*" Barbette screeched. "*It's Buddy!*"

He lifted his hand in a lukewarm salute, not knowing if Rase would come out next, his arms full of beer, his heart full of murder. Cheri gave him a canary-eating grin and Graig rumbled and laughed.

"Son of a bitch, if it ain't old mountain man Buddy. We figured you skipped out and we'd never see you again."

"I just come back to pick up my stuff at the trailer. I'm headin out, actually. Goin a—west. Heard about a job." That was in case Rase asked where he had gone. Rase was capable of following him to Alaska. Another good reason to work on a boat.

Vernon Clarence was pulling at his sleeve. He seemed a different child, the dull face animated, his eyes bright and bold.

"Buddy," he said. "Buddy. Buddy. Buddy, guess what?"

"What? I see you still got your arm in that red cast."

"Buddy." And he pulled hard. "I want a tell you somethin. A secret."

Buddy crouched down and Vernon Clarence's sticky lips came close to his ear. He whispered loudly and happily.

"Buddy, *the wufs ate daddy*." He laughed, paused to watch the effect this news would have. Buddy, without any effort, looked astonished. Vernon Clarence continued to unload his momentous news.

"And Graig says not to tell nobody. Graig is our daddy now. And no wufs can eat him because he is their friend! And they won't eat *us* because he is our new daddy!"

"Congratulations," he whispered back to Vernon Clarence and stood up. Something very bad had happened to Rase.

Graig was looking at him. He had to have guessed what Vernon Clarence had whispered. Buddy extended one hand helplessly as if there was nothing to say, found himself looking into the mountain man's eyes. The old merry twinkle was extinguished. A hard, alpha stare had taken its place. Cheri must have told him her version of what had happened the night Vernon Clarence's arm was broken and Graig now saw him as a rival.

He meant to say something mollifying, add an exit line and get the hell out of Wamsutter but he began to back away and when he opened his mouth what he blurted was, "I see you got your own pack now."

Issue 171, 2004

Ben Okri

✠

The Dream-Vendor's August

Ajegunle Joe spent the evening reading the letters from the few subscribers he had left. Without a single exception they called him a fraud and demanded back their money. When he had finished reading he was very depressed. He went to a bar and got quite drunk, but that didn't improve anything. So he went to his favorite hotel to look for a cheap prostitute. That didn't help either. He kept hearing the subscribers in his head. In the end he paid the woman for her time and left more depressed than he had arrived. He got home, lit two mosquito coils, and climbed into bed. He forgot to lock the door. Soon he was snoring.

He dreamed about a woman with a rugged face and indifferent eyes. All through the dream he didn't have an erection. When he woke up it was with the certainty that someone had been in the room while he was asleep. He saw the open door and soon found that large quantities of printing paper, his tubes of printing ink, his transistor radio, his pornographic magazines, and a book he much valued called *The Ten Wonders of Africa*, were missing.

He sat on the bed. He stared at the almanacs of long-bearded mystics on the wall. Somewhere in him was the feeling that a pain he had lived with had suddenly edged toward the unbearable. He had the taste of tangerines in his mouth. He was two weeks into the month of August.

When July passed with its thunderous downpours, and when August advanced with its dry winds and browning elephant grass, Joe felt himself at the mercy of a cyclical helplessness. Two years earlier, around the same time, Joe lost a woman he had been planning to marry. They had met one day to discuss their future together. Joe had catarrh. He made the mistake of blowing his nose in her presence, the act of which produced a long and disgusting sound. She didn't show her disapproval, but afterward all talk of marriage was avoided. When later on he learned that she had become engaged to another man, Joe was shattered. He went around in a daze. He no longer walked with his former arrogant swing. He became clumsy and unsure of himself. He lost his job. One night in a bar when he tried to sound like his former arrogant self, he got involved in a fight and had two of his front teeth knocked into his mouth. Then he took to strangling his laughter.

It was after the woman left his life, after his birthday in September, that he got another job in a small printing press. He took correspondence courses in psychology and salesmanship and earned himself two diplomas. He developed an unusual interest in the occult and in mysticism. His thoughts became too deep for him and his dreams became more mysterious. He gradually experienced himself being taken over by a new personality. He took to writing down his visions and dreams: then he began publishing them as cheap pamphlets. The first pamphlet was called *Mysteries of Orumaka*. Quite a few people bought it and he was encouraged by the modest sales. With the help of his boss he printed pamphlets like: *How to Sleep Soundly, How to Have Powerful Dreams, How to Fight Witches and Wizards*, and *How to Banish Poverty from Your Life*. The pamphlets achieved some limited popularity but they didn't make him any money. Sometimes when there wasn't much work at the printing press Ajegunle Joe would take bundles of his pamphlets to sell on the molue buses. It was in the Christmas of that year that it occurred to him to set up a correspondence course on how people could improve their lives. He discussed it with his boss and they agreed to split profits. Two adverts were placed in the newspapers and soon they had subscribers. The correspondence course was named: "Turn Life Into Money."

And then came the following August. Tax inspectors took a sudden interest in him. His mother fell ill and he had to go home and see her. When he got back the landlord had taken it into his head to increase the rent. It was an August of elections, political fevers and riggings. Ajegunle Joe's dreams became so violent that he wrote and printed a treasonable tract called: *The Farce Which Will Become History*. Nobody bought the tract and one night the printer's shop was raided by soldiers, who carried away all existing copies. The police got hold of Joe the next day, and he was jailed for two weeks without any charges being brought against him. Then, suddenly, he was released. He wrote to all the newspapers about his arrest, but because no one knew him, and everyone was afraid, his letters were never published. What made matters worse was that his boss suddenly opted out of their joint venture, deducted half the losses from Joe's salary, and then gave him the sack. But what saved Joe was that the new personality had taken him over completely. He spent the rest of the year selling his pamphlets in the day and occasionally working at the docks in the night.

This August was no better. Business had been worse than usual. Printing paper was scarce. And he felt stale. Nothing moved in him that morning. He found himself at the point where his faith in his own correspondence course had reached its lowest.

He got up from the bed and opened the window. He went to the toilet and then had a shower. Back in his room he lit a stick of incense. He fetched a tumbler of water, breathed deeply, and drank, facing the east. He sat in one of his chairs. He intoned some vowel sounds and then he meditated on an empty stomach. By the time he had finished meditating and sealing his morning prayers with occultic signs, he had begun to accept the reality of his losses. He made some food and ate. He was about to start cleaning his room when he heard someone calling to him from outside.

"Is Jungle Joe in? Jungle Joe! Your friend is here."

His friend, Cata-cata, knocked and came into the room. They called him by that name because he used to be a hard-headed generator of confusion. He had quieted down now; he was even thinking of marriage. He used to be a boxer, but after being knocked out in the first round of an unmemorable featherweight match, he seemed to settle for the anonymity of being a ladies man. He was tall and solemn; he had a wide nose and narrow eyes. He wore a Ghanian print shirt and khaki trousers. He worked regular night shifts at the docks. In the daytime he fished. He smiled broadly at Joe when he came into the room. He had two mangoes in his hand. He had a Ghanian woman with him. She was robust, and her body was slow in its thick sweaty sensuality. She had fleshy lips, a kind face, and she smiled a lot. She carried an orange and two bottles of small stout.

"How are you Joe?" Cata-cata said, slapping his friend on the back.

"Not too good."

"Why, what's happened?"

"Everything."

"Have you met my friend?" Cata-cata said to the Ghanian woman. She was still smiling.

"Well, this is Ajegunle Joe, occultist and dreamer. Joe, this is my girlfriend, Sarah."

They greeted one another. The Ghanian woman avoided meeting Joe's eyes. They were all still standing. Cata-cata offered Joe a mango.

"No, thank you, my friend. Things are so bad I don't have a mouth for fruits," Joe said.

"That's a shame."

"Cata-cata, I've just been robbed."

"When?" Cata-cata said, taking a seat and indicating to Sarah that she do the same. She sat on the bed.

"Today. When I was asleep."

"You mean they robbed you when you were asleep?"

"Yes," said Joe, dryly.

"What sort of sleep is that? You must have been drinking too much."

Cata-cata laughed in the direction of the woman.

"I think I left the door open," said Joe unsmilingly.

"What did they take?"

"Pamphlets. Clothes. They took the transistor radio and . . ."

"That radio?" interrupted Cata-cata, laughing again in the direction of the woman.

"They must have been desperate . . ."

"And worst of all," said Joe, "they took that book that I got. *The Ten Wonders of Africa.*"

"I'm sorry to hear that," said Cata-cata with laughter still on his face.

Ajegunle Joe nodded. He was feeling in bad humor. He sat on a stool and kept eyeing the woman. Looks very ripe, he thought. Then he felt bitter that for two years he had been without a regular woman.

"I can't offer you drinks," Joe said suddenly.

"What is drinks between friends, eh? Besides, we brought our own."

The Ghanian woman crossed her legs. Then she put the bottles of stout on the table. There was a long silence. There was some embarrassment in the air. Cata-cata kept trying to catch Joe's eyes.

"So how is the course doing?"

"Bad," said Joe, staring grimly at his friend. Cata-cata made signs for Joe to leave the room. Joe pretended not to notice. He continued with what he was saying.

"One of my subscribers ran into trouble," he said in an even voice.

"How?"

"She followed my instructions and got sacked. She wants her money back."

"What instructions?" Cata-cata said, gesticulating furiously.

"In the first lesson I instructed them to look fearlessly at people in the eye and to speak up forcefully. Well, her boss didn't like it when she did."

Cata-cata laughed again. The Ghanian woman laughed as well. She looked very youthful when she laughed and her breasts rocked. Joe remained dour.

When the general laughter had subsided Cata-cata said, with more intentionality than was needed: "Joe, aren't you going out? It's going to rain soon, you know."

"It's not supposed to rain in August."

"But it's going to rain, anyway," Cata-cata said, glaring at Joe.

"So why should I go out if it's going to rain soon, eh?"

He knew Cata-cata was referring to their usual arrangement. I've been robbed, Joe thought, and all my friend can think about is sex.

"Because you can go out and come back before it rains, that's why."

"I see," said Joe.

Cata-cata, surprised at his friend's incomprehension, looked from Joe to the woman and back again.

"You know what I mean," he said, with some desperation.

"I don't know," Joe replied, sweating in pretended ignorance. "How can I know when I've been robbed, eh? And all the subscribers want their money back. I don't know anything, my friend."

Joe was very serious. Look at all that is happening to me, he thought, and all he wants to do is make love to this woman in my room.

"By the way," Joe said aloud, "what is wrong with your room, eh?"

Cata-cata was alarmed. He stammered. He had a regular girlfriend; she had a key to his room; and she made it a habit to turn up at the oddest hours. There was even talk of marriage between them. He wanted the Ghanian woman quickly, on the side. He couldn't risk the use of his own room, and Joe knew this well.

"I have a relative staying," Cata-cata said, almost pleadingly.

Ajegunle Joe stared at him unsympathetically. Cata-cata suddenly stood up.

"I want to talk to you outside," he said to Joe.

They both went out.

"You're a bastard!" Cata-cata said, the moment they were outside.

"Things are hard," Joe said.

"What are you trying to do? Spoil my fun, eh?"

"Things are bad."

"So what? Aren't we friends? Look. Relax. We'll go fishing later."

"What will that do for me?"

"You might catch a fish. You've never caught a fish."

"A fish won't pay my rent. A fish won't get those thieves."

"You are mad."

"Rubbish."

They were silent for a moment. They could see the back of the

Ghanian woman through the window. She fidgeted. She played with the orange.

"You know she likes you."

"Who?"

"Sarah. I've done a build up of you. I can tell she likes you. Have her afterward. She won't mind."

"How do you know?"

"What do you mean? She is a good, fun-loving woman."

"I don't want her afterward," Joe said, looking at her through the window.

"What do you want then, eh?"

"Money."

"Money?"

"Lend me some money."

"More? You owe me ten already."

"Give me another ten."

"I am not a bank."

"Give me ten. I'll sell some pamphlets today. I'll pay you back when some subscriptions come in."

"And when will that be?"

"Today, tomorrow, soon."

"You've been saying that for two years now."

"Lend me ten."

"Okay."

"Things are hard."

"Things are always hard for you."

"They'll get better."

"When do you want it?"

"Now."

"Now?"

"Yes."

Cata-cata gave Joe the ten naira. They went back in without exchanging another word.

The Ghanian woman had started peeling the orange with her fingers when they both came in. Cata-cata sat down on the bed next to her. He put his arm round her.

Joe said, "I'm going to check my post office box before it rains. Do you want some stamps?"

"No."

Ajegunle Joe looked at the woman as she ate the orange. With her palm she wiped the juice that flowed down the sides of her mouth.

Struck by the fleshiness of her thighs, noticing the succulence of her lips, Joe said: "Have you read any of my pamphlets?"

"No," said the woman.

"You should. There are many powers in this world."

"Leave her alone," Cata-cata said, caressing her neck.

"They call me the Dream-Vendor," Joe said, "because I am at the mercy of my dreams. I am the man who runs the Cosmic Power Correspondence Course. Have you ever heard of it?"

"Leave her alone," Cata-cata said. "She can't read and she doesn't have any money to subscribe. Leave the poor girl alone."

"Yes, I have," the woman said.

Both men turned toward her.

"My younger brother is taking your course. He thinks it's all right. Every morning he looks into the mirror and says strange things. He drinks a glass of water, breathes deeply and starts making funny noises. He is always asking me the direction of the east. He is going to university in Ghana next year. He always smells of bad incense."

Ajegunle Joe was surprised. He beamed. He held up his head. He was so amazed that he didn't say anything. His throat kept moving. His mood immediately improved and he wore his battered galoshes and the greatcoat he had bought cheaply from among the stolen goods at the docks. He bustled around the room. He moved with a forced swing that tossed the bulk of the coat one way and another. The swagger suited him fine.

He said: "People need advice. People need power. To see far is the only way to win the battles of this terrible life."

The Ghanian woman said: "My brother takes several other courses. About five of them. Every night he does a different thing. Sometimes he mixes up all the instructions. He is too serious. I think he is going mad."

She had finished eating the orange. Her eyes shone brilliantly. She stopped smiling.

Ajegunle Joe didn't seem to have heard what she said, because he went on to deck himself out with his talismanic necklaces. He made a show of wearing his three rings. He explained their powers as he wore them. One of them was called "The Ring of Merlin." It was supposed to have been brought to Africa by Portuguese sailors. It had the magic number 7 in green; it was guaranteed to make him invisible in time of danger. Then there was "The Ring of Master Eckhart." He was a German mystic. This ring, Joe said, had been additionally treated by a Spanish divine. The third one, with its red triangle, was "The Ring of Aladdin." It had been found on the dead body of Isaac Newton.

"For every act there is an equal and opposite reaction," Joe said. He winked at his friend. He bared the gap in his front teeth in a smile to the woman.

He said: "Nothing stays still. Do it gently, but think of my poor bed."

He swung the back of his coat and made for the door. Soon he had the sky opening above him.

He paused just outside his room. He stood still, listening. He heard the bed creak.

He heard Cata-cata say: *"What are you waiting for?"*

Then the window was slammed shut.

Joe went up the street, toward the main road. The air was dense and unpleasant with the smell of the evaporating gutters. It was August and the bushes near uncompleted houses were thickly filmed with dust, and no trees were in bloom.

The main road was cluttered with multiple traffic jams. Drivers sweated at the steering wheels: they looked as if they were undergoing the most perverse of punishments. Joe felt a peculiar freedom walking past the vehicles in the standstill, so he began to stride. In the second lesson of his correspondence course, Joe says: "The way you carry yourself is the way you want people to think of you." When Joe cuts down the road he looks like an amiable scarecrow. He walks too stylishly. People sometimes say that too much style betrays hunger.

. . .

There was chaos at the post office. Queues stretched out from the building and down the road. Joe checked his box: there weren't any subscriptions, but there were inquiries about his catalogue. He joined the end of the queue and it was a while before he got anywhere near the counter. He heard someone in the queue saying that the post office workers were so underpaid that they were now sabotaging the post. When he got to the counter it took some time, and some shouting, before any of the clerks paid him any attention.

The clerk said: "Why are you shouting as if you are in your mother's kitchen?"

"God punish you for saying that," Joe said.

An argument ensued and Joe got so worked up he felt his heart hammering unnaturally against his ribs. He quieted down. The clerk went on abusing him. Joe suffered the abuses in silence. He bought his stamps. He was counting his change when he suddenly felt a searing sensation in his crotch. He pushed his way out through the crowd; but the crowd pushed back on him. He found himself being squashed to the metallic frame of the door and he was overcome with panic. He started shouting, swearing, fighting his way out.

He was on his way back home when the sky came closer to the ground. Petty traders and stall-owners rushed to clear their goods. Joe continued to stride on stylishly. There was commotion everywhere. Thunder exploded overhead. The road was lit in a moment's incandescence. The sky darkened and lightning split the air. The rain pelted down in a hurry. Gutters began to overflow and vehicles, avoiding the potholes, splashed mud all over Ajegunle Joe's greatcoat. He was soon thoroughly drenched and he had to run all the way home with water squelching in his galoshes.

Cata-cata and the woman had gone when Joe got back. Water ran down his back, along his spine. He shivered. He found the key under the doormat.

It was hot in the room. Joe undressed, dried himself, and wore fresh clothes all through the sex smells of the heated room. He couldn't open the window; the rain would come in. So he lit a stick of incense.

Cata-cata and the Ghanian woman had left the orange peelings and the mango seeds on the center table. The two bottles of stout were empty. The bed was very rough. Flies had come into the room. Joe became very despondent. He changed the sheets and climbed into bed. He slept through the steady drone of the falling rain. He dreamed that the rain had been falling for a long time and the great voice of thunder spoke intermittently from the sky. People were wailing and there was a beautiful music pervading the world. He felt he knew the music, though he had never heard it before.

And then a midget with a large head and red eyes came to him and said: "How are you?"

"Fine," Joe said.

"Good."

"How long has it been raining?" Joe asked the midget.

"Forty days."

Joe stared at the midget. The music stopped, the rain increased.

The midget said: "Open your eyes."

"They are open," Joe said.

"No they're not. Open them."

Joe opened his eyes and woke up. The rain was heavier and water had been flowing into his room from beneath the door. Joe stayed in bed. He turned over and listened to his stomach rumbling. He fell back asleep and the midget came to him again.

"I told you your eyes were shut," the midget said.

"You did."

"How can you see me if they are shut?"

"Faith," said Joe.

The midget laughed.

"I like you," the midget said.

"I don't know you," Joe said, "but I like you too."

"You talk in riddles."

"I'm sorry," said Joe.

"I hate people who are sorry," the midget said.

"But you just said you liked me."

"I do. That's why I'm going to give you something. But when I come and ask for it, you must give it back."

"That's fine," said Joe.

The midget put something in Joe's palm and closed the fingers over it. Joe opened his hand and a blue light flashed in his eyes, but Joe didn't see anything.

"You didn't give me anything," Joe said.

"Yes I did. But it's flown away now. I didn't ask you to look at it, did I?"

"What was it?" Joe asked.

"Wisdom."

Joe was quiet for a moment.

"Why don't you give me something else then?"

The midget gave him something and told him to put it away. Joe put it in his pocket. The midget grinned and then disappeared.

When Joe woke up it had stopped raining. He spent some of the evening looking at his finances, which were very low. Then he tried to do some more work on the fifteenth lesson of his correspondence course. He had been writing on the theme of adversity and he couldn't find anything more to say on the subject. All he had written was: "Adversity is the secret way to the center, to the base and springboard. Train your muscles before you leap. Train your head before you soar." The pile of manuscript lay beside him on the bed. He tried to think about adversity, but he succeeded only in thinking about women. He thought about sex, without getting hot. He soon fell back asleep.

Ajegunle Joe spent the morning sweeping the water out from his room. Centipedes and worms had come in with the water. He caught the worms, to use sometime for fishing, and put them in a bottle. In the afternoon he took large quantities of his pamphlets and went out. At the main road bus conductors shouted their destination and there was commotion as people rushed to embark. Joe was astonished to find that a bus stop had materialized at the top of his street. With the bus stop had also come Ogogoro retailers, corn-roasters, petty traders, prostitutes, pickpockets. Ajegunle Joe bought himself a tumbler of Ogogoro and drank it slowly. He surveyed the bickering crowd, unable to believe his luck. When he finished the Ogogoro he began selling his pamphlets. In three hours he made thirty naira, selling off the pamphlets he brought with him. He went home and fetched some more; but by the time he got back most of the crowd had gone.

In the evening Joe went to a bar near his place for a quiet celebratory drink. He had been drinking heavily for a while, turning words and phrases on adversity in his head, when he noticed a woman sitting alone at a corner table. She looked familiar. Her face was bruised and puffed under the eyes. She had a plaster on her forehead, bandages on her left arm, and a wound just above her left ankle. She wore a black dress and white high-heeled shoes. Every time Joe dropped his tumbler and looked in her direction he was convinced she had just looked away. This went on till Joe eventually caught her eye. It was the Ghanian woman. She stared at him totally without recognition. He ordered two small bottles of stout, picked up his drink, and went over to join her.

"What happened to you?"

"None of ya business."

"Aren't you Sarah, Cata-cata's woman?"

"Don't talk to me."

"Don't you remember me?"

"Eh, so what?"

"What have I done to you, eh?"

"Birds of a feather . . ."

"What feather?"

". . . shit together."

"Hah! Sarah! What is this, eh?"

She stared stubbornly through him. He got up and opened one of the bottles of stout at the counter. When he got back she was smiling. She looked almost ghoulish with her puffed eyes, and her deranged, upturned lips.

"So how are you?" Joe asked.

"Shut up and pour me some of the stout," she said.

"Sarah! Take it easy."

"You men are like paper."

He poured out her drink. She finished the tumbler of stout in a single gulp. She took out a cigarette and lit it. She stared at him.

"Talk to me," she said, with glinting eyes.

Joe couldn't think of anything to say. After she had finished the two bottles of stout Joe went and got her three more.

"I can't finish three," she said.

Joe stared at the ring she had on her middle finger. It was a large red ring with the white face of a little tiger.

"What sort of ring is that, eh?"

"Protection," she said.

"What sort of protection?"

"From stupid men like ya friend," she said.

"Sarah, tell me what happened. Did you quarrel?"

She played with her ring. She drank down another bottle, wiped her mouth, and then she went to the toilet. When she came back she told him what had happened. After she and Cata-cata had finished in Joe's room they went to the bus stop. Cata-cata was seeing her off home when suddenly a woman stepped out from the crowd and blocked their path. The woman turned out to be Cata-cata's regular girlfriend.

"You should have seen her. She was just like a witch," Sarah said.

"And what happened?"

"What do you think happened? She started shouting. Cursing. Screaming. And you should have seen Cata-cata. He's big for nothing. He was begging her. Begging her. In public. And then he began to lie about me to my own very face. He said I was just a friend. And then he said I was your new girlfriend. He denied me to my own face."

"Then what happened?"

"His girlfriend scratched his face and spat in his eyes. The next thing was that both of them were fighting. In public. She picked up a stick and knocked him on the head. He slapped her. You should have heard her scream. Just like a witch. Quickly she ran and picked up a stone. He grabbed her and slapped her again. She dropped the stone and threw sand in his eyes. He went mad. He started hitting everywhere and he slapped me and then I too joined the fight. I joined her. Both of us jumped on him and he beat us and then a soldier came with a whip and flogged us and we ran. That friend of yours is a coward. He and his woman went home and settled their quarrel."

Joe stared at her incredulously. He went and bought two bottles of beer for himself. He drank while staring at her. She didn't seem to notice his gaze.

"Cata-cata is my best friend, but I'm not like that. Big people don't need courage. I protect my friends."

"Shit," she said.

"I can help you," he said solemnly.

"Help yourself."

They fell silent.

Then Sarah said: "Why do you men like thin girls with big breasts, eh?"

Joe thought for a long time before he said: "I like girls like you."

She stared at him from reddened eyes. She stood up.

"Where are you going now?"

She picked up the two remaining bottles of stout.

Then she said: "Men are always asking stupid questions."

They went out together.

He had hardly shut the window and locked the door when he felt her kissing his neck. He felt the full softness of her wet lips. He felt hot, but he didn't feel right. He felt very hot, a great yearning ached in him, he began to tremble. She kissed his face over and he noticed that she had a freckled tongue. He reached down under her pants and he was blasted by the surprising texture of her pubic hair. She was richly wet. He took off her clothes and saw that she had beads round her waist. He spent a long time kissing her breasts and playing with the circlets of hair round her nipples. Her breasts quivered. He took off his magic rings and his clothes and they went to bed. She was hot and her eyes were heavy-lidded. She still had her strange ring on. She struck him as one of those fortunate women who feel deeply their own arousal and whom it takes little touches to satisfy. He didn't like the women who were remote from their own desires, whom he would make love to from sunrise to sundown with them still seeking their elusive climaxes.

He fingered her and kissed her. He went up her, but it wasn't right. He couldn't understand. She was wet and willing, half-sunken in euphoria, waiting, it seemed, for a mere full penetration, but he wasn't hard. So he tried. He tried to dissolve himself into her desire, to feel the spell-breaking reality of her nakedness. He breathed in her potent, shameless body smells. And she waited. And he tried.

Then eventually he said: "I think something is wrong."

"What?"

"I don't know."

"You don't want to do it?"

"I want to do it wickedly, but . . . it's not hard."

She played with his private part desultorily, impatiently, wrenching it to both sides, dragging it down, talking gruffly to it, but still nothing came of her efforts. Suddenly she got out of bed. She dressed furiously.

"You and ya friend are completely useless," she said.

Ajegunle Joe started to apologize, to suggest alternatives, but she slapped him hard on the face. Before he could recover she had gone out into the August night, leaving behind her two unopened bottles of stout.

Ajegunle Joe stared at the door. He sat on the bed. Then he got dressed. He wore his red, long-billed cap. He went out and bought himself a large tumbler of Ogogoro. He spent the evening staring at the almanacs of the long-bearded mystics, without seeing them. He fell asleep with the red cap still on his head.

Joe spent the next two days in misery. He went to a petty chemist and bought an ointment for gonorrhea and tablets for "increased virility." They were expensive. They did not solve his problem. And his problem did not help the sales of his pamphlets. On the third day when he got up to do his improvised sales talk on the molue buses, his mouth was dry, his voice was thin and unconvincing, and people laughed at him. He also found, to his chagrin, that he had serious competitors. Some of them sold pamphlets foretelling the future, complete guides to palm-reading, even pamphlets that professed herbal cures for everything from leprosy to rheumatism. Humiliated, carried away by the intensity of competition, Joe began to denounce the regime, the society, policemen, soldiers. He made predictions of violent riots in the north, and tribal cannibalism in the south. It was unfortunate for him, however, that there were two policemen in mufti on the bus. But it was fortunate for him that he was only thrown off; he would otherwise most certainly have spent the rest of August in prison. Joe was not particularly bothered by the manhandling. The policemen were northerners; besides, he always believed that when people didn't like a dream he offered, it was usually because the dream was true.

After Joe had been thrown off the molue bus he headed homewards. He was wearing his red, long-billed cap, a jacket too large at the shoulders, his three talismanic rings, a shabby pair of blue trousers, and his galoshes. He was an unhappy sight. He went past a mechanic's workshop and an herbalist's signboard. Next to the board there was a red-painted shed. The door of the shed opened slowly as Ajegunle Joe went past. Then a chicken with a red cloth tied to its foot came out, and then went back into the shed. Joe should have remembered the fourteenth lesson of his own correspondence course, which says: "Every human being has got something to be afraid of, in the form of signs." But Joe didn't remember. Without thinking, he sneaked into the shed.

It was dark inside. He smelt animal blood, stale palm wine, and excellent cooking. When his eyes got used to the darkness he saw shelves on which were candles, bones, bundles of spiders' webs, jars, bottles, snakeskins. Something brushed against his galoshes and he screamed, jumping backward. It was a turtle. Then he saw the numerous snails on the walls. A lizard regarded him from a niche.

"Is anybody in?"

He heard a cough. Then he noticed the other room in the shed, partitioned by an antelope screen. Someone was in the room, in the half-light, eating. Joe smelt smoked shrimps, fried plantain, bush meat, and he salivated.

"Who is there?" he said.

The chicken went out of the room, past the partition. A door opened. He heard water being poured into a glass.

The lights came on suddenly and then a voice said: "The minute I saw your red cap I knew you were mine! Come in. Sit down. My name is Aringo. I am the most underrated herbalist in this God-forsaken city."

Joe went into the inner room.

"So. Yes. What do you want? You have family problems? A strange illness? Is someone stealing your job from you? You have woman problems? Sit down! If you have money, I can cure anything."

Joe sat on a stool. The herbalist stared at him expectantly. He had a bony, rugged face, and blazing eyes. He sweated gloriously. He wore a red soutane and he had beads around his neck. He had a long tongue which kept showing when he spoke.

"Talk! Talk! What's your problem? Have you come just to look at me? That costs money, you know," the herbalist said, baring his yellow teeth.

Joe was stuck for words.

The herbalist, increasing the volume of his voice, said: "Look, mister man, I don't have time to stare at you. Can't you speak, eh? Have you got mosquitoes in your brain, eh?"

Joe still couldn't find anything to say. He stammered beneath his breath.

"Did someone beat you up, eh? I can give you medicine for fighting. You will be able to fight three men for seven days non-stop and you won't even be tired. You won't even sweat. That medicine costs ten naira, but it's guaranteed."

Joe's continued silence began to exasperate the herbalist, who stood up suddenly. He strode up and down the inner room with the quick, angular movements of a cricket. That was when Joe noticed the figure of a warrior juju in a dark corner of the room. It was covered in candle wax, bits of kola nuts, native chalk, feathers of birds. It glistened with libations.

It looked very menacing, very attentive, standing there in the dark.

The herbalist said: "Get up. Come and see this."

The herbalist took the cover off a clay pot. Joe got up and went over. Something large and red pumped at the bottom of the pot.

"This is a crocodile's heart. Come and look at this."

He showed Joe an earthenware pot: there was a snake curled up in its transparent liquid.

"Now. Tell me your problem and I will help you."

It took some time before Joe managed to say, in a whisper: "It's woman problem."

"Ah-*hah*! So it's *woman problem*, eh?"

"Yes."

"What kind of woman problem? You don't have a woman, or is there one in particular . . ."

"I tried to do it but I couldn't do it," Joe said, hurriedly.

"What couldn't you do? Tell me. Don't be afraid."

"It wouldn't stand up."

"You mean you had a woman there, naked, and it wouldn't stand up?"

"Yes," Joe said in a whisper.

"I didn't hear you."

"Yes."

"You should have said so. It's a small problem. Is that all you were whispering to me? Is that what you are ashamed of, eh?"

"Yes."

"Do you think you are the first person to suffer it?"

"No."

"The English people have a name for it. They call it *impotence*."

"I know."

"So you know? I see."

He gave Joe a severe look.

"Take down your trousers," the herbalist suddenly commanded.

"*What?*"

"I said take down your trousers. Let me see what's wrong with you."

"But . . ."

"But what? What's wrong with you, eh? You think you are special, eh? This month alone I have circumcised two white men. I have treated three Lebanese men for gonorrhea. Not to mention the Portuguese women. So you think you are special, eh? Okay. Go! Leave my shed! Get out and carry your *impotence* with you!"

Joe coyly lowered his trousers and his underpants. The herbalist inspected him.

"Is it this tiny thing you're ashamed of, eh?"

Joe was silent. The herbalist continued with his inspection and then said: "You are lucky. You don't have gonorrhea."

He straightened. Joe pulled up his trousers. He looked defeated.

The herbalist said: "How much have you got?"

Joe stammered. The herbalist did not press the point.

He said: "In this my shed I have everything you need. I can give you the sexual power of a horse, or of a hippopotamus. They cost differently, of course. Talk to me. What do you want to fuck like? A tiger? A lion? You want to do it like a cat, or quickly like a dog? I have different things for women, too. If you both want to be powerful in bed, all it takes is money."

"If I want to do it like a bull, how much will that cost?" Joe risked asking.

The herbalist eyed him disdainfully.

He said: "You won't be able to afford that one. I sold that medicine to a Portuguese man last month. He came back three times for more. So. Which one do you want?"

There was another silence.

"Will the medicine work immediately?"

"Yes. Guaranteed."

Another silence.

Then the herbalist suddenly, sharply, said: "Take off those rings! Take them off!"

Joe started.

"Take them off! *Now*! Unless you have come here to *challenge* me."

Joe still didn't understand what was happening. The herbalist bent over and pulled off his red soutane. His chest and stomach were covered in weird scarifications. He had a bulbous navel.

"If you want my treatment, take off those rings," the herbalist said, reaching for a cutlass, which he waved menacingly in the air.

Joe took off the rings and put them in his coat pocket. The herbalist still waved the cutlass as if he might use it.

He said: "They are useless rings. Quack rings. I have got better ones. I have got one that shows you if you are healthy and it flashes before there is danger. I have got a ring that will make any woman you want come to you. I have got another one that you wear only when you are discussing a lot of money. That one costs a lot. I have even got one of King Solomon's rings. I won't sell it. So. Which one do you want, eh?"

"I'll have the medicine of an antelope," Joe said eventually.

The herbalist was relieved.

"It costs thirty naira. Not a kobo more, not a kobo less."

Joe had only thirty-five naira on him.

"Okay," he said, weakly.

His course of treatment consisted of having to wash in murky herbal water, rubbing the afflicted part with a dark, grainy ointment, and drinking a tasteless pot of soup in which had been supposedly sprinkled the grindings of an antelope's testicles. Then a fire was built in the backyard which he had to extinguish with his urine. When he finished the course of treatment nothing happened. Joe gave it some time and then he got angry and demanded his money back; but people were knocking on the outside door.

The herbalist, having already lost interest in him, said: "Be patient. Go home and be patient. I've got other customers at the door."

"You are a crook. You are a thief," Joe shouted.

The herbalist's face darkened, his nose flared; but he went to a niche, came back, and gave Joe his business card.

"Go home. If by Saturday nothing happens, come and burn down my shed."

Joe took the card and stamped out of the shed. He felt nauseous, cheated, and foolish.

Joe caught a bus home.

He got a seat at the back, near the window. The traffic moved slowly. The road and pavement were full of trinket sellers, hawkers of smoked fish, petty traders of bread and boiled eggs. Without being aware of it, Joe had been watching a girl who sold oranges. Now and again the girl broke out and sang: "Sweet orange re-o!" She had a clear, beautiful voice.

It wasn't long before Joe became aware that he had been staring at her. She had browned teeth. Her face was pale with dried sweat. She had on a single wrapper and a loose blouse. She caught his eye and came over to sell him some oranges. He didn't know how to refuse, so he bought two. When the girl went back to singing of her sweet oranges Joe felt something in him. The traffic eased. Joe smiled. Beneath his coat, he felt the quiet salute of desire.

He was tremulous with desperation when he got off the bus. He went to the bar in search of Sarah. She wasn't there. He ordered a few bottles of beer and he waited. The longer he waited the more unbearable his desire became. He suffered such an unabated hardness that he was forced to go home and change into his mud-splattered greatcoat. He went from one bar to another, hoping to find Sarah. He didn't find her. All night he was hard and it began to hurt in its hardness. He couldn't meditate, couldn't sleep. He tossed and turned, worried that the herbalist had given him an unusually strong dose of the antelope medicine. In the morning he was still hard. It was in the evening that he began to approach normality. And by then it had become clear that the only way he could find the Ghanian woman was through his friend, Cata-cata.

He chose an unfortunate time to pay a visit. When he knocked on the door and went in, he saw his friend's room in disarray. Clothes were scattered all over the bed. On the cupboard there was a boxing glove that had been cut up grotesquely. There were torn photographs on the table. Cata-cata sat on a chair exhaling cigarette smoke like an enraged bull. He had scratches on his neck, and a cut on his forehead.

"What happened to you, my friend?"

"Nothing."

"Nothing?"

"Woman problem, as usual."

Joe laughed.

"What's so funny?"

"Nothing."

They were silent, till Joe said: "Did they beat you up again?"

"Who?"

"The women."

"What women?"

"Nothing."

"What women?"

"Forget it."

Joe went and sat on the bed.

"Have you seen Sarah?"

"Why?"

"I want to talk to her."

"Why?"

"Why not?"

"She's my woman."

"What about the one you've got?"

"None of your business."

"I want to talk to her."

"About what?"

"About her brother, the one taking my course."

"Leave her alone."

"You're selfish."

"Go and find your own woman, my friend."

They were silent. Then Cata-cata put out his cigarette. He laughed.

"You should have seen those two big women fighting. They went at one another like hungry tigers. Fought and scratched. I hate women fighting, so I reconciled them. You know what I did afterward, eh?"

"What?"

"I brought them home. And enjoyed both of them. Together."

"Lie!" said Joe.

"True. I swear."

"Lie!"

"How do you know it's a lie, eh? Were you there?"

"The Ghanian woman told me . . ."

"What . . ."

Cata-cata leaped up from the chair and rushed at Joe. He grabbed his friend by the collar of the greatcoat and shook him, wrenched him up, and threw him against the wall. Cata-cata went at him again, grabbed him round the neck, and pulled back his left fist. His eyes were deranged with jealousy. Then he suddenly relaxed. He lowered his fist. He went and sat down on the chair. He lit another cigarette. Neither of them spoke for a while. Joe stayed where he was with his back against the wall.

"I'm sorry, my friend."

Joe was silent.

"Don't be angry. Me and my woman quarreled before you arrived."

Joe didn't move.

"So you are angry with me? Can't you forgive and forget? Okay. I will tell you where you can find her."

Cata-cata told him; Joe still didn't speak. Cata-cata went out and bought three placatory bottles of beer: Joe continued with the sulky silence.

It was only when Cata-cata asked Joe to forget the money he owed, that Joe said: "You don't know, and I won't tell you."

He went to the door.

"Let's go fishing," Cata-cata said.

"Tomorrow," Joe said, shutting the door behind him.

They set out early in the morning on Saturday. Joe had cleaned out his room and sprinkled Dettol on the floor and over the walls. He had also been to the post office. He found four subscriptions to his course, paid for in postal orders. They set out with their fishing rods and tackles, their box of fish hooks, their jar of earthworms and insects. Cata-cata had brought some tangerines and oranges along with the three conciliatory bottles of beer. Not one word passed between them.

They caught two buses to get to FESTAC Estate along the Bada-

gry road. Cata-cata had taken Joe fishing there before. The last time
the short pier had been full of rubbish. When they arrived it was surprising for them to find the pier clean: it had been washed by the August rain.

It was a clear and hot day. The river water was brown and there
were canoes in the distance. Crabs scuttled around the pier.

Joe lay flat on his back and watched the clear sky while Cata-cata
fished.

"The fishes are asleep."

"Maybe," Joe said.

"Did I tell you about the dream I had last night, eh?"

"No."

"I dreamed that I caught a fish, an electric fish, a big one. I clob-
bered it, but it wouldn't die. I threw a brick on its head, and do you
know what happened, eh?"

"No."

"The brick scattered into pieces. And the fish was crying. It
wouldn't stop crying. In the end I threw the fish back into the
river."

"It's a good thing you did," Joe said.

"I think so."

"Do you want a beer?"

"No, but help yourself."

Joe took a bottle. The beer was still chilled. He opened the bottle
with his teeth and drank steadily through half of it. He burped. He
looked across the river. On the other shore there were palm trees and
huts. An eagle flew past low along the river.

Joe said, "Too many competitors and not enough money."

"True."

"This life is a financial problem."

"You're right."

"But a man must fly."

"A man is not a bird."

Joe didn't say anything. He finished the bottle of beer.

"Did you go and see Sarah?" Cata-cata asked.

"Yes."

"What happened?"

"At first she didn't want to talk to me. Then we agreed to meet tonight."

"I see."

Joe looked across the river. He saw the trees against the sky. He saw the river softly rippling, softly flowing. He felt the wind cool beneath the warmth of the day. He felt peaceful. He was happy to see the crabs scuttling along the shore. He fell asleep and dreamed that he was paddling a canoe in a green bottle.

Then the midget with the big head and red eyes came to him and said: "How are you?"

"I don't know. But how are you?"

"I am not feeling all that well."

"What's wrong? Can I help?" Joe asked.

"Yes. I want you to give me back that thing I gave you. My life has been hell without it."

"Please let me keep it. I will give you anything else you ask for."

"If you want it, keep it."

Joe didn't like the way the midget said that; so he gave the midget what he asked for.

"Thank you," said the midget.

"Thank you," said Joe.

"I am always happy to see you."

"Thank you."

"Don't thank me."

"Okay. Tell me, what was that thing you gave me?"

"Bad luck," the midget said, cheerfully.

"You are a true friend," said Joe.

"So are you. Except for one thing. You've got your eyes always shut. Open them."

Joe opened his eyes. Cata-cata was leaning over him.

"You've been talking in your sleep."

"It's a small problem."

"Have a tangerine."

Joe peeled the tangerine and ate it. He felt light. He felt possessed of a secret wonder. The tangerine was cool in his mouth. He thought about prison. He thought about Sarah. He felt he had to turn off his thinking. He tried to, but he only succeeded in having an idea for his sixteenth lesson. He would call it: "Turning Experience into Gold."

Wells Tower

⌖

The Brown Coast

Bob Munroe woke up on his face. He had rolled over in the night and now his arms were pinned beneath him. They were numb and rubbery and, in that dark, cloudy time between sleep and waking, Bob wondered if someone hadn't come along and stolen his arms in the night. The thought registered dimly, as if it were someone else thinking it someplace far from here. To have no arms would be a bad thing, surely, but it would not be the worst thing. Bob would get along.

Of more immediate concern were the little bits of cracker that had worked their way beneath the waistband of Bob's underpants. He had come in late, his back hurting from the long bus ride down, and had stretched out on the floor with a brick of saltines. He must have crushed the saltines while he slept because the crumbs were all over him, up his shirt, stuck in the creases of his skin. He could feel a big piece of cracker sitting in the crack of his ass, and this was a feeling worse than the prickly sensation returning to his fingers, worse than the ache in his jaw from sleeping on it wrong. He could almost see that crumb, porous and obdurate and pointed on one end like a valentine. Yet his arms were slow in responding. He couldn't get his brain to make his body work, couldn't reach down there with a half-dead hand and fetch that crumb out of there. Waking up for the first time in this empty house, Bob felt the hot white morning congealing on him. His heart beat hard against the floor, and he sensed that not far below, not too far down in the sandy soil, death was reaching up for him.

Outside the kitchen door was the patio Bob was supposed to be down here rectifying. Pale, leggy plants stuck through the holes in the bricks. The roots of pine and palm trees had found their way beneath the patio and fouled things up, pulled the bricks out of true, made it so the lawn chairs wouldn't sit right.

This house had once been the joint property of his father and his uncle Randall, who was wasting no time putting it on the market now that Bob's father was dead. It was an investment his father had been railroaded into sight unseen, and Bob couldn't recall his father coming down here more than once or twice. The way the deed worked out, ownership conveyed exclusively to Randall, and Bob wondered whether he hadn't been banking on this turn of events all along.

Randall lived where Bob lived, several hours north. When Bob's father was dying, Randall had made a promise that he would do what he could to make sure things turned out all right for Bob. In the weeks after the funeral, Randall had made a point of stopping by frequently to condole with him, though his sympathies usually took the form of showing up around dinnertime and staying long enough to finish off whatever beers Bob had in the fridge. There was something disquieting about his uncle, how his oiled hair always showed the furrows of a recent combing and how he wore braces on his teeth, though he was well into his middle years.

Bob had not been close with his father, so it was puzzling for Bob and also for his wife, Vicky, when his father's death touched off in him an angry lassitude that seemed to curdle Bob's enthusiasm for work and married life. He had fallen into a bad condition and, in addition to several minor miscalculations, had made three major fuck-ups that would be a long time in smoothing over. He had reported to work under the influence of alcohol, committed a calamitous oversight on a house he'd been helping to build and was dismissed soon after. One week after that, he'd rear-ended a local real-estate developer, who as a result of the collision developed a clicking in his jaw and sued away Bob's lean inheritance.

Worst of all, he had tried to blunt oncoming feelings of hopelessness by trysting with a lonely woman he'd met in traffic school. Even at the time, it had seemed like a pointless enterprise: the two of them dry-mouthed and distracted, their joyless minstrations only making things worse.

Then one day, when they were driving into town, Vicky looked up and saw the phantom outline of a woman's footprint on the windshield over the glove box. She slipped her sandal off, saw that the print did not match her own and told Bob that he was no longer welcome in their home.

Bob spent two months on Randall's couch before Randall got the idea to send him south. "Hole up at the beach house for a while," Randall had said. "This damn thing's just a bump in the road. You need a little time to recombobulate is all."

Bob did not want to go. Vicky was already beginning to soften on her demands for a divorce, and he was sure that with time she'd open her door to him again. But Vicky encouraged him to leave and, things being how they were, he thought it best not to be contrary. Anyway, it was a generous offer on Randall's part, though Bob was not surprised that when Randall dropped him off at the bus station he handed him a list of jobs already written out.

Randall's house was not a nice place—a cinderblock cottage with a badly flaking pink paint job, the ruins of a previous owner's doomed ambition to make the house seem cheery. The jaundiced linoleum that covered the living room floor had been improperly glued and was coming loose, curling back on itself at a long seam running the length of the room. The wood paneling in the living room had shrugged up over the course of many moist summers, and now the walls looked like a relief map of some unfriendly, mountainous territory. "Fix walls," it said in the note.

In the gloomy, windowless hall, Randall had hung the taxidermied bodies of some things he'd killed. An armadillo. A deer's head and, just beside it, that same deer's ass as well. A square of plywood with a row of purple, leathery things nailed to it which Bob figured out were turkey beards. Above the kitchen sink was a clumsy painting of a Budweiser can with Randall's prominent signature in the bottom right corner. Randall had done a good job with the letters, but he'd had to stretch out the can's midsection to accommodate them, so it bulged in the middle, like a snake swallowing a rat.

In a dark corner of the living room, an old aquarium burbled away. It was huge—as long as a casket and three feet deep—and empty except for a bottle of hair tonic, a waterlogged bat and some other things floating on the surface. The water was thick and murky, the color of moss, but still the aerator breathed a futile sigh of bubbles through the tank. Bob clicked it off. Then he stepped into his flip-flops and went outside.

The house was at the northern tip of a small island. It had given Bob a little jolt of hope and excitement when Randall had described it to him. He liked beaches, how each day the tide scoured the sand and left it clean, how people generally came to the coast because they wanted to have a good time. What confounded Bob was that this island did not seem to have any beach at all. Instead of beach, the land here met the water in a marshy skirt that hummed with mosquitoes and smelled terribly of fart gas. The nearest decent beach, a man on the bus had said, was on another island three miles out to sea and cost twelve dollars to get to on a boat.

Bob crossed the cockeyed patio. Tiny lizards scattered from his path. He followed the sound of waves to the end of the yard, through a stand of loblolly pine trees, limbless and spectral. He stepped from the pines onto a road paved with oyster shells. A pair of white-haired women in a yellow golf cart rolled silently past. "Hidy," one of them said to Bob.

"All right, now," he said. And then he was startled by the sound of metal clanking on metal and a man yelling. "Goddamn shit! Shit-box," he hollered. The man was standing in his driveway, half-vanished down the open hood of a Pontiac, walloping something with something.

The white-haired women were not far away. "Good gracious," one of them said. "Mercy," said the other. They continued on their way, and the man sang out a furious syncopation of *motherfuckers*. Rising from the hollows of the engine compartment, his words flattened the soft silence of the morning and hiked Bob's heart rate up. It occurred to Bob to go and yank the sawed-off broom handle that was holding up the hood, but he did not.

He walked over. "Would you mind shutting the hell up with that cussing," he said. "It's really fucking up the morning."

The man pulled his head out of the hood and looked at Bob. He had a jowly face, and his eyes were red and weary. "Who the hell are you?" the man asked in a tone more mystified than hostile.

"Bob," Bob said. "I'm staying over there."

"At Randall Munroe's? I know Randall. I did a couple of things to his cat."

Bob made a puzzled face.

"Derrick Treat. I'm a veterinarian, that's how I make my money."

"Well I didn't mistake you for a car mechanic," Bob said.

"You got that right. Can't get this turkey to crank. Fuck it anyhow. It's pretty much got cancer of the car."

What it had was nothing more than a bad spark plug. Bob pulled a decent looking one out of a tractor Derrick had rusting in the backyard. Then the car cranked fine. "That's a pretty thing," Derrick said, listening to the engine go. "Some kind of mechanicking mother-fucker, ain't you?"

Bob said he wasn't, but Derrick clapped him on the back, cocked an ear to the engine again and crowed with pleasure. "Come on in the house and let me get you a glass of compensation," Derrick said.

Bob told him thanks and everything, but he meant to go have a look at the water.

"Shit, the water'll keep." Derrick hustled Bob inside the house.

Derrick's home was just like Randall's. Same dark hall, same bad paneling warping and splintering up. In the living room, a woman was sitting back in a recliner reading a magazine and having a cigarette. She was pretty, but she had spent too much time in the sun and had pruned up and gone dark, like a turkey beard.

"Bob, this is Claire," Derrick said. "This fellow got the car running."

Claire smiled at Bob. "Well that's something," she said, shaking Bob's hand and not minding the grease. "New out here?"

Bob said he was, and she told him welcome. She said he should come by anytime and that the door was always open and that she meant that.

Bob followed Derrick to the kitchen. Derrick pulled two jelly jars from the freezer and called to the living room. "You need a drink, baby doll?" Claire said she did, and Derrick pulled out a third jar. He poured a dollop of vodka into each one and then filled them up the rest of the way with champagne. "Claire calls it a Polack Holiday," Derrick said, handing a drink to Bob. "Her people are from over there so I guess she knows."

They went back to the living room, and Bob sat on the sofa. Derrick sat on the arm of the recliner with his arm around Claire.

"What do you do, Bob?" Claire asked him.

"I don't do anything now," Bob said. He knocked back his drink and a hot flower blossomed in his stomach. "Used to be a carpenter."

"But what?" Claire asked.

"But I messed this thing up and got let go. I built a staircase that wasn't any good."

"That doesn't sound right," Claire said. "That doesn't sound like anything to get fired about."

Bob explained what it took to build a staircase, how you've got to cut the risers exactly the same height. "Even a sixteenth of an inch difference and people will stumble on it. Mine was a half-inch or so off on every step, and a granddad broke his leg on it and then a grandma broke her hip. Confused the shit out of them. Then a lawyer went over with a tape measure and got the story right there."

"Oops," Derrick said. "Should've measured it yourself."

"Yeah, well," Bob said, faintly peeved to be hearing advice from a man so inept he couldn't even diagnose a sour sparkplug. Bob's jar was empty, and the frost on the glass was turning to sweat. "It was nice meeting you folks, but I think I better push on."

"Shit, man, you just got here," Derrick said. The phone rang in the kitchen. Derrick told Bob to stay put and went after the phone. Claire dipped a brown finger in her drink and then stuck the finger in her mouth. A saw-edged scar ran down the back of her hand, standing out pink and tender on the skin there, which was the color of a pot roast.

"You should stick around, at least to eat with Derrick and me," she said. "I'm making eggs and salmon cakes."

Derrick was on the phone, speaking in a loud, incautious expert's voice. "Do what? Did you take a look, can you see the head? Uh-huh. Sounds like she's fixing to domino. I'll be over."

Derrick came back into the living room. "Gotta take a trip over the bridge," he said. "I've got to go pull something out of a horse's pussy."

"What kind of a thing?" Bob asked.

"I dunno," Derrick said. "A baby horse, I hope."

Derrick showed Bob where to cut across the yard to get down to the sea. It was much hotter now, and the sun glared down through the gray sky like a flashlight behind a sheet. He walked across a dead garden and through a salt-burned hedge. He slapped along in his flip-flops, woozy from the cocktail and with a heat headache coming on. At the top of a dirt embankment, he stopped and saw the water. It lay in bands of blue and green and took the sun's light in a speckled glow. A slow wind was blowing in towards land, putting divots on the water like a giant plate of hammered brass. No sand here, but rising up from the marsh was a long tongue of smooth rock that stretched some distance out into the sea.

Bob started going down the bank, but it was steep and the simplest thing was to ride down it on your ass. When he got to the bottom he had sand in his shorts and skeins of shore weeds looped between his toes.

The sea had a tonic effect on Bob. A clean wind rolled off the water. It cut the stagnant dampness of the day and dried the sweat on his face and chest. Bob scrambled along the spit of rock. He took the salt into his lungs and savored the itchy feeling it gave him in his chest. He touched the long grasses waving in the water like women's hair. He paused to look at barnacles, their tiny feathery hands combing blindly for invisible prey. The gulls were crying, and pelicans cast long shadows on the water.

Not far from the water's edge, Bob nearly put his foot into a deep tidepool in the rock. It was big as a bathtub and deeper than Bob could see. A pair of crimson starfish clung to the edge. He fished them out. They were hard and spiny in his hands. He stretched out the belly of his T-shirt and dropped them in.

Deeper down, Bob saw a beautiful fish hovering in the water. It was big and blue, and its fins tapered into brilliant yellow filaments that hung behind it in an undulating train. Bob put his hands in the water, and the starfish dropped from his shirt. The fish did not move, even as Bob reached his hands down beside it. It flapped the little fins below its silver gills, like a horse switching flies, but it stayed quite still.

He made a grab at it, astonishing himself when his thumb caught under its gill plate, and flipped it up out of the hole. It jerked and bounced across the rock, and Bob felt a shot of panic ricochet through his belly. He pulled his shirt off and grabbed it up with that. Then he sprinted up the bank, with the swaddled fish buckling and twisting against his chest. It was a violent and vital sensation, and Bob wondered for a moment if it was anything like this when a woman had a baby inside her.

Bob ran across Derrick's yard. Claire was in a bikini on the concrete porch. She waved to him and he yelled hey but didn't stop. He ran with his flip-flops in his hand, and the oyster shells on the road hurt his feet.

He made it back to his house, busted open the screen door and dumped the fish into the aquarium. It sank and then slowly floated to the surface, regarding Bob with an untenanted, passive eye. This seemed to Bob like a hell of a swindle, after he'd torn ass home to get the thing there in good health.

"Uh-uh. Bull*shit*," Bob told the fish in a tone of stern pity.

He placed his palm beneath it and swept the foul water through its gills, and soon it stirred again. He pulled out the bottle of hair tonic and the bat and dropped them on the floor. The fish drifted indifferently to one end of the tank and nibbled at a pencil that was standing in the corner.

He ladled out most of the old green water with a saucepan, leaving just enough to keep the fish covered. He cleaned out the rest of the junk: bottle caps, a doll's head and almost two dollars in change. Then he got a soup pot from the kitchen and carried clean water from the narrow tidal creek that ran past Randall's house. It took him half an hour, toting the sloshing pot back and forth, but when the aquarium was full and clean Bob stood back and beheld it, gratified.

The fish swam in contented circles and did not seem to mind the tiny white crabs that had come in with the clean water. The seams were sweating little threads of seawater, and Bob patched them as best he could with some plumber's putty he found under the sink.

That night he borrowed a folding cot from Derrick and Claire and set it up in the living room. He put a lamp behind the aquarium and turned it on. He did not like it in this house, its odors of old meals, how the place hummed with the shrill songs of insects that breezed in through the absent windowscreens. Lying there waiting for sleep to come, it brought him some calm to see his fish, so large and placid, floating in the tank. With the aquarium lit up and the house dark, the fish seemed to hang in the air at the far end of the room. For a while, it swam in a lazy circle, hugging the glass and peering out at Bob with a large, gold-rimmed eye. Then it stopped in the middle of the tank, shivered, and began blowing from its mouth a milky, diaphanous sac. Bob sat up in bed to watch. The sac trembled in the water but held its form. When it had grown to the size of a basketball, the fish glided inside and went to sleep.

In the morning Bob went and stood on the patio. He got angry, first at Randall, for not weeding this pitiful square of bricks and letting it go, and then at the fact of this monkey-ass job. He had built five homes, from the foundation forms to the trimwork on the eaves. He'd put up a house for himself and Vicky and, when she first saw it finished, she couldn't stop laughing because it looked so good. It struck him then that disgrace was not some vague condition of the spirit; it had a concrete savor. It felt like hard bricks in your hand, a creaking ache in your knees, like sun on your face and nobody around to give a goddamn whether you had something cool to drink.

This patio was a mess, not even half worth fixing for the little money Randall had vaguely promised. Hell, maybe he would weed it, but he wasn't going to mess with tearing up those bricks or setting them level; Randall's note could fuck itself. He kicked up a splotch of moss with his toe and, he had to admit, there was something that felt all right about the clean patch of brick it left. So he ripped up saw grass and pokeweed and nettle. He liked the sound of the weeds tearing out. He stayed at it all morning.

With all the weeds gone, the patio did not look good. It was tidy, but now the big swells where the tree roots lay were easier and more unpleasant to see. He took up the bricks. With his bare hands, he snatched out the thin, pale roots that lay underneath and used Randall's rusty ax to chop up the big ones. It took the rest of the day, and by the time Bob knocked off in the afternoon he was aching and had a bad sunburn deepening on his face and arms. He went inside and mixed up some old Kool-Aid, which hardly masked the sulfurous bite of the water that ran from the tap. Then he walked down towards the water and brought the soup pot with him.

Derrick was out in his yard, and Bob wished he'd cut through the bushes on the other side of Derrick's house. But Derrick got out of his chair and waved Bob over. He had on a green plastic visor and a pair of the tiniest jean shorts that Bob had ever seen on a man. "Hey, man," Derrick said. "What're you doing?"

"I thought I'd go get my feet wet," Bob said. "I've been toting bricks all day."

"Shit, go on," said Derrick. "I was up at six A.M. today working on a shih tzu with a damn bowel occlusion. I'd rather be toting bricks any day. Dag, I'd pay you to *let* me tote bricks." Derrick narrowed his eyes at Bob. "What's that boil pot for?"

"I dunno," Bob said. "I was maybe going to stash some sea life in it."

"Huh," Derrick said. "Let me grab you this old dipnet Claire's got. Hold on."

Derrick went into the house and came back out with the net. "I'll come on down with you, if that's all right," Derrick said.

They skitched down the bank and got out on the spit. The sun was hovering above the horizon and was slick and smooth as a canned peach. Bob dipped a foot in the water and it felt warm and mild.

"I'm getting in," Bob said, unbuckling his belt.

Derrick was brushing off a spot on the rock and was slowly getting down on it. "In the water? To swim?" Derrick asked.

"Yes," Bob said. He shucked his shorts and waded in.

"What, nude?"

"Yes," Bob said. "How God intended." When he pushed out into the water, he was amazed at how hot and thick it was, like baby oil, almost. Even when he stopped moving, the water buoyed him up and wouldn't let him sink.

"All right," Derrick said. "But don't laugh at my small pecker." Derrick peeled off his shorts and disappeared on the far side of the spit. Bob heard a messy splash and Derrick cussing.

Bob swam out until his feet couldn't touch. He dived down through the green water and floated for a moment in the mantle of coolness where the sun's hard beams didn't reach. That would be an okay place to stay, if you could only find a way to linger there. But already he was rising back into the warm thickness, and in a moment he felt the surface break across his shoulders.

Claire was picking her way down through the grass. She wore a fake-palm skirt and a leopard-print bikini top.

"Back up, girl," Derrick called out. "We're in our altogether here."

"Heavens," she said. "Well, show me something good."

She waved to Bob. As natural as an athlete, she shrugged off her top and pushed her skirt down. Across her breasts and oval hips, her skin looked soft and new and white as shortening. Bob floated off the tip of the spit, looking at her and combing the water with his sore hands. He watched her ease into the low green curl. He considered for a moment the many miles that lay between him and his own wife, and what it would take to cinch that distance up again. A lot of talking, a lot of work was what it would take, more than a hundred patios. It was a discouraging thought, and Bob slipped beneath the water with the weight of it.

With the sun beginning to fall, Bob crawled from the water and got his shorts back on. Derrick and Claire were still far out in the water, their heads vanishing beneath the swells, their voices distant and wordless. He looked in the tidepool. A ring of vermilion minnows hung near the surface in a quivering halo. He went after them with Derrick's net but they flicked away from him and disappeared into the hole. He netted a small octopus and a steel-blue crab and dumped them in the pot. Farther down, Bob saw a golden eel twisting in the water. He had heard about an eel that would clamp its jaws on you and stay like that for life. He drew his hands out of the hole.

When Derrick was out he came and had a look. "*Anguilla Rostrata*," he said. "American eel. You know the thing about these? These and European eels, they both start out as babies in the Sargasso Sea. Some ride the Gulf Stream up this way and some fag off to Europe. You can eat these. You want to eat it?"

"No," Bob said. "I want to keep it."

Derrick dipped the net a couple of times, called the eel a cocksucker and then hauled it out. Once out in the air, it wriggled from the net. Derrick clutched at it with his hands, and the eel nipped at Derrick's ear. He dropped it in the pot. "You just lost the rights on that son of a bitch, Bob," Derrick said, rubbing his earlobe. "He's got an appointment with some hot coals."

But Bob picked up the pot and lugged it home.

The week wore on and Bob fell into a good rhythm, working in the days, jawing with the neighbors on evenings when he felt like it, spending time down by the water when he did not. He brought back remarkable things for the aquarium: anemones, sea horses, a small dogfish. One day he and Derrick rode the Pontiac to a pier down the coast and caught hardhead catfish on porkrind bottom-rigs. They made dinner at Randall's cottage. Bob watched Claire skin the fish. She blanched them in hot water and then nailed their heads to a cutting board, peeling the skin away, revealing the snowy flesh beneath. She knew how to break the head from the body so the guts came loose with it.

They sat on the patio and ate off paper plates.

"Look at you, Bob, this is mighty sharp," Claire said, surveying how he'd done the bricks. "I'd like to get you over and handyman up a few things for me. Derrick? The man is hell with pussycats, but he is bad to jackleg a thing, no offense, baby doll."

"I know it," Derrick said. "My father used to like saying I was so dick-fingered I couldn't brush my teeth without poking out my eye."

Bob pulled a tiny bone from his lips and flicked it into the dark yard. "I'll probably split in a couple of days," he said. "Maybe you'll look after those fish in there when I'm gone."

The next night he walked to the store in the island's little village and called home on the pay phone. A big halide bulb buzzed at the top of the telephone pole, and moths tumbled in the light like confetti. He plunked a handful of quarters into the slot. For a moment he waited. A man picked up.

"Hey, Randall," Bob said.

"Buddy," Randall said. "What's the word?"

"I don't know," Bob said. "I fixed your patio. Slapped some paint on those cabinets, too."

"Thank you, my man. That's a lifesaver. Would've done it myself but, you know, that thing with my shoulder. That's great." There was a pause, and then Randall sneezed into the phone. "How's that paneling look?"

"It looks fucked up," Bob said. "And it's going to stay fucked up. I can't hump a bunch of sheetrock back from the store in a damn wheelbarrow."

"You can't get hold of a truck or something? Rent one?" Randall said. "Or maybe they deliver. Hell, I don't know, Bob, figure it out. You make it hard for somebody to do you a favor."

"What are you up to in my house?" Bob said.

Bob heard Randall saying something that he couldn't make out. Vicky got on and said hello.

"Hey, Vick," he said.

"Well, how is it?"

"Real great," Bob said. "I struck oil in the yard. I got a magic dog who every day he licks off the dishes and shits a gold watch. I got people on call to put grapes in my mouth. But, anyway, I think I'm getting ready to get ready to come on back."

"Huh," she said. "We have to talk about some things."

Bob asked what things, and Vicky didn't say at first. She said she loved him and that she spent a lot of time worrying over him. She told him in a gentle, pious tone that she pitied him for sabotaging his shot at happiness with her and for the other unwise things he'd done. She said she did not like being without him, but that she could not think of a reason to take him back again, though she'd tried hard to. From the sound of it, she had everything written down with dates and witnesses and the worst parts underlined. Bob listened to all of this and he felt himself get cold.

"Why don't you tell me about why that shitbird Randall's up in my house," he said. "Why don't we talk about something like that."

"He's *your* family, remember?" Vicky took her mouth away from the phone for a second, and when she came back her voice was hitched up a register. "You've got some kind of gall, saying that to me."

Bob tried hard to get an apology to take root, but Vicky wouldn't answer, and he suspected she was holding the phone away from her face. Then he got back to the subject of his uncle, which felt like solid ground, and began to deliver some grandiose pronouncements about what he planned on doing to him if he didn't mind his business.

"That's really terrific," Vicky's voice said. "You're going to threaten people? Chop somebody's head off? Is that what that's supposed to mean?"

Bob watched a mouse scamper out from behind the soda machine. It was eating a coupon.

"It means what it's supposed to mean," Bob said, with regret already rising in his voice.

"Right," Vicky said. And she hung up before he could give her a reason not to, before he could tell her any of the things he'd really called to say.

Bob walked home with the sunset nearly dead. He went past the town's one bar and heard men and women laughing. He turned at the chamber of commerce, which was just an old converted garage where they'd hung out a wooden shingle with some crooked letters burned into it instead of a sign. Past the post office, he picked up the road home and followed it back out of town.

Bob was getting into bed when Derrick came over. He opened the door without knocking. "Oh, no," Bob said out loud.

Derrick staggered into the house on splayed legs, fried to the hat. He squinted around the room for a long second or before he spotted Bob sitting up on the cot. "Muhfugh," Derrick said. "You'n me ridin' to Tampa and party."

Bob started to protest, but Derrick was in no condition to listen. He pointed a limp finger at Bob. He took three steps and his foot caught the curled edge of the linoleum divide. His head hit the floor with a hollow smack.

Bob lay awake in the darkness awhile, and soon the door opened again. It was Claire. She saw where Derrick was lying, and she kissed her hand and laid it on his cheek.

"We can let him stay like that," she said. "I brought this thing for you."

She clicked on a lamp. She was holding a glass salad bowl filled with water, a brown speckled thing lying on the bottom. Its spongy body was studded with thorny reddish nodes; to Bob, it looked like the turd of someone who'd been eating rubies.

"What is it?" Bob asked.

"Not sure," she said. "It's ugly as death isn't it? I thought it would be nice, make the other fish feel good about themselves." She pushed back the cover on the aquarium and dumped the thing in.

Claire knelt beside Bob's cot and let go with a big acid belch. "You need me to get in there with you?" she said.

"There's not anything going on in here," Bob said, but then he drew the covers back. The cot squealed under their shared weight. Bob felt her breath on his neck, felt her hand on his belly. But the hand stopped there, and soon they were asleep.

.   .   .

Bob woke up early. Derrick lay on the floor snoring in a deep, braying drone. The room smelled sweet and boozy with his breath. In the night, Claire had slipped down beside her husband. She'd drawn an old raincoat over the two of them, and she slept holding one of Derrick's big thumbs in her fist. When Bob stirred, her eyes opened for an instant and closed again.

The sun was still low in the sky. It slanted in through the windows and washed the room in bright, brittle light. Bob glanced at the far end of the room and saw that things were not all right with his aquarium. He couldn't see the eel or the fantastic fish with the long yellow fins. He walked over and saw that they were all floating together, making an unsteady, fleshy terrain on the surface of the tank. In the middle of the empty water was the sluglike thing Claire had brought. It stretched and flexed happily, moving unencumbered behind the glass.

Bob thought he might throw up. He made a fist and drove it hard into the center of the glass. That didn't satisfy him, so he hit it twice more, putting the full weight of his body behind it. The tank rocked back and then pitched forward off the stand, hitting the floor with a wet cymbal clap. Glass flew, and dead and dying creatures washed through the room.

Claire jumped up when the water hit her. Derrick, whose cheek had been flush against the floor, sat up and spit out a mouthful of aquarium water even before he had his eyes open all the way. Then he looked down at the crab that had fetched up on his lap, then up at Bob and Claire with a question on his face that seemed to have no feasible answer. He said, "What in the fuck is going on in this living room?"

Bob tried to speak, and was mortified by the painful thickness that had gathered in his throat. He said that Claire's gift had ruined his fish and pointed at the thing, which had gotten caught up in a spray of blue dust near the baseboard. He said that the tank had gotten tipped over and that was why everything was wet.

"Oh, Lord," Claire said. "Oh, my."

Bob reached down and picked up a dead periwinkle and pinched it between his thumb and forefinger until he heard its shell give way.

"Sea cucumber," Derrick said. "I could of told you. Those things are bad with company." This kind spooked easily, Derrick explained, and when they got the urge they put out a cloud of toxic juice and killed everything nearby. "Waste of all this seafood," Derrick said. "Should've got my go ahead, honey."

"Yes, evidently," she said. "I'm so sorry. What a wicked thing." She knelt and tipped the sea cucumber into a dirty coffee cup.

"Smush that thing," Bob said.

"Put it in the toilet," Derrick said.

"No," said Claire. "I'm going to chuck it back in the sea." And holding the cup before her like a candle, she led the two men outside.

Derrick and Bob walked together. Derrick had a purple knot on his cheek from the floor, and he kept a hand on it as he bumped along through the saw grass. "How all was it with Claire last night?" he said to Bob.

"It wasn't any way, there wasn't anything," he said.

"Uh-huh. She said she was thinking about trying to enjoy you. She does pretty much what she likes."

The three of them walked out onto the spit, and as they reached the end a catamaran sailboat swung out from the sound side of the island. A handsome man with big arms and dark hair sat at the rudder, and a pretty woman with bobbed hair and a T-shirt with French stripes lay across the canvas. They smiled and waved to Derrick and Bob and Claire. And looking at these strangers' faces, Bob experienced something like a déjà vu, a tiny surge of hope and recognition. He had the delirious thought that perhaps these people had come for him. They beckoned, and he could see himself climbing aboard. He could feel the boat thrumming along through the waves, way out past sight of land where the sky is a vast benign bubble and each direction is as good as any other. He thought of distant beaches with sand like flour, where few people cared to go. He thought of how this young man probably knew of a system for keeping things together, for having a boat and nice wife with French stripes and that it wouldn't seem like anything complicated once it was explained in plain words. He thought about how far this sea must stretch, and how once he got out in it, he might just gently dissipate, like a drop of oil radiating in a rainbow across a giant puddle.

The man and woman on the boat saw Bob reaching toward them and the grin on his face that didn't look right. They saw the woman beside him drop her arm like a softball pitcher and then fling something from the coffee cup she held in her hand. They watched it wobble in the air like a ball of dark mercury, though, as they waited for the sound of the splash, a warm wind came off the land and pushed the boat back from the shore.

Issue 161, 2002

Julie Orringer

✠

When She Is Old and I Am Famous

There are grape leaves, like a crown, on her head. Grapes hang in her hair, and in her hands she holds the green vines. She dances with both arms in the air. On her smallest toe she wears a ring of pink shell.

Can someone tell her, please, to go home? This is my Italy and my story. We are in a vineyard near Florence. I have just turned twenty. She is a girl, a gangly teen, and she is a model. She is famous for almost getting killed. Last year, when she was fifteen, a photographer asked her to dance on the rail of a bridge and she fell. A metal rod beneath the water pierced her chest. Water came into the wound, close to her heart, and for three weeks she was in the hospital with an infection so furious it made her chant nonsense. All the while she got thinner and more pale, until, when she emerged, they thought she might be the best model there ever was. Her hair is wavy and long and buckeye-brown, and her blue eyes have a stunned, sad look to them. She is five feet eleven inches tall and weighs one hundred and thirteen pounds. She has told me so.

This week she is visiting from Paris, where she lives with her father, my Uncle Claude. When Claude was a young man he left college to become the darling of a great couturier, who introduced him to the sequin-and-powder world of Paris drag. Monsieur M. paraded my uncle around in black-and-white evening gowns, high-heeled pumps and sprayed-up diva hairdos. I have seen pictures in his attic back in Fernald, Indiana, my uncle leaning over some balustrade in a cloud of pink chiffon, silk roses at his waist. One time he appeared in *Vogue*, in a couture photo spread. All this went on for years, until I was six, when a postcard came asking us to pick him up at the Chicago airport. He came off the plane holding a squirming baby. Neither my mother nor I knew anything about his having a child, or even a female lover. Yet there she was, my infant cousin, and here she is now, in the vineyard doing her grape-leaf dance for my friends and me.

Aïda. That is her terrible name. *Ai-ee-duh*: two cries of pain and one of stupidity. The vines tighten around her body as she spins, and Joseph snaps photographs. She knows he will like it, the way the leaves cling, and the way the grapes stain her white dress. We are trespassing here in a vintner's vines, spilling the juice of his expensive grapes, and if he sees us here he will surely shoot us. What an end to my tall little cousin. Between the purple stains on her chest, a darker stain spreads. Have I mentioned yet that I am fat?

Isn't it funny, how I've learned to say it? I am fat. I am not skin or muscle or gristle or bone. What I am, the part of my body that I most am, is fat. Continuous, white, lighter than water, a source of energy. No one can hold all of me at once. Does this constitute a crime? I know how to carry myself. Sometimes I feel almost graceful. But all around I hear the thin people's bombast: *Get Rid of Flabby Thighs Now! Avoid Holiday Weight-Gain Nightmares! Lose Those Last Five Pounds!* What is left of a woman once her last five pounds are gone?

I met Drew and Joseph in my drawing class in Florence. Joseph is a blond sculptor from Manhattan, and Drew is a thirty-seven-year-old painter from Wisconsin. In drawing class we had neighboring easels, and Drew and I traded roll-eyed glances over Joe's loud Walkman. We both found ourselves drawing in techno-rhythm. When we finally complained to him, he told us he started wearing it because Drew and I talked too much. I wish that were true. I hardly talk to anyone, even after three months in Florence.

One evening as the three of us walked home from class we passed a billboard showing Cousin Aïda in a gray silk gown, and when I told them she was my cousin they both laughed as if I had made some sort of feminist comment. I insisted that I was telling the truth. That was a mistake. They sat me down at a café and made me talk about her for half an hour. Joseph wondered whether she planned to complete her schooling or follow her career, and Drew had to know whether she suffered from eating disorders and skewed self-esteem. It would have been easier if they'd just stood in front of the billboard and drooled. At least I would have been able to anticipate their mute stupor when they actually met her.

Aïda rolls her shoulders and lets her hair fall forward, hiding her face in shadow. They can't take their eyes off her. Uncle Claude would scold her for removing her sun hat. I have picked it up and am wearing it now. It is gold straw and it fits perfectly. What else of hers could I put on? Not even her gloves.

"Now stand perfectly still," Joseph says, extending his thumb and index finger as if to frame her. He snaps a few pictures then lets the camera drop. He looks as if he would like to throw a net over her. He will show these pictures of Aïda to his friends back home, telling them how he slept with her between the grapevines. This will be a lie, I hope. "Dance again," he says, "this time slower."

She rotates her hips like a Balinese dancer. "Like this?"

"That's it," he says. "Nice and slow." Surreptitiously he adjusts his shorts.

When Drew looks at my cousin I imagine him taking notes for future paintings. In Wisconsin he works as a professional muralist, and here he is the best drawing student in our class, good even at representing the foot when it faces forward. I am hopeless at drawing the foot at any angle. My models all look like they are sliding off the page. I've seen photographs of Drew's murals, twenty-foot-high paintings on the sides of elementary schools and parking structures, and his figures look as though they could step out of the wall and crush your car. He does paintings of just the feet. I can tell he's studying Aïda's pink toes right now. Later he will draw her, at night in his room, while his upstairs neighbor practices the violin until the crack of dawn. "If she didn't live there, I'd have to hire her to live there," he tells me. She may keep him up all night, but at least she makes him paint well.

There are certain things I can never abide: lack of food, lack of sleep and Aïda. But she is here in Italy on my free week because our parents thought it would be fun for us. "Aïda doesn't get much rest," my mother told me. "She needs time away from that business in France."

I told my mother that Aïda made me nervous. "Her name has an umlaut, for crying out loud."

"She's your cousin," my mother said.

"She's been on the covers of twelve magazines."

"Well, Mira"—and here her voice became sweet, almost reverent—"you are a future Michelangelo."

There's no question about my mother's faith in me. She has always believed I will succeed, never once taking into account my failure to represent the human figure. She says I have a "style." That may be true, but it does not make me the next anybody. Sometimes I freeze in front of the canvas, full of the knowledge that if I keep painting, sooner or later I will fail her.

My cousin always knew how important she was, even when she was little. Over at her house in Indiana I had to watch her eat ice-cream bars while I picked at my Sunmaid raisins. I tried to be nice because my mother had said, "Be nice." I told her she had a pretty name, that I knew she was named after a character from a Verdi opera, which my mom and I had listened to all the way from Chicago to Indiana. Aïda licked the chocolate from around her lips, then folded the silver wrapper. "I'm not named after the *character*," she said. "I'm named after the *entire opera*."

The little bitch is a prodigy, a skinny Venus, a genius. She knows how to shake it. She will never be at a loss for work or money. She is a human dollar sign. Prada has made millions on her. And still her eyes remain clear and she gets enough sleep at night.

Joseph has run out of film. "You have beautiful teeth," he says hopelessly.

She grins for him.

Drew looks at me and shakes his head, and I am thankful.

.   .   .

When she's tired of the dance, Aïda untwines the vines from her body and lets them fall to the ground. She squashes a plump grape between her toes, looking into the distance. Then, as though compelled by some sign in the sky, she climbs to the top of a ridge and looks down into the valley. Joseph and Drew follow to see what she sees, and I have no choice but to follow as well. Where the vines end, the land slopes down into a bowl of dry grass. Near its center, surrounded by overgrown hedges and flower beds, the vintner's house rises, a sprawling two-story villa with a crumbling tile roof. Aïda inhales and turns toward the three of us, her eyes steady. "That's where my mother lives," she announces.

It is such an astounding lie, I cannot even bring myself to respond. Aïda's mother was the caterer at a party Uncle Claude attended during his "wild years"; my own mother related the story to me years ago as a cautionary tale. When Aïda was eight weeks old her mother left her with Claude, and that was that. But Aïda's tone is earnest and forthright, and both Joseph and Drew look up, confused.

"I thought you lived with your dad in Paris," Joseph says. He shoots a hard glance at me as if I've been concealing her whereabouts all this time.

"She does," I say.

Aïda shrugs. "My mother's family owns this whole place."

"This is news." Joseph looks at me, and I shake my head.

"My mom and I aren't very close," Aïda says and sits down. She ties a piece of grass into a knot, then tosses it down the hill. "Actually, the last time I saw her I was three." She draws her legs up and hugs her knees, and her shoulders rise and fall as she sighs. "It's not the kind of thing you do in Italy, tote around your bastard kid. It would have been a *vergogna* to the *famiglia*, as they say." Aïda looks down at the stone house in the valley.

Joseph and Drew exchange a glance, seeming to decide how to handle this moment. I find myself wordless. It's true that Aïda's mother didn't want to raise her. I don't doubt that it would have been a disgrace to her Catholic family. What baffles me is how Aïda can make up this story when she knows that *I* know it's bullshit. What does she expect will happen? Does she think I'll pretend to believe her? Joseph's eyebrows draw together with concern. I can't tell what he's thinking.

Aïda stands and dusts her hands against her dress, then begins to make her way down the slope. Joe gives us a look, shakes his head as if ashamed of himself, and then follows her.

"Where the hell do you think you're going?" I call to Aïda.

She turns, and the wind lifts her hair like a pennant. Her chin is set hard. "I'm going to get something from her," she says. "I'm not going back to France without a memento."

"Let's stop this now, Aïda," I say. "You're not related to anyone who lives in that house." In fact, it didn't look as if anyone lived there at all. The garden was a snarl of overgrown bushes, and the windows looked blank like sightless eyes.

"Go home," she says. "Joe will come with me. And don't pretend you're worried. If I didn't come back, you'd be glad."

She turns away and I watch her descend toward the villa, my tongue dry in my mouth.

These past days Aïda has been camping on my bedroom floor. Asleep she looks like a collapsed easel, something hard and angular lying where it shouldn't. Yesterday morning I opened one eye to see her fingering the contents of a blue tin box, my private cache of condoms. When I sat up and pushed the mosquito netting aside, she shoved the box back under the bed.

"What are you doing?" I asked.

The color rose in her cheeks.

"It's none of my business," I said. "But if you meet a guy."

She gave an abbreviated "ha" like the air had been punched out of her. Then she got up and began to look for something in her suitcase. Very quietly she said, "Of course, you're the expert."

"What's that supposed to mean?" I said.

She turned around and smiled with just her lips. "Nothing."

"Listen, shitweed, I may not be the next *Vogue* cover girl, but that doesn't mean I sleep alone every night."

"Whatever you say." She shook out a teeny dress and held it against herself.

"For God's sake," I said. "Do you have to be primo bitch of the whole universe?"

She tilted her head, coy and intimate. "You know what I think, Mira?" she said. "I think you're a vibrator cowgirl. I think you're riding the mechanical bull."

I had nothing to say. But something flew at her and I knew I had thrown it. She ducked. A glass candlestick broke against the wall.

"Fucking psycho!" she shouted. "Are you trying to kill me?"

"Get a hotel room," I said. "You're not staying here."

"Fine with me. I'll sleep in a ditch and you can sleep alone."

Her tone was plain and hard, eggshell white, but for a split second her lower lip quivered. It occurred to me for the first time that she might feel shunted off, that she might see me as a kind of babysitter she had to abide while her father had a break from her. Quickly I tried to replay in my mind all the names she had called me, that day and throughout our kid years, so I could shut out any thoughts that would make me feel sorry for her. "Get out of my room," I said. She picked her way across the glass and went into the bathroom. Door-click, faucet-knob squeak and then her scream, because in my apartment there is no hot water to be had, ever, by anyone.

Drew and I shuffle sideways down a rock hill toward the dried-up garden. Fifty yards below, my cousin sidles along the wall of the house. I cannot imagine how she plans to enter this fortress or what she will say if someone sees her. There's a rustle in a bank of hedges, and we see Joseph creeping along, his camera bag banging against his leg. He disappoints me. Back in New York he works in a fashion photographer's darkroom, and he speaks of commercial photography as if it were the worst imaginable use for good chemicals and photo paper.

For three months he's photographed nothing in Florence but water and cobblestones. Today he follows Aïda as if she were leading him on a leash.

Aïda freezes, flattening herself against the house wall. It seems she's heard something, although there's still no one in the garden. After a moment she moves toward a bank of curtained French doors and tries a handle. The door opens, and she disappears inside. Joseph freezes. He waits until she beckons with her hand, then he slides in and closes the door behind him. They're gone. I am not about to go any farther. The sun is furious and the vines too low to provide any shelter. A bag containing lunch for four people hangs heavy on my back. I am the only one who has not brought any drawing tools. It was somehow understood that I would carry the food.

"We might as well wait here," Drew says. "Hopefully they'll be out soon."

"I hope." The bag slides off my shoulders and falls into the dust.

Drew reaches for the lunch. "I would have carried this for you," he says. His eyes rest for a moment on mine, but I know he is only trying to be polite.

There was a time when I was the one who got the attention, when my body was the one everyone admired. In junior high, where puberty was a kind of contest, you wanted to be the one with the tits out to here. I had my bra when I was nine, the first in our grade, which made me famous among my classmates. My mother, a busty lady herself, told me she was proud to see me growing up. I believed my breasts were a gift from God, and even let a few kids have an accidental rub at them. It wasn't until high school, when the novelty wore off and they grew to a D-cup, that I started to see things as they really were. Bathing suits did not fit right. I spilled out of the tops of sundresses. I looked ridiculous when running or jumping. Forget cheerleading. I began smashing those breasts down with sports bras, day and night.

It doesn't matter what the Baroque masters thought. The big breasts, the lush bodies, those are museum pieces now, and who cares if they stand for fertility and plenty, wealth and gluttony, or the fullest bloom of youth? Rubens's nudes made of cumulus clouds, Titian's milky, half-dressed beauties overflowing their garments, Lorenzo Lotto's big intelligent-eyed Madonnas—they have their place, and it is on a wall. No one remembers that a tiny breast meant desolation and deserts and famine.

Take Aïda on the billboard in Florence, wearing a gray Escada gown held up by two thin strands of rhinestones. Where the dress dips low at the side, there is a shadow like a closed and painted eyelid, just the edge of Aïda's tiny breast, selling this $6,000 dress. That is what you can do today with almost nothing.

The fact is, Aïda guessed right when she said I was a virgin. There were other girls at my high school, fat girls, who would go out by the train tracks at night and take off all their clothes. There were some who would give hand jobs. There were others who had sex for the first time when they were eleven. Few of these girls had dates for homecoming, and none of them held hands at school with the boys they met by the tracks at night. At the time, I would rather have died than be one of them.

But sometimes I think about how it might have been for those girls, who got to touch and be touched and to live with exciting varieties of shame. When I look at my drawings of men and women, there's a stiffness there, a glassiness I'm afraid comes from too little risk. It makes me dislike myself and perhaps it makes me a bad artist. Can these things be changed now that I am, in most ways, grown up? Is there a remedy for how I conducted my life all those years? Where do I begin?

Drew lies back on his elbows and whistles "Moon River." I wish I could relax. Somewhere below, my cousin stalks an artifact of her non-mother. I picture the tall, cool rooms with their crumbling ceilings and threadbare tapestries woven in dark colors. Maybe she will burn the place down. In another few months, I imagine, she will need to do something to get herself on the evening news. Being on a billboard can't be enough for her.

I put on Aïda's sun hat and tie its white ribbons beneath my chin. Just as I'm wondering if either of us will speak to the other all afternoon, Drew asks if I've decided to submit any works for display in the Del Reggio Galléry in Rome.

"*What* works?" I say. "You've seen my sliding people. Maybe I could do a little installation with a basket underneath each painting to catch the poor figure when she falls off the page."

"You have a talent, Mira. People criticize *my* work for being too realistic."

"But I don't plan to draw them expressionistically. They just come out that way. It's artistic stupidity, Drew, not talent."

"Well, then, I guess you'd better quit now," he says, shrugging. He picks up some fallen grapes, waxy and black, and throws them into the hammock of my skirt. "How about another profession? Sheepherding? Radio announcing? Hat design?"

"There's a fine idea." The words come out clipped and without humor. A dry silence settles between us, and I'm angry at myself for being nervous and at him for bringing up the exhibition. He knows his work will go into the show.

At times I think it would be terrible to have him touch me. I can imagine the disappointment he would show when I removed my dress. One hopes to find a painter who likes the old masters, like in the personal columns I've read in *The Chicago Tribune*: Lusty DWM w/taste for old wine and Rubens seeks SWF with full-bodied flavor. Would I ever dare to call?

"So what do you think of my little cousin?" I ask.

"Why?" he says. "What do you think of her?"

"She's had a hard past," I say, in an attempt at magnanimity. Because if I answered the question with honesty, I would blast Aïda to Turkmenistan. All our lives she has understood her advantage over me, and has exercised it at every turn. When I pass her billboard in town I can feel her gleeful disdain. No matter how well you paint, she seems to say, you will remain invisible next to me.

Perhaps because Drew is older I thought of him as enlightened in certain ways; but I saw how he looked at my cousin today with plain sexual appetite. I hand him a plum from our lunch bag and turn my face away from the sun because I am hot and tired and want to be far away from here.

. . .

As we eat, we hear the foreign-sounding *ee-oo* of an Italian police siren in the distance. Dread kindles in my chest. I imagine Aïda being wrested into handcuffs by a brown-shirted Italian policeman, and the shamefaced look she'll give Joseph as her lie comes crashing down. Will I be too sorry later to say I told her so? I can almost hear my mother's phone diatribe: *You let her break into a house with some boy? And just watched the police haul her off to an Italian jail?* Drew and I get to our feet. The house below is quiet and still. A boxy police car sweeps into the lane, dragging a billow of dust behind it. It roars down the hill and screeches to a stop somewhere in front of the house, where we can no longer see it. After a moment someone pounds on the front door.

Drew says, "We'd better go down."

"They'll see us."

"Suit yourself." He flicks the pit of his plum into the grapevines and starts down the hill.

I follow him toward the front of the house until we see the paved area where the car is parked. He is about to step onto the piazza. Panicked, I take his arm and pull him behind a stand of junipers at the side of the driveway. There are just enough bushes to hide both of us. The shadows are deep but there are places to look through the branches, and we can see the police officer who had been pounding on the front door. The other officer sits quietly in the car, engrossed in a map.

"This is ridiculous," Drew says. "We have to go in."

"No way," I whisper. "There's enough trouble already. What's the minimum penalty for breaking and entering in this country?"

Drew shakes his head. "Tell me I came to Florence to stand in a bush."

The front door opens slightly, and the policeman goes inside. After a few minutes the officer with the map gets out and goes to the door, then into the house. Everything is still. A bird I can't name alights near Drew's hand and bobs on a thin branch. We stand together in the dust. The heat coming off his body has an earthy smell like the beeswax soap nuns sell in the marketplace. If I extended my hand just a centimeter, I could touch his arm.

"Uh-oh," he says softly.

There are Aïda and Joseph being led from the house by the police-men. Aïda's hair is mussed as if there has been a struggle, and her dress hangs crooked at the shoulder. Joseph walks without looking at her. A woman in a black dress—a housekeeper from the looks of her—curses at them from the doorway. They're not in handcuffs, but the police aren't about to let them go, either. Just as the first police-man opens the car door, a chocolate-colored Mercedes appears at the top of the drive. The steel-haired housekeeper stiffens and points. "*La padrona di casa*," she says.

They hold Aïda and Joseph beside the police car, waiting for the Mercedes to descend into the piazza. When the car arrives and the dust clears, the lady of the house climbs out. She squares herself to-ward the scene in front of her villa. She is tall and lean. Her hair is caught in the kind of knot the Italian women wear, heavy and sweep-ing and low on the neck. Beneath her ivory jacket her shoulders are businesslike. She looks as if she would be more at home in New York or Rome than out here on this grape farm. She lowers her black sun-glasses. With a flick of her hand toward Aïda and Joseph, she asks who the two criminals might be.

Aïda raises her chin and looks squarely at the woman. "*La vostra dottore*," she says. Your doctor.

The policemen roar with laughter.

The maid tells her padrona that Aïda was apprehended in the boudoir, trying on shoes. She had tried on nearly ten pairs before she was caught.

"You like my shoes?" the woman asks in English. She tilts her head, scrutinizing Aïda. "You look familiar to me."

"She's a model," Joseph says.

"Ah!" the woman says. "And you? You are a model too?" Her mouth is thin and agile.

"A photographer," Joe says.

"And you were trying on shoes also in my house?"

There is a silence. Joseph looks at Aïda for some clue as to what she wants him to say or do. Aïda looks around, and I almost feel as if she is looking for me, as if she thinks I might come out and save her now. Her eyes begin to dart between the padrona and the policemen, and her mouth opens. She lets her eyes flutter closed, then collapses against a policeman in an extremely realistic faint.

"Poor girl," the woman says. "Bring her into the house."

The police look disapproving, but they comply. One of them grabs her under the shoulders and the other takes her feet. Like an imperial procession they all enter the house, and the housekeeper closes the door behind them.

"She must be sick," Drew whispers. "Does she eat?"

"In a manner of speaking."

He climbs out of our hiding place and starts down toward the house. I have to follow him. I picture being home in bed, lying on my side and looking at the blank wall, a desert of comfort, no demands or disappointment. As I navigate the large stones at the edge of the piazza, my foot catches in a crevice and I lose my balance. There's a snap, and pain shoots through my left ankle. I come down hard onto my hip.

Drew turns around. "You okay?"

I nod, sideways, from the ground. He comes back to offer me his hand. It's torture getting up. My body feels as if it weighs a thousand pounds. When I test the hurt ankle, the pain makes my eyes water. I let go of Drew's hand and limp toward the door.

"Are you going to make it?" Drew asks.

"Sure," I say, but the truth is there's something awfully wrong. The pain tightens in a band around my lower leg. Drew rings the doorbell, and in a few moments the housekeeper opens the door. Her eyes are small and stern. She draws her gray brows together and looks at Drew. In his perfect Italian, he tells her that our friends are inside and that we would like to ask forgiveness of the lady of the house. She throws her hands heavenward and wonders aloud what will happen next. But she holds the door open and beckons us inside.

The entry hall is cool and dark like a wine cavern itself. There is a smell of fennel and coffee and dogs, and the characteristic dampness of Florentine architecture. Supporting myself against the stone wall, I creep along behind Drew, past tall canvases portraying the vintner's family, long-faced men and women arrayed in brocade and velvet and gold. The style is almost more Dutch than Italian, with angular light and deep reds and blues. In one portrait a seventeenth-century version of our padrona holds a lute dripping with flower garlands. She looks serene and pastoral, certainly capable of mercy. I take this for a good sign. We move past these paintings toward a large sunny room facing the back garden, whose French doors I recognize as the ones Aïda slipped through not long ago. My cousin is stretched out on a yellow chaise longue with Joseph at her side. The policemen are nowhere to be seen. I imagine them drinking espresso in the kitchen with the inevitable cook. La Padrona sits next to Aïda with a glossy magazine open on her lap, exclaiming at what she sees. "Ah, yes, here you are again," she says. "God, what a gown." It's as though royalty has come for a visit. She seems reluctant to look away from the photographs when the maid enters and announces us as friends of the signorina.

"More friends?"

"Actually, Mira's my cousin," Aïda explains. "And that's Drew. He's another student."

Drew gives our padrona a polite nod. Then he goes to Aïda and crouches beside her chaise longue. "We saw you faint," he says. "Do you need some water?"

"She'll be fine," Joseph says, and gives him a narrow-eyed look.

Drew stands, raising his hands in front of him. "I asked her a simple question."

The padrona clears her throat. "Please make yourself comfortable," she says. "Maria will bring you a refreshment." She introduces herself as Pietà Cellini, the wife of the vintner. She says this proudly, although from the state of their house it seems the family wines haven't been doing so well in recent years. As she speaks she holds Aïda's hand in her own. "Isn't she remarkable, your cousin?" she asks. "So young."

"I'm awfully sorry about all this," I say. "We should be getting home."

"She's darling," says Signora Cellini. "My own daughter went to study in Rome two years ago. She's just a little older than Aïda. Mischievous, too."

"Is that so?" I say. The pain in my ankle has become almost funny. My head feels weightless and poorly attached.

"Aïda was just showing me her lovely pictures in *Elle*," our host says. "The poor girl had a shock just now, all those police. I'm afraid our housemaid was quite rude."

"I'm sure she was just protecting your house," I say.

Aïda sips water from a porcelain cup. Joseph takes it from her when she's finished and sets it down on a tiny gilt table. "Is that better?" he asks.

"You're so nice." Aïda pats his arm. "I'm sure it was just the heat."

Black flashes crowd the edges of my vision. The ankle has begun to throb. I look past them all, through the panes of the French doors and out into the garden, where an old man digs at a bed of spent roses. Dry-looking cuttings lie on the ground, and bees dive and hover around the man. He is singing a song whose words I cannot hear through the glass. I rest my forehead against my hand, wondering how I can stand to be here a moment longer. Aïda laughs, and Joseph's voice joins hers. It seems she has done this intentionally, in reparation for the thrown candlestick or the words I said to her, or even because all my life I have had a mother and she has had none. What a brilliant success I would be if I could paint the scene in this sunny room, glorious Aïda in careful disarray, the two men repelled by one another and drawn to her, the elegant woman leaning over her with a porcelain cup. Sell it. Retire to Aruba. I can already feel the paint between my fingers, under my nails, sliding beneath my fingertips on the canvas. And then I hear the padrona's voice coming from what seems a great distance, calling not Aïda's name but my own. "Mira," she says, "Good God. What happened to your ankle?"

In defiance of all my better instincts, I look down. At first it seems I am looking at a foreign object, some huge red-and-purple swelling where my ankle used to be. It strains against the straps of my sandal as if threatening to burst. "I got hurt," I say, blinking against a contracting darkness, and then there is silent nothing.

. . .

It is nighttime. I do not recall getting back to the apartment, nor do I remember undressing or getting into bed. The room is quiet. There is a bag of crushed ice on my ankle, and an angel bending over it as if it had already died. Translucent wings rise from the angel's back, and its face is inclined over my foot. Its hair shines blue in the moonlight. It murmurs an incomprehensible prayer.

The mosquito netting fills with wind and then hangs limp again, brushing Aïda's shoulders. Her face is full of concentration. She touches the swollen arch of my foot. I can hardly feel it. You could help me if you wanted to, she might say now. You have lived longer than I have and could let me know how it is, but you don't. You let me dance and giggle and look like an idiot. You like it. You wish it. Is she saying this?

"How did we get home?" I ask her. My voice sounds full of sleep.

"You're awake," she says. "You sure messed up your ankle."

"It feels like there are bricks on my chest."

"Signora Cellini gave you Tylenol with codeine. It knocked you out."

Sweet drug. My wisdom-tooth friend. One should have it around. "Where are the guys?"

"Home. We made quite a spectacle."

"You did."

"That's what I do, Cousin Mira."

"*I* don't."

"Was I the only one to faint today?" She raises her eyebrows at me.

"Well, I didn't do it on purpose."

"You'll have to go to a doctor tomorrow."

"So be it. This is your fault, you know," I tell her. I mean for it to be severe, but the last part comes out *falyuno*. I am almost asleep again and grateful for that. With my eyelids half-closed I can see the wings rising from her shoulders again, and her feet might be fused into one, and who knows, she might after all be sexless and uninvolved with the commerce of this world, and I might be the Virgin Mary, receiving the impossible news.

The next morning Aïda calls a cab and we go down to the university infirmary, where an American nurse named Betsy feels my ankle and shakes her head. "X-ray," she says, her blond ponytail swinging back and forth. "This looks ugly." My ankle, if I were to reproduce it on a canvas, would require plenty of aquamarine and ocher and Russian red. The doctor handles me gently. He tells the technician to take plenty of pictures. In another room the doctor puts my films up on a lighted board. He shows me a hairline fracture, which looks to me like a tiny mountain range etched into my bone. He does not understand why I smile when he gives me the bad news. How can I explain to him how apt it is? Drew would recommend a self-portrait.

When I return to the waiting room wearing a fiberglass cast from toes to mid-calf, I find Aïda holding a croissant on a napkin. I feel as if I will faint from hunger.

"Hi, gimp," she says. There's a smirk. I'd like to whack her with my new weapons. Instead we head for the door and walk down Via Rinaldi toward a trattoria where I can find some breakfast. The sun is out, and the *zanzare*. Big, fat ones. Unlike American mosquitoes, these actually hurt when they bite. It's the huge proboscis. At least my ankle is safe from that for a while.

The doctor has prescribed normal activity, with caution until I learn to use the crutches better. It's my first time on them—I always wanted them when I was a kid, but somehow managed to escape injury—and I think I will stay home as long as possible. Time to paint. No more vineyards. Aïda can do what she likes for the last two days of her visit.

At the trattoria we have a marble-topped table on the sidewalk, and a kind waiter looks at me with pity. He brings things we do not order, a little plate of biscotti and tiny ramekins of flavored butter for our *pane*. Aïda twirls her hair and looks at her feet. She is quiet today and has neglected to put on the customary makeup: something to make her lips shine, a thin dark line around the eyes, a pink stain on the cheeks. She looks almost plain, like anyone else's cousin. She actually eats the free biscotti.

Our waiter sets espresso cups on the table. Aïda's growth will be stunted forever by the staggering amount of caffeine she has consumed in Florence. Of course, her father doesn't allow it back home. "Does it hurt?" she asks, pointing to the ankle.

"Not so much anymore," I say. "All that good pain medicine."

"Too bad about the cast. I really mean it. They itch something awful."

Great.

"Now, can I ask you one question, Aïda?" I say.

"One." She lifts her cup and grins at her sneakers.

"What was all that malarkey about your mother? I mean, for God's sake."

There's a long silence. Her lips move slightly as if she's about to answer, but no words come. She sets the cup down and begins to twist her hands, thin bags of bones, against each other. The knuckles crack. "*I* don't know," she says finally. "It was just something to say."

"A little ridiculous, don't you think? Making Joseph break into the house with you?"

"I didn't make anyone do anything." She frowns. "He could have stayed behind with you."

"You sorcered him, Aïda. You knew you were doing it."

Aïda picks up her tiny spoon and stirs the espresso, her eyes becoming serious and downcast. "I did look up my actual mother once," she says.

The admission startles me. I sit up in the iron chair. "When?"

"Last year. After the accident. I imagined dying without ever knowing her, and that was too scary. I didn't tell my dad about it, because you know, he wants me to see him as *both* parents."

"But how did you find her?"

"There was a government agency. France has tons of them, they're so socialized. A man helped me locate a file, and there she was, I mean her name and information about her. Her parents' address in Rouen. My grandparents, can you believe it?"

I imagine a white-haired lady somewhere on an apple farm, wondering to whom the high, clear voice on the phone could belong. It sounds like the voice of a ghost, a child she had who died when she was twelve. She answers the girl's questions with fear in her chest. Does a phone call from a spirit mean that one is close to death?

"They gave me her phone number and address. She was living in Aix-en-Provence. I took a bus there and stood outside her apartment building for hours, and when it rained I stood in someone's vestibule. I didn't even know which window was hers. It's just as well, I guess. She wouldn't have wanted to see me anyhow."

I don't want to believe this story. It seems designed to make me pity her. Yet there's an embarrassment in her face that suddenly makes her look very young, like a child who has admitted to a misdeed. "Are you going to try again?" I ask.

"Maybe sometime," she says. "Maybe after my career."

"That might be a long time," I say.

"Probably not," she says, her eyes set on something in the distance. "I'll have a few good years, and I'd better make enough money to retire on. I don't know what other job I could do."

I consider this. "So what will you do with yourself afterward?"

"I don't know. Go to Morocco with my father. Have kids. Whatever people do."

I think of those pictures of my uncle in couture evening gowns, his skin milky, his waist slender as a girl's. His graceful fingers hold roses or railings or *billets-doux*. His hair hangs long and thick, a shiny mass down his back. He now wears turtlenecks and horn-rimmed glasses; there are veins on the backs of his hands, and his beautiful hair is gone. I wonder how this can happen to Aïda. She seems eternal, the exception to a rule. Can she really be mortal? Even when she fell off the bridge and chanted fever-songs, I knew she would survive to see international fame. In the glossy pages of Signora Cellini's magazines and those of women all over the world, she will never, never change.

But here on the sidewalk at the trattoria she bites a hangnail, and looks again at my foot. "We should get you home," she says. "You need some rest." I wonder if she will survive what will happen to her. I wonder if she will live to meet her mother. There are many things I would ask her if only we liked each other better.

One afternoon, perhaps a month after Aïda's return to Paris, I buy a bottle of inexpensive Chianti and a round loaf of bread and head down to the ancient marketplace by the Arno. There, in the shadow of a high colonnade, the tall bronze statue of Il Porcelino guards the empty butcher stalls. It's easy to move around on the crutches now, although the cobbled streets provide a challenge. I wear long loose dresses to hide my cast.

At the center of the piazza the white-robed Moroccans have spread their silver and leather goods on immaculate sheets. They sing prices as I pass. Because I have some *lire* in my pocket, I buy a thin braided bracelet of leather. Perhaps I will send it to my cousin. Perhaps I will keep it for myself. Down by the river, pigeons alight on the stones and groom their feathers. I sit with my legs dangling over a stone ledge and uncork my round-bellied bottle, and the wine tastes soft and woody. It's bottled by the Cellinis. It's pretty good, certainly not bad enough to make them go broke. I drink to their health and to the health of people everywhere, in celebration of a rather bizarre occurrence. Two days ago I sold a painting. The man who bought it laughed aloud when I said he had made a bad choice. He is an opera patron and food critic from New York City, the godson of my painting professor back in the States. He attended our winter exhibition last January, and happened to be visiting Rome when the Del Reggio Gallery was showing our work.

It is not a painting of Aïda dancing in the grapevines, her hair full of leaves. It is not an unapologetic self-portrait, nor a glowing Tuscan landscape. It is a large sky-blue square canvas with two Chagall-style seraphim in the foreground, holding a house and a tree and a child in their cupped hands. It is called *Above the Farm*. In slightly darker blue, down below, you can make out the shadow of a tornado. Why he bought this painting, I do not know. But there's one thing I can tell you: those angels have no feet.

Although it's interesting to think of my painting hanging in this man's soaring loft in Manhattan, it makes me sad to think I will never see it again. I always feel comforted, somehow, looking at that child standing by his house and tree, calm and resigned to residence in the air. Five hundred feet off the ground, he's still the same boy he was when he stood on the earth. I imagine myself sitting on this ledge with Aïda, when she is old and I am famous. She will look at me as if I take up too much space, and I will want to push her into the Arno. But perhaps by then we will love ourselves less fiercely. Perhaps the edges of our mutual hate will have worn away, and we will have already said the things that need to be said.

Issue 149, 1998

Rick Bass

The Hermit's Story

An ice storm, following seven days of snow; the vast fields and drifts of snow turning to sheets of glazed ice that shine and shimmer blue in the moonlight as if the color is being fabricated not by the bending and absorption of light but by some chemical reaction within the glossy ice; as if the source of all blueness lies somewhere up here in the north—the core of it beneath one of those frozen fields; as if blue is a thing that emerges, in some parts of the world, from the soil itself, after the sun goes down.

Blue creeping up fissures and cracks from depths of several hundred feet; blue working its way up through the gleaming ribs of Ann's buried dogs; blue trailing like smoke from the dogs' empty eye sockets and nostrils—blue rising like smoke from chimneys until it reaches the surface and spreads laterally and becomes entombed, or trapped—but still alive, and smoky—within those moonstruck fields of ice.

Blue like a scent trapped in the ice, waiting for some soft release, some thawing, so that it can continue spreading.

It's Thanksgiving. Susan and I are over at Ann's and Roger's house for dinner. The storm has knocked out all the power down in town—it's a clear, cold, starry night, and if you were to climb one of the mountains on snowshoes and look forty miles south toward where town lies, instead of seeing the usual small scatterings of light—like fallen stars, stars sunken to the bottom of a lake, but still glowing—

you would see nothing but darkness—a bowl of silence and darkness in balance for once with the mountains up here, rather than opposing or complementing our darkness, our peace.

As it is, we do not climb up on snowshoes to look down at the dark town—the power lines dragged down by the clutches of ice—but can tell instead just by the way there is no faint glow over the mountains to the south that the power is out: that this Thanksgiving, life for those in town is the same as it always is for us in the mountains, and it is a good feeling, a familial one, coming on the holiday as it does—though doubtless too the townspeople are feeling less snug and cozy about it than we are.

We've got our lanterns and candles burning. A fire's going in the stove, as it will all winter long and into the spring. Ann's dogs are asleep in their straw nests, breathing in that same blue light that is being exhaled from the skeletons of their ancestors just beneath and all around them. There is the faint, good smell of cold-storage meat—slabs and slabs of it—coming from down in the basement, and we have just finished off an entire chocolate pie and three bottles of wine. Roger, who does not know how to read, is examining the empty bottles, trying to read some of the words on the labels. He recognizes the words *the* and *in* and *USA*. It may be that he will never learn to read—that he will be unable to—but we are in no rush, and—unlike his power lifting—he has all of his life in which to accomplish this. I for one believe that he will learn it.

Ann has a story for us. It's about one of the few clients she's ever had, a fellow named Gray Owl, up in Canada, who owned half a dozen speckled German shorthaired pointers, and who had hired Ann to train them all at once. It was eleven years ago, she says—her last good job.

She worked the dogs all summer and into the autumn, and finally had them ready for field trials. She took them back up to Gray Owl—way up in Saskatchewan—driving all day and night in her old truck, which was old even then, with dogs piled up on top of each other, sleeping and snoring: dogs on her lap, dogs on the seat, dogs on the floorboard. How strange it is to think that most of us can count on one hand the number of people we know who are doing what they most want to do for a living. They invariably have about them a kind of wildness and calmness both, possessing somewhat the grace of animals that are fitted intricately and polished into this world. An academic such as myself might refer to it as a kind of "biological confidence." Certainly I think another word for it could be *peace*.

Ann was taking the dogs up there to show Gray Owl how to work them: how to take advantage of their newly found talents. She could be a sculptor or some other kind of artist, in that she speaks of her work as if the dogs are rough blocks of stone whose internal form exists already and is waiting only to be chiseled free and then released by her beautiful into the world.

Basically, in six months, the dogs had been transformed from gangling, bouncy puppies into six raging geniuses, and she needed to show their owner how to control them, or rather, how to work with them. Which characteristics to nurture, which ones to discourage. With all dogs, Ann said, there was a tendency, upon their leaving her tutelage—unlike a work of art set in stone or paint—for a kind of chitinous encrustation to set in, a sort of oxidation, upon the dogs leaving her hands and being returned to someone less knowledgeable and passionate, less committed than she. It was as if there were a tendency in the world for the dogs' greatness to disappear back into the stone.

So she went up there to give both the dogs and Gray Owl a checkout session. She drove with the heater on and the window down; the cold Canadian air was invigorating, cleaner, farther north. She could smell the scent of the fir and spruce, and the damp alder and cottonwood leaves beneath the many feet of snow. We laughed at her when she said it, but she told us that up in Canada she could taste the fish in the streams as she drove alongside creeks and rivers.

She listened to the only radio station she could pick up as she drove, but it was a good one. She got to Gray Owl's around midnight. He had a little guest cabin but had not heated it for her, uncertain as to the day of her arrival, so she and the six dogs slept together on a cold mattress beneath mounds of elk hides: their last night together. She had brought a box of quail with which to work the dogs, and she built a small fire in the stove and set the box of quail next to it.

The quail muttered and cheeped all night and the stove popped and hissed and Ann and the dogs slept for twelve hours straight, as if submerged in another time, or as if everyone else in the world was submerged in time—encased in stone—and as if she and the dogs were pioneers, or survivors of some kind: upright and exploring the present, alive in the world, free of that strange chitin.

She spent a week up there, showing Gray Owl how his dogs worked. She said he scarcely recognized them afield, and that it took a few days just for him to get over his amazement. They worked the dogs both individually and, as Gray Owl came to understand and appreciate what Ann had crafted, in groups. They traveled across snowy hills on snowshoes, the sky the color of snow, so that often it was like moving through a dream, and except for the rasp of the snowshoes beneath them, and the pull of gravity, they might have believed they had ascended into some sky-place where all the world was snow.

They worked into the wind—north—whenever they could. Ann would carry birds in a pouch over her shoulder—much as a woman might carry a purse—and from time to time would fling a startled bird out into that dreary, icy snow-scape—and the quail would fly off with great haste, a dark feathered buzz bomb disappearing quickly into the teeth of cold, and then Gray Owl and Ann and the dog, or dogs, would go find it, following it by scent only, as always.

Snot icicles would be hanging from the dogs' nostrils. They would always find the bird. The dog, or dogs, would point it, at which point Gray Owl or Ann would step forward and flush it—the beleaguered bird would leap into the sky again—and then once more they would push on after it, pursuing that bird toward the horizon as if driving it with a whip. Whenever the bird wheeled and flew downwind, they'd quarter away from it, then get a mile or so downwind from it and push it back north.

When the quail finally became too exhausted to fly, Ann would pick it up from beneath the dogs' noses as they held point staunchly, put the tired bird in her game bag and replace it with a fresh one, and off they'd go again. They carried their lunch in Gray Owl's daypack, as well as emergency supplies—a tent and some dry clothes—in case they should become lost, and around noon each day (they could rarely see the sun, only an eternal ice-white haze, so that they relied instead only on their rhythms within) they would stop and make a pot of tea on the sputtering little gas stove. Sometimes one or two of the quail would die from exposure, and they would cook that on the stove and eat it out there in the tundra, tossing the feathers up into the wind as if to launch one more flight, and feeding the head, guts and feet to the dogs.

Perhaps seen from above their tracks would have seemed aimless and wandering, rather than with the purpose, the focus that was burning hot in both their and the dogs' hearts—perhaps someone viewing the tracks could have discerned the pattern, or perhaps not—but it did not matter, for their tracks—the patterns, direction and tracing of them—were obscured by the drifting snow sometimes within minutes after they were laid down.

Toward the end of the week, Ann said, they were finally running all six dogs at once—like a herd of silent wild horses through all that snow—and as she would be going home the next day, there was no need to conserve any of the birds she had brought, and she was turning them loose several at a time: birds flying in all directions; the dogs, as ever, tracking them to the ends of the earth.

It was almost a whiteout that last day, and it was hard to keep track of all the dogs. Ann was sweating from the exertion as well as the tension of trying to keep an eye on, and evaluate, each dog—the sweat was freezing on her in places, so that it was as if she were developing an ice skin. She jokingly told Gray Owl that next time she was going to try to find a client who lived in Arizona, or even South America. Gray Owl smiled and then told her that they were lost, but no matter, the storm would clear in a day or two.

They knew it was getting near dusk—there was a faint dulling to the sheer whiteness—a kind of increasing heaviness in the air, a new density to the faint light around them—and the dogs slipped in and out of sight, working just at the edges of their vision.

The temperature was dropping as the north wind increased—"No question about which way south is; we'll turn around and walk south for three hours, and if we don't find a road, we'll make camp," Gray

Owl said—and now the dogs were coming back with frozen quail held gingerly in their mouths, for once the birds were dead, they were allowed to retrieve them, though the dogs must have been puzzled that there had been no shots. Ann said she fired a few rounds of the cap pistol into the air to make the dogs think she had hit those birds. Surely they believed she was a goddess.

They turned and headed south—Ann with a bag of frozen birds over her shoulder, and the dogs—knowing that the hunt was over now—all around them, once again like a team of horses in harness, though wild and prancey.

After an hour of increasing discomfort—Ann's and Gray Owl's hands and feet numb, and ice beginning to form on the dogs' paws, so that the dogs were having to high-step—they came in day's last light to the edge of a wide clearing: a terrain that was remarkable and soothing for its lack of hills. It was a frozen lake, which meant—said Gray Owl—they had drifted west (or perhaps east) by as much as ten miles.

Ann said that Gray Owl looked tired and old and guilty, as would any host who had caused his guest some unasked-for inconvenience. They knelt down and began massaging the dogs' paws and then lit the little stove and held each dog's foot, one at a time, over the tiny blue flame to help it thaw out.

Gray Owl walked out to the edge of the lake ice and kicked at it with his foot, hoping to find fresh water beneath for the dogs; if they ate too much snow, especially after working so hard, they'd get violent diarrhea and might then become too weak to continue home the next day, or the next, or whenever the storm quit.

Ann said she could barely see Gray Owl's outline through the swirling snow, even though he was less than twenty yards away. He kicked once at the sheet of ice, the vast plate of it, with his heel, then disappeared below the ice.

Ann wanted to believe that she had blinked and lost sight of him, or that a gust of snow had swept past and hidden him, but it had been too fast, too total: she knew that the lake had swallowed him. She was sorry for Gray Owl, she said, and worried for his dogs—afraid they would try to follow his scent down into the icy lake, and be lost as well—but what she was most upset about, she said—to be perfectly honest—was that Gray Owl had been wearing the little day-pack with the tent and emergency rations. She had it in her mind to try to save Gray Owl, and to try to keep the dogs from going through the ice— but if he drowned, she was going to have to figure out how to try to get that daypack off of the drowned man and set up the wet tent in the blizzard on the snowy prairie and then crawl inside and survive. She would have to go into the water naked, so that when she came back out—if she came back out—she would have dry clothes to put on.

The dogs came galloping up, seeming as large as deer or elk in that dim landscape against which there was nothing else to give them perspective, and Ann whoaed them right at the lake's edge, where they stopped immediately as if they had suddenly been cast with a sheet of ice.

Ann knew they would stay there forever, or until she released them, and it troubled her to think that if she drowned, they too would die—that they would stand there motionless, as she had commanded them, for as long as they could, until at some point—days later, perhaps—they would lie down, trembling with exhaustion—they might lick at some snow, for moisture—but that then the snows would cover them, and still they would remain there, chins resting on their front paws, staring straight ahead and unseeing into the storm, wondering where the scent of her had gone.

Ann eased out onto the ice. She followed the tracks until she came to the jagged hole in the ice through which Gray Owl had plunged. She was almost half again lighter than he, but she could feel the ice crackling beneath her own feet. It sounded different, too, in a way she could not place—it did not have the squeaky, percussive resonance of the lake-ice back home—and she wondered if Canadian ice froze differently or just sounded different.

She got down on all fours and crept closer to the hole. It was right at dusk. She peered down into the hole and dimly saw Gray Owl standing down there, waving his arms at her. He did not appear to be swimming. Slowly, she took one glove off and eased her bare hand down into the hole. She could find no water, and tentatively, she reached deeper.

Gray Owl's hand found hers and he pulled her down in. Ice broke as she fell but he caught her in his arms. She could smell the wood smoke in his jacket from the alder he burned in his cabin. There was no water at all, and it was warm beneath the ice.

"This happens a lot more than people realize," he said. "It's not really a phenomenon; it's just what happens. A cold snap comes in October, freezes a skin of ice over the lake—it's got to be a shallow one, almost a marsh. Then a snowfall comes, insulating the ice. The lake drains in fall and winter—percolates down through the soil"—he stamped the spongy ground beneath them—"but the ice up top remains. And nobody ever knows any differently. People look out at the surface and think, *Aha, a frozen lake*." Gray Owl laughed.

"Did you know it would be like this?" Ann asked.

"No," he said, "I was looking for water. I just got lucky."

Ann walked back to shore beneath the ice to fetch her stove and to release the dogs from their whoa command. The dry lake was only about eight feet deep, but it grew shallow quickly, closer to shore, so that Ann had to crouch to keep from bumping her head on the overhead ice, and then crawl; and then there was only space to wriggle, and to emerge she had to break the ice above her by bumping and then battering it with her head and elbows, like the struggles of some embryonic hatchling; and when stood up, waist-deep amid sparkling shards of ice—it was nighttime, now—the dogs barked ferociously at her, but remained where she had ordered them to stay—and she was surprised at how far off course she was when she climbed out; she had traveled only twenty feet but already the dogs were twice that far away from her. She knew humans had a poorly evolved, almost nonexistent sense of direction, but this error—over such a short distance—shocked her. It was as if there were in us a thing—an impulse, a catalyst—that denies our ever going straight to another thing. Like dogs working left and right into the wind, she thought, before converging on the scent.

Except that the dogs would not get lost, while she could easily imagine herself and Gray Owl getting lost beneath the lake, walking in circles forever, unable to find even the simplest of things: the shore.

She gathered the stove and dogs. She was tempted to try to go back in the way she had come out—it seemed so easy—but considered the consequences of getting lost in the other direction, and instead followed her original tracks out to where Gray Owl had first dropped through the ice. It was true night now and the blizzard was still blowing hard, plastering snow and ice around her face like a mask. The dogs did not want to go down into the hole, so she lowered them to Gray Owl and then climbed gratefully back down into the warmth herself.

The air was a thing of its own—recognizable as air, and breathable, as such, but with a taste and odor, an essence, unlike any other air they'd ever breathed. It had a different density to it, so that smaller, shallower breaths were required; there was very much the feeling that if they breathed in too much of the strange, dense air, they would drown.

They wanted to explore the lake, and were thirsty, but it felt like a victory simply to be warm—or rather, not cold—and they were so exhausted that instead they made pallets out of the dead marsh grass that rustled around their ankles, and they slept curled up on the tiniest of hammocks, to keep from getting damp in the pockets and puddles of dampness that still lingered here and there.

All eight of them slept as if in a nest, heads and arms draped across other ribs and hips, and it was, said Ann, the best and deepest sleep she'd ever had—the sleep of hounds, the sleep of childhood—and how long they slept, she never knew, for she wasn't sure, later, how much of their subsequent time they spent wandering beneath the lake, and then up on the prairie, homeward again—but when they awoke, it was still night, or night once more, and clearing, with bright stars visible through the porthole, their point of embarkation; and even from beneath the ice, in certain places where for whatever reasons—temperature, oxygen content, wind scour—the ice was clear rather than glazed they could see the spangling of stars, though more dimly; and strangely, rather than seeming to distance them from the stars, this phenomenon seemed to pull them closer as if they were up in the stars, traveling the Milky Way—or as if the stars were embedded in the ice.

It was very cold outside—up above—and there was a steady stream, a current like a river of the night's colder, heavier air plunging down through their porthole, as if trying to fill the empty lake with that frozen air—but there was also the hot muck of the earth's massive respirations breathing out warmth and being trapped and protected beneath that ice, so that there were warm currents doing battle with the lone cold current.

The result was that it was breezy down there, and the dogs' noses twitched in their sleep as the images brought by these scents painted themselves across their sleeping brains in the language we call dreams but which, for the dogs, and perhaps for us, were reality: the scent of an owl *real*, not a dream; the scent of bear, cattail, willow, loon, *real*, even though they were sleeping, and even though those things were not visible: only over the next horizon.

The ice was contracting, groaning and cracking and squeaking up tighter, shrinking beneath the great cold—a concussive, grinding sound, as if giants were walking across the ice above—and it was this sound that had awakened them. They snuggled in warmer among the rattly dried yellowing grasses and listened to the tremendous clashings, as if they were safe beneath the sea and were watching waves of starlight sweeping across their hiding place; or as if they were in some place, some position, where they could watch mountains being born.

After a while the moon came up and washed out the stars. The light was blue and silver and seemed, Ann said, to be like a living thing. It filled the sheet of ice just above their heads with a shimmering cobalt light, which again rippled as if the ice were moving, rather than the earth itself, with the moon tracking it—and like deer drawn by gravity getting up in the night to feed for an hour or so before settling back in, Gray Owl and Ann and the dogs rose from their nests of straw and began to travel.

"You didn't—you know—*engage?*" Susan asks: a little mischievously, and a little proprietary, perhaps.

Ann shakes her head. "It was too cold," she says. I sneak a glance at Roger, but cannot read his expression. Is he in love with her? Does she own his heart?

"But you would have, if it hadn't been so cold, right?" Susan asks, and Ann shrugs. "He was an old man—in his fifties—and the dogs were around. But yeah, there was something about it that made me think of . . . those things," she says, careful and precise as ever.

"I would have done it anyway," Susan says, "Even if it was cold, and even if he was a hundred."

"We walked a long way," Ann says, eager to change the subject. "The air was damp down there and whenever we'd get chilled, we'd stop and make a little fire out of a bundle of dry cattails." There were little pockets and puddles of swamp gas pooled here and there, she said, and sometimes a spark from the cattails would ignite one of those, and all around these little pockets of gas would light up like when you toss gas on a fire—these little explosions of brilliance, like flashbulbs—marsh pockets igniting like falling dominoes, or like children playing hopscotch—until a large-enough flash-pocket was reached—sometimes thirty or forty yards away from them, by this point—that the puff of flame would blow a chimney-hole through the ice, venting the other pockets, and the fires would crackle out—the scent of grass smoke sweet in their lungs—and they could feel gusts of warmth from the little flickering fires, and currents of the colder, heavier air—sliding down through the new vent holes and pooling around their ankles. The moonlight would strafe down through those rents in the ice, and shards of moon-ice would be glittering and spinning like diamond-motes in those newly vented columns of moonlight; and they pushed on, still lost, but so alive.

The mini-explosions were fun, but they frightened the dogs, and so Ann and Gray Owl lit twisted bundles of cattails and used them for torches to light their way, rather than building warming fires: though occasionally they would still pass through a pocket of methane and a stray ember would fall from their torches, and the whole chain of fire and light would begin again, culminating once more with a vent-hole being blown open and shards of glittering ice tumbling down into their lair . . .

What would it have looked like, seen from above—the orange blur-rings of their wandering trail beneath the ice; and what would the sheet of lake-ice itself have looked like that night—throbbing with the ice-bound, subterranean blue and orange light of moon and fire? But

again, there was no one to view the spectacle: only the travelers themselves, and they had no perspective, no vantage or loft from which to
view or judge themselves. They were simply pushing on from one fire
to the next, carrying their tiny torches. The beauty in front of them
was enough.

They knew they were getting near a shore—the southern shore,
they hoped, as they followed the glazed moon's lure above—when
the dogs began to encounter shore birds that had somehow found
their way beneath the ice through small fissures and rifts and were
taking refuge in the cattails. Small winter birds—juncos, nuthatches,
chickadees—skittered away from the smoky approach of their
torches; only a few later-migrating (or winter-trapped) snipe held
tight and steadfast, and the dogs began to race ahead of Gray Owl
and Ann, working these familiar scents—blue and silver ghost-
shadows of dog-muscle weaving ahead through slants of moonlight.

The dogs emitted the odor of adrenaline when they worked, Ann
said—a scent like damp fresh-cut green hay—and with nowhere to
vent, the odor was dense and thick around them, so that Ann wondered if it too might be flammable, like the methane: if in the dogs'
passions they might literally immolate themselves.

They followed the dogs closely with their torches. The ceiling was
low—about eight feet, as if in a regular room—so that the tips of their
torches' flames seared the ice above them, leaving a drip behind them
and transforming the milky, almost opaque cobalt and orange ice behind them—wherever they passed—into wandering ribbons of clear
ice, translucent to the sky—a script of flame, or buried flame, ice-
bound flame—and they hurried to keep up with the dogs.

Now the dogs had the snipe surrounded, as Ann told it, and one
by one the dogs went on point—each dog freezing as it pointed to the
birds hiding places—and it was the strangest scene yet, Ann said,
seeming surely underwater; and Gray Owl moved in to flush the
birds, which launched themselves with vigor against the roof of the
ice above, fluttering like bats; but the snipe were too small, not powerful enough to break through those frozen four inches of water
(though they could fly four thousand miles to South America each
year, and then back to Canada six months later—is freedom a lateral

component, or a vertical one?) and as Gray Owl kicked at the clumps of frost-bent cattails where the snipe were hiding and they burst into flight only to hit their heads on the ice above them, the snipe came tumbling back down, raining limp and unconscious back to their soft grassy nests.

The dogs began retrieving them, carrying them gingerly, delicately—not preferring the taste of snipe, which ate only earthworms—and Ann and Gray Owl gathered the tiny birds from the dogs, placed them in their pockets, and continued on to the shore, chasing that moon—the ceiling lowering to six feet, then four, then to a crawl space—and after they had bashed their way out (with elbows, fists and forearms) and stepped back out into the frigid air, they tucked the still-unconscious snipe into little crooks in branches, up against the trunks of trees and off the ground, out of harm's way, and passed on, south—as if late in their own migration—while the snipe rested, warm and terrified and heart-fluttering, but saved, for now, against the trunks of those trees.

Long after Ann and Gray Owl and the pack of dogs had passed through, the birds would awaken—their bright dark eyes luminous in the moonlight—and the first sight they would see would be the frozen marsh before them with its chain of still-steaming vent-holes stretching back across all the way to the other shore. Perhaps these were birds that had been unable to migrate due to injuries, or some genetic absence. Perhaps they had tried to migrate in the past but had found either their winter habitat destroyed, or the path down there so fragmented and fraught with danger that it made more sense—to these few birds—to ignore the tuggings of the stars and seasons and instead to try to carve out new lives, new ways-of-being, even in such a stark and severe landscape: or rather, in a stark and severe period—knowing that lushness and bounty was still retained within that landscape. That it was only a phase; that better days would come. That in fact (the snipe knowing these things with their blood, ten-million-years-in-the-world), the austere times were the very thing, the very imbalance, which would summon the resurrection of that frozen richness within the soil—if indeed that richness, that magic, that hope, did still exist beneath the ice and snow. Spring would come like its own green fire, if only the injured ones could hold on.

And what would the snipe think or remember, upon reawakening and finding themselves still in that desolate position, desolate place and time, but still alive, and with hope?

Would it seem to them that a thing like grace had passed through, as they slept—that a slender winding river of it had passed through and rewarded them for their faith and endurance?

Believing, stubbornly, that that green land beneath them would blossom once more. Maybe not soon; but again.

If the snipe survived, they would be among the first to see it. Perhaps they believed that the pack of dogs, and Gray Owl's and Ann's advancing torches, had only been one of winter's dreams. Even with the proof—the scribings—of grace's passage before them—the vent-holes still steaming—perhaps they believed it was only one of winter's dreams.

It would be curious to tally how many times any or all of us reject, or fail to observe, moments of grace. Another way in which I think Susan and I differ from most of the anarchists and militia members up here is that we believe there is still green fire in the hearts of our citizens, beneath this long snowy winter—beneath the chitin of the insipid. That there is still something beneath the surface: that our souls and spirits are still of more worth, more value, than the glassine, latticed ice-structures visible only now at the surface of things. We still believe there's something down there beneath us, as a country. Not that we're better than other countries, by any means—but that we're luckier. That ribbons of grace are still passing through and around us—even now, and for whatever reasons, certainly unbeknownst to us, and certainly undeserved, unearned.

Gray Owl, Ann and the dogs headed south for half a day until they reached the snow-scoured road on which they'd parked. The road looked different, Ann said, buried beneath snowdrifts, and they didn't know whether to turn east or west. The dogs chose west, and so Gray Owl and Ann followed them. Two hours later they were back at their truck, and that night they were back at Gray Owl's cabin; by the next night Ann was home again. She says that even now she still sometimes has dreams about being beneath the ice—about living beneath the ice—and that it seems to her as if she was down there for much longer than a day and a night; that instead she might have been gone for years.

It was twenty years ago, when it happened. Gray Owl has since died, and all of those dogs are dead now, too. She is the only one who still carries—in the flesh, at any rate—the memory of that passage.

Ann would never discuss such a thing, but I suspect that it, that one day-and-night, helped give her a model for what things were like for her dogs when they were hunting and when they went on point: how the world must have appeared to them when they were in that trance, that blue zone, where the odors of things wrote their images across the dogs' hot brainpans. A zone where sight, and the appearance of things—*surfaces*—disappeared, and where instead their essence—the heat molecules of scent—was revealed, illuminated, circumscribed, possessed.

I suspect that she holds that knowledge—the memory of that one day-and-night—especially since she is now the sole possessor—as tightly, and securely, as one might clench some bright small gem in one's fist: not a gem given to one by some favored or beloved individual but, even more valuable, some gem found while out on a walk—perhaps by happenstance, or perhaps by some unavoidable rhythm of fate—and hence containing great magic, great strength.

Such is the nature of the kinds of people living, scattered here and there, in this valley.

Issue 147, 1998

James Lasdun

⚭

Snow

My great-uncle Dominic, the inventor, took me into the small workshop that stood between the back of his house and the large kitchen garden behind it. "This will amuse you," he said, pointing to a box-shaped contraption with what looked like a headlamp encased in it. "It's called a stroboscope. They are going to become very popular." He switched on an electric drill, and brought it into the flashing, acetylene-blue light of the contraption. With his free hand he adjusted the frequency of the flashing, and I watched, enchanted, as the drill bit appeared to slow gradually down to a complete halt. "There, you see," he said, "it renders the most violent things harmless. Touch the drill, go on . . ."

Such was his solicitude, however, that before I had raised my small hand a fraction, he clutched it with his own. "Now let this serve as a lesson to you. Watch . . ." He brought a piece of wood from the workbench to the motionless drill-bit. A harsh rasping came as the one contacted the other, a flashlit spray of sawdust plumed out in a staggered curve, and in a trice the innocent piece of metal had bitten clean through the inch-thick piece of wood. "There you are. If something looks peaceful then leave it alone or else you get crucified. The stroboscope makes machines look still because it only illuminates one point in their cycle. Terrible accidents happen in factories where they have flickering neon lights . . . Now I must go and have a nap before Inge and I go out."

Uncle Dominic was a man of extraordinary mildness. Family legend has it that his only retort to the irresponsible nurse in whose charge his son drowned forty-five years ago was, "If this sort of thing happens again you'll have to go." He made his fortune when the patent for a guidance device he had invented was purchased by an aeronautical company, which then adapted it for use in naval missiles. After the war he calculated that he had been instrumental in the deaths of some twenty thousand people. The fact haunted him. He wrote countless letters to the press warning scientists to guard their discoveries from the military, and was much ridiculed for them. In an oddly inverted piece of *folie de grandeur*, he papered his workshop with the dead and wounded of Hiroshima, as if he had been personally responsible for the carnage. The projects he worked on became increasingly trifling, as his concern over their possible abuse grew more obsessive. That winter he had perfected a machine for feeding minced chicken, at twelve-hourly intervals, to Salome, his beloved Persian Blue, so that he and his second wife Inge could take short holidays without troubling the neighbors to look after the animal.

He had also built the prototype of a hair-plaiting device for Inge, and as we returned from the cold workshop to the warm house, we heard Inge shouting from the bedroom upstairs—"Come and get this wretched machine out of my hair. It's stuck—" Uncle Dominic quickened his pace, then checked himself. "I mustn't run," he said to me, "you go and help her."

Inge, twenty-six years my great-uncle's junior, sat at her dressing table in a blue silk *peignoir* embroidered with tiny bright humming birds, the plaiting device sticking incongruously from her long golden hair. "Ah. Little Thomas," she said, "how sweet you are . . ." I stood behind her disentangling the golden strands from the silver tines of the device as gently as I could. "None of his machines work these days," she whispered, as Uncle Dominic's footsteps approached the door.

He fell instantly asleep on the bed, while Inge had me brush her hair with her soft, ivory-handled hairbrush, and plait it with my own hands. I can remember wanting to tell her how lovely I thought she was, but having the courage only to let my all-licensed hands linger in that gleaming floss some moments longer than were necessary. She coiled the braid into a bun, and fixed it with two tourmaline pins. "Now go," she said, "while I dress," and kissed me on my forehead.

I saw them off from the front entrance; my great-uncle immaculate in evening dress, the black of his tall gaunt frame and the silver hair repeated in his tipped ebony stick; Inge's sable stole collecting the first white crystals of the frozen evening. "We won't be long," she called to me from the bottom of the marble steps. "Anne-Marie will look after you. If Mr. Morpurgo arrives before we do, then . . . offer him a drink." She climbed into the car giggling at the thought, and they drove off to their cocktail party.

I sat on the living-room sofa drawing Christmas cards for them, while Anne-Marie—or Claire or Gabrielle—buffed silver knives and piled them on a salver where they gleamed like fish spilt from a net.

Mr. Morpurgo, their dinner guest, did arrive before Dominic and Inge. He wore, as I remember, a yellow suit with pieces of brown suede clasping the shoulders and elbows. His face was a porous, piecemeal assemblage of unrelated features that could never agree on one expression. Smiles dissolved into scowls then into parodies of misery, swiftly, and with no apparent reason. He was the kind of man who awakens in children their first sensations of snobbery. I offered him a drink, and when he asked jovially if I was joining him, I declined with a delicious sense of disdain. He addressed me as "little man," but I knew he had only been invited out of pity, because his wife had left him, and it was Christmas Eve, and he happened to live across the garden. He tried to flirt with the au pair, but she feigned ignorance of English. He put on a French accent, as if that would help, and she quickly found an excuse to leave the room. He wandered about picking up and examining ornaments from shelves, and when I intimated that the silver-and-glass-framed wedding portrait of Dominic and Inge he'd pulled from its hook was fragile and perhaps rather special to them, he made a great show of replacing it exactly as he'd found it, smirking at me while he did so. "Whatever the little man says," he added, and in an attempt to amuse, clicked his heels together and saluted me.

The slam of the front door brought in Dominic and Inge, rosy-cheeked and vibrant from their cocktail party. As they greeted Mr. Morpurgo, apologizing for their lateness, I watched the powdery snow on Inge's stole melting into tiny seed pearls that clung, sparkling, to the wet tips of fur. The arrowheads of her pale blue high heels were rimmed with moisture, and I remember this pleasing me, because it meant the snow was settling.

At dinner, Mr. Morpurgo tried to draw out my Uncle Dominic on the subject of his pacifism. "Go on, admit it," he kept saying, with what was presumably intended to be a roguish grin, "you're deluding yourself. No real progress has ever been made in the name of peace or love. Greed, aggression and lust—that's what motivates people. We're beasts really—I'm one, I don't deny it. I organize my life and work accordingly. Stab your neighbor before he stabs you, that's the only way. Admit it, go on . . ." Out of courtesy, Uncle Dominic made a token defense of his position; the lazy, tail-swishing defense a horse makes against a mildly irritating fly, and it seemed entirely proper to me that he should not waste energy doing battle with so unworthy an adversary.

After dinner he dozed on the living-room sofa, Salome dozing on his lap, while Inge and Mr. Morpurgo played backgammon, quietly accusing one another of cheating, and giggling quietly so as not to wake Uncle Dominic. Mr. Morpurgo risked a stab at his sleeping host—"That's how he preserves his illusions is it—by sleeping most of his life, and only waking up for the good bits?" Inge smiled sadly at her husband and said nothing.

As ever, no effort was made to send me to bed, although Mr. Morpurgo twice expressed his amazement at "the little man's stamina." I went, eventually, in the wake of Uncle Dominic who, roused by the bite of Salome's claws, declared himself a little sleepy and retired, wishing us all a happy Christmas. When Inge came up to say goodnight, she let me unpin her hair, unfurl it, and separate the three golden locks which she rustled back into one disheveled tress before returning to Mr. Morpurgo.

I found myself very suddenly wide awake long before the dawn of Christmas Day. I left opening my stocking until my great-uncle and aunt would have woken, and I could open it on their bed, the quilt wrapped about my shoulders, while they received my tribute of delight in return for their generosity. Through my bedroom window the dark blue sky with its sprinkling of stars coaxed pale shades of silver from the snow-covered garden and surrounding houses. The snow on the garden was pristine, except for a dotted line that ran across the center from our house to the one opposite, like the perforations between two stamps seen from their white, shiny backs.

I put on my slippers, went downstairs to investigate, and yes, parallel with two sets of snowed-over footprints leading out from the back door, past my great-uncle's workshop, was a set cut freshly into the crisp snow, the arrow heads pointing back into our house.

The significance of these footprints remained in chrysalis within me until the recent death of my great-uncle reminded me of the occasion; though by then I, like everyone else except perhaps Uncle Dominic, knew all about Inge's affair. The sight thus provided me with no sorrowful descent into knowledge. It did, however, give rise to a tableau which now seems a peculiarly expressive coda to my Uncle Dominic's life.

The busy Christmas morning rituals on the day itself demanded I put the image of the footprints temporarily out of mind. At lunch, though, it rose once more from its suppression. The ten or twelve assembled relatives had finished eating, and we were leaning back in our chairs telling stories and sipping *eiswein*. Whether it was an excess of that extraordinary distillation of frost-corrupted grapes, or the air's intoxicating fragrance of tangerine peel, burnt brandy, and cigar smoke, or the way the candle flames were splintered and multiplied in the table's debris of silver cutlery and dishes, I don't know; but something released in me the image of those tracks again, catalyzing a thought that seemed to me astoundingly clever, and well worth the immediate attention of the company.

"Uncle Dominic," I called out in my shrill voice. The table hushed, and my great-uncle's eyelids opened a crack. "Your stroboscope is like snow. There were footprints leading to the back door this morning when I got up, and I've just thought . . ." but to my chagrin the relatives at once resumed their conversations in unnecessarily loud voices. I piped louder, but my ingenious explanation—that all the action happens *between* the footprints, so that only the moments of stillness are made visible by the snow—was drowned by my relatives' voices that rose with mine, fell briefly at intervals when they thought I'd given up, then rose in chorus again as I persisted, so that all my Uncle Dominic was allowed to hear were the disjointed words that rang out during the brief pauses.

He looked perplexed for a moment, but made no attempt to hear more than the babble permitted and soon let his eyelids drop again. I was finally silenced by Inge's mother who asked me, with a fatuous (though unreturned) grin at her daughter, whether I thought those footprints might have been Father Christmas's. Mortified by this snub, I fell into a sulk from which I did not recover until I had flown back to my parents, who worked in a place where Christmas is not celebrated, and where snow has never been seen.

Issue 104, 1987

Malinda McCollum

⌖

The Fifth Wall

Sam's Tackle Box was wall-to-wall merchandise, packed so tight it fooled most customers into thinking everything for sale was already on display. But Elana Hall wasn't fooled. Though the store stunk of bait and brine, she could still catch the sour odor of methamphetamine, which Sam himself cooked regularly in a well-vented room above the sales floor.

Elana came to the Tackle Box with her daughter, Jeanette, every week, though neither had much affection for fish. Still, the kid went wild in the place, and broke away from her mother as soon as they passed through the door. Elana, troubled and aching, paused next to an arrangement of musky lures and watched her go. Weren't children's senses supposed to be more acute than adults'? Shouldn't Sam's reek and clutter be too much for her girl? A dim memory surfaced from her own past, a trip to New York City, to Chinatown, the smell of fish so overwhelming that she begged her dad to return to Des Moines straightaway. The fact that her daughter could handle Sam's—the fact that she sometimes seemed to love it—suggested that Jeanette was already leaving childhood behind. Physical senses dulling, their loss soon to be offset by increased insight and guile. A pain pulsed behind Elana's eyes. It frightened her, this coming Jeanette. This clever spy replacing her dreamy little tot, who understood and wanted not much at all.

"Friends!" Sam's third wife called from behind the register. Her name was Janice, and she wore studded wristbands, a leotard and a long, low ponytail, as if any minute she might either punch somebody or pull out a sticky mat and pop into Downward-Facing Dog.

Elana allowed a thin smile of anticipation. Janice pushed a button beneath the counter, and they both listened to a faint bell ring overhead. There was the solid sound of boots hitting the floor. A door closing. The *ee-aw* of the stairs. Then Sam himself, from behind a green curtain on the side wall, still handsome and imposing at sixty. And Elana as happy to see him as when she was a kid at the Ceilidh, when he'd grab her to join a Gordon dance with his now-dead first wife and her dad.

She moved toward him quickly. But out from an aisle ran her daughter, crashing into his legs. Sam lifted Jeanette, and she opened up to flaunt her horrible new braces.

"Mom said they make me look beautiful!" she squealed.

"Your mom's a real sweet lady," Sam said smoothly. "Your mom's something else, that's for sure." He set the girl down. "In fact, I'd like to talk to your mom in private. I have an idea for your birthday present that I need to float."

"We got some Fuzz-E-Grubs in," Janice called enticingly. "I haven't put them out yet, but I'll let you take a look."

Her daughter rushed to the counter, and Elana followed Sam though an aisle of rigs and out a rear screen door to the Mirage. Thirty years ago he'd created it by fencing off half his parking lot and planting oak trees and grass. The last six months saw the addition of motion-sensitive lights and barbed wire. The lights were designed to function only at night, but through the years the oaks had grown aggressively, and the Mirage was overhung with a dense awning of leaves that nearly blocked the sun. As Elana and Sam entered, individual floods clicked on and spotlighted their movements—her sitting in a ratty mesh lounger, him hauling himself into the bass boat he'd parked on blocks.

This was in June, during a summer when the seventeen-year cicadas emerged from underground. The trees were filled with buzz, males drumming their abdomens while females laid eggs and died. But in spite of the noise, the headache Elana had been fronting all day stepped back. Around Sam, things settled into place. He took over whatever story you were telling so you could sit down and shut up.

She rolled her sleeve to her elbow. Sam unsnapped the boat's cover and climbed into the hold. A month ago she'd lost her job at Hy-Vee for spitting at a customer who complained about her bagging pace. Jeanette's braces came next. Still, even without cash, Sam kept advancing her. She knew he had a reason for stringing her along—the man was no saint—but she figured that being aware of it meant that she was complicit. Being complicit in her own destruction made the danger seem less.

Sam climbed down from the boat with a syringe and a strip of tubing. When he offered them, she shook her head.

"Do you mind?" she asked. "My eyes are wrecked."

Obligingly, he bent to her, circling her bicep with tube. She bit one end and tasted rubber. Sam slapped the crook of her arm, until he stopped.

First came the Nip. Then the Whirl. Elana pumped her fists and rose from the chair, head bobbing, until she bumped a low branch and loosed a rain of cicada shells. Sighing, Sam plucked the molted skins from her hair.

"Seventeen years ago," he said, pinching a dry skin to dust. "Where was Elana then?" Her head rang as images flashed from that summer. Third place in Jig at a dancing comp in Chicago. Pink champagne from the gas station, drunk in Greenwood Park. The driver's ed teacher, Mr. Hunt, yelling about her lead foot and rolling stops.

"That was not a full stop!" she croaked now, remembering his hoarse voice from the passenger seat. "In California maybe that half-assed stop would fly. But not here, I assure you, not here!"

Sam cast a sharp eye upon her. "Funny you mention California," he said. "You ever been?"

"Un uh. Un uh." She stepped away from him, to give everything its space.

Sam carefully retucked his shirt before lowering himself into her chair. "Let me be straight," he said. "I'm not one for cutting off people. But I can't see as to how you're going to pay this large debt you've acquired."

So this was the day! A flicker of fear, but the speed transformed it to energy. "Maybe we can brainstorm," she said brightly.

"I'll start." Sam stroked his beard, the pale gray of it strange against his hard, tanned face. "Let me paint the big picture. Demand is high, which is good, but the bad news is I can't keep up on my own. Most operations around here are sourced in southern Cal. It's time for me to plug into that game. The catch is that that particular pipeline is no secret to anyone, narcs included, and they've got the highways between here and L.A. all staked out. Some unfortunates try the bus as safe passage. Remember that guy nabbed on Greyhound with ten pounds of crank in his socks?"

"What about flying?"

"X-rays, dogs. No, the road is the only way to go. The one question: What's the best cover?"

He went on to describe his strategy of outfitting a vehicle and its passengers as if the whole enterprise were an innocent family trip. Plenty of luggage in the trunk, plenty of snacks in a cooler, guidebooks and maps prominently displayed. The problem was, he said, that even if he and Janice tricked themselves out as tourists, the disparity in their ages made them appear suspect. It wasn't Janice, he continued, but himself. There was a criminal air about him that he'd never been able to shake. That, along with a tendency to get shifty-eyed in authority's presence, meant that he'd be forced to sit this trip out.

Elana tried to stay with his speech, but the meth jumped her ahead to his as-yet unspoken proposal that she go to California in his place. The idea both terrified and attracted her. That's how it was with most things those days.

"I want to give you the chance to clear your debt," Sam said, leaning forward to set his elbows on his knees. "I'll forgive everything if Jeanette rides to California with Janice."

"No," she said automatically.

"Imagine. A cop pulls them over. What's this? A mother and daughter taking a summer trip. What could be nicer? More straight up?"

"A good mother wouldn't risk her kid that way." But already she perceived a slight inner crumbling. "How could I be a good mother and let her go?"

"A good mother wants what's best for her child. Think. What do you want for Jeanette?"

She envisioned an island with coconuts and wild horses.

"For her to end up somewhere else," she said.

"Right," said Sam. "Somewhere else entirely. This trip could show her a lot of different ways to live." He reclined in the chair. "Besides, you know I loved your father. I'd never do anything to hurt his only grandkid."

"What about me?" she heard herself whine. "I'm his only daughter. Look what you've done to me."

Sam stood and took hold of her wrist. At first she thought he was comforting her, but as his grip tightened she received the real message: Pain.

"You dug your own hole," he said evenly. "I brought the shovel, but you put it to dirt."

"Without the shovel I couldn't have gone very deep," she pointed out.

"Don't be stupid."

"I'm not stupid," she mumbled. "I'm weak." Then some sort of aural hallucination overtook her, reducing their discussion to one word—*California!*—cried with delight. *California! California! California!* With each repetition the word sounded less strange and the voice more familiar, until she recognized it as her daughter's, from inside the store. Was it possible that her daughter had stumbled into her consciousness, discovering a decision she thought she hadn't yet made?

"I'm going to California!" Jeanette cried. Elana wrenched away from Sam and peered through the screen. Her daughter ran toward her, braids flying, so quickly there was no time for warning.

Jeanette crashed into the door at full speed. Dazed, she tried to pull away, but her braces were tangled in the screen.

"Oh dear," Janice said, behind her. "I'll get pliers."

Jeanette screamed. The sound pierced Elana, but before she could move, Sam was kneeling before the door.

"Honey," he said urgently, "calm down, or you'll hurt yourself even worse. How about I give you the rest of your birthday present? Then play you a little something on my pipes?"

Jeanette's next sob stopped in her throat. "Okay," she said, sniffling.

Sam ambled toward his boat, the motion lights flashing like he was a paparazzo's prey. After a moment, Elana willed herself toward her daughter. Jeanette's lips were stretched back from her mouth. Her gums and teeth were flat against the wire, like a caged monkey in a lab.

"Sweet pea," Elana told her. "I'm going to open this door really slowly. You walk forward when I do." When she turned the handle and pulled, Jeanette inched over the threshold into the Mirage. Elana held her hand and squatted opposite the screen.

"Your hand thwet," her daughter said in an accusing tone, tongue thrusting against the screen.

"I'm sweating," Elana said quickly. "You scared the crap out of me with that wail." She let go to wipe her palm on her jeans, then clutched Jeanette's hand again. "Why did you say you're going to California?

"Janith thaid you thaid okay. For my birthday."

"That really sounds fun?"

"Your faith ith weird."

"You ought to see yours," Elana said. She licked her lips. "So you want to go? You wouldn't miss not having me along?"

Before her daughter could answer, Sam returned, a purple plastic suitcase in his hand. When he unzipped the case, it was stuffed with new clothes. He removed a pair of red canvas platform sneakers for Jeanette's approval. They were far too high for an eight-year-old girl.

"I love them!" her daughter exclaimed.

"Let me see those," said Elana.

"Careful," Sam said, handing her a sneaker. It was surprisingly light, and when she examined the sole, she saw it had been cut out and reglued. If she had a knife she could wedge the tip in and peel back the rubber, but even without a knife she knew what was inside. A hollowed-out platform. An empty two-inch space. They were going to stash meth in her daughter's shoes. It was wicked enough to make her woozy. Though if cops found drugs on Jeanette—she caught herself reasoning—they'd know her daughter was an unwitting pawn. The nearest adult would be the one accountable. And Elana would be miles away. If the cops came after her next, she could explain that an old family friend had offered the trip as a gift. How could she be expected to know the journey's true aim?

She wanted to ask Jeanette leading questions, but her daughter was transfixed by the sight of Sam. Whistling, he sat in the lounger and assembled his bagpipes, fitting the melody pipe and drones to their stocks. Jeanette watched him fixedly, until Janice returned with the pliers and a small pair of wire snips.

Catching sight of the tools, Jeanette stiffened. "Nooo," she moaned.

"It's all right," Janice said. "I'm just going to untwist the wire and maybe cut away a bit of screen."

"Mom," Jeanette whispered.

"We need to get you out," Elana reassured her, squeezing her hand. "Would you feel better if I do it?"

Her daughter gave her a wary look. "What about Tham?"

He halted his assembling. "My fingers are too big, honey," he said. "I can't get in there."

"Do you want me to do it?" Elana asked again.

Something bleak descended onto her daughter, darkening her thin face.

"No," she said at last. "Janith can."

The other woman nudged Elana from her spot. When the pliers opened, Elana looked away. She switched her attention to the lounger, where Sam was tuning his pipes. First a note on the chanter. Followed by a note from the tenor drone, not quite there. He adjusted the sliding joints and again played the chanter. Then another near miss. More adjustments, and the drone became shorter. Once more, the original note. The tenor note, played in response, remained a hairsbreadth off-key.

Elana's shirt was soaked in sweat. "Isn't it close enough?" she asked angrily.

Without responding, Sam mouthed the blowpipe and started "Scotland the Brave." The low notes thrummed in her chest the way they did as a child, when during the summer Sam and her dad practiced in the yard. She'd listen from the attic where she slept. All the heat in the house rose there, and she'd remove her nightgown and throw the sheets on the floor to get cool. She'd close her eyes and hold herself rigid, in order to catch the tiniest draft if it passed. Most nights she'd be awake for hours. The heat rarely broke before dawn.

Now here was the same tune, the same player. She tried to bring back the sensation of being still. But the secret was gone.

"Finished," Janice announced, shaking out her wrist.

Jeanette didn't respond. She stared at Sam, who puffed his cheeks and pressured the bag beneath his arm. Noticing this, Elana slipped behind her daughter and eased her away from the door. Then she bent to her ear.

"You know, baby, they call California the Golden State because they discovered gold there, yes, and because of all the yellow sand too, of course, but golden also because everybody wants to go there, to *be* there, and myself, I never have, so I think you're really very lucky, you're luckier than me, and—"

"Quit talking," Jeanette snapped. "I want to hear."

An hour later, Elana walked Grand Avenue alone. Out of a passing car, a driver tossed a lit cigarette. Elana pinched it from the sidewalk, hand trembling as she brought it to her lips. She nursed the stub for five blocks before throwing it away.

Once home, she tore open an envelope of lime Jell-O. She wet her finger and poked inside, licking off whatever stuck. After the dark streets, the kitchen seemed snug and intimate. Blue bowls dried in a wooden drainer, an herb garden grew in Styrofoam cups on the sill. Elana switched on the television. Let the thing glow and roar for a while.

She poured the rest of the Jell-O into a teacup. Onscreen, an interior designer instructed his viewers not to forget the ceiling in their decorating plans. "Very important," the man declared. "*The ceiling is your fifth wall.*" The show cut to footage of a sloppy angel-themed mural, but Elana couldn't get past the words. If the ceiling was truly the fifth wall, then the floor, Lord help her, must be the sixth. At the thought, all six walls began moving closer. She fled, with her teacup, to the yard.

There, the cicadas' singing had taken on a rowdy, boastful aspect. Elana paced the perimeter of her bricked-up patio. Her daughter was staying with Sam and Janice and would leave at sunrise. They were aiming for Ogallala by noon.

She'd done a terrible, evil thing. But suddenly, under the black sky, she felt blessed. Her debt was paid. More important, she'd finally hit rock bottom. After this, she and Jeanette could begin again. No more drugs. No Tackle Box. No Sam. She breathed, imagining clarity as a glittering steam free for her to inhale.

Back in the kitchen, she turned off the television and went to survey her daughter's room. Her sweet love! Hot tears spilled to her cheeks, and she staggered onto her daughter's bed. The body was exhausted, but the mind galloped. Even with closed eyes, she could see Jeanette's monkey face. Despairing, she looked to the ceiling for solace. In one corner hung a thread of lint, twitching in a feeble breeze.

Jeanette's riding shotgun, next to Janice, and her mouth hurts. In her pocket there's wax to protect cheeks from braces, but wax is nothing, it's really a joke. Her mother said to try aspirin, but Jeanette doesn't ever take it, and she doesn't ask Janice for anything now. The truth is she thinks this must be what it feels like to be older. The ache makes her feel tired and wise.

Janice says, Out here, in spring, people set fires to their lawns. Burn off winter weeds so grass comes back green and strong.

Jeanette thinks Janice is sort of ugly, with those droopy eyes and her bad skin.

Sometimes on windy days, Janice says, the fires get big and take houses.

Jeanette ignores her, looking up at a barn as red as soup, with wooden slats that let sunlight through.

Just over the hill, Janice slams the brakes hard. Tea splashes from the mug she's holding onto her sweater and the legs of Jeanette's jeans.

Look, she says.

Jeanette does. The sky's purple with sunrise. Thick haze drifts over the road.

Unless you want to go crazy, Janice says, make sure you're often in the presence of beauty. Or in the presence of ugliness if it is the truth.

Jeanette shivers because her mind's been read. She says, I think you're ugly sometimes.

I'm true. And truthfully, sometimes you're ugly too.

But I'm not true, Jeanette says.

Janice sips tea. Dishonesty has its own kind of beauty, she says. Especially if it reveals a deeper truth.

Can we have tacos for lunch? Jeanette asks her.

What?

Can we have tacos?

Why do I bother, Janice sighs, but with affection in her voice, maybe. She pulls Jeanette close and twists a piece of her hair to its root.

Like she was attacked by a drunken boxer, Elana hurt. Fever burned in her eyeballs and the membranes of her nose. Lying in her daughter's bed, she chewed on a piece of lip until it ripped free. The new morning filtered in, bringing no hope whatsoever. When she pressed a thumb to her lip, it came back with blood. The promises she made to herself? Ha. Overnight the blessing she received had been withdrawn.

Sam lived in one half of a duplex a few blocks from the store. Elana hesitated on his porch before ringing the bell. He'd instructed her to lie low until Janice and Jeanette returned. He planned to close the Tackle Box and spend the weekend piping at the Highland Games. Nobody was supposed to contact anybody. There would be no postcards or calls from the road.

When the door opened, Sam was already wearing his kilt. He looked angry, but unsurprised.

"What are you doing here?" he said. "We had a deal."

"I don't want her to go," Elana said.

"You know they've already left. Why did you come?"

She opened her mouth to answer, but lacked the energy to speak.

"Say, 'I'm powerless to face real life.' Say, 'I'm a junkie who's sold out my soul.'"

There was no call for him to talk like that. Her indignation gave her a moment's strength. "I don't feel powerless," she said slowly. "Not at all. Desperate, maybe. Like I could do anything. Even call the police."

Sam glared at her. "You'll get busted and lose her forever."

"In this life," she said, "all of us have things to lose."

"You dead-eyed . . ." For an instant she thought he'd hit her, but somehow he regained control. "What am I doing?" he said, straining for an affable tone. "You and me, we're friends. For a long time now. We should help each other through this rough patch."

"I could use some help," she said.

"There's no reason to go through this alone. It will be a hard week for both of us." He smiled tensely. "How about this? Why don't you come with me to the games? Might be a nice diversion for you."

So he understood that it was safer to have her near. To keep her addled and quiet. Good.

Once she was inside, Sam said offhandedly, "Check out the third drawer in the john." There she found a glassine envelope and a kit. The tubing in her mouth tasted like a pacifier. Two fingers rapped against her skin sounded like trying to shake ketchup out. After she fixed, the exhilaration of the previous night made a more muted return. It was like if she squinted, she could see an end point to everything, looming in the distance like some far-flung sign. One last week, she vowed. One last week, and she was through.

On the way to the Games, she jabbered to Sam about her redecorating plans for Jeanette's room, the wonders she'd work on that fucked ceiling—wait—*fifth wall*. He listened in silence.

"Here," he said finally, when they pulled into the fairgrounds' dusty parking field. He gave her a small baggie of pills. "In case you want to bring it down."

The entrance to the Games was flagged by banners announcing the weekend's reuniting clans. Sam paid her admission, and they entered the gauntlet of exhibitors and vendors peddling everything from bangers to medieval swords. In one spacious booth, a falconer in black gloves attended a hawk tied with bungee cord to a steel V-framed perch. As Elana approached, she saw the man fasten a silver bell to the hawk's leg. Above the bell, the bird's plumage was cream and brown, its posture freakily erect. Elana stepped closer.

The hawk appeared sleek-bodied and hungry. He was a fearsome creature, even tied.

The falconer glanced at her. Then at Sam.

"What do you throw a drowning bagpipe player?" he asked.

Sam sighed before answering. "His bagpipes."

"You got it," the falconer said, standing tall. "Cheers. You know, they say the Scots have a good sense of humor because it's free." He reached behind him for a whiskey-filled quaich, but Sam declined his offer and took Elana's arm.

"Go ahead," she said. "I think I'll hang out here a while."

"Let's go." He increased the strength of his hold.

"Ow," Elana said, loudly.

The falconer's eyebrows lifted. Across the row, a pretzel vendor paused as she counted a man's change. Sam assessed the scene. After a moment, he released Elana and brushed some dust from his shirt-front. "Be at the stage in half an hour," he said, through his teeth.

"Don't worry, Pops," the falconer cracked. "I'll keep an eye on her." Beside him, the hawk lifted both wings until they nearly met overhead. Sam gave man and bird a measured gaze before finally walking away.

The falconer laughed. "Is your daddy piping today?"

"He's not my daddy," Elana said. "But he's piping for Highland Dancing." She accepted the quaich and drank. "You may not believe it, but I used to dance myself. Many years ago."

"I bet you were something in your hornpipe suit." The falconer was too young for her, but he had a sly manner that made her feel indulgent of his youth and aroused.

"What about you?" she asked, returning the cup. "You hunt or you only do the Games?"

"We fly most days. Even if it's just driving around the neighborhood with my arm stuck out, hunting sparrows from the glove."

She stared wide-eyed at the hawk. "You fly this thing at sparrows?"

"Other days we go to the country with a couple ferrets. Loose the ferrets to flush the jacks out of their holes. Then this beauty wastes them." He clapped his hands. "Rabbit stew all around."

"Wouldn't it be easier to use a gun?"

"Always easier to use a gun. But I'm not about easy." He shook his head, grinning. "No, I take my pleasure in the process." He bent toward her. "And if I may ask, what do you take your pleasure in?"

She shrugged. "I'd say product. Mostly."

"That was my guess," he said. "But maybe I can change your mind." He assumed a wide stance and cleared his throat. "There's this process called manning. It's when you train the raptor to tolerate your presence. Convincing her it's in her best interest to stick around."

She was interested. "How's it work?"

"Like you might bind her wings in a sock so she can't fly off at the sight of you."

"I'm not going anywhere," Elana said.

The falconer seemed amused. "Then onto the unconventional ways." He lowered his voice. "I know one way to cut the manning time in half. Learned it from an Arab fellow over in Cairo. Seeling, he called it."

"I'm listening," she whispered back.

The falconer placed a glove over her face. It was large enough to cover all her features. She let her tongue flick out and taste the grain.

"In seeling," he said, "you sew a raptor's eyes shut with a single piece of thread."

She punched away the glove. "What the hell?"

The falconer blinked. "Don't get the wrong idea." He gestured to the hawk, who observed him blankly. "There's no master/slave thing happening here."

"I hope that bird claws out your eyeballs!" Elana cried.

"You got the wrong idea," the falconer insisted. "I live my whole life around hers."

Elana swiveled wildly. People were gathering, and in the distance, she saw a man with a red security sash take note. Meanwhile, the falconer pleaded for understanding. The hawk stretched, extending its tail feathers in a fan. Elana broke into a panicky jog that carried her past the athletics field, the Exhibition Hall, and a Campbell Clan Reunion before she arrived, sweating, at the outdoor dancing stage. The competition hadn't started, but the stage was crowded with girls practicing jumps and high steps. The girls wore gray sweatpants under their kilts, and their hair was twisted into what looked like painful buns.

She made her way to a patch of lawn near the front of the amphitheater. Beside her, a couple on a blanket fed each other fresh shortbread and shared a cup of lemon tea. Elana's pulse felt erratic, and her forearms itched. She choked down two Valium, but forbade herself from scratching. It was small punishment for her flirting. For flirting while her child might be in danger. She wept softly at the idea.

"Your daughter up there?" the male half of the couple asked, mistaking her tears for pride.

"Where?" she said eagerly, before catching herself. "I mean, no, I don't have any kids." Mentioning Jeanette would only lead to further questions: How old? What's she like? Where is she now?

"Sorry," the man said. "None of my business."

"Nope, no kids yet," she repeated. "Maybe someday."

Over the loudspeaker, the MC called for Novices to gather. He introduced three judges, who assumed center seats. Finally he brought on Sam, who appeared with a wink and his bagpipes, hitting his spot at the rear of the stage.

The first group competed in the Fling. Elana tried to lose herself in the kids' goofy missteps, but without luck. Denying her daughter's existence had left her sick. Why didn't she mention Jeanette and, if the man asked further, explain that she was at camp? She considered leaning over now and telling him, but he would think she was crazy.

Onstage, Sam ended the tune with a flurry of grace notes. He counted *one-two-three*, and the little girls bowed. Next, a cluster of Intermediates mounted the stage, one of whom looked so much like Jeanette—the braids, the braces, the hyper air—that Elana had to lower her eyes. The action was enough to ease her into sleep.

In mid-Nebraska, there's a red school bus parked way off the road, and that's where they pause for a while. Janice's girlfriend lives there. She and Janice sprawl on beanbags and smoke clove cigarettes, listening to Joni Mitchell's *Blue*.

Come here, Janice says.

Jeanette sits beside her, and Janice twists her into a yoga position, feet behind her head. Jeanette's back against the wall keeps her upright. Her tailbone's rock hard on the floor.

Can you imagine? the girlfriend says. I mean, really.

Great popularity in her future, Janice says.

Yeah? Jeanette wonders.

No, Janice says. No popularity. Your fate is to always be alone.

Hey, the girlfriend says, pissed, don't saddle the poor kid with that.

I'm liberating her, says Janice. Being alone you're free to take risks. You're beholden to no one. That's the kind of people the world needs.

Not nice, the girlfriend says, rising from the beans. Not nice *at all!* She adjusts her vest and wobbles out of the bus.

Janice sighs. Women. Then she crawls toward the door, calling Kelly? Honey?

Jeanette watches her go, not worrying, because she knows she'll return. But soon she hears glass break, a door slam, a car start and drive away.

The problem: she has flexibility, but not strength. Her arms are trapped by her thighs, and she doesn't have enough muscle to lift her feet over her head. Lift, she mutters, lift! Nothing. Joni sings about kissing a pig on some street.

A few minutes later an older girl saunters in, buttoning a plaid cover onto a Bermuda bag. She stops and studies the scene before setting down her purse and grabbing Jeanette's shoes. Her freed feet *thunk-thunk* on the floor.

Thanks, Jeanette says, toes stinging. She tries to stand, but the girl says no. Always end with the Corpse pose, the girl says. She tells Jeanette to lie on her back, arms out to the side. Make your legs heavy, she says. Open your shoulders. Now relax and let your tongue settle down.

Elana started awake. Onstage the Premier class had just finished Flora's Fancy, and held their skirts out stiffly, like clean white tents.

Sam whispered *one-two-three* from his corner. The girls performed lovely bows. It was the final dance of the morning, and Sam lumbered off the stage.

Red-faced from anger and lack of breath, he came to where Elana was sitting. "Nodding off up here in front of everyone," he chastised her.

"I can't do this," she said. "We have to stop it. Something terrible's going to happen on this trip."

"Come on," Sam said, yanking her to her feet. "There's another piper for the afternoon session. I'm off until tomorrow. Let's split."

On the way to the car, they passed the falconer. Elana ducked her head and tried to hurry by.

"Hey, Pops," the falconer called. "What do you have when a piper is buried to his neck in sand?"

Sam pivoted toward him. The falconer's hopeful smile began to fade. It took Sam three steps to cover the distance between them. Then, with a neat jab, he slammed the hawk. The bird's feet stuttered before it dropped like a rock from the perch, swinging upside-down from its cord.

"Not enough sand," said Sam. He kept his fist clenched, like the falconer was next. But the anguished man was cradling the hawk, trying to revive it, and eventually Sam's fingers relaxed.

Back in the car, Elana tried to organize her thinking, but the wind speeding through the windows left her thoughts in disarray. She couldn't pin down her fear. It was a subtle, sneaky dread.

"I want out of this," she finally said. "Why are you getting me deeper in?"

"You want out?" Sam shouted suddenly, slamming the wheel. "Bullshit. You're working this situation for all it's worth. Threatening to spill the beans, faking second guesses. Anything so I'll keep you tweaking until that poor girl gets back."

"For one week, Sam. One last week. When she gets back, it's over."

His eyes rolled. "Honey, deep down you think you've hit the jackpot. You think you've discovered the way to get your shit for free." He sounded an ugly snort. "The last week? It's the first of many weeks. Check yourself. You'll see."

She did, imagining her daughter's return. The car pulling up, her daughter bursting from the side door, sunglasses atop her head like a crown. Her daughter running to her. She hugging Jeanette, then holding her at arm's length to soak her in. Then, as she saw herself in this vision, she kneeled eagerly to untie her daughter's platform shoes.

Elana vomited onto the floor mat. What emerged was watery and green.

The drive continued, but Sam took a hand from the wheel to rub her back as she heaved. "Calm yourself," he crooned, "everything's fine." His voice like a lullaby. "You know, your dad and I had some talks before he passed. He was worried. Your troubles had been going on for so long. He knew you'd never quit. He knew I was getting into the business. We both knew you'd find your demons somewhere."

A dark spot appeared in her vision. "Don't you say it," she warned. "Even if it's true."

"In the end we figured: Why not Sam? If I was the one, at least I could manage your intake. Adjust the potency, if need be."

"You think I believe," she choked, "that my dad asked you to string me out?"

"He trusted me," Sam went on. "He knew I'd been looking out for you all your life. Just today, in fact, I was remembering when I used to play your dancing comps. You never caught on, but I'd always play a bit faster for your group. Get you jumping higher. Get the blood to your cheeks."

The car stopped, and when she lifted her head, she saw they'd arrived at the Tackle Box. When she faced Sam, his expression was fond.

"I'll always protect you, Elana. And if I'm still around when you're gone, I'll protect your daughter too."

Her throat burned. "When I'm gone?"

"You've picked a dangerous life." He gazed at her ruefully.

"You plan on killing me, Sam?"

He chuckled. "I don't think my involvement will be required."

"Go ahead," she challenged him. "Sew my eyes shut while you're at it. Sew them shut so I can't see your broke-down lying face!"

"There's a face you don't want to see," he agreed. "But we both know that face isn't mine."

He helped her from the car to the Tackle Box entrance, where he ushered her in, flipping on one weak light. Dumbly, Elana followed him through the dim aisles and out to the Mirage. Sam steered her to a lounger and offered a beer.

"Upstairs if you need me," he said then, heading back into the store. "Duty, it always seems to call."

The bottle rested cold in her lap, and soon she was plagued by chills. In the trees, the cicadas droned loudly. She struggled out of the lounger and into the Tackle Box. Disoriented by the dim light, she made her slow way to the store's telephone. She stared at it for a while before lifting the receiver. Nothing. When she examined the base, she saw the cord to the wall jack was gone.

There was footfall on the stairs. A moment later, Sam stepped from behind his green curtain and saw the dead phone in her hand.

"Oh, honey," he said, smiling faintly. "Why do you bother to try?"

The pope is coming to Denver tomorrow for a conference of Catholic youth. Janice pleads with front desks from North Platte to Loveland, but the motels are packed with clean teens. Fine, Janice declares, we'll keep driving. All the way to California if need be!

By Utah, she's exhausted. The road's straight, so she decides to let Jeanette take the wheel. Jeanette sits on top of her new purple suitcase, with Janice at shotgun, her foot on the pedal until she sets cruise control. Then it's Jeanette alone. The thrill reminds Jeanette of mornings when her mom is sleeping, when the whole house is hers. She drinks coffee and gets the paper and cuts the herb garden. After a while she wakes her mom with a cup of spearmint brew.

When Jeanette sees a roadside phone, she turns off cruise and slides from the suitcase until her shoe hits the brake.

I want to call home, she announces.

No time, says Janice. No money. No need. She reaches over and lightly beats Jeanette's leg. Let's go.

I'm not a drum.

My sweet bongo, Janice sings. My little snare. She returns Jeanette to her perch, presses the pedal and turns the car back to the road.

After cruise control's set, Jeanette shuts her eyes for one second. Two seconds. Three. The dark part's not that bad. She's only scared when her eyes open again.

When she spots a shooting star, she pokes Janice. Did you see?

Janice squints at the windshield. Make a wish, she says.

Jeanette watches another star drop. And another. Then she thinks she's crazy because there are dozens, there are hundreds, exploding like bulbs. When one falls onto the hood, she slides for the brake.

Then she's standing on the hot road. From there, she can see the stars are fireflies. Swarms of fireflies. She catches one. Through her fingers come bleary light.

Janice gets out and stands beside her, and Jeanette tells her how once her mom killed some fireflies and smeared them on Jeanette's cheeks.

Your mother, Janice frowns. I don't know.

Don't move, her mom had told her. Then she had run inside. She came back with the medicine cabinet's ripped-off mirror. She held it up so Jeanette could see her own face glow.

First the sky was a ceiling of black vinyl. Then it became the sky she remembered—endless blue.

"Welcome back," a voice said.

Elana rose from a pillow of wadded rags. Sam was at the other end of the boat, rolling up the cover. At the sight of him, she vaguely recalled a speed-fueled Tea Party, with her climbing into the bass boat and chucking paraphernalia onto the grass. Then Sam wrestling her to the deck. Pushing pills past her stiff lips. Black vinyl snapped tight above. And finally sleep, a long one, utterly free of dreams.

"Quite a night," said Sam. For once, he looked his age.

"I thought I was dead," she said. "The pills, I mean. Forced overdose, I thought."

He crossed the deck to enfold her in what felt like a poor replica of a hug.

"Such paranoia," he said. "Not necessary. The goal is to get through this with no drama, no fuss. You think I want a body on my hands? And an orphan? The whole deal would blow apart." He embraced her more tightly, his beard roughing her skin. "Yeah, yesterday I was trying to make you a little scared. To get you behaving. But the truth is I need you alive." He stepped back and rubbed his hands briskly. "Now quit worrying. You need a morning shot?"

She said no. Whatever he'd given her was still in her blood. She pushed past him into the Tackle Box and found the bathroom, where she massaged her gums with toothpaste and sprayed Janice's perfume. She was dirty, but she vowed not to take a bath until her daughter returned.

The drive to the Highland Games was a silent one, and the silence continued as they walked through the fairgrounds. Elana noticed the falconer's absence from his former post and found herself wishing him good health.

They were late, but there was a seat in the front row. Sam left her there and hurried to fix his bagpipes and take the stage. The Lilt was the first number, danced by the Intermediates, and as they lined up, Elana spotted the girl who resembled Jeanette a second time. The girl could pass for Jeanette's sister, in fact, and seeing her, Elana wished she were. It wasn't fair to have only one child. Alone, with no siblings to comfort her or boost her anger, the only child was compelled to forgive.

When the dance ended, the couple beside her stood and moved back several rows. Elana wondered if she stunk, if the perfume was too much. But then another family hurried to the rear, and following their nervous glances, she saw a good-sized swarm of yellow jackets overhead.

"They'll only sting you once," the MC chortled, noticing the minor exodus. "Pay no mind." A group of Premiers took the stage for the Irish Jig.

Elana studied the swarm above her. It was flattening like a chunk of butter heated in a pan. The yellow jackets looped in larger, lower circles until they were streaming lazily over the theater's front half. A few landed on her arm, but she didn't flick them. Unlike most of the audience, who dashed, swatting madly, to the back.

There was a brief conference at the MC's table, with the judges and Sam. Then the MC returned to his microphone. "We're going to keep going," he announced. "The girls are okay, okay up here. Those little suckers are avoiding the stage." He paused. "Plenty of seats in the back though, if anyone would be more comfortable there."

She stayed where she was. The Jig was her favorite dance. Sam launched into it, and the dancers shook their fists and stomped their feet, a burlesque of angry workers crushing snakes. All smiled broadly, except for a single girl whose grim expression truly matched the dance's intent.

A cluster of yellow jackets settled at the base of Elana's neck, tickling beneath her chin. Another grouped loosely near her wrist. She didn't flinch. In her mind, she was mapping Sam's speed against a steady rhythm. At last she could hear it—he was rushing the Jig! Her mouth fell open when suddenly he pushed the tempo faster. Yet the grim girl met him, sweat beading on her muscled calves.

Then all at once, Sam slipped the blowpipe from his mouth. The Jig trailed off with a tired squawk. Most of the dancers halted immediately, except for the grim girl, who performed a few steps without a tune. But then she paused too, and looked where everyone was looking. At Elana. Like she was on stage.

Such anxious faces! She wanted to tell them not to worry, but feared disturbing the things on her tongue.

"Easy now," Sam called. His voice quivered like an old man's.

It was amazing, all these creatures moving through her, even as she remained still.

Norman Rush

⁂

Instruments of Seduction

The name she was unable to remember was torturing her. She kept coming up with Bechamel, which was ridiculously wrong yet somehow close. It was important to her that she remember. A thing in a book by this man lay at the heart of her secret career as a seducer of men—three hundred and twelve of them. She was a seducer, not a seductress. The male form of the term was active. A seductress was merely someone who was seductive and who might or might not be awarded a victory. But a seducer was a professional, a worker, and somehow a record of success was embedded in the term. "Seducer" sounded like a credential. Game was afoot tonight. Remembering the name was part of preparation. She had always prepared before tests.

Male or female, you couldn't be considered a seducer if you were below a certain age, had great natural beauty, or if you lacked a theory of what you were doing. Her body of theory began with a scene in the book she was feeling the impulse to reread. The book's title was lost in the mists of time. As she remembered the scene, a doctor and perhaps the woman of the house are involved together in some emergency lifesaving operation. The woman has to assist. The setting is an apartment in Europe, in a city. The woman is not attractive. The doctor is. There has been shelling or an accident. The characters are disparate in every way and would never normally be appropriate for one another. The operation is described in upsetting detail. It's touch and go. When it's over, the doctor and the woman fall into one another's arms—to their own surprise. Some fierce tropism compels them. Afterward they part, never to follow up. The book was from the French. She removed the Atmos clock from the living room mantel and took it to the pantry to get it out of sight.

The scene had been like a flashbulb going off. She had realized that, in all her seductions up to that point, she had been crudely and intuitively using the principle that the scene made explicit. Putting it bluntly, a certain atmosphere of allusion to death, death fear, death threats, mystery pointing to death, was, in the right hands, erotic, and could lead to a bingo. Of course, that was hardly all there was to it. The subject of what conditions conduce—that was her word for it— to achieving a bingo, was immense. One thing, it was never safe to roll your *r*'s. She thought, Everything counts: chiaroscuro, no giant clocks in evidence and no wrist-watches either, music or its absence, what they can assume about privacy and *le futur*. That was critical. You had to help them intuit you were acting from appetite, like a man, and that when it was over you would be yourself and not transformed before their eyes into a love-leech, a limbless tube of longing. You had to convince them that what was to come was, no question about it, a transgression, but that for you it was about at the level of eating between meals.

She was almost fifty. For a woman, she was old to be a seducer. The truth was that she had been on the verge of closing up shop. The corner of Bergen County they lived in was scorched earth, pretty much. Then Frank had been offered a contract to advise African governments on dental care systems. They had come to Africa for two years.

In Botswana, where they were based, everything was unbelievably conducive. Frank was off in the bush or advising as far away as Lusaka or Gwelo for days and sometimes weeks at a time. So there was space. She could select. Gaborone was comfortable enough. And it was full of transient men: consultants, contractors, travelers of all kinds, seekers. Embassy men were assigned for two-year tours and knew they were going to be rotated away from the scene of the crime sooner rather than later. Wives were often absent. Either they were slow to arrive or they were incessantly away on rest and recreation in the United States or the Republic of South Africa. For expatriate men, the local women were a question mark. Venereal disease was pandemic and local attitudes toward birth control came close to being surreal. She had abstained from Batswana men. She knew why. The very attractive ones seemed hard to get at. There was a feeling of danger in the proposition, probably irrational. The surplus of more familiar white types was a simple fact. In any case, there was still time. This place had been designed with her in mind. The furniture the government provided even looked like it came from a bordello. And Botswana was unnerving in some overall way there was only one word for: conducive. The country depended on copper and diamonds. Copper prices were sinking. There were too many diamonds of the wrong kind. Development projects were going badly and making people look bad, which made them nervous and susceptible. What was there to do at night? There was only one movie house in town. The movies came via South Africa and were censored to a fare-thee-well— no nudity, no blue language. She suspected that for American men the kind of heavyhanded dummkopf censorship they sat through at the Capitol Cinema was in fact stimulating. Frank was getting United States Government money, which made them semiofficial. She had to admit there was fun in foiling the eyes and ears of the embassy network. She would hate to leave.

Only one thing was sad. There was no one she could tell about her life. She had managed to have a remarkable life. She was ethical. She never brought Frank up or implied that Frank was the cause in any way of what she chose to do. Nor would she ever seduce a man who could conceivably be a recurrent part of Frank's life or sphere. She assumed feminists would hate her life if they knew. She would like to talk to feminists about vocation, about goal-setting, about using one's mind, about nerve and strength. Frank's ignorance was one of her feats. How many women could do what she had done? She was modestly endowed and now she was even old. She was selective. Sometimes she felt she would like to tell Frank, when it was really over, and see what he said. She would sometimes let herself think he would be proud, in a way, or that he could be convinced he should be. There was no one she could tell. Their daughter was a cow and a

Lutheran. Her gentleman was late. She went into the pantry to check the time.

For this evening's adventure she was perhaps a little too high-priestess, but the man she was expecting was not a subtle person. She was wearing a narrowly-cut white silk caftan, a seed-pod necklace, and sandals. The symbolism was a little crude: silk, the ultra-civilized material, over the primitive straight-off-the-bush necklace. Men liked to feel things through silk. But she wore silk as much for herself as for the gentlemen. Silk energized her. She loved the feeling of silk being slid up the backs of her legs. Her nape hairs rose a little as she thought about it. She had her hair up, in a loose, flat bun. She was ringless. She had put on and then taken off her scarab ring. Tonight she wanted the feeling that bare hands and bare feet would give. She would ease off her sandals at the right moment. She knew she was giving up a proven piece of business—idly taking off her ring when the occasion reached a certain centigrade. Men saw it subliminally as taking off a wedding ring and as the first act of undressing. She had worked hard on her feet. She had lined her armpits with tissue which would stay just until the doorbell rang. With medical gentlemen, hygiene was a fetish. She was expecting a doctor. Her breath was immaculate. She was proud of her teeth, but then she was married to a dentist. She thought about the Danish surgeon who brought his own boiled-water ice cubes to cocktail parties. She had some bottled water in the refrigerator, just in case it was indicated.

Her gentleman was due and overdue. Everything was optimal. There was a firm crossbreeze. The sightlines were nice. From where they would be sitting they would look out at a little pad of healthy lawn, the blank wall of the inner court, and the foliage of the tree whose blooms still looked to her like scrambled eggs. It would be self-evident that they would be private here. The blinds were drawn. Everything was secure and cool. Off the hall leading to the bathroom, the door to the bedroom stood open. The bedroom was clearly a working bedroom, not taboo, with a night light on and an oscillating fan performing on low. He would sit on leather; she would sit half-facing, where she could reach the bar trolley, on sheepskin, her feet on a jennet-skin karosse. He should sit in the leather chair because it was regal but uncomfortable. You would want to lie down. She would be in a slightly more reclining mode. Sunset was on. Where was her gentleman? The light was past its peak.

The doorbell rang. Be superb, she thought.

The doctor looked exhausted. He was greyfaced. Also, he was older than the image of him she had been entertaining. But he was all right. He had nice hair. He was fit. He might be part Indian, with those cheekbones and being from Vancouver. Flats were never a mistake. He was not tall. He was slim.

She led him in. He was wearing one of the cheaper safari suits, with the S-for-something embroidery on the left breast pocket. He had come straight from work, which was in her favor.

When she had him seated, she said, "Two slight catastrophes to report, doctor. One is that you're going to have to eat appetizers from my own hand. As the British say, my help are gone. My cook and my maid are sisters. Their aunt died. For the second time, actually. Tebogo is forgetful. In any case, they're in Mochudi for a few days and I'm alone. Frank won't be home until Sunday. *And*, the Webers are off for tonight. They can't come. We're on our own. I hope we can cope."

He smiled weakly. The man was exhausted.

She said, "But a cool drink, quick, wouldn't you say? What would you like? I have everything."

He said it should be anything nonalcoholic, any kind of juice would be good. She could see work coming. He went to wash up.

He took his time in the bathroom, which was normally a good sign. He looked almost crisp when he came back, but something was the matter. She would have to extract it.

He accepted iced rooibos tea. She poured Bombay gin over crushed ice for herself. Men noticed what you drank. This man was not strong. She was going to have to underplay.

She presented the appetizers, which were genius. You could get through a week on her collations if you needed to, or you could have a few select tastes and go on to gorge elsewhere with no one the wiser. But you would remember every bite. She said "You might like these. These chunks are bream fillet, poached, from Lake Ngami. No bones.

Vinaigrette. They had just started getting these down here on a regular basis on ice about a year ago. AID had a lot of money in the Lake Ngami fishery project. Then the drought struck, and Lake Ngami, poof, it's a damp spot in the desert. This is real Parma ham. I nearly had to kill someone to get it. The cashews are a little on the tangy side. That's the way they like them in Mozambique, apparently. They're good."

He ate a little, sticking to mainstream items like the gouda cheese cubes, she was sorry to see. Then he brought up the climate, which made her writhe. It was something to be curtailed. It led the mind homeward. It was one of the three deadly *W*'s: weather, wife, and where to eat—in this country, where not to eat. She feigned sympathy. He was saying he was from British Columbia so it was to be expected that it would take some doing for him to adjust to the dry heat and the dust. He said he had to remind himself that he'd only been here four months and that ultimately his mucous membrane system was supposed to adapt. But he said he was finding it wearing. Lately he was dreaming about rain. A lot, he said.

Good! she thought. "Would you like to see my tokoloshi?" she asked, crossing her legs.

He stopped chewing. She warned herself not to be reckless.

"Dream animals!" she said. "Little effigies. I collect them. The Bushmen carve them out of softwood. They use them as symbols of evil in some ceremony they do. They're turning up along with all the other Bushman artifacts, the puberty aprons and so on, in the craft shops. Let me show you."

She got two tokoloshi from a cabinet.

"They call these the evil creatures who come to you at night in dreams. What you see when you look casually is this manlike figure with what looks like the head of a fox or rabbit or zebra, at first glance. But look at the clothing. Doesn't this look like a clerical jacket? The collar shape? They're all like that. And look closely at the animal. It's actually a spotted jackal, the most despised animal there is because of its taste for carrion. Now look in front at this funny little tablet that looks like a huge belt buckle with these x-shapes burned into it. My theory is that it's a Bushman version of the Union Jack. If you notice on this one, the being is wearing a funny belt. It looks like a cartridge belt to me. Some of the tokoloshi are smoking these removable pipes. White tourists buy these things and think they're cute. I think each one is a carved insult to the West. And we buy loads of them. I do. The black areas like the jacket are done by charring the wood with hot nails and things."

He handled the carvings dutifully and then gave them back to her. He murmured that they were interesting.

He took more tea. She stood the tokoloshi on an end table halfway across the room, facing them. He began contemplating them, sipping his tea minutely. Time was passing. She had various mottoes she used on herself. One was: Inside every suit and tie is a naked man trying to get out. She knew they were stupid, but they helped. He was still in the grip of whatever was bothering him.

"I have something that might interest you," she said. She went to the cabinet again and returned with a jackal-fur wallet, which she set down on the coffee table in front of him. "This is a fortune-telling kit the witch doctors use. It has odd things inside it." He merely looked at it.

"Look inside it," she said.

He picked it up reluctantly and held it in his hand, making a face. He was thinking it was unsanitary. She was in danger of becoming impatient. The wallet actually was slightly fetid, but so what? It was an organic thing. It was old.

She reached over and guided him to open and empty the wallet, touching his hands. He studied the array of bones and pebbles on the tabletop. Some of the pebbles were painted or stained. The bones were knucklebones, probably opossum, she told him, after he showed no interest in trying to guess what they were. She had made it her business to learn a fair amount about Tswana divination practices, but he wasn't asking. He moved the objects around listlessly.

She lit a candle, though she felt it was technically premature. It would give him something else to stare at if he wanted to and at least he would be staring in her direction, more or less.

The next segment was going to be taxing. The pace needed to be meditative. She was fighting impatience.

She said, "Africa is so strange. You haven't been here long, but you'll see. We come here as . . . bearers of science, the scientific attitude. Even the dependents do, always telling the help about nutrition and weaning and that kind of thing.

"Science so much defines us. One wants to be scientific, or at least not *un*scientific. Science is our religion, in a way. Or at least you begin to feel it is. I've been here nineteen months . . ."

He said something. Was she losing her hearing or was the man just unable to project? He had said something about noticing that the tokoloshi weren't carrying hypodermic needles. He was making the point, she guessed, that the Batswana didn't reject Western medicine. He said something further about their attachment to injections, how they felt you weren't actually treating them unless they could have an injection, how they seemed to love injections. She would have to adapt to a certain lag in this man's responses. I am tiring, she thought.

She tried again, edging her chair closer to his. "Of course, your world is different. You're more insulated, at the Ministry, where everyone is a scientist of sorts. You're immersed in science. That world is . . . safer. Are you following me?"

He said he wasn't sure that he was.

"What I guess I mean is that one gets to want to really *uphold* science. Because the culture here is so much the opposite. So relentlessly so. You resist. But then the first thing you know, very peculiar things start happening to you. Or you talk to some of the old settler types, whites, educated people from the protectorate days who decided to stay on as citizens, before the government made that such an obstacle course. The white settlers are worse than your everyday Batswana. They accept everything supernatural, almost. At first you dismiss it as a pose."

She knew it was strictly pro forma, but she offered him cigarettes from the caddy. He declined. There was no way she could smoke, then. Nothing tonight was going to be easy. Bechamel was right next door to the name she was trying to remember: why couldn't she get it?

"But it isn't a pose," she said. "Their experiences have changed them utterly. There is so much witchcraft. It's called *muti*. It's so routine. It wasn't so long ago that if you were going to open a business you'd go to the witch doctor for good luck rites with human body parts as ingredients. A little something to tuck under the cornerstone of your bottle store. People are still being killed for their parts. It might be a windpipe or whatever. It's still going on. Sometimes they dump the body onto the railroad tracks after they've taken what they need, for the train to grind up and disguise. Recently they caught somebody that way. The killers threw this body on the track but the train was late. They try to keep it out of the paper, I know that for a fact. But it's still happening. An undertow."

She worked her feet out of her sandals. Normally she would do one and let an intriguing gap fall before doing the other. She scratched an instep on an ankle.

She said, "I know a girl who's teaching in the government secondary in Bobonong who tells me what a hard time the matron is having getting the girls to sleep with their heads out of the covers. It seems they're afraid of *bad women* who roam around at night, who'll scratch their faces. These are women called *baloi* who go around naked, wearing only a little belt made out of human neckbones. Naturally, anyone would say what a fantasy this is. Childish.

"But I really did once see a naked woman dodging around near some rondavels late one night, out near Mosimane. It was only a glimpse. No doubt it was innocent. But she did have something white and shimmering around her waist. We were driving past. You begin to wonder."

She waited. He was silent.

"Something's bothering you," she said.

He denied it.

She said, "At any rate, don't you think it's interesting that there are no women members of the so-called traditional doctor's association? I know a member, what an oaf! I think it's a smoke screen association. They want you to think they're just a benign bunch of herbalists trying out one thing or another a lot of which ought to be in the regular pharmacopeia if only white medical people weren't so narrow-minded. They come to seminars all jolly and humble. But if you talk to the Batswana, you know that it's the women, the witches, who are the really potent ones."

Still he was silent.

"Something's happened, hasn't it? To upset you. If it's anything I've said, please tell me." A maternal tone could be death. She was flirting with failure.

He denied that she was responsible in any way. It seemed sincere. He was going inward again, right before her eyes. She had a code name for failures. She called them case studies. Her attitude was that every failure could be made to yield something of value for the future. And it was true. Some of her best material, anecdotes, references to things, aphrodisiana of all kinds, had come from case studies. The cave paintings at Gargas, in Spain, of mutilated hands . . . handprints, not paintings . . . stencils of hundreds of hands with joints and fingers missing. Archaeologists were totally at odds as to what all that meant. One case study had yielded the story of fat women in Durban buying tainted meat from butchers so as to contract tapeworms for weight loss purposes. As a case study, if it came to that, tonight looked unpromising. But you could never tell. She had an image for case studies: a grave robber, weary, exhausted, reaching down into some charnel mass and pulling up some lovely ancient sword somehow miraculously still keen that had been overlooked. She could name case studies that were more precious to her than bingoes she could describe.

She had one quiver left. She meant arrow. She hated using it.

She could oppose her silence to his until he broke. It was difficult to get right. It ran counter to being a host, being a woman, and to her own nature. The silence had to be special, not wounded, receptive, with a spine to it, maternal, in fact.

She declared silence. Slow moments passed.

He stirred. His lips stirred. He got up and began pacing.

He said, "You're right." Then for a long time he said nothing, still pacing.

"You read my mind!" he said. "Last night I had an experience . . . I still . . . it's still upsetting. I shouldn't have come, I guess."

She felt sorry for him. He had just the slightest speech defect, which showed up in noticeable hesitations. This was sad.

"Please tell me about it," she said perfectly.

He paced more, then halted near the candle and stared at it.

"I hardly drink," he said. "Last night was an exception. Phoning home to Vancouver started it, domestic nonsense. I won't go into that. They don't understand. No point in going into it. I went out. I went drinking. One of the hotel bars, where Africans go. I began drinking. I was drinking and buying drinks for some of the locals. I drank quite a bit.

"All right. These fellows are clever. Bit by bit I am being taken over by one, this one fellow, George. I can't explain it. I didn't like him. He took me over. That is, I notice I'm paying for drinks but this fellow's passing them on to whomever he chooses, his friends. But I'm buying. But I have no say.

"We're in a corner booth. It's dark and loud, as usual. This fellow, his head was shaved, he was strong-looking. He spoke good English, though. Originally, I'd liked talking to him, I think. They flatter you. He was a combination of rough and smooth. Now he was working me. He was a refugee from South Africa, that always starts up your sympathy. Terrible breath, though. I was getting a feeling of something being off about the ratio between the number of drinks and what I was laying out. I think he was taking something in transit.

"I wanted to do the buying. I took exception. All right. Remember that they have me wedged in. That was stupid, but I was, I allowed it. Then I said I was going to stop buying. George didn't like it. This man had a following. I realized they were forming a cordon, blocking us in. Gradually it got nasty. Why wouldn't I keep buying drinks, didn't I have money, what was my job, didn't the Ministry pay expatriates enough to buy a few drinks? So on ad nauseam."

His color was coming back. He picked up a cocktail napkin and touched at his forehead.

He was looking straight at her now. He said, "You don't know what the African bars are like. Pandemonium. I was sealed off. As I say, his friends were all around.

"Then it was all about apartheid. I said I was Canadian. Then it was about Canada the lackey of America the supporter of apartheid. I'm not political. I was scared. All right. When I tell him I'm really through buying drinks he asks me how much money have I got left, exactly. I tell him again that I'm through buying drinks. He says not to worry, he'll sell me something instead. All right. I knew I was down to about ten pula. And I had dug in on buying drinks, the way you will when you've had a few too many. No more buying drinks, that was decided. But he was determined to get my money, I could damned well see that.

"He said he would sell me something I'd be very glad to know. Information. All right. So then comes a long runaround on what kind of information. Remember that he's pretty well three sheets to the wind himself. It was information I would be glad to have as a doctor, he said.

"Well, the upshot here was that this is what I proposed, so as not to seem totally stupid and taken. I would put all my money down on the table in front of me. I took out my wallet and made sure he could see that what I put down was all of it, about ten pula, change and everything. All right. And I would keep the money under the palm of my hand. And he would whisper the information to me and if I thought it was a fair trade I would just lift my hand. Of course, this was all just facesaving on my part so as not to just hand over my money to a thug. And don't think I wasn't well aware it might be a good idea at this stage of things to be seen getting rid of any cash I had, just to avoid being knocked down on the way to my car."

"This is a wonderful story," she said spontaneously, immediately regretting it.

"It isn't a story," he said.

"You know what I mean," she said. "I mean, since I see you standing here safe and sound I can assume the ending isn't a tragedy. But please continue. Really."

"In any event. There we are. There was more back and forth over what kind of information this was. Finally he says it's not only something a doctor would be glad of. He is going to tell me the secret of how they are going to make the revolution in South Africa, a secret plan. An actual plan.

"God knows I have no brief for white South Africans. I know a few professionally, doctors. Medicine down there is basically about up to 1950, by our standards, despite all this veneer of the heart transplants. But the doctors I know seem to be decent. Some of them hate the system and will say so.

"I go along. Empty my wallet, cover the money with my hand.

"Here's what he says. They had a sure way to drive out the whites. It was a new plan and was sure to succeed. It would succeed because they, meaning the blacks, could bring it about with only a handful of men. He said that the Boers had won for all time if the revolution meant waiting for small groups to grow into bands and then into units, batallions and so on, into armies that would fight the Boers. The Boers were too intelligent and had too much power. They had corrupted too many of the blacks. The blacks were divided. There were too many spies for the Boers among them. The plan he would tell me would take less than a hundred men.

"Then he asked me, if he could tell me such a plan would it be worth the ten pula. Would I agree that it would? I said yes."

"This is extraordinary!" she said. *Duhamel!* she thought, triumphant. The name had come back to her: *Georges Duhamel*. She could almost see the print. She was so grateful.

"Exciting!" she said, gratitude in her voice.

He was swearing. "Well, this is what he says. He leans over, whispers. The plan is simple. The plan is to assemble a shock force, he called it. Black people who are willing to give their lives. And this is all they do: *they kill doctors*. That's it! They start off with a large first wave, before the government can do anything to protect doctors. They simply kill doctors, as many as they can. They kill them at home, in their offices, in hospitals, in the street. You can get the name of every doctor in South Africa through the phone book. Whites need doctors, without doctors they think they are already dying, he says. Blacks in South Africa have no doctors to speak of anyway, especially in the homelands where they are all being herded to die in droves. Blacks are dying of the system every day regardless, he says. But whites would scream. They would rush like cattle to the airports, screaming. They would stream out of the country. The planes from Smuts would be jammed full. After the first strike, you would continue, taking them by ones and twos. The doctors would leave, the ones who were there and still alive. No new ones would come, not even Indians. He said it was like taking away water from people in a desert. The government would capitulate. That was the plan.

"I lifted my hand and let him take the money. He said I was paying the soldiery and he thanked me in the name of the revolution. Then I was free to go."

He looked around dazedly for something, she wasn't clear what. Her glass was still one third full. Remarkably, he picked it up and drained it, eating the remnants of ice.

She stood up. She was content. The story was a brilliant thing, a gem.

He was moving about. It was hard to say, but possibly he was leaving. He could go or stay.

They stood together in the living room archway. Without prelude, he reached for her, awkwardly pulled her side against his chest, kissed her absurdly on the eye, and with his free hand began squeezing her breasts.

Denis Johnson

※

Train Dreams

1.

In the summer of 1917 Robert Grainier took part in an attempt on the life of a Chinese laborer caught, or anyway accused of, stealing from the company stores of the Spokane International Railway in the Idaho Panhandle.

Three of the railroad gang put the thief under restraint and dragged him up the long bank toward the bridge under construction fifty feet above the Moyea River. A rapid singsong streamed from the Chinaman voluminously. He shipped and twisted like a weasel in a sack, lashing backward with his one free fist at the man lugging him by the neck. As this group passed him, Grainier, seeing them in some distress, lent assistance and found himself holding one of the culprit's bare feet. The man facing him, Mr. Sears, of Spokane International's management, held the prisoner almost uselessly by the armpit and was the only one of them, besides the incomprehensible Chinaman, to talk during the hardest part of their labors: "Boys, I'm damned if we ever see the top of this heap!" Then we're hauling him all the way? was the question Grainier wished to ask, but thought it better to save his breath for the struggle. Sears laughed once, his face pale with fatigue and horror. They all went down in the dust and got righted, went down again, the Chinaman speaking in tongues and terrifying the four of them to the point that whatever they may have had in mind at the outset, he was a deader now. Nothing would do but to toss him off the trestle.

They came abreast of the others, a gang of a dozen men pausing in the sun to lean on their tools and wipe at sweat and watch this thing. Grainier held on convulsively to the Chinaman's horny foot, wondering at himself, and the man with the other foot let loose and sat down gasping in the dirt and got himself kicked in the eye before Grainier took charge of the free-flailing limb. "It was just for fun. For fun," the man sitting in the dirt said, and to his confederate there he said, "Come on, Jel Toomis, let's give it up." "I can't let loose," this Mr. Toomis said, "I'm the one's got him by the neck!" and laughed with a gust of confusion passing across his features. "Well, I've got him!" Grainier said, catching both the little demon's feet tighter in his embrace. "I've got the bastard, and I'm your man!"

The party of executioners got to the midst of the last completed span, sixty feet above the rapids, and made every effort to toss the Chinaman over. But he bested them by clinging to their arms and legs, weeping his gibberish, until suddenly he let go and grabbed the beam beneath him with one hand. He kicked free of his captors easily, as they were trying to shed themselves of him anyway, and went over the side, dangling over the gorge and making hand-over-hand out over the river on the skeleton form of the next span. Mr. Toomis's companion rushed over now, balancing on a beam, kicking at the fellow's fingers. The Chinaman dropped from beam to beam like a circus artist downward along the crosshatch structure. A couple of the work gang cheered his escape, while others, though not quite certain why he was being chased, shouted that the villain ought to be stopped. Mr. Sears removed from the holster on his belt a large old four-shot black-powder revolver and took his four, to no effect. By then the Chinaman had vanished.

Hiking to his home after this incident, Grainier detoured two miles to the store at the railroad village of Meadow Creek to get a bottle of Hood's Sarsaparilla for his wife, Gladys, and their infant daughter, Kate. It was hot going up the hill through the woods toward the cabin, and before getting the last mile he stopped and bathed in the river, the Moyea, at a deep place upstream from the village.

It was Saturday night, and in preparation for the evening a number of the railroad gang from Meadow Creek were gathered at the hole, bathing with their clothes on and sitting themselves out on the rocks to dry before the last of the daylight left the canyon. The men left their shoes and boots aside and waded in slowly up to their shoulders, whooping and splashing. Many of the men already sipped whiskey from flasks as they sat shivering after their ablutions. Here and there an arm and hand clutching a shabby hat jutted from the surface while somebody got his head wet. Grainier recognized nobody and stayed off by himself and kept a close eye on his boots and his bottle of sarsaparilla.

Walking home in the falling dark, Grainier almost met the Chinaman everywhere. Chinaman in the road. Chinaman in the woods. Chinaman walking softly, dangling his hands on arms like ropes. Chinaman dancing up out of the creek like a spider.

He gave the Hood's to Gladys. She sat up in bed by the stove, nursing the baby at her breast, down with a case of the salt rheum. She could easily have braved it and done her washing and cut up potatoes and trout for supper, but it was their custom to let her lie up with a bottle or two of the sweet-tasting Hood's tonic when her head ached and her nose stopped, and get a holiday from such chores. Grainier's baby daughter, too, looked rheumy. Her eyes were a bit crusted and the discharge bubbled pendulously at her nostrils while she suckled and snorted at her mother's breast. Kate was four months old, still entirely bald. She did not seem to recognize him. Her little illness wouldn't hurt her as long as she didn't develop a cough out of it.

Now Grainier stood by the table in the single-room cabin and worried. The Chinaman, he was sure, had cursed them powerfully while they dragged him along, and any bad thing might come of it. Though astonished now at the frenzy of the afternoon, baffled by the violence, at how it had carried him away like a seed in a wind, young Grainier still wished they'd gone ahead and killed that Chinaman before he'd cursed them.

He sat on the edge of the bed.

"Thank you, Bob," his wife said.

"Do you like your sarsaparilla?"

"I do. Yes, Bob."

"Do you suppose little Kate can taste it out your teat?"

"Of course she can."

Many nights they heard the northbound Spokane International train as it passed through Meadow Creek, two miles down the valley. To-night the distant whistle woke him, and he found himself alone in the straw bed.

Gladys was up with Kate, sitting on the bench by the stove, scrap-ing cold boiled oats off the sides of the pot and letting the baby suckle this porridge from the end of her finger.

"How much does she know, do you suppose, Gladys? As much as a dog-pup, do you suppose?"

"A dog-pup can live by its own after the bitch weans it away," Gladys said.

He waited for her to explain what this meant. She often thought ahead of him.

"A man-child couldn't do that way," she said, "just go off and live after it was weaned. A dog knows more than a babe until the babe knows its words. But not just a few words. A dog raised around the house knows some words, too—as many as a baby."

"How many words, Gladys?"

"You know," she said, "the words for its tricks and the things you tell it to do."

"Just say some of the words, Glad." It was dark and he wanted to keep hearing her voice.

"Well, fetch, and come, and sit, and lay, and roll over. Whatever it knows to do, it knows the words."

In the dark he felt his daughter's eyes turned on him like a cor-nered brute's. It was only his thoughts tricking him, but it poured something cold down his spine. He shuddered and pulled the quilt up to his neck.

All of his life Robert Grainier was able to recall this very moment on this very night.

2.

Forty-one days later, Grainier stood among the railroad gang and watched while the first locomotive crossed the one-hundred-twelve-foot interval of air over the sixty-foot-deep gorge, traveling on the bridge they'd made. Mr. Sears stood next to the machine, a single engine, and raised his four-shooter to signal the commencement. At the sound of the gun the engineer tripped the brake and hopped out of the contraption, and the men shouted it on as it trudged very slowly over the tracks and across the Moyea to the other side, where a second man waited to jump aboard and halt it before it ran out of track. The men cheered and whooped. Grainier felt sad. He couldn't think why. He cheered and hollered too. The structure would be called "Eleven-Mile Cutoff Bridge" because it eliminated a long curve around the gorge and through an adjacent pass and saved the Spokane International's having to look after that eleven-mile stretch of rails and ties.

Grainier's experience on the Eleven-Mile Cutoff made him hungry to be around other such massive undertakings, where swarms of men did away with portions of the forest and assembled structures as big as anything going, knitting massive wooden trestles in the air of impassable chasms, always bigger, longer, deeper. He went to northwestern Washington in 1920 to help make repairs on the Robinson Gorge Bridge, the grandest yet. The conceivers of these schemes had managed to bridge a space 208 feet deep and 804 feet wide with a railway capable of supporting an engine and two flatcars of logs. The Robinson Gorge Bridge was nearly thirty years old, wobbly and terrifying—nobody ever rode the cars across, not even the engineer. The brakeman caught it at the other end.

When the repairs were done, Grainier moved higher into the forest with the Simpson Company and worked getting timber out. A system of brief corduroy roads worked all over the area. The rails were meant only for transporting timber out of the forest; it was the job of the forty-some-odd men whom Grainier had joined to get the logs by six-horse teams within cable's reach of the railway landing.

At the landing crouched a giant engine the captain called a donkey, an affair with two tremendous iron drums, one paying out cable and the other winding it in, dragging logs to the landing and sending out the hook simultaneously to the choker, who noosed the next log. The engine was an old wood-burning steam colossus throbbing and booming and groaning while its vapors roared like a falls, the horses over on the skid road moving gigantically in a kind of silence, their noises erased by the commotion of steam and machinery. From the landing the logs went onto railroad flatcars, and then across the wondrous empty depth of Robinson Gorge and down the mountain to the link with all the railways of the American continent.

Meanwhile Robert Grainier had passed his thirty-fifth birthday. He missed Gladys and Kate, his Li'l Girl and Li'l Li'l Girl, but he'd lived thirty-two years a bachelor before finding a wife, and easily slipped back into a steadying loneliness out here among the countless spruce.

Grainier himself served as a choker—not on the landing, but down in the woods, where sawyers labored in pairs to fell the spruce, limbers worked with axes to get them clean, and buckers cut them into eighteen-foot lengths before the chokers looped them around with cable to be hauled out by the horses. Grainier relished the work, the straining, the heady exhaustion, the deep rest at the end of the day. He liked the grand size of things in the woods, the feeling of being lost and far away, and the sense he had that with so many trees as wardens, no danger could find him. But according to one of the fellows, Arn Peeples, an old man now, formerly a jim-crack sawyer, the trees themselves were killers, and while a good sawyer might judge ninety-nine times correctly how a fall would go, and even by remarkable cuts and wedging tell a fifty-tonner to swing around uphill and light behind him as deftly as a needle, the hundredth time might see him smacked in the face and deader than a rock, just like that. Arn Peeples said he'd once watched a five-ton log jump up startled and fly off the cart and tumble over six horses, killing all six. It was only when you left it alone that a tree might treat you as a friend. After the blade bit in, you had yourself a war.

Cut off from anything else that might trouble them, the gang, numbering sometimes over forty and never fewer than thirty-five men, fought the forest from sunrise until suppertime, felling and bucking the giant spruce into pieces of a barely manageable size, accomplishing labors, Grainier sometimes thought, tantamount to the pyramids, changing the face of the mountainsides, talking little, shouting their communications, living with the sticky feel of pitch in their beards, sweat washing the dust off their long johns and caking it in the creases of their necks and joints, the odor of pitch so thick it abraded their throats and stung their eyes, and even overlaid the stink of beasts and manure. At day's end the gang slept nearly where they fell. A few rated cabins. Most stayed in tents: These were ancient affairs patched extensively with burlap, most of them; but their canvas came originally from infantry tents of the Civil War, on the Union side, according to Arn Peeples. He pointed out stains of blood on the fabric. Some of these tents had gone on to house U.S. Cavalry in the Indian campaigns, serving longer, surely, than any they sheltered, so reckoned Arn Peeples.

"Just let me at that hatchet, boys," he liked to say. "When I get to chopping, you'll come to work in the morning and the chips won't yet be settled from yesterday . . .

"I'm made for this summer logging," said Arn Peeples. "You Minnesota fellers might like to complain about it. I don't get my gears turning smooth till it's over a hundred. I worked on a peak outside Bisbee, Arizona, where we were only eleven or twelve miles from the sun. It was a hundred and sixteen degrees on the thermometer, and every degree was a foot long. And that was in the shade. And there wasn't no shade." He called all his logging comrades "Minnesota fellers." As far as anybody could ascertain, nobody among them had ever laid eyes on Minnesota.

Arn Peeples had come up from the Southwest and claimed to have seen and spoken to the Earp brothers in Tombstone; he described the famous lawmen as "crazy trash." He'd worked in Arizona mines in his youth, then sawed all over logging country for decades, and now he was a frail and shrunken gadabout, always yammering, staying out of the way of hard work, the oldest man in the woods.

His real use was occasional. When a tunnel had to be excavated, he served as the powder monkey, setting charges and blasting his way deeper and deeper into a bluff until he came out the other side, men clearing away the rubble for him after each explosion. He was a superstitious person and did each thing exactly the way he'd done it in the Mule Mountains in south Arizona, in the copper mines.

"I witnessed Mr. John Jacob Warren lose his entire fortune. Drunk and said he could outrun a horse." This might have been true. Arn Peeples wasn't given to lying, at least didn't make claims to know many famous figures, other than the Earps, and, in any case, nobody up here had heard of any John Jacob Warren. "Wagered he could outrun a three-year-old stallion! Stood in the street swaying back and forth with his eyes crossed, that drunk, I mean to say—the richest man in Arizona!—and he took off running with that stallion's butt-end looking at him all the way. Bet the whole Copper Queen Mine. And lost it, too! *There's* a feller I'd like to gamble with! Of course he's busted down to his drop-bottoms now, and couldn't make a decent wager."

Sometimes Peeples set a charge, turned the screw to set it off, and got nothing for his trouble. Then a general tension and silence gripped the woods. Men working half a mile away would somehow get an understanding that a dud charge had to be dealt with, and all work stopped. Peeples would empty his pockets of his few valuables—a brass watch, a tin comb, and a silver toothpick—lay them on a stump, and proceed into the darkness of his tunnel without looking back. When he came out and turned his screws again and the dynamite blew with a whomp, the men cheered and a cloud of dust rushed from the tunnel and powdered rock came raining down over everyone.

It looked certain Arn Peeples would exit this world in a puff of smoke with a monstrous noise, but he went out quite differently, hit across the back of his head by a dead branch falling off a tall larch—the kind of snag called a "widow-maker" with just this kind of misfortune in mind. The blow knocked him silly, but he soon came around and seemed fine, complaining only that his spine felt "knotty amongst the knuckles" and "I want to walk suchways—crooked." He had a number of dizzy spells and grew dreamy and forgetful over the course of the next few days, lay up all day Sunday racked with chills and fever, and on Monday morning was found in his bed deceased, with the covers up under his chin and "such a sight of comfort," as the captain said, "that you'd just as soon not disturb him—just lower him down into a great long wide grave, bed and all." Arn Peeples had said a standing tree might be a friend, but it was from just such a tree that his death had descended.

Arn's best friend, Billy, also an old man, but generally wordless, mustered a couple of remarks by the grave mound: "Arn Peeples never cheated a man in his life," he said. "He never stole, not even a stick of candy when he was a small, small boy, and he lived to be pretty old. I guess there's a lesson in there for all of us to be square, and we'll all get along. In Jesus' name, amen." The others said, "Amen." "I wish I could let us all lay off a day," the captain said. "But it's the company, and it's the war." The war in Europe had created a great demand for spruce. An armistice had actually been signed eighteen months before, but the captain believed an armistice to be only a temporary thing until the battles resumed and one side massacred the other to the last man.

That night the men discussed Arn's assets and failings and went over the details of his final hours. Had the injuries to his brain addled him, or was it the fever he'd suddenly come down with? In his delirium he'd shouted mad words—"RIGHT REVEREND RISING ROCKIES!" he'd shouted—"forerunner grub holdup feller! Caution! Caution!"— and called out to the spirits from his past, and said he'd been paid a visit by his sister and his sister's husband, though both, as Billy said he knew for certain, had been many years dead.

Billy's jobs were to keep the double drum's engine watered and lubricated and to watch the cables for wear. This was easy work, old man's work. The outfit's real grease monkey was a boy, twelve-year-old Harold, the captain's son, who moved along before the teams of horses with a bucket of dogfish oil, slathering it across the skids with a swab of burlap to keep the huge logs sliding. One morning, Wednesday morning, just two days after Arn Peeple's death and burial, young Harold himself took a dizzy spell and fell over onto his work, and the horses shied and nearly overturned the load, trying to keep from trampling him. The boy was saved from a mutilated death by the lucky presence of Grainier himself, who happened to be standing aside waiting to cross the skid road and hauled the boy out of the way by the leg of his pants. The captain watched over his son all afternoon, bathing his forehead with spring water. The youth was feverish and crazy, and it was this malady that had laid him out in front of the big animals.

That night old Billy also took a chill and lay pitching from side to side on his cot and steadily raving until well past midnight. Except for his remarks at his friend's graveside, Billy probably hadn't let go of two or three words the whole time the men had known him, but now he kept the nearest ones awake, and those sleeping farther away in the camp later reported hearing from him in their dreams that night, mostly calling out his own name—"Who is it? Who's there?" he called. "Billy? Billy? Is that you, Billy?"

Harold's fever broke, but Billy's lingered. The captain acted like a man full of haunts, wandering the camp and bothering the men, catching one whenever he could and poking his joints, thumbing back his eyelids and prying apart his jaws like a buyer of livestock. "We're finished for the summer," he told the men Friday night as they lined up for supper. He'd calculated each man's payoff—Grainier had sent money home all summer and still had four hundred dollars coming to him.

By Sunday night they had the job shut up and the last logs down the mountain, and six more men had come over with chills. Monday morning the captain gave each of his workers a four-dollar bonus and said, "Get out of this place, boys." By this time Billy, too, had survived the crisis of his illness. But the captain said he feared an influenza epidemic like the one in 1897. He himself had been orphaned then, his entire family of thirteen siblings dead in a single week. Grainier felt pity for his boss. The captain had been a strong leader and a fair one, a blue-eyed, middle-aged man who trafficked little with anybody but his son Harold, and he'd never told anyone he'd grown up without any family.

This was Grainier's first summer in the woods, and the Robinson Gorge was the first of several railroad bridges he worked on. Years later, many decades later, in fact, in 1962 or 1963, he watched young ironworkers on a trestle where U.S. Highway 2 crossed the Moyea River's deepest gorge, every bit as long and deep as the Robinson. The old highway took a long detour to cross at a shallow place; the new highway shot straight across the chasm, several hundred feet above the river. Grainier marveled at the youngsters swiping each other's hard hats and tossing them down onto the safety net thirty or forty feet below, jumping down after them to bounce crazily in the netting, clambering up its strands back to the wooden catwalk. He'd been a regular chimpanzee on the girders himself, but now he couldn't get up on a high stool without feeling just a little queasy. As he watched them, it occurred to him that he'd lived almost eighty years and had seen the world turn and turn.

Some years earlier, in the mid-1950s, Grainier had paid ten cents to view the World's Fattest Man, who rested on a divan in a trailer that took him from town to town. To get the World's Fattest Man onto this divan they'd had to take the trailer's roof off and lower him down with a crane. He weighed in at just over a thousand pounds. There he sat, immense and dripping sweat, with a mustache and goatee and one gold earring like a pirate's, wearing shiny gold short pants and nothing else, his flesh rolling out on either side of him from one end of the divan to the other and spilling over and dangling toward the floor like an arrested waterfall, while out of this big pile of himself poked his head and arms and legs. People waited in line to stand at the open doorway and look in. He told each one to buy a picture of him from a stack by the window there for a dime.

Later in his long life Grainier confused the chronology of the past and felt certain that the day he'd viewed the World's Fattest Man— that evening—was the very same day he stood on Fourth Street in Troy, Montana, twenty-six miles east of the bridge, and looked at a railway car carrying the strange young hillbilly entertainer Elvis Presley. Presley's private train had stopped for some reason, maybe for repairs, here in this little town that didn't even merit its own station. The famous youth had appeared in a window briefly and raised his hand in greeting, but Grainier had come out of the barbershop across the street too late to see this. He'd only had it told to him by the townspeople standing in the late dusk, strung along the street beside the deep bass of the idling diesel, speaking very low if speaking at all, staring into the mystery and grandeur of a boy so high and solitary.

Grainier had also once seen a wonder horse, and a wolf-boy, and he'd flown in the air in a biplane in 1927. He'd started his life story on a train ride he couldn't remember, and ended up standing around outside a train with Elvis Presley in it.

3.

When a child, Grainier had been sent by himself to Idaho. From precisely where he'd been sent he didn't know, because his eldest cousin said one thing and his second-eldest another, and he himself couldn't remember. His second eldest cousin also claimed not to be his cousin at all, while the first said yes, they were cousins—their mother, whom Grainier thought of as his own mother as much as theirs, was actually his aunt, the sister of his father. All three of his cousins agreed Grainier had come on a train. How had he lost his original parents? Nobody ever told him.

When he disembarked in the town of Fry, Idaho, he was six—or possibly seven, as it seemed a long time since his last birthday and he thought he may have missed the date, and couldn't say, anyhow, where it fell. As far as he could ever fix it, he'd been born sometime in 1886, either in Utah or in Canada, and had found his way to his new family on the Great Northern Railroad, the building of which had been completed in 1892. He arrived after several days on the train with his destination pinned to his chest on the back of a store receipt. He'd eaten all of his food the first day of his travels, but various conductors had kept him fed along the way. The whole adventure made him forget things as soon as they happened, and he very soon misplaced this earliest part of his life entirely. His eldest cousin, a girl, said he'd come from northeast Canada and had spoken only French when they'd first seen him, and they'd had to whip the French out of him to get room for the English tongue. The other two cousins, both boys, said he was a Mormon from Utah. At so early an age it never occurred to him to find out from his aunt and uncle who he was. By the time he thought to ask them, many years had passed and they'd long since died, both of them.

His earliest memory was that of standing beside his uncle Robert Grainier, the First, standing no higher than the elbow of this smoky-smelling man he'd quickly got to calling Father, in the mud street of Fry within sight of the Kootenai River, observing the mass deportation of a hundred or more Chinese families from the town. Down at the street's end, at the Bonner Lumber Company's railroad yard, men with axes, pistols, and shotguns in their hands stood by saying very little while the strange people clambered onto three flatcars, jabbering like birds and herding their children into the midst of themselves, away from the edges of the open cars. The small, flatfaced men sat on the outside of the three groups, their knees drawn up and their hands locked around their shins, as the train left Fry and headed away to someplace it didn't occur to Grainier to wonder about until decades later, when he was a grown man and had come very near killing a Chinaman—had wanted to kill him. Most had ended up thirty or so miles west, in Montana, between the towns of Troy and Libby, in a place beside the Kootenai River that came to be called China Basin. By the time Grainier was working on bridges, the community had dispersed, and only a few lived here and there in the area, and nobody was afraid of them anymore.

The Kootenai River flowed past Fry as well. Grainier had patchy memories of a week when the water broke over its banks and flooded the lower portion of Fry. A few of the frailest structures washed away and broke apart downstream. The post office was undermined and carried off, and Grainier remembered being lifted up by somebody, maybe his father, and surfacing above the heads of a large crowd of townspeople to watch the building sail away on the flood. Afterwards some Canadians found the post office stranded on the lowlands one hundred miles downriver in British Columbia.

Robert and his new family lived in town. Only two doors away a bald man, always in a denim oversuit, always hatless—a large man, with very small, strong hands—kept a shop where he mended boots. Sometimes when he was out of sight little Robert or one of his cousins liked to nip in and rake out a gob of beeswax from the mason jar of it on his workbench. The mender used it to wax his thread when he sewed on tough leather, but the children sucked at it like candy.

The mender, for his part, chewed tobacco like many folks. One day he caught the three neighbor children as they passed his door. "Look here," he said. He bent over and expectorated half a mouthful into a glass canning jar nestled up against the leg of his table. He picked up this receptacle and swirled the couple inches of murky spit it held. "You children want a little taste out of this?"

They didn't answer.

"Go ahead and have a drink!—if you think you'd like to," he said.

They didn't answer.

He poured the horrible liquid into his jar of beeswax and glopped it all around with a finger and held the finger out toward their faces and hollered, "Take some any time you'd like!" He laughed and laughed. He rocked in his chair, wiping his tiny fingers on his denim lap. A vague disappointment shone in his eyes as he looked around and found nobody there to tell about his maneuver.

In 1899 the towns of Fry and Eatonville were combined under the name of Bonners Ferry. Grainier got his reading and numbers at the Bonners Ferry schoolhouse. He was never a scholar, but he learned to decipher writing on a page, and it helped him to get along in the world. In his teens he lived with his eldest cousin Suzanne and her family after she married, this following the death of their parents, his aunt and uncle Helen and Robert Grainier.

He quit attending school in his early teens and, without parents to fuss at him, became a layabout. Fishing by himself along the Kootenai one day, just a mile or so upriver from town, he came on an itinerant bum, a "boomer," as his sort was known, holed up among some birches in a sloppy camp, nursing an injured leg. "Come on up here. Please, young feller," the boomer called. "Please—please! I'm cut through the cords of my knee, and I want you to know a few things."

Young Robert wound in his line and laid the pole aside. He climbed the bank and stopped ten feet from where the man sat up against a tree with his legs out straight, barefoot, the left leg resting over a pallet of evergreen limbs. The man's old shoes lay one on either side of him. He was bearded and streaked with dust, and bits of the woods clung to him everywhere. "Rest your gaze on a murdered man," he said.

"I ain't even going to ask you to bring me a drink of water," the man said. "I'm dry as boots, but I'm going to die, so I don't think I need any favors." Robert was paralyzed. He had the impression of a mouth hole moving in a stack of leaves and rags and matted brown hair. "I've got just one or two things that must be said, or they'll go to my grave . . .

"That's right," he said. "I been cut behind the knee by this one feller they call Big-Ear Al. And I have to say, I know he's killed me. That's the first thing. Take that news to your sheriff, son. William Coswell Haley, from St. Louis, Missouri, has been robbed, cut in the leg, and murdered by the boomer they call Big-Ear Al. He snatched my roll of fourteen dollars off me whilst I slept, and he cut the strings back of my knee so's I wouldn't chase after him. My leg's stinking," he said, "because I've laid up here so long the rot's set in. You know how that'll do. That rot will travel till I'm dead right up to my eyes. Till I'm a corpse able to see things. Able to think its thoughts. Then about the fourth day I'll be all the way dead. I don't know what happens to us then—if we can think our thoughts in the grave, or we fly to Heaven, or get taken to the Devil. But here's what I have to say, just in case:

"I am William Coswell Haley, forty-two years old. I was a good man with jobs and prospects in St. Louis, Missouri, until a bit more than four years ago. At that time my niece Susan Haley became about twelve years of age, and, as I was living in my brother's house in those days, I started to get around her in her bed at night. I couldn't sleep—it got that way, I couldn't stop my heart from running and racing—until I'd got up from my pallet and snuck to the girl's room and got around her bed, and just stood there quiet. Well, she never woke. Not even one night when I rustled her covers. Another night I touched her face and she never woke, grabbed at her foot and didn't get a rise. Another night I pulled at her covers, and she was the same as dead. I touched her, lifted her shift, did every little thing I wanted. Every little thing. And she never woke.

"And that got to be my way. Night after night. Every little thing. She never woke.

"Well, I came home one day, and I'd been working at the candle factory, which was an easy job to acquire when a feller had no other. Mostly old gals working there, but they'd take anybody on. When I got to the house, my sister-in-law Alice Haley was sitting in the yard on a wet winter's day, sitting on the greasy grass. Just plunked there. Bawling like a baby.

" 'What is it, Alice?'

" 'My husband's took a stick to our little daughter Susan! My husband's took a stick to her! A stick!'

" 'Good God, is she hurt,' I said, 'or is it just her feelings?'

" 'Hurt? Hurt?' she cries at me—'My little girl is dead!'

"I didn't even go into the house. Left whatever-all I owned and walked to the railway and got on a flatcar, and I've never been a hundred yards from these train tracks ever since. Been all over this country. Canada, too. Never a hundred yards from these rails and ties.

"Little young Susan had a child in her, is what her mother told me. And her father beat on her to drive that poor child out of her belly. Beat on her till he'd killed her."

For a few minutes the dying man stopped talking. He grabbed at breaths, put his hands to the ground either side of him and seemed to want to shift his posture, but had no strength. He couldn't seem to get a decent breath in his lungs, panting and wheezing. "I'll take that drink of water now." He closed his eyes and ceased struggling for air. When Robert got near, certain the man had died, William Haley spoke without opening his eyes: "Just bring it to me in that old shoe."

4.

The boy never told anyone about William Coswell Haley. Not the sheriff, or his cousin Suzanne, or anyone else. He brought the man one swallow of water in the man's own boot, and left William Haley to die alone. It was the most cowardly and selfish of the many omissions that might have been counted against him in his early years. But maybe the incident affected him in a way nobody could have traced successfully, because Robert Grainier settled in and worked through the rest his youth as one of the labor pool around town, hiring out to the railroad or to the entrepreneurial families of the area, the Eatons, the Frys, or the Bonners, finding work on the crews pretty well whenever he needed, because he stayed away from drink or anything unseemly and was known as a steady man.

He worked around town right through his twenties—a man of whom it might have been said, but nothing was ever said of him, that he had little to interest him. At thirty-one he still chopped firewood, loaded trucks, served among various gangs formed up by more enterprising men for brief jobs here and there.

Then he met Gladys Olding. One of his cousins, later he couldn't remember which one to thank, took him to church with the Methodists, and there she was, a small girl just across the aisle from him, who sang softly during the hymns in a voice he picked out without any trouble. A session of lemonade and pastries followed the service, and there in the courtyard she introduced herself to him casually, with an easy smile, as if girls did things like that every day, and maybe they did—Robert Grainier didn't know, as Robert Grainier stayed away from girls. Gladys looked much older than her years, having grown up, she explained to him, in a house in a sunny pasture, and having spent too much time in the summer light. Her hands were as rough as any fifty-year-old man's.

They saw each other frequently, Grainier forced, by the nature of their friendship, to seek her out almost always at the Methodist Sunday services and at the Wednesday night prayer group. When the summer was full on, Grainier took her by the river road to show her the acre he'd acquired on the short bluff above the Moyea. He'd bought it from young Glenwood Fry, who had wanted an automobile and who eventually got one by selling many small parcels of land to other young people. He told her he'd try some gardening here. The nicest place for a cabin lay just down a path from a sparsely overgrown knoll he could easily level by moving around the stones it was composed of. He could clear a bigger area cutting logs for a cabin, and pulling at stumps wouldn't be urgent, as he'd just garden among them, to start. A half-mile path through a thick woods led into a meadow cleared some years back by Willis Grossling, now deceased. Grossling's daughter had said Grainier could graze a few animals there as long as he didn't run a real herd over the place. Anyway he didn't want more than a couple sheep and a couple goats. Maybe a milk cow. Grainier explained all this to Gladys without explaining why he was explaining. He hoped she guessed. He thought she must, because for this outing she'd put on the same dress she usually wore to church.

This was on a hot June day. They'd borrowed a wagon from Gladys's father and brought a picnic in two baskets. They hiked over to Grossling's meadow and waded into it through daisies up to their knees. They put out a blanket beside a seasonal creek trickling over the grass and lay back together. Grainier considered the pasture a beautiful place. Somebody should paint it, he said to Gladys. The buttercups nodded in the breeze and the petals of the daisies trembled. Yet further off, across the field, they seemed stationary.

Gladys said, "Right now I could just about understand everything there is." Grainier knew how seriously she took her church and her Bible, and he thought she might be talking about something in that realm of things. "Well, you see what I like," he said.

"Yes, I do," she said.

"And I see what I like very, very well," he said, and kissed her lips.

"Ow," she said. "You got my mouth flat against my teeth."

"Are you sorry?"

"No. Do it again. But easy does it."

The first kiss plummeted him down a hole and popped him out into a world he thought he could get along in—as if he'd been pulling hard the wrong way and was now turned around headed downstream. They spent the whole afternoon among the daisies kissing. He felt glorious and full of more blood than he was supposed to have in him.

When the sun got too hot, they moved under a lone jack pine in the pasture of jeremy grass, he with his back against the bark and she with her cheek on his shoulder. The white daisies dabbed the field so profusely that it seemed to foam. He wanted to ask for her hand now. He was afraid to ask. She must want him to ask, or surely she wouldn't lie here with him, breathing against his arm, his face against her hair—her hair faintly fragrant of sweat and soap . . . "Would you care to be my wife, Gladys?" he astonished himself by saying.

"Yes, Bob, I believe I would like it," she said, and she seemed to hold her breath a minute; then he sighed, and both laughed.

When, in the summer of 1920, he came back from the Robinson Gorge job with four hundred dollars in his pocket, riding in a passenger car as far as Coeur d'Alene, Idaho, and then in a wagon up the Panhandle, a fire was consuming the Moyea Valley. He rode through a steadily thickening haze of wood smoke into Bonners Ferry and found the little town crowded with residents from along the Moyea River who no longer had any homes.

Grainier searched for his wife and daughter among the folks sheltering in town. Many had nothing to do now but move on, destitute. Nobody had word of his family.

He searched among the crowd of some one hundred or so people camping at the fairgrounds among tiny collections of the remnants of their worldly possessions, random things, dolls and mirrors and bridles, all waterlogged. These had managed to wade down the river and through the conflagration and out the southern side of it. Others, who'd headed north and tried to outrun the flames, had not been heard of since. Grainier questioned everyone, but got no news of his wife and daughter, and he grew increasingly frantic as he witnessed the refugees' strange happiness at having got out alive and their apparent disinterest in the fate of anyone who might have failed to.

The northbound Spokane International was stopped in Bonners and wouldn't move on until the fire was down and a good rain had soaked the Panhandle. Grainier walked the twenty miles out along the Moyea River Road toward his home with a handkerchief tied over his nose and mouth to strain the smoke, stopping to wet it often in the river, passing through a silvery snow of ash. Nothing here was burning. The fire had started on the river's east side not far above the village of Meadow Creek and worked north, crossed the river at a narrow gorge bridged by flaming mammoth spruce trees as they fell, and devoured the valley. Meadow Creek was deserted. He stopped at the railroad platform and drank water from the barrel there and went quickly on without resting. Soon he was passing through a forest of charred, gigantic spears that only a few days past had been evergreens. The world was gray, white, black, and acrid, without a single live animal or plant, no longer burning and yet still full of the warmth and life of the fire. So much ash, so much choking smoke—it was clear to him miles before he reached his home that nothing could be left of it, but he went on anyway, weeping for his wife and daughter, calling, "Kate! Gladys!" over and over. He turned off the road to look in on the homesite of the Andersens, the first one past Meadow Creek. At first he couldn't tell even where the cabin had stood. Their acreage looked like the rest of the valley, burned and silent except for the collective hiss of the very last remnants of combustion. He found their cookstove mounding out of a tall drift of ashes where its iron legs had buckled in the heat. A few of the biggest stones from the chimney lay strewn nearby. Ash had buried the rest.

The farther north he hiked, the louder came the reports of cracking logs and the hiss of burning, until every charred tree around him still gave off smoke. He rounded a bend to hear the roar of the conflagration and see the fire a half mile ahead like a black and red curtain dropped from a night sky. Even from this distance the heat of it stopped him. He collapsed to his knees, sat in the warm ashes through which he'd been wading, and wept.

Ten days later, when the Spokane International was running again, Grainier rode it up into Creston, B.C., and back south again the evening of the same day through the valley that had been his home. The blaze had climbed to the ridges either side of the valley and stalled halfway down the other side of the mountains, according to the reports Grainier had listened to intently. It had gutted the valley along its entire length like a campfire in a ditch. All his life Robert Grainier would remember vividly the burned valley at sundown, the most dreamlike business he'd ever witnessed waking—the brilliant pastels of the last light overhead, some clouds high and white, catching daylight from beyond the valley, others ribbed and gray and pink, the lowest of them rubbing the peaks of Bussard and Queen mountains; and beneath this wondrous sky the black valley, utterly still, the train moving through it making a great noise but unable to wake this dead world.

The news in Creston was terrible. No escapees from the Moyea Valley fire had appeared there.

Grainier stayed at his cousin's home for several weeks, not good for much, sickened by his natural grief and confused by the situation. He understood that he'd lost his wife and little girl, but sometimes the idea stormed over him, positively stormed into his thoughts like an irresistible army, that Gladys and Kate had escaped the fire and that he should look for them everywhere in the world until he found them. Nightmares woke him every night: Gladys came out of the black landscape onto their homesite, dressed in smoking rags and carrying their daughter, and found nothing there, and stood crying in the waste.

In September, thirty days after the fire, Grainier rented a pair of horses and a wagon and set out up the river road carting a heap of supplies, intending to put up shelter on his acre and wait all winter for his family to return. Some might have called it an ill-considered plan, but the experiment had the effect of bringing him to his senses. As soon as he entered the remains he felt his heart's sorrow blackened and purified, as if it were an actual lump of matter from which all the hopeful, crazy thinking was burning away. He drove through a layer of ash deep enough, in some places, that he couldn't make out the roadbed any better than if he'd driven through winter snows. Only the fastest animals and those with wings could have escaped this feasting fire.

After traveling through the waste for several miles, scarcely able to breathe for the reek of it, he quit and turned around and went back to live in town.

Not long after the start of autumn, businessmen from Spokane raised a hotel at the little railroad camp of Meadow Creek. By spring a few dispossessed families had returned to start again in the Moyea

Valley. Grainier hadn't thought he'd try it himself, but in May he camped alongside the river, fishing for speckled trout and hunting for a rare and very flavorful mushroom the Canadians called morel, which sprang up on ground disturbed by fire. Progressing north for several days, Grainier found himself within a shout of his old home and climbed the draw by which he and Gladys had habitually found their way to and from the water. He marveled at how many shoots and flowers had sprouted already from the general death.

He climbed to their cabin site and saw no hint, no sign at all of his former life, only a patch of dark ground surrounded by the black spikes of spruce. The cabin was cinders, burned so completely that its ashes had mixed in with a common layer all about and then been tamped down by the snows and washed and dissolved by the thaw.

He found the woodstove lying on its side with its legs curled up under it like a beetle's. He righted it and pried at the handle. The hinges broke away and the door came off. Inside sat a chunk of birch, barely charred. "Gladys!" he said out loud. Everything he'd loved lying ashes around him, but here this thing she'd touched and held.

He poked through the caked mud around the grounds and found almost nothing he could recognize. He scuffed along through the ashes and kicked up one of the spikes he'd used in building the cabin's walls, but couldn't find any others.

He saw no sign of their Bible, either. If the Lord had failed to protect even the book of his own Word, this proved to Grainier that here had come a fire stronger than God.

Come June or July this clearing would be grassy and green. Already foot-tall jack pine sprouted from the ashes, dozens of them. He thought of poor little Kate and talked to himself again out loud: "She never even growed up to a sprout."

Grainier thought he must be very nearly the only creature in this sterile region. But standing in his old homesite, talking out loud, he heard himself answered by wolves on the peaks in the distance, these answered in turn by others, until the whole valley was singing. There were birds about, too, not foraging, maybe, but lighting to rest briefly as they headed across the burn.

Gladys, or her spirit, was palpably near. A feeling overcame him that something belonging to her and the baby, to both of them, lay around here to be claimed. What thing? He believed it might be the chocolates Gladys had bought in a red box, chocolates cupped in white paper. A crazy thought, but he didn't bother to argue with it. Once every week, she and the tyke had sucked one chocolate apiece. Suddenly he could see those white cups scattered all around him. When he looked directly at any one of them, it disappeared.

Toward dark, as Grainier lay by the river in a blanket, his eye caught on a quick thing up above, flying along the river. He looked and saw his wife Gladys's white bonnet sailing past overhead. Just sailing past.

He stayed on for weeks in this camp, waiting, wanting many more such visions as that of the bonnet, and the chocolates—as many as wanted to come to him; and he figured as long as he saw impossible things in this place, and liked them, he might as well be in the habit of talking to himself, too. Many times each day he found himself deflating on a gigantic sigh and saying, "A pretty mean circumstance!" He thought he'd better be up and doing things so as not to sigh quite as much.

Sometimes he thought about Kate, the pretty little tyke, but not frequently. Hers was not such a sad story. She'd hardly been awake, much less alive.

He lived through the summer off dried morel mushrooms and fresh trout cooked up together in butter he bought at the store in Meadow Creek. After a while a dog came along, a little red-haired female. The dog stayed with him, and he stopped talking to himself because he was ashamed to have the animal catch him at it. He bought a canvas tarp and some rope in Meadow Creek, and later he bought a nanny goat and walked her back to his camp, the dog wary and following this newcomer at a distance. He picketed the nanny near his lean-to.

He spent several days along the creek in gorges where the burn wasn't so bad, collecting willow whips from which he wove a crate about two yards square and half as tall. He and the dog walked to Meadow Creek and he bought four hens, also a rooster to keep them in line, and carted them home in a grain sack and cooped them up in the crate. He let them out for a day or two every now and then, penning them frequently so the hens wouldn't lay in secret places, not that there were many places in this destruction even to hide an egg.

The little red dog lived on goat's milk and fish heads and, Grainier supposed, whatever she could catch. She served as decent company when she cared to, but tended to wander for days at a time.

Because the ground was too bare for grazing, he raised his goat on the same laying mash he fed the chickens. This got to be expensive. Following the first frost in September he butchered the goat and jerked most of its meat.

After the second frost of the season, he started strangling and stewing the fowls one by one over the course of a couple of weeks, until he and the dog had eaten them all, the rooster, too. Then he left for Meadow Creek. He had grown no garden and built no structure other than his lean-to.

As he got ready to depart, he discussed the future with his dog. "To keep a dog in town it ain't my nature," he told the animal. "But you seem to me elderly, and I don't think an elderly old dog can make the winter by your lonely up around these hills." He told her he would pay an extra nickel to bring her aboard the train a dozen miles into Bonners Ferry. But this must not have suited her. On the day he gathered his few things to hike down to the platform at Meadow Creek, the little red dog was nowhere to be found, and he left without her.

The abbreviated job a year earlier at Robinson Gorge had given him money enough to last through the winter in Bonners Ferry, but in order to stretch it Grainier worked for twenty cents an hour for a man named Williams who'd contracted with Great Northern to sell them one thousand cords of firewood for two dollars and seventy-five cents each. The steady daylong exertions kept him and seven other men warm through the days, even as the winter turned into the coldest seen in many years. The Kootenai River froze hard enough that one day they watched, from the lot where wagons brought them logs of birch and larch to be sawn and split, a herd of two hundred cattle being driven across the river on the ice. They moved onto the blank white surface and churned up a snowy fog that first lost them in itself, then took in all the world north of the riverbank, and finally rose high enough to hide the sun and sky.

Late that March Grainier returned to his homesite in the Moyea Valley, this time hauling a wagon-load of supplies.

Animals had returned to what was left of the forest. As Grainier drove along in the wagon behind a wide, slow, sand-colored mare, clusters of orange butterflies exploded off the blackish-purple piles of bear-sign and winked and fluttered magically like leaves without trees. More bears than people traveled the muddy road, leaving tracks straight up and down the middle of it; later in the summer they would forage in the low patches of huckleberry he already saw coming back on the blackened hillsides.

At his old campsite by the river he raised his canvas lean-to and went about chopping down five dozen burned spruce, none of them bigger around than his own hatsize, acting on the generally acknowledged theory that one man working alone could handle a house log about the circumference of his own head. With the rented horse he got the timber decked in his clearing, then had to return the outfit to the stables in Bonners Ferry and hop the train back to Meadow Creek.

It wasn't until a couple of days later, when he got back to his old home—now his new home—that he noticed what his labors had prevented his seeing: It was full on spring, sunny and beautiful, and the Moyea Valley showed a lot of green against the dark of the burn. The ground about was healing. Fireweed and jack pine stood up about thigh high. A mustard-tinted fog of pine pollen drifted through the valley when the wind came up. If he didn't yank this crop of new ones, his clearing would return to forest.

He built his cabin about eighteen by eighteen, laying out lines, making a foundation of stones in a ditch knee-deep to get down below the frost line, scribing and hewing the logs to keep each one flush against the next, hacking notches, getting his back under the higher ones to lift them into place. In a month he'd raised four walls nearly eight feet in height. The windows and roof he left for later, when he could get some milled lumber. He tossed his canvas over the east end to keep the rain out. No peeling had been required, because the fire had managed that for him. He'd heard that fire-killed trees lasted best, but the cabin stank. He burned heaps of jack pine needles in the middle of the dirt floor trying to change the odor's character, and felt after a while that he'd succeeded.

In early June the red dog appeared, took up residence in a corner, and whelped a brood of four pups that appeared quite wolfish.

Down at the Meadow Creek store he spoke about this development with a Kootenai Indian named Bob. Kootenai Bob was a steady man who had always refused liquor and worked frequently at jobs in town, just as Grainier did, and they'd known each other for many years. Kootenai Bob said that if the dog's pups had come out wolfish, that would be quite strange. The Kootenais had it that only one pair in a wolf den ever made pups—that you couldn't get any of the he-wolves to mate except one, the chief of the wolf tribe. And the she-wolf he chose to bear his litters was the only bitch in the pack who ever came in heat. "And so I tell you," Bob said, "that therefore your wandering dog wouldn't drop a litter of wolves." But what if she'd encountered the wolf pack at just the moment she was coming into heat, Grainier wanted to know—might the king wolf have mounted her then, just for the newness of the experience? "Then perhaps, perhaps," Bob said. "Might be. Might be you've got yourself some dog-of-wolf. Might be you've started your own pack, Robert."

Three of the pups wandered off immediately as the little dog weaned them, but one, a dis-coordinated male, stayed around and was tolerated by its mother. Grainier felt sure this dog was got of a wolf, but it never even whimpered in reply when the packs in the distance, some as far away as the Selkirks on the British Columbia side, sang at dusk. The creature needed to be taught its nature, Grainier felt. One evening he got down beside it and howled. The little pup only sat on its rump with an inch of pink tongue jutting stupidly from its closed mouth. "You're not growing the direction of your own nature, which is to howl when the others do," he told the mongrel. He stood up straight himself and howled long and sorrowfully over the gorge, and over the low quiet river he could hardly see across this close to nightfall . . . Nothing from the pup. But often, thereafter, when Grainier heard the wolves at dusk, he laid his head back and howled for all he was worth, because it did him good. It flushed out something heavy that tended to collect in his heart, and after an evening's program with his choir of British Columbian wolves he felt warm and buoyant.

He tried telling Kootenai Bob of this development. "Howling, are you?" the Indian said. "There it is for you, then. That's what happens, that's what they say: There's not a wolf alive that can't tame a man."

The pup disappeared before autumn, and Grainier hoped he'd made it across the line to his brothers in Canada, but he had to assume the worst: food for a hawk, or for the coyotes.

Many years later—in 1930—Grainier saw Kootenai Bob on the very day the Indian died. That day Kootenai Bob was drunk for the first time in his life. Some ranch hands visiting from across the line in British Columbia had managed to get him to take a drink by fixing up a jug of shandy, a mixture of lemonade and beer. They'd told him he could drink this with impunity, as the action of the lemon juice would nullify any effect of the beer, and Kootenai Bob had believed them, because the United States was by now more than a decade into Prohibition, and the folks from Canada, where liquor was still allowed, were considered experts when it came to alcohol. Grainier found old Bob sitting on a bench out front of the hotel in Meadow Creek toward evening with his legs wrapped around an eight-quart canning pan full of beer—no sign of lemonade by now—lapping at it like a thirsty mutt. The Indian had been guzzling all afternoon, and he'd pissed himself repeatedly and no longer had the power of speech. Sometime after dark he wandered off and managed to get himself a mile up the tracks, where he lay down unconscious across the ties and was run over by a succession of trains. Four or five came over him, until late next afternoon the gathering multitude of crows prompted someone to investigate. By then Kootenai Bob was strewn for a quarter mile along the right-of-way. Over the next few days his people were seen plying along the blank patch of earth beside the rails, locating whatever little tokens of flesh and bone and cloth the crows had missed and collecting them in brightly, beautifully painted leather pouches, which they must have taken off somewhere and buried with a fitting ceremony.

5.

At just about the time Grainier discovered a rhythm to his seasons—summers in Washington, spring and fall at his cabin, winters boarding in Bonners Ferry—he began to see he couldn't make it last. This was some four years into his residence in the second cabin.

His summer wages gave him enough to live on all year, but he wasn't built for logging. First he became aware how much he needed the winter to rest and mend; then he suspected the winter wasn't long enough to mend him. Both his knees ached. His elbows cracked loudly when he straightened his arms, and something hitched and snapped in his right shoulder when he moved it the wrong way; a general stiffness of his frame worked itself out by halves through most mornings, and he labored like an engine through the afternoons, but he was well past thirty-five years, closer now to forty, and he really wasn't much good in the woods any more.

When the month of April arrived in 1925, he didn't leave for Washington. These days there was plenty of work in town for anybody willing to get around after it. He felt like staying closer to home, and he'd come into possession of a pair of horses and a wagon—by a sad circumstance, however. The wagon had been owned by Mr. and Mrs. Pinkham, who ran a machine shop on Highway 2. He'd agreed to help their grandson Henry, known as Hank, an enormous youth in his late teens, certainly no older than his early twenties, to load sacks of cornmeal aboard the Pinkham's wagon; this favor a result of Grainier's having stopped in briefly to get some screws for a saw handle. They'd only loaded the first two sacks when Hank sloughed the third one from his shoulder onto the dirt floor of the barn and said, "I am as dizzy as anything today," sat on the pile of sacks, removed his hat, flopped over sideways, and died.

His grandfather hastened from the house when Grainier called him and went to the boy right away, saying, "Oh. Oh. Oh." He was open-mouthed with uncomprehension. "He's not gone, is he?"

"I don't know, sir. I just couldn't say. He sat down and fell over. I don't even think he said anything to complain," Grainier told him.

"We've got to send you for help," Mr. Pinkham said.

"Where should I go?"

"I've got to get Mother," Pinkham said, looking at Grainier with terror on his face. "She's inside the house."

Grainier remained with the dead boy but didn't look at him while they were alone.

Old Mrs. Pinkham came into the barn flapping her hands and said, "Hank? Hank?" and bent close, taking her grandson's face in her hands. "Are you gone?"

"He's gone, isn't he?" her husband said.

"He's gone! He's gone!"

"He's gone, Pearl."

"God has him now," Mrs. Pinkham said.

"Dear Lord, take this boy to your bosom . . ."

"You could seen this coming ever since!" the old woman cried.

"His heart wasn't strong," Mr. Pinkham explained. "You could see that about him. We always knew that much."

"His heart was his fate," Mrs. Pinkham said. "You could've looked right at him any time you wanted and seen this."

"Yes," Mr. Pinkham agreed.

"He was that sweet and good," Mrs. Pinkham said. "Still in his youth. Still in his youth!" She stood up angrily and marched from the barn and over to the edge of the roadway—U.S. Highway 2—and stopped.

Grainier had seen people dead, but he'd never seen anybody die. He didn't know what to say or do. He felt he should leave, and he felt he shouldn't leave.

Mr. Pinkham asked Grainier a favor, standing in the shadow of the house while his wife waited in the yard under a wild mixture of clouds and sunshine, looking amazed and, from this distance, as young as a child, and also very beautiful, it seemed to Grainier. "Would you take him down to Helmer's?" Helmer was in charge of the cemetery and, with Smithson the barber's help, often prepared corpses for the ground. "We'll get poor young Hank in the wagon. We'll get him in the wagon, and you'll go ahead and take him for me, won't you? So I can tend to his grandmother. She's gone out of her mind."

Together they wrestled the heavy dead boy aboard the wagon, resorting after much struggle to the use of two long boards. They inclined them against the wagon's bed and flopped the corpse up and over, up and over, until it rested in the conveyance. "Oh—oh—oh—oh—" exclaimed the grandfather with each and every nudge. As for Grainier, he hadn't touched another person in several years, and even apart from the strangeness of this situation, the experience was something to remark on and remember. He giddyapped Pinkham's pair of old mares, and they pulled young dead Hank Pinkham to Helmer's cemetery.

Helmer, too, had a favor to ask of Grainier, once he'd taken the body off his hands. "If you'll deliver a coffin over to the jail in Troy and pick up a load of lumber for me at the yard on Main, then take the lumber to Leona for me, I'll pay you rates for both jobs separate. Two for the price of one. Or come to think of it," he said, "one job for the price of two, that's what it would be, ain't it, sir?"

"I don't mind," Grainier told him.

"I'll give you a nickel for every mile of it."

"I'd have to stop at Pinkham's and bargain a rate from them. I'd need twenty cents a mile before I saw a profit."

"All right then. Ten cents and it's done."

"I'd need a bit more."

"Six dollars entire."

"I'll need a pencil and a paper. I don't know my numbers without a pencil and a paper."

The little undertaker brought him what he needed, and together they decided that six-and-a-half dollars was fair.

For the rest of the fall and even a ways into winter, Grainier leased the pair and wagon from the Pinkhams, boarding the mares with their owners, and kept himself busy as a freighter of sorts. Most of his jobs took him east and west along Highway Two, among the small communities there that had no close access to the railways.

Some of these errands took him down along the Kootenai River, and traveling beside it always brought into his mind the image of

William Coswell Haley, the dying boomer. Rather than wearing away, Grainier's regret at not having helped the man had grown much keener as the years had passed. Sometimes he thought also of the Chinese railroad hand he'd almost helped to kill. The thought paralyzed his heart. He was certain the man had taken his revenge by calling down a curse that had incinerated Kate and Gladys. He believed the punishment was too great.

But the hauling itself was better work than any he'd undertaken, a ticket to a kind of show, to an entertainment comprised of the follies and endeavors of his neighbors. Grainier was having the time of his life. He contracted with the Pinkhams to buy the horses and wagon in installments for three hundred dollars.

By the time he'd made this decision, the region had seen over a foot of snow, but he continued a couple more weeks in the freight business. It didn't seem a particularly bad winter down below, but the higher country had frozen through, and one of Grainier's last jobs was to get up the Yahk River Road to the saloon at the logging village of Sylvanite, in the hills above which a lone prospector had blown himself up in his shack while trying to thaw out frozen dynamite on his stove. The man lay out on the bartop, alive and talking, sipping free whiskey and praising his dog. His dog's going for help had saved him. For half a day the animal had made such a nuisance of himself around the saloon that one of the patrons had finally noosed him and dragged him home and found his master extensively lacerated and raving from exposure in what remained of his shack.

Much that was astonishing was told of the dogs in the Panhandle and along the Kootenai River, tales of rescues, tricks, feats of super-canine intelligence and humanlike understanding. As his last job for that year, Grainier agreed to transport a man from Meadow Creek to Bonners who'd actually been shot by his own dog.

The dog-shot man was a bare acquaintance of Grainier's, a surveyor for Spokane International who came and went in the area, name of Peterson, originally from Virginia. Peterson's boss and comrades might have put him on the train into town the next morning if they'd waited, but they thought he might perish before then, so Grainier hauled him down the Moyea River Road wrapped in a blanket and half sitting up on a load of half a dozen sacks of wood chips bagged up just to make him comfortable.

"Are you feeling like you need anything?" Grainier said at the start.

Grainier thought Peterson had gone to sleep. Or worse. But in a minute the victim answered: "Nope. I'm perfect."

A long thaw had come earlier in the month. The snow was melted out of the ruts. Bare earth showed off in the woods. But now, again, the weather was freezing, and Grainier hoped he wouldn't end up bringing in a corpse dead of the cold.

For the first few miles he didn't talk much to his passenger, because Peterson had a dented head and crazy eye, the result of some mishap in his youth, and he was hard to look at.

Grainier steeled himself to glance once in a while in the man's direction, just to be sure he was alive. As the sun left the valley, Peterson's crazy eye and then his entire face became invisible. If he died now, Grainier probably wouldn't know it until they came into the light of the two gas lamps either side of the doctor's house. After they'd moved along for nearly an hour without conversation, listening only to the creaking of the wagon and the sound of the nearby river and the clop of the mares, it grew dark.

Grainier disliked the eeriness of the shadows, the spindly silhouettes of birch trees, and the clouds strung around the yellow half-moon. It all seemed designed to frighten the child in him. "Sir, are you dead?" he asked Peterson.

"Who? Me? Nope. Alive," said Peterson.

"Well, I was wondering—do you feel as if you might go on?"

"You mean as if I might die?"

"Yessir," Grainier said.

"Nope. Ain't going to die tonight."

"That's good."

"Even better for *me*, I'd say."

Grainier now felt they'd chatted sufficiently that he might raise a matter of some curiosity to him. "Mrs. Stout, your boss's wife, there. She said your dog shot you."

"Well, she's a very upright lady—to my way of knowing, anyways."

"Yes, I have the same impression of her right around," Grainier said, "and she said your dog shot you."

Peterson was silent a minute. In a bit, he coughed and said, "Do you feel a little warm patch in the air? As if maybe last week's warm weather turned around and might be coming back on us?"

"Not as such to me," Grainier said. "Just holding the warm of the day the way it does before you get around this ridge."

They continued along under the rising moon.

"Anyway," Grainier said.

Peterson didn't respond. Might not have heard.

"Did your dog really shoot you?"

"Yes, he did. My own dog shot me with my own gun. Ouch!" Peterson said, shifting himself gently. "Can you take your team a little more gradual over these ruts, Mister?"

"I don't mind," Grainier said. "But you've got to get your medical attention, or anything could happen to you."

"All right. Go at it like the Pony Express, then, if you want."

"I don't see how a dog shoots a gun."

"Well, he did."

"Did he use a rifle?"

"It weren't a cannon. It weren't a pistol. It were a rifle."

"Well, that's pretty mysterious, Mr. Peterson. How did that happen?"

"It was self-defense."

Grainier waited. A full minute passed, but Peterson stayed silent.

"That just tears it then," Grainier said, quite agitated. "I'm pulling this team up, and you can walk from here, if you want to beat around and around the bush. I'm taking you to town with a hole in you, and I ask a simple question about how your dog shot you, and you have to play like a bunkhouse lout who don't know the answer."

"All right!" Peterson laughed, then groaned with the pain it caused him. "My dog shot me in self-defense. I went to shoot *him*, at first, because of what Kootenai Bob the Indian said about him, and he slipped the rope. I had him tied for the business we were about to do." Peterson coughed and went quiet a few seconds. "I ain't stalling you now! I just got to get over the hurt a little bit."

"All right. But why did you have Kootenai Bob tied up, and what has Kootenai Bob got to do with this, anyways?"

"Not Kootenai Bob! I had the *dog* tied up. Kootenai Bob weren't nowhere near this scene I'm relating. He was before."

"But the *dog*, I say."

"And say I also, the *dog. He's* the one I ties. *He's* the one slips the rope, and I couldn't get near him—he'd just back off a step for every step I took in his direction. He knew I had his end in mind, which I decided to do on account of what Kootenai Bob said about him. That dog *knew* things—because of what happened to him, which is what Kootenai Bob the Indian told me about him—that animal all of a sudden *knew* things. So I swung the rifle by the barrel and butt-ended that old pup to stop his sass, and wham! I'm sitting on my very own butt-end pretty quick. Then I'm laying back, and the sky is traveling away from me in the wrong direction. Mr. Grainier, I'd been shot! Right here!" Peterson pointed to the bandages around his left shoulder and chest. "By my own dog!"

Peterson continued: "I believe he did it because he'd been confabulating with that wolf-girl person. If she is a person. Or I don't know. A creature is what you can call her, if ever she was created. But there are some creatures on this earth that God didn't create."

"Confabulating?"

"Yes. I let that dog in the house one night last summer because he got so yappy and wouldn't quit. I wanted him right by me where I could beat him with a kindling should he irritate me one more time. Well, next morning he got up the wall and out through the window like a bear clawing up a tree, and he started working that porch, back and forth. Then he started working that yard, back and forth, back and forth, and off he goes, and down to the woods, and I didn't see him for thirteen days. All right. All right—Kootenai Bob stopped by the place one day a while after that. Do you know him? His name is Bobcat such and such, Bobcat Ate a Mountain or one of those rooty-toot Indian names. He wants to beg you for a little money, wants a pinch of snuff, little drink of water, stops around twice in every season or so. Tells me—you can guess what: Tells me the wolf-girl has been spotted around. I showed him my dog and says this animal was gone thirteen days and come back just about wild and hardly knew me. Bob looks him in the face, getting down very close, you see, and says, 'I am goddamned if you hadn't better shoot this dog. I can see that girl's picture on the black of this dog's eyes. This dog has been with the wolves, Mr. Peterson. Yes, you better shoot this dog before you get a full moon again, or he'll call that wolf-girl person right into your home, and you'll be meat for wolves, and your blood will be her drink like whiskey.' Do you think I was scared? Well, I was. 'She'll be blood-drunk and running along the roads talking in your own voice, Mr. Peterson,' is what he says to me. 'In your own voice she'll go to the window of every person you did a dirty to, and tell them what you did.' Well, I know about the girl. That wolf-girl was first seen many years back, leading a pack. Stout's cousin visiting from Seattle last Christmas saw her, and he said she had a bloody mess hanging down between her legs."

"A bloody mess?" Grainier asked, terrified in his soul.

"Don't ask me what it was. A bloody mess is all. But Bob the Kootenai feller said some of them want to believe it was the afterbirth or some part of a wolf-child torn out of her womb. You know they believe in Christ."

"What? Who?"

"The Kootenais—in Christ, and angels, devils, and creatures God didn't create, like half-wolves. They believe just about anything funny or witchy or religious they hear about. The Kootenais call animals to be people. 'Coyote-person,' 'Bear-person,' and such a way of talking."

Grainier watched the darkness on the road ahead, afraid of seeing the wolf-girl. "Dear God," he said. "I don't know where I'll get the strength to take this road at night anymore."

"And what do you think?—I can't sleep through the night, myself," Peterson said.

"God'll give me the strength, I guess."

Peterson snorted. "This wolf-girl is a creature God didn't create. She was made out of wolves and a man of unnatural desires. Did you ever get with some boys and jigger yourselves a cow?"

"What!"

"When you was a boy, did you ever get on a stump and love a cow? They all did it over where I'm from. It's not unnatural down around that way."

"Are you saying you could make a baby with a cow, or make a baby with a wolf? You? Me? A person?"

Peterson's voice sounded wet from fear and passion. "I'm saying it gets dark, and the moon gets full, and there's creatures God did not create." He made a strangling sound. "God!—this hole in me hurts when I cough. But I'm glad I don't have to try and sleep through the night, waiting on that wolf-girl and her pack to come after me."

"But did you do like the Indian told you to? Did you shoot your dog?"

"No! *He* shot *me*."

"Oh," Grainier said. Mixed up and afraid, he'd entirely forgotten that part of it. He continued to watch the woods on either side, but that night no spawn of unnatural unions showed herself.

For a while the rumors circulated. The sheriff had examined the few witnesses claiming to have seen the creature and had determined them to be frank and sober men. By their accounts, the sheriff judged her to be a female. People feared she'd whelp more hybrid pups, more wolf-people, more monsters who eventually, logically, would attract the lust of the Devil himself and bring down over the region all manner of evil influence. The Kootenais, wedded as they were known to be to pagan and superstitious practice, would fall prey completely to Satan. Before the matter ended, only fire and blood would purge the valley . . .

But these were the malicious speculations of idle minds, and, when the election season came, the demons of the silver standard and the railroad land-snatch took their attention, and the mysteries in the hills around the Moyea Valley were forgotten for a while.

6.

Not four years after his wedding and already a widower, Grainier lived in his lean-to by the river below the site where his home had been. He kept a campfire going as far as he could into the night and often didn't sleep until dawn. He feared his dreams. At first he dreamed of Gladys and Kate. Then only of Gladys. And finally, by the time he'd passed a couple of months in solitary silence, Grainier dreamed only of his campfire, of tending it just as he had before he slept—the silhouette of his hand and the charred length of lodgepole he used as a poker—and was surprised to find it gray ash and butt-ends in the morning, because he'd watched it burn all night in his dreams.

And three years later still, he lived in his second cabin, precisely where the old one had stood. Now he slept soundly through the nights, and often he dreamed of trains, and often of one particular train: He was on it; he could smell the coal smoke; a world went by. And then he was standing in that world as the sound of the train died away. A frail familiarity in these scenes hinted to him that they came from his childhood. Sometimes he woke to hear the sound of the Spokane International fading up the valley and realized he'd been hearing the locomotive as he dreamed.

Just such a dream woke him in December his second winter at the new cabin. The train passed northward until he couldn't hear it any-more. To be a child again in that other world had terrified him, and he couldn't get back to sleep. He stared around the cabin in the dark. By now he'd roofed his home properly, put in windows, equipped it with two benches, a table, a barrel stove. He and the red dog still bedded on a pallet on the floor, but for the most part he'd made as much a home here as he and Gladys and little Kate had ever enjoyed. Maybe it was his understanding of this fact, right now, in the dark, after his nightmare, that called Gladys back to visit him in spirit form. For many minutes before she showed herself, he felt her moving around the place. He detected her presence as unmistakably as he would have sensed the shape of someone blocking the light through a window, even with his eyes closed.

He put his right hand on the little dog stretched beside him. The dog didn't bark or growl, but he felt the hair on her back rise and stiffen as the visitation began to manifest itself visibly in the room, at first only as a quavering illumination, like that from a guttering candle, and then as the shape of a woman. She shimmered, and her light shook. Around her the shadows trembled. And then it was Gladys—nobody else—flickering and false, like a figure in a motion picture.

Gladys didn't speak, but she broadcast what she was feeling: She mourned for her daughter, whom she couldn't find. Without her baby she couldn't go to sleep in Jesus or rest in Abraham's bosom. Her daughter hadn't come across among the spirits, but lingered here in the world of life, a child alone in the burning forest. But the forest isn't burning, he told her. But Gladys couldn't hear. Before his sight she was living again her last moments: The forest burned, and she had only a minute to gather a few things and her baby and run from the cabin as the fire smoked down the hill. Of what she'd snatched up, less and less seemed worthy, and she tossed away clothes and valuables as the heat drove her toward the river. At the lip of the bluff she held only her Bible and her red box of chocolates, each pinned against her with an elbow, and the baby clutched against her chest with both her hands. She stooped and dropped the candy and the heavy book at her feet while she tied the child inside her apron, and then she was able to pick them up again. Needing a hand to steady her along the rocky bluff as they descended, she tossed away the Bible rather than the chocolates. This uncovering of her indifference to God, the Father of All—this was her undoing. Twenty feet above the water she kicked loose a stone, and not a heartbeat later she'd broken her back on the rocks below. Her legs lost all feeling and wouldn't move. She was only able to pluck at the knot across her bodice until the child was free to crawl away and fend for itself, however briefly, along the shore. The water stroked at Gladys until by the very power of its gentleness, it seemed, it lifted her down and claimed her, and she drowned. One by one from eddy pools and from among the rocks, the baby plucked the scattered chocolates. Eighty-foot-long spruce jutting out over the water burned through and fell into the gorge, their clumps of green needles afire and trailing smoke like pyrotechnical snakes, their flaming tops hissing as they hit the river. Gladys floated past it all, no longer in the water but now overhead, seeing everything in the world. The moss on the shingled roof of her home curled and began to smoke faintly. The logs in the walls stressed and popped like large-bore cartridges going off. On the table by the stove a magazine curled, darkened, flamed, spiraled upward, and flew away page by page, burning and circling. The cabin's one glass window shattered, the curtains began to blacken at the hems, the wax melted off the jars of tomatoes, beans, and Canada cherries on a shelf above the steaming kitchen tub. Suddenly all the lamps in the cabin were lit. On the table a metal-lidded jar of salt exploded, and then the whole structure ignited like a match head.

Gladys had seen all of this, and she made it his to know. She'd lost her future to death, and lost her child to life. Kate had escaped the fire.

Escaped? Grainier didn't understand this news. Had some family downriver rescued his baby daughter? "But I don't see how they could have done, not unbeknownst to anybody. Such a strange and lucky turn would have made a big story for the newspapers—like it made for the Bible, when it happened to Moses."

He was talking out loud. But where was Gladys to hear him? He sensed her presence no more. The cabin was dark. The dog no longer trembled.

7.

Thereafter, Grainier lived in the cabin, even through the winters. By most Januaries, when the snow had deepened, the valley seemed stopped with a perpetual silence, but as a matter of fact it was often filled with the rumble of trains and the choirs of distant wolves and the nearer mad jibbering of coyotes. Also his own howling, as he'd taken it up as a kind of sport.

The spirit form of his departed wife never reappeared to him. At times he dreamed of her, and dreamed also of the loud flames that had taken her. Usually he woke in the middle of this roaring dream to find himself surrounded by the thunder of the Spokane International going up the valley in the night.

But he wasn't just a lone eccentric bachelor who lived in the woods and howled with the wolves. By his own lights, Grainier had amounted to something. He had a business in the hauling.

He was glad he hadn't married another wife, not that one would have been easy to find, but a Kootenai widow might have been willing.

That he'd taken on an acre and a home in the first place he owed to Gladys. He'd felt able to tackle the responsibilities that came with a team and wagon because Gladys stayed in his heart and in his thoughts.

He boarded the mares in town during winters—two elderly logging horses in about the same shape and situation as himself, but smart with the wagon, and more than strong enough. To pay for the outfit he worked in the Washington woods one last summer, very glad to call it his last. Early that season a wild limb knocked his jaw crooked, and he never quite got the left side hooked back properly on its hinge again. It pained him to chew his food, and that accounted more than anything else for his lifelong skinniness. His joints went to pieces. If he reached the wrong way behind him, his right shoulder locked up as dead as a vault door until somebody freed it by putting a foot against his ribs and pulling on his arm. "It takes a great deal of pulling," he'd explain to anyone helping him, closing his eyes and entering a darkness of bone torment, "more than that—pull harder— a great deal of pulling now, greater, greater, you just have to *pull*—" until the big joint unlocked with a sound between a pop and a gulp. His right knee began to wobble sideways out from under him more and more often; it grew dangerous to trust him with the other end of a load. "I'm got so I'm joined up too tricky to pay me," he told his boss one day. He stayed out the job, his only duty tearing down old coolie shacks and salvaging the better lumber, and when that chore was done he went back to Bonners Ferry. He was finished as a woodsman.

He rode the Great Northern to Spokane. With nearly five hundred dollars in his pocket, more than plenty to pay off his team and wagon, he stayed in a room at the Riverside Hotel and visited the county fair, a diversion that lasted only half an hour, because his first decision at the fairgrounds was a wrong one.

In the middle of a field, two men from Alberta had parked an airplane and were offering rides in the sky for four dollars a passenger— quite a hefty asking price, and not many took them up on it. But Grainier had to try. The young pilot—just a kid, twenty or so at the most, a blond boy in a brown oversuit with metal buttons up the front—gave him a pair of goggles to wear and boosted him aboard. "Climb on over. Get something under your butt," the boy said.

Grainier seated himself on a bench behind the pilot's. He was now about six feet off the ground, and already that seemed high enough. The two wings on either side of this device seemed constructed of the frailest stuff. How did it fly when its wings stayed still?—by making its own gale evidently, propelling the air with its propeller, which the other Albertan, the boy's grim father, turned with his hands to get it spinning.

Grainier was aware only of a great astonishment, and then he was high in the sky, while his stomach was somewhere else. It never did catch up with him. He looked down at the fairgrounds as if from a cloud. The earth's surface turned sideways, and he misplaced all sense of up and down. The craft righted itself and began a slow, rackety ascent, winding its way upward like a wagon around a mountain. Except for the churning in his gut, Grainier felt he might be getting accustomed to it all. At this point the pilot looked backward at him, resembling a raccoon in his cap and goggles, shouting and baring his teeth, and then he faced forward. The plane began to plummet like a hawk, steeper and steeper, its engine almost silent, and Grainier's organs pushed back against his spine. He saw the moment with his wife and child as they drank Hood's Sarsaparilla in their little cabin on a summer's night, then another cabin he'd never remembered before, the places of his hidden childhood, a vast golden wheat field, heat shimmering above a road, arms encircling him, and a woman's voice crooning, and all the mysteries of this life were answered. The present world materialized before his eyes as the engine roared and the plane leveled off, circled the fairgrounds once, and returned to earth, landing so abruptly Grainier's throat nearly jumped out of his mouth.

The young pilot helped him overboard. Grainier rolled over the side and slid down the barrel of the fuselage. He tried to steady himself with a hand on a wing, but the wing itself was unsteady. He said, "What was all that durn hollering about?"

"I was telling you, 'This is a nosedive!'"

Grainier shook the fellow's hand, said, "Thank you very much," and left the field.

He sat on the large porch out front of the Riverside Hotel all afternoon until he found an excuse to make his way back up the Panhandle—an excuse in Eddie Sauer, whom he'd known since they were boys in Bonners Ferry and who'd just lost all his summer wages in taverns and bawdy environs and said he'd made up his mind to walk home in shame.

Eddie said, "I was rolled by a whore."

"Rolled! I thought that meant they killed you!"

"No, it don't mean they killed you or anything. I ain't dead. I only wish I was."

Grainier thought Eddie and he must be the same age, but the loose life had put a number of extra years on Eddie. His whiskers were white, and his lips puckered around gums probably nearly toothless. Grainier paid the freight for both of them, and they took the train together to Meadow Creek, where Eddie might get a job on a crew.

After a month on the Meadow Creek rail-and-ties crew, Eddie offered to pay Grainier twenty-five dollars to help him move Claire Thompson, whose husband had passed away the previous summer, from Noxon, Montana, over to Sandpoint, Idaho. Claire herself would pay nothing. Eddie's motives in helping the widow were easily deduced, and he didn't state them. "We'll go by road number 200," he told Grainier, as if there were any other road.

Grainier took his mares and his wagon. Eddie had his sister's husband's Model T Ford. The brother-in-law had cut away the rumble seat and built onto it a flat cargo bed that would have to be loaded judiciously so as not to upend the entire apparatus. Grainier rendezvoused with Eddie early in the morning in Troy, Montana, and headed east to the Bullhead Lake road that would take them south to Noxon, Grainier preceding by half a mile because his horses disliked the automobile, and also seemed to dislike Eddie.

A little German fellow named Heinz ran an automobile filling station on the hill east of Troy, but he, too, had something against Eddie, and refused to sell him gas. Grainier wasn't aware of this problem until Eddie came roaring up behind with his horn squawking and nearly stampeded the horses. "You know, these gals have seen all kinds of commotion," he told Eddie irritably when they'd pulled to the side of the dusty road and he'd walked back to the Ford. "They're used to anything, but they don't like a horn. Don't blast that thing around my mares."

"You'll have to take the wagon back and buy up two or three jugs of fuel," Eddie said. "That old schnitzel-kraut won't even talk to me."

"What'd you do to him?"

"I never did a thing! I swear! He just picks out a few to hate, and I'm on the list."

The old man had a Model T of his own out front of his place. He had its motor's cover hoisted and was half-lost down its throat, it seemed to Grainier, who'd never had much to do with these explosive machines. Grainier asked him, "Do you really know how that motor works inside of there?"

"I know everything." Heinz sputtered and fumed somewhat like an automobile himself, and said, "I'm God!"

Grainier thought about how to answer. Here seemed a conversation that could go no further.

"Then you must know what I'm about to say."

"You want gas for your friend. He's the Devil. You think I sell gas to the Devil?"

"It's me buying it. I'll need fifteen gallons, and jugs for it, too."

"You better give me five dollars."

"I don't mind."

"You're a good fellow," the German said. He was quite a small man. He dragged over a low crate to stand on so he could look straight into Grainier's eyes. "All right. Four dollars."

"You're better off having that feller hate you," Grainier told Eddie when he pulled up next to the Ford with the gasoline in three olive military fuel cans.

"He hates me because his daughter used to whore out of the barbershop in Troy," Eddie said, "and I was one of her happiest customers. She's respectable over in Seattle now," he added, "so why does he hold a grudge?"

They camped overnight in the woods north of Noxon. Grainier

slept late, stretched out comfortably in his empty wagon, until Eddie brought him to attention with his Model T's yodeling horn. Eddie had bathed in the creek. He was going hatless for the first time Grainier ever knew about. His hair was wild and mostly gray and a little of it blond. He'd shaved his face and fixed several nicks with plaster. He wore no collar, but he'd tied his neck with a red and white necktie that dangled clear down to his crotch. His shirt was the same old one from the Saturday Trade or Discard at the Lutheran church, but he'd scrubbed his ugly working boots, and his clean black pants were starched so stiffly his gait seemed to be affected. This sudden attention to terrain so long neglected constituted a disruption in the natural world, about as much as if the Almighty himself had been hit in the head, and Eddie well knew it. He behaved with a cool, contained hysteria.

"Terrence Naples has took a run at Mrs. Widow," he told Grainier, standing at attention in his starched pants and speaking strangely, moving just his lips so as not to disturb the plaster dabs on his facial wounds, "but I told old Terrence it's going to be my chance now with the lady, or I'll knock him around the county on the twenty-four-hour plan. That's right, I had to threaten him. But it's no idle boast. I'll thrub him till his bags bust. I'm too horrible for the young ones, and she's the only go—unless I'd like a Kootenai gal, or I migrate down to Spokane, or go crawling over to Wallace." Wallace, Idaho, was famous for its brothels and for its whores, an occasional one of whom could be had for keeping house with on her retirement. "And I knew old Claire first, before Terrence ever did," he said. "Yes, in my teens I had a short, miserable spell of religion and taught the Sunday school class for tots before services, and she was one of them tots. I think so, anyway. I seem to remember, anyway."

Grainier had known Claire Thompson when she'd been Claire Shook, some years behind him in classes in Bonners Ferry. She'd been a fine young lady whose looks hadn't suffered at all from a little extra weight and her hair's going gray. Claire had worked in Europe as a nurse during the Great War. She'd married quite late and been widowed within a few years. Now she'd sold her home and would rent a house in Sandpoint along the road running up and down the Idaho Panhandle.

The town of Noxon lay on the south side of the Clark Fork River and the widow's house lay on the north, so they didn't get a chance even to stop over at the store for a soda, but pulled up into Claire's front yard and emptied the house and loaded as many of her worldly possessions onto the wagon as the horses would pull, mostly heavy locked trunks, tools, and kitchen gear, heaping the rest aboard the Model T and creating a pile as high up as a man could reach with a hoe, and at the pinnacle two mattresses and two children, also a little dog. By the time Grainier noticed them, the children were too far above him to distinguish their age or sexual type. The work went fast. At noon Claire gave them iced tea and sandwiches of venison and cheese, and they were on the road by one o'clock. The widow herself sat up front next to Eddie with her arm hooked in his, wearing a white scarf over her head and a black dress she must have bought nearly a year ago for mourning, laughing and conversing while her escort tried to steer by one hand. Grainier gave them a good start, but he caught up with them frequently at the top of the long rises, when the auto labored hard and boiled over, Eddie giving it water from gallon jugs the children—boys, it seemed—filled from the river. The caravan moved slowly enough that the children's pup was able to jump down from its perch atop the cargo to chase gophers and nose at their burrows, then clamber up the road bank to a high spot and jump down again between the children, who sat stiff-armed with their feet jutting out in front, hanging onto the tiedowns on either side of them.

At a neighbor's a few hours along they stopped to take on one more item, a two-barreled shotgun Claire Thompson's husband had given as collateral on a loan. Apparently Thompson had failed to pay up, but in honor of his death the neighbor's wife had persuaded her husband to return the old .12 gauge. This Grainier learned after pulling the mares to the side of the road, where they could snatch at grass and guzzle from the neighbor's spring box.

Though Grainier stood very near them, Eddie chose this moment to speak sincerely with the widow. She sat beside him in the auto shaking the gray dust from her head kerchief and wiping her face. "I mean to say," he said—but must have felt this wouldn't do. He opened his door quite suddenly and scrambled out, as flustered as if the auto were sinking in a swamp, and raced around to the passenger's side to stand by the widow.

"The late Mr. Thompson was a fine feller," he told her. He spent a tense minute getting up steam, then went on: "The late Mr. Thompson was a fine feller. Yes."

Claire said, "Yes?"

"Yes. Everybody who knew him tells me he was an excellent feller and also a most . . . excellent feller, you might say. So they say. As far as them who knew him."

"Well, did you know him, Mr. Sauer?"

"Not to talk to. No. He did me a mean bit of business once . . . But he was a fine feller, I'm saying."

"A mean bit of business, Mr. Sauer?"

"He runned over my goat's picket and broke its neck with his wagon! He was a sonofabitch who'd sooner steal than work, wadn't he? But I mean to say! Will you marry a feller?"

"Which feller do you mean?"

Eddie had trouble getting a reply lined up. Meanwhile, Claire opened her door and pushed him aside, climbing out. She turned her back and stood looking studiously at Grainier's horses.

Eddie came over to Grainier and said to him, "Which feller does she *think* I mean? This feller! Me!"

Grainier could only shrug, laugh, shake his head.

Eddie stood three feet behind the widow and addressed the back of her: "The feller I mentioned! The one to marry! I'm the feller!"

She turned, took Eddie by the arm, and guided him back to the Ford. "I don't believe you are," she said. "Not the feller for me." She didn't seem upset anymore.

When they traveled on, she sat next to Grainier in his wagon. Grainier was made desperately uncomfortable because he didn't want to get too near the nose of a sensitive woman like Claire Shook, now Claire Thompson—his clothes stank. He wanted to apologize for it, but couldn't quite. The widow was silent. He felt compelled to converse. "Well," he said.

"Well what?"

"Well," he said, "that's Eddie for you."

"That's not Eddie for *me*," she said.

"I suppose," he said.

"In a civilized place, the widows don't have much to say about who they marry. There's too many running around without husbands. But here on the frontier, we're at a premium. We can take who we want, though it's not such a bargain. The trouble is you men are all worn down pretty early in life. Are you going to marry again?"

"No," he said.

"No. You just don't want to work any harder than you do now. Do you?"

"No, I do not."

"Well then, you aren't going to marry again, not ever."

"I was married before," he said, feeling almost required to defend himself, "and I'm more than satisfied with all of everything's been left to me." He did feel as if he was defending himself. But why should he have to? Why did this woman come at him waving her topic of marriage like a big stick? "If you're prowling for a husband," he said, "I can't think of a bigger mistake to make than to get around me."

"I'm in agreement with you," she said. She didn't seem particularly happy or sad to agree. "I wanted to see if your own impression of you matched up with mine is all, Robert."

"Well, then."

"God needs the hermit in the woods as much as He needs the man in the pulpit. Did you ever think about that?"

"I don't believe I am a hermit," Grainier replied, but when the day was over, he went off asking himself, Am I a hermit? Is this what a hermit is?

Eddie became pals with a Kootenai woman who wore her hair in a mop like a cinema vamp and painted her lips sloppy red. When Grainier first saw them together, he couldn't guess how old she was, but she had brown, wrinkled skin. Somewhere she had come into possession of a pair of hexagonal eyeglasses tinted such a deep blue that behind them her eyes were invisible, and it was by no means certain she could see any objects except in the brightest glare. She must have been easy to get along with, because she never spoke. But whenever Eddie engaged in talk she muttered to herself continually, sighed and grunted, even whistled very softly and tunelessly. Grainier would have figured her for mad if she'd been white.

"She probly don't even speak English," he said aloud, and realized that nobody else was present. He was all alone in his cabin in the woods, talking to himself, startled at his own voice. Even his dog was off wandering and hadn't come back for the night. He stared at the firelight flickering from the gaps in the stove and at the enclosing shifting curtain of utter dark.

8.

Even into his last years, when his arthritis and rheumatism sometimes made simple daily chores nearly impossible and two weeks of winter in the cabin would have killed him, Grainier still spent every summer and fall in his remote home.

By now it no longer astonished him to understand that the valley wouldn't slowly, eventually resume its condition from before the great fire. Though the signs of destruction were fading, it was a very different place now, with different plants and therefore with different animals. The gorgeous spruce had gone. Now came almost exclusively jack pine, which tended to grow up scraggly and mean. He'd been hearing the wolves less and less often, from farther and farther away. The coyotes grew numerous, the rabbits increasingly scarce. From long stretches of the Moyea River through the burn, the trout had gone.

Maybe one or two people wondered what drew him back to this hard-to-reach spot, but Grainier never cared to tell. The truth was he'd vowed to stay, and he'd been shocked into making this vow by something that happened about ten years after the region had burned.

This was in the two or three days after Kootenai Bob had been killed under a train, while his tribe still toured the tracks searching out the bits of him. On these three or four crisp autumn evenings, the Great Northern train blew a series of long ones, sounding off from the Meadow Creek crossing until it was well north, proceeding slowly through the area on orders from the management, who wanted to give the Kootenai tribe a chance to collect what they could of their brother without further disarrangement.

It was mid-November, but it hadn't yet snowed. The moon rose near midnight and hung above Queen Mountain as late as ten in the morning. The days were brief and bright, the nights clear and cold. And yet the nights were full of a raucous hysteria.

These nights, the whistle got the coyotes started, and then the wolves. His companion the red dog was out there, too—Grainier hadn't seen her for days. The chorus seemed the fullest the night the moon came full. Seemed the maddest. The most pitiable.

The wolves and coyotes howled without letup all night, sounding in the hundreds, more than Grainier had ever heard, and maybe other creatures too, owls, eagles—what, exactly, he couldn't guess—surely every single animal with a voice along the peaks and ridges looking down on the Moyea River, as if nothing could ease any of God's beasts. Grainier didn't dare to sleep, feeling it all to be some sort of vast pronouncement, maybe the alarms of the end of the world.

He fed the stove and stood in the cabin's doorway half-dressed and watched the sky. The night was cloudless and the moon was white and burning, erasing the stars and making gray silhouettes of the mountains. A pack of howlers seemed very near, and getting nearer, baying as they ran, perhaps. And suddenly they flooded into the clearing and around it, many forms and shadows, voices screaming, and several brushed past him, touching him where he stood in his doorway, and he could hear their pads thudding on the earth. Before his mind could say "these are wolves come into my yard," they were gone. All but one. And she was the wolf-girl.

Grainier believed he would faint. He gripped the doorjamb to stay on his feet. The creature didn't move, and seemed hurt. The general shape of her impressed him right away that this was a person—a female—a child. She lay on her side panting, a clearly human creature with the delicate structure of a little girl, but she was bent in the arms and legs, he believed, now that he was able to focus on this dim form in the moonlight. With the action of her lungs there came a whistling, a squeak, like a frightened pup's.

Grainier turned convulsively and went to the table looking for—he didn't know. A weapon? He'd never kept a shotgun. Perhaps a piece of kindling to beat at the thing's head. He fumbled at the clutter on the table and located the matches and lit a hurricane lamp and found such a weapon, and then went out again in his long johns, barefoot, lifting the lantern high and holding his club before him, stalked and made nervous by his own monstrous shadow, so huge it filled the whole clearing behind him. Frost had built on the dead grass, and it skirled beneath his feet. If not for this sound he'd have thought himself struck deaf, owing to the magnitude of the surrounding silence. All the night's noises had stopped. The whole valley seemed to reflect his shock. He heard only his footsteps and the wolf-girl's panting complaint.

Her whimpering ceased as he got closer, approaching cautiously so as not to terrify either this creature or himself. The wolf-girl waited, shot full of animal dread and perfectly still, moving nothing but her eyes, following his every move but not meeting his own gaze, and the breath smoking before her nostrils.

The child's eyes sparked greenly in the lamplight like those of any wolf. Her face was that of a wolf, but hairless.

"Kate?" he said. "Is it you?" But it was.

Nothing about her told him that. He simply knew it. This was his daughter.

She stayed stock-still as he drew even closer. He hoped that some sign of recognition might show itself and prove her to be Kate. But her eyes only watched in flat terror, like a wolf's. Still. Still and all. Kate she was, but Kate no longer. Kate-no-longer lay on her side, her left leg akimbo, splintered and bloody bone jutting below the knee; just a child spent from crawling on threes and having dragged the shattered leg behind her. He'd wondered sometimes about little Kate's hair, how it might have looked if she'd lived; but she'd scratched herself nearly bald. It grew out in a few patches.

He came within arm's reach. Kate-no-longer growled, barked, snapped as her father bent down toward her, and then her eyes glassed and she so faded from herself he believed she'd expired at his approach. But she lived, and watched him.

"Kate. Kate. What's happened to you?"

He set down the lamp and club and got his arms beneath her and lifted. Her breathing came rapid, faint, and shallow. She whimpered once in his ear and snapped her jaws but didn't otherwise struggle. He turned with her in his embrace and made for the cabin, now walking away from the lamplight and thus toward his own monstrous shadow as it engulfed his home and shrank magically at his approach. Inside, he laid her on his pallet on the floor. "I'll get the lamp," he told her.

When he came back into the cabin, she was still there. He set the lamp on the table where he could see what he was doing, and prepared to splint the broken leg with kindling, cutting the top of his long johns off himself around the waist, dragging it over his head, tearing it into strips. As soon as he grasped the child's ankle with one hand and put his other on the thigh to pull, she gave a terrible sigh, and then her breathing slowed. She'd fainted. He straightened the leg as best he could and, feeling that he could take his time now, he whittled a stick of kindling so that it cupped the shin. He pulled a bench beside the pallet and sat himself, resting her foot across his knee while he applied the splint and bound it around. "I'm not a doctor," he told her. "I'm just the one that's here." He opened the window across the room to give her air.

She lay there asleep with the life driven half out of her. He watched her a long time. She was as leathery as an old man. Her hands were curled under, the back of her wrists calloused stumps, her feet misshapen, as hard and knotted as wooden burls. What was it about her face that seemed so wolflike, so animal, even in repose? He couldn't say. The face just seemed to have no life behind it when the eyes were closed. As if the creature would have no thoughts other than what it saw.

He moved the bench against the wall, sat back, and dozed. A train going through the valley didn't wake him, but only entered his dream. Later, near daylight, a much smaller sound brought him around. The wolf-girl had stirred. She was leaving.

She leaped out the window.

He stood at the window and watched her in the dawn effulgence, crawling and pausing to twist sideways on herself and snap at the windings on her leg as would any wolf or dog. She was making no great speed and keeping to the path that led to the river. He meant to track her and bring her back, but he never did.

9.

In the hot, rainless summer of 1935, Grainier came into a short season of sensual lust greater than any he'd experienced as a younger man.

In the middle of August it seemed as if a six-week drought would snap; great thunderheads massed over the entire Panhandle and trapped the heat beneath them while the atmosphere dampened and ripened; but it wouldn't rain. Grainier felt made of lead—thick and worthless. And lonely. His little red dog had been gone for years, had grown old and sick and disappeared into the woods to die by herself, and he'd never replaced her. On a Sunday he walked to Meadow Creek and hopped the train into Bonners Ferry. The passengers in the lurching car had propped open the windows, and any lucky enough to sit beside one kept his face to the sodden breeze. The several who got off in Bonners dispersed wordlessly, like beaten prisoners. Grainier made his way toward the county fairgrounds, where a few folks set up shop on Sunday, and where he might find a dog.

Over on Second Street, the Methodist congregation was singing. The town of Bonners made no other sound. Grainier still went to services some rare times, when a trip to town coincided. People spoke nicely to him there, people recognized him from the days when he'd attended almost regularly with Gladys, but he generally regretted going. He very often wept in church. Living up the Moyea with plenty of small chores to distract him, he forgot he was a sad man. When the hymns began, he remembered.

At the fairgrounds he talked to a couple of Kootenais—one a middle-aged squaw, and the other a girl nearly grown. They were dressed to impress somebody, two half-breed witch-women in fringed blue buckskin dresses with headbands dangling feathers of crow, hawk, and eagle. They had a pack of very wolfish pups in a feed sack, and also a bobcat in a willow cage. They took the pups out one at a time to display them. A man was just walking away and saying to them, "That dog-of-wolf will never be Christianized."

"Why is that thing all blue?" Grainier said.

"What thing?"

"That cage you've got that old cat trapped up in."

One of them, the girl, showed a lot of white in her, and had freckles and sand-colored hair. When he looked at these two women, his vitals felt heavy with yearning and fear.

"That's just old paint to keep him from gnawing out. It sickens this old bobcat," the girl said. The cat had big paws with feathery tufts, as if it wore the same kind of boots as its women captors. The older woman had her leg so Grainier could see her calf. She scratched at it, leaving long white rakes on the flesh.

The sight so clouded his mind that he found himself a quarter mile from the fairgrounds before he knew it, without a pup, and having seen before his face, for some long minutes, nothing but those white marks on her dark skin. He knew something bad had happened inside him.

As if his lecherous half-thoughts had blasted away the ground at his feet and thrown him down into a pit of universal sexual mania, he now found that the Rex Theater on Main Street was out of its mind, too. The display out front consisted of a large bill, printed by the local newspaper, screaming of lust:

One Day Only Thursday August 22
The Most Daring Picture of the Year
"Sins Of Love"
Nothing Like It Ever Before!

SEE **Natural Birth**
An Abortion
A Blood Transfusion
A Real Caesarian Operation
IF YOU FAINT EASILY—DON'T COME IN!
TRAINED NURSES AT EACH SHOW

On the Stage—Living Models Featuring

Miss Galveston
Winner of the Famous Pageant of Pulchritude
In Galveston, Texas

No One Under 16 Admitted

Matinee
Ladies Only

Night
Men Only

In Person
Professor Howard Young
Dynamic Lecturer on Sex.
Daring Facts Revealed

The Truth About Love.
Plain Facts About Secret Sins
No Beating About the Bush!

Grainier read the advertisement several times. His throat tightened and his innards began to flutter and sent down his limbs a palsy which, though slight, he felt sure was rocking the entire avenue like a rowboat. He wondered if he'd gone mad and maybe should start visiting an alienist.

Pulchritude!

He felt his way to the nearby railroad platform through a disorienting fog of desire. *The Sins of Love* would come August 22, Thursday. Beside the communicating doors of the passenger-car he rode out of town, there hung a calendar that told him today was Sunday, August 11.

At home, in the woods, the filthiest demons of his nature beset him. In dreams Miss Galveston came to him. He woke up fondling himself. He kept no calendar, but in his very loins he marked the moments until Thursday, August 22. By day he soaked almost hourly in the frigid river, but the nights took him over and over to Galveston.

The dark cloud over the Northwest, boiling like an upside-down ocean, blocked out the sun and moon and stars. It was too hot and muggy to sleep in the cabin. He made a pallet in the yard and spent the nights lying on it naked in an unrelieved blackness.

After many such nights, the cloud broke without rain, the sky cleared, the sun rose on the morning of August 22. He woke up all dewy in the yard, his marrow thick with cold—but when he remembered what day had come, his marrow went up like kerosene jelly, and he blushed so hard his eyes teared and the snot ran from his nose. He began walking immediately in the direction of the road, but turned himself around to wander his patch of land frantically. He couldn't find the gumption to appear in town on this day—to appear even on the road to town for anyone to behold, thickly melting with lust for the Queen of Galveston and desiring to breathe her atmosphere, to inhale the fumes of sex, sin, and pulchritude. It would kill him! Kill him to see it, kill him to be seen! There in the dark theater full of disembodied voices discussing plain facts about secret sins he would die, he would be dragged down to Hell and tortured in his parts eternally before the foul and stinking President of all Pulchritude. Naked, he stood swaying in his yard.

His desires must be completely out of nature; he was the kind of man who might couple with a beast, or—as he'd long ago heard it phrased—jigger himself a cow.

Around behind his cabin he fell on his face, clutching at the brown grass. He lost touch with the world and didn't return to it until the sun came over the house and the heat itched in his hair. He thought a walk would calm his blood, and he dressed himself and headed for the road and over to Placer Creek, several miles, never stopping. He climbed up to Deer Ridge and down the other side and up again into Canuck Basin, hiked for hours without a break, thinking only: Pulchritude! Pulchritude!—Pulchritude will be the damning of me, I'll end up snarfing at it like a dog at a carcass, rolling in it like a dog will, I'll end up all grimed and awful with pulchritude. Oh that Galveston would allow a parade of the stuff! That Galveston would take this harlot of pulchritude and make a queen of her!

At sunset, all progress stopped. He was standing on a cliff. He'd found a back way into a kind of arena enclosing a body of water called Spruce Lake and now looked down on it hundreds of feet below him, its flat surface as still and black as obsidian, engulfed in the shadow of surrounding cliffs, ringed with a double ring of evergreens and reflected evergreens. Beyond, he saw the Canadian Rockies still sunlit, snow peaked, a hundred miles away, as if the earth were in the midst of its creation, the mountains taking their substance out of the clouds. He'd never seen so grand a prospect. The forests that filled his life were so thickly populous and so tall that generally they blocked him from seeing how far away the world was, but right now it seemed clear there were mountains enough for everybody to get his own. The curse had left him, and the contagion of his lust had drifted off and settled into one of those distant valleys.

He made his way carefully down among the boulders of the cliff, reaching the lakeside in darkness, and slept there curled up under a blanket he made out of spruce boughs, on a bed of spruce, exhausted and comfortable. He missed the display of pulchritude at the Rex that night, and never knew whether he'd saved himself or deprived himself.

Grainier stayed at home for two weeks afterward and then went to town again, and did at last get himself a dog, a big male of the far-north sledding type, who was his friend for many years.

Grainier himself lived over eighty years, well into the 1960s. In his time he'd traveled west to within a few dozen miles of the Pacific, though he'd never seen the ocean itself, and as far east as the town of Libby, forty miles inside Montana. He'd had one lover—his wife Gladys—owned one acre of property, two horses, and a wagon. He'd never been drunk. He'd never purchased a firearm or spoken into a telephone. He'd ridden on trains regularly, many times in automobiles, and once on an aircraft. During the last decade of his life he watched television whenever he was in town. He had no idea who his parents might have been, and he left no heirs behind him. Almost everyone in those parts knew Robert Grainier, but when he passed away in his sleep sometime in November of 1968, he lay dead in his cabin through the rest of the fall, and through the winter, and was never missed. A pair of hikers happened on his body in the spring. Next day the two returned with a doctor, who wrote out a certificate of death, and, taking turns with a shovel they found leaning against the cabin, the three of them dug a grave in the yard, and there lies Robert Grainier.

The day he bought the sled dog in Bonners Ferry, Grainier stayed overnight at the house of Dr. Sims, the veterinarian, whose wife took in lodgers. The doctor had come by some tickets to the Rex Theater's current show, a demonstration of the talents of Theodore the Wonder Horse, because he'd examined the star of it—that is, the horse, Theodore—in a professional capacity. Theodore's droppings were bloody, his cowboy master said. This was a bad sign. "Better take this ticket and go wonder at his wonders," the Doctor told Grainier, pressing one of his complimentary passes on the lodger, "because in half a year I wouldn't wonder if he was fed to dogs and rendered down to mucilage."

Grainier sat that night in the darkened Rex Theater amid a crowd of people pretty much like himself—his people, the hard people of the northwestern mountains, most of them quite a bit more impressed with Theodore's master's glittering getup and magical lariat than with Theodore, who showed he could add and subtract by knocking on the stage with his hooves and stood on his hind legs and twirled around and did other things that any of them could have trained a horse to do.

The wonder-horse show that evening in 1935 included a wolf-boy. He wore a mask of fur, and a suit that looked like fur but was really something else. Shining in the electric light, silver and blue, the wolf-boy frolicked and gamboled around the stage in such a way the watchers couldn't be sure if he meant to be laughed at.

They were ready to laugh in order to prove they hadn't been fooled. They had seen and laughed at such as the Magnet Boy and the Chicken Boy, at the Professor of Silly and at jugglers who beat themselves over the head with Indian pins that weren't really made of wood. They had given their money to preachers who had lifted their hearts and baptized scores of them and later rolled around drunk in the Kootenai village and fornicated with squaws. Tonight, faced with the spectacle of this counterfeit monster, they were silent at first. Then a couple made remarks that sounded like questions, and a man in the dark honked like a goose, and people let themselves laugh at the wolf-boy.

But they hushed, all at once and quite abruptly, when he stood utterly still at center stage, his arms straight out from his shoulders, and went rigid, and began to tremble with a massive inner dynamism. Nobody present had ever seen anyone stand so still and yet so strangely mobile. He laid his head back until his scalp contacted his spine, that far back, and opened his throat, and a sound rose in the auditorium like a wind coming from all four directions, low and terrifying, rumbling up from the ground beneath the floor, and it gathered into a roar that sucked at the hearing itself, and coalesced into a voice that penetrated into the sinuses and finally into the very minds of those hearing it, taking itself higher and higher, more and more awful and beautiful, the originating ideal of all such sounds ever made, of the foghorn and the ship's horn, the locomotive's lonesome whistle, of opera singing and the music of flutes and the continuous moan-music of bagpipes. And suddenly it all went black. And that time was gone forever.

Mary Robison

※

Likely Lake

His doorbell rang and Buddy peered through the viewer at a woman in the courtyard. She had green eyes and straight black hair, cut sharply like a fifties Keely Smith. He knew her. She did bookkeeping or something for the law partners next door, especially at tax times. He also remembered her from his wife's yard sale, although that was a couple years ago and the wife was now his ex. She'd bought a jewelry case and a halogen lamp. He could picture her standing on the walk there—her nice legs and the spectator pumps she wore. She'd driven a white VW Bug in those days. But it must have died because later he had noticed her arriving for work in cabs.

He had lent her twenty bucks, in fact. Connie was her name. Last June, maybe, when his garden was at its peak. He'd been out there positioning the sprinkler, first thing in the morning, when a cab swerved up and she was in back. She had rolled down her window and started explaining to him. She was coming in to work early but had ridden the whole way without realizing she'd brought an empty handbag. She *showed* it to him—a beige clutch. She even undid the clasp and held the bag out the window.

Now she waved a twenty as Buddy opened the door.

"That isn't necessary, Connie," he said.

She thanked him with a nod for remembering her name. She said, "Don't give me any argument." She came close and tucked the bill into his shirt pocket. "You see here?" she said. "This is already done."

"Well, I thank you," Buddy said. He stroked the pocket, smoothing the folded money flat. It was a blue cotton shirt he'd put on an hour earlier when he got home from having his hair cut.

She was still close and wearing wonderful perfume, but he didn't think he should remark on that. He kept his eyes level and waited as if she were a customer and he a clerk. He said, "So, are you still in the neighborhood? I rarely see you."

"They haven't needed me." She pretended a pout. "Nobody's needed me." She stepped back. It was the first week of September, still mild. She wore a fitted navy dress with a white collar and had a red cardigan sweater over her arms. Her large shapely legs were in sheer stockings.

"We have one last problem," she said. She held up a finger.

He looked at her, his eyebrows lifted.

Her hand fell and she gazed off and spoke as if reading, as if her words were printed over in the sky there to the right. "I have a crush on you," she said. "Such a crush on you, Buddy. The worst, most ungodly crush."

"No, you don't. You couldn't."

"*The, worst, crush.*"

"Well," Buddy said. "Well dee well-dell-dell."

He owned the house—a two-story, Lowcountry cottage. It was set on a lane that led into Indian Town and beyond that were the roads and highways into north Pennsylvania. He sat on a divan near a window in the living room now and, in the noon light, looked through some magazines and at a book about birds.

He had a view from this window. Behind the house stood a tall ravine and Buddy could see through its vines and trees to the banks of Likely Lake.

His son had died after an accident there. Three years ago, August. Matthew. When he was two days short of turning twenty-one. His Jet Ski had hit a fishing boat that slid out of an inlet. The August after that, Buddy's wife left him.

He had stopped going out—what his therapist referred to as "isolating." He knocked the walls off his son's bedroom suite and off the room where Ruthie used to sew and he converted the whole upper floor into a studio. He began bringing all his assignments home. He was a draftsman, the senior draftsman at Qualitec, a firm of electro-mechanical engineers he had worked with for years.

"Beware of getting out of touch," his therapist had warned. "It happens gradually. It creeps over you by degrees. When you're not in-teracting with people, you start losing the beat. Then blammo. Sud-denly, you're that guy in the yard."

"I'm who?" asked Buddy.

"The guy with the too-short pants," said the therapist.

He would *dissuade* the Connie woman, Buddy told himself now as he poked around in the kitchen. He yanked open a drawer and consid-ered its contents, extracted a vegetable peeler, put it back in its place. He would dissuade her nicely. He didn't want to make her feel like a bug. "Let her down easy," he said aloud and both the cats spurted in to study him. Buddy had never learned to tell the cats apart. They were everyday cats, middle sized and yellow. Matt's girlfriend, Shay, had presented them as kittens, for a birthday present, the same week he died. The cats stayed indoors now and kept close to Buddy. He called one of them Bruce and the other Bruce's Brother.

He went into a utility closet off the kitchen now and rolled out a canister vacuum. He liked vacuuming. He liked jobs he could quickly complete. And he wanted things just-so when Elise came over to-night. She had changed things for him in the months since they had met. Everything was different because of her.

One way to go with the Connie woman, he was thinking, would be to parenthetically mention Elise. That might have its effect. Or a stronger method would be to say, "My girlfriend is the jealous type," or some such.

The cats padded along into the dining area and watched as Buddy positioned the vacuum and unwound its mile of electric cord. "Don't ever touch a plug like this," he told them. "It is hot, hot, hot."

. . .

Elise phoned from work around two. She was a group counselor at Cherry Trees, a psychiatric hospital over in the medical park. Buddy saw his therapist in another building on the grounds and he had met Elise there, in fact, in the parking area. It was on a snowy day last February when he'd forgotten and left his fog lights burning. She had used yellow jumper cables to rescue him. Buddy had invited her to go for coffee and the two of them drove off in his black Mercury, zooming along the Old Post Highway to get the car battery juiced.

They ended up having lunch at a French place, where Elise put on horn-rimmed glasses and read from the menu aloud. Without the glasses, she reminded him of Jean Arthur—her figure, the freckles and bouncy, curly hair. Elise's French was awful and full of oinky sounds but Buddy liked her for trying it anyway. He liked her laugh, which went up and came down.

"Vincent escaped," she said now on the phone. "He broke out somehow. From right in the middle of a Life Challenges Meeting."

"I'm fortunate I don't know what that is," Buddy said.

"The problem for *me* is, with Vincent loose and Security looking for him, I can't take my people outside. Which means no Smoke Walk."

"Right, because you're the only one with a lighter. So that they have to trail along behind you."

"Well they're not dogs. But they're getting mighty grumpy. And being critical of Vincent. They think he should be shot."

"Hard to know whose side to take," said Buddy.

"That it is," Elise said, and told him she had to go.

This flower garden was Buddy's first, but *gorgeous*. He no longer understood people who spoiled and killed plants. The therapist had suggested gardening, so one Saturday when Elise was free, she and Buddy went to Tristie's Arboretum and bought starter materials. She also helped shape the garden. They put in a design like a collar around the court and walk.

Buddy had watered, fed, and misted his flowers. With each day they bloomed, grew large, stood tall. "What more could I ask of you?" he asked them. "Nuts and fruit?"

He thought he might recruit Elise to help lay in winter pansies around the side porch if that didn't seem boring. She was good at a hundred things. She could play bridge and poker and shuffle cards. She could play the piano. She liked listening to jazz and she *knew* most of it. They'd dress up and go dancing at Sky Mountain or at the Allegheny Club where there was an orchestra. Elise had beautiful evening clothes. She'd take him to all kinds of things—to midnight movies or a raunchy comedy club. Last spring they'd even taken a train trip to New Orleans for Jazz Fest.

From close by, Buddy heard a woman's voice and froze. It might be Connie's. He didn't feel up to another encounter with her, just yet. She seemed interesting and he liked her. She certainly was a handsome woman. She had mentioned peeking out her office window, how she always found herself watching for him. That was flattering, but still. He'd felt jarred by it. What if he were just out on some stupid errand, grabbing the paper or the mail out of the box, if he hadn't shaved or his shirt was on sideways?

The voice came a second time. It was *not* Connie's. However, the next one might be, he warned himself. He shook off his gloves and poked his tools back in their wire caddy. It was four something. She probably got off work pretty soon.

As he scrubbed his hands, he rehearsed telling Elise the Connie story. Elise was coming over for dinner after she finished her shift.

He started organizing the food he had bought earlier at the farmer's market. He got out a lemon and some lettuce in cello wrap, a net bag of radishes, a plum tomato. He heaped what he wanted of that into a wooden bowl; returned to the refrigerator and ripped a few sprigs of parsley. "Less like a picnic," he said to himself. He arranged a serving plate with slices of honey-baked ham; another with deviled egg halves and used the parsley for garnish. He knew he was not a great cook. With the exception of the jumbo shrimp he had grilled for Elise and her mom on July 4th. Those were delicious.

He carried the serving dishes into the dining room. It was too *soon* but he wanted to try the food to see how it looked set on the table. He got out a big linen tablecloth, gripped it by the ends, and flapped it hugely in the air to wave out the folds.

The cats somersaulted in. They leapt onto the sideboard. They stood poised and still and gazed at the platter of ham.

"Scary monster," Buddy told them, but sighed and dropped the tablecloth. He marched the ham back to the kitchen and hid it deep inside the refrigerator.

Elise knew a lot, in his opinion. She'd earned a degree in social psych and she was popular with the patients at Cherry Trees. Maybe he would skip complaining to her about Connie. That could only cause worry. He should be more circumspect. Why bother Elise?

He did call, but merely to ask how she was doing and to confirm their dinner plans. "I don't want anything," he said when she came to the phone.

"They sent Martha to the Time Out Room," Elise said. "The woman admitted last Saturday? You should see her now, though. Calm and quiet. Like she's had some realizations. Or been given back her doll."

"Who else is in your group?" Buddy asked. "I know you've told me."

"Well, it's evil and immoral that I did and I'll probably roast in hell for it. Donna, with the mysterious migraines. She's been here the longest. Next is Lorraine, the obsessive one who bought a hundred clear plastic tote bags. Barry, the ER nurse. He's tired, is all that's wrong with that man. And there's Doug, the Pilot Error guy. Martha. Vincent. Oh, and the new girl. I love her! She reminds me of somebody. Kim Novak maybe."

"Then I love her too," Buddy said.

"Or she's one of the Gabors. With her collar turned up? Always dancing and singing with a scarf tied on her wrist, like this is a musical. I have to go, Buddy."

"I know you do," he said. "How'd they make out with Vincent? They captured him yet?"

"No, unfortunately. But he has been seen." She said, "Well, of course, he's been seen! At practically every patient's window. And in their closets. Or he's standing right beside them in the mirror."

"Don't make jokes," Buddy said.

"No, I have to," said Elise, and she clicked off.

Buddy had the dinner table all prepared and he wanted to start the candles. He had read on the carton that the wicks would flame more evenly if lighted once in advance. He went hunting for stick matches, which weren't where they were supposed to be, in the cabinet over the stove. The sun was going down, and he glanced through the sliding glass doors to the side porch. Connie was here, sitting in the swing, mechanically rocking an end of it. She held a cigarette and was staring ardently at the floor.

Buddy forgot himself for a second. He wasn't sure what to do. He crept out of the room, turned around and came back.

"Nine one one," he said to the cats before he slid the door and took himself outside.

"So, what's shaking?" he asked. He made an unconcerned walk across the porch and to the railing. Half the sky had grown purple. There were red clouds twisted like a rope above the lake.

Connie went on gazing at the floorboards but stopped the swing with the heels of her shoes. They were snakeskin or lizard, very dark maroon. "Don't be mad," she said.

"I'm not," said Buddy.

"I like to sit in strange places, don't you? Especially if it's someone else's place. I play a little game of seeing what effect it has on them."

The curve of her throat when she looked up now was lovely. That surprised Buddy out of making a comment on the game.

"I wonder if it's ever occurred to you," she said. "These past two summers. The drought, right? You've heard about it on the news. You probably aren't aware that I live in Langley. My father and I. You always hear it called 'Scrap Pile' but it's Langley. It is poor and it's all wrecked. Of course, my father didn't guess that would *happen* when he inherited our house. This is only about eight miles—"

"Isn't that . . . Crabapple?" Buddy asked.

"No, it isn't. Crabapple's about twelve miles. Or was, it hardly exists anymore. But you wouldn't go there, so that's part of my point."

Buddy shuffled over and lowered next to her in the swing.

"When I'm coming to work?" She spoke straight into his face. "It gets greener. And greener. Until it's this lush—I don't know what. There's no drought here. You folks don't have a drought."

Buddy was nodding slowly. "I'm ashamed to admit it . . ."

Connie exhaled smoke and now rearranged something in herself, as if she were closing one folder and opening the next. "I feel very embarrassed. About the confession I made to you earlier," she said.

"Oh," he said and laughed once. "It's not like I could mind."

"Horseshit." She rose in her seat and flicked her cigarette expertly across the porch into a huddle of savanna shrubs.

"Connie, my girlfriend is a counselor over at Cherry Trees."

"What about it?" she asked and Buddy winced.

"Sorry," he said, as they both nodded and shrugged.

"You people." Her hand worked in the air. She clutched at nothing, let it go.

She said, "I am happy about this much. I've finally been at my job long enough that I've earned some time off for the things I enjoy. Such as travel."

"Where to?" Buddy asked.

"I'm thinking Belize," Connie said, and after a moment, "I've heard you don't really go anywhere. Mr. Secrest or someone said. No, it was he. He knew your wife. He said you hardly ever go out since your son died."

"That's mostly correct."

She said, "I didn't mean it as a criticism."

The phone began ringing and—certain the caller was Elise—Buddy apologized, scooted off the swing and hurried inside.

"I'll never get out of here," Elise said. "I know it ruins our plans. There's no alternative."

"It doesn't matter. We'll do it tomorrow."

"Everyone's so spooked. I wouldn't dare leave. And the nurses have them so doped up on sedatives. You should see this, Buddy. They could *hurt* themselves. It's like they're walking on shipboard."

He was smiling.

"It's because we're now told that Vincent is inside the hospital. So there's an all-out search," she said. "Anyway, I did one thing. I raced over to Blockbuster and rented them a movie—*The Matrix* is what they voted for. That is helping. It's got them focused. All in their pajamas, all in the Tomorrow Room with their bed pillows, doubled up on the couches and lying over chairs."

"*I* want to do that. That's sounds great!"

"No, you're not invited," said Elise.

She giggled at something on her end and said to Buddy, "You remember how I said they're always nicknaming the psychiatrists? I just heard, 'Here comes Dr. Post-It Note accompanying Drs. Liar and Deaf.'"

"My therapist looks like Al Haig."

"See, that's what I mean. That's why you don't belong here," Elise said.

"I'll call you later on," she told him.

From where he stood, he'd been viewing his dining-room setup. His table had crystal, candlesticks, and thirty red chrysanthemums in a vase. He hadn't realized, until the line went dead, how very sharp was his disappointment.

He had stepped down off the porch to inspect the walkway where a couple slate tiles had strayed out of line. He was stooped over, prompting a piece back into place with his shoe. Here were weeds. Here were ants, too, crawling in a long contorted file.

Connie watched him, smoking hard and unhappily, still in the swing. "I need to say a few things. About my feelings," she said.

He stuffed his hands in his pockets and rejoined her on the porch. He leaned on the far railing, facing her. They were quiet a moment. "I'm sorry. I'm an oaf," he said.

She answered that silently and with a brief, sarcastic smile.

He said, "I do want to hear."

She looked at the ceiling.

"Okay, I probably just don't understand then, Connie." He

brought his hands from his pockets, bunched his fingers, and consulted them. "Is it that you have a kind of *fantasy* about me?"

"God, no!" she said and clicked her tongue. "It's actually a little more adult than that." She pronounced the word "*aah*—dult."

Her smile grew reproachful. "So you know all about my feelings."

"Oh, I don't think that."

She said, "Since you're Mister Perfect." She began fussing with the cultured pearl in her ear. "Bet you wish I'd kept my feelings to my own fuckin' self."

It was one of the unhappiest conversations Buddy could recall. "I really don't think any of that," he said.

Connie's long legs were folded now with her feet tucked to the side. She had the grace of someone who had been an athlete or a dancer. And she used her hands prettily, holding one in the other or touching the prim white collar on her dress. Her hair was fascinating—a gleaming black. But there was sorrow in her eyes, or so Buddy thought. They moved slowly, when they did move. Her gaze seldom shifted. Her eyes were heavy, and gave an impression of defeat.

He was thinking, patting his fingertips. He said, "I'll tell you a few things about myself. The morning Matt died, by the time I arrived at the ICU and could locate Ruthie, my wife, she was standing with her face to a wall, clenching her diaphragm like she'd run a marathon and couldn't breathe. So I tiptoed over and tapped her on the shoulder to show I was there. Only she didn't feel it or was too distressed. At any rate, she didn't acknowledge. I wasn't sure. I just stayed there waiting. Until, when she finally did turn, she looked straight through me. So, what I did? I gave her this huge *tick-tock* wave. Like, hidee-ho."

He smoothed his hair a few times. "How much have I thought about that! It was just a bad moment probably, a slipup, but it might've paved the way for this second thing, a situation I found myself in."

He said, "My son was riding his Jet Ski, I don't know what you heard about it."

Connie's head moved, no.

Buddy's head nodded. "On the lake. He crashed into a fishing boat that had a couple of high-school boys. No one else was killed but damn near. I found it hard. Hard to stop picturing. Then this urge came that if I could talk to someone I didn't know very well. Have a plain conversation with no mention of my son. So, for some reason I chose a woman who's the floor rep at Zack's Print Shop. We'd exchanged a few words. I doubt if she remembered my name. I gave her some information, the first call. I told her their sign—for the rear parking whatchumajiggy—had fallen down. Then I started calling with everything you could name—a TV contest, or foreseeing a weather problem. Or call and make some joke about Zack. Ten, fifteen times a day. Sitting in a spindly chair there with the phone, not even comfortable. And my poor wife, having to overhear all of this, was just beside herself. As to why I kept harassing this woman. Who, finally, when it got too much, went downtown and filed a restraining order."

"Man!" Connie said.

"She did indeed," said Buddy.

He got up. The cats were yowling and hopping at the glass door. "I have to stop for a second and give them dinner. I'll be right back."

"Go," Connie said, "go," and signaled with a flick of her hand that she understood.

While he was filling the dish with Science Diet, he had caught her figure in the shadows, descending the porch stairs.

Buddy rocked on his shoes. A light switched on at the lawyers' place next door.

He watched as the cats chowed. He refreshed their water.

He stood in the center of the kitchen and waited, without going to a window, for the effect of a taxicab's headlights out on the lane.

It was quiet where Elise was. She almost had to whisper. "This is eerie. All the patients' colored faces in the TV light? It's despicable that I'm always canceling on you. It's the worst thing I do. It's what destroyed every relationship I've had."

"Oh God, let that be true," Buddy said.

He was flicking a stub of paper around on the countertop, to no end. "Are you ever nervous around me?" he asked Elise.

"What?"

"Nervous *about* me, I mean. Because of the way I bothered that woman."

"Don't insult me," Elise said.

"Excuse me?"

"I'm a smart person. One of the smart ones. They insisted on textbooks where I went to school."

"Oh," he said.

There was a pause between them. Buddy paced up and back a step, holding the phone. The room was overly warm and the cats had taken to the cool of the floor tiles.

"I should go," Elise said. "I really have to pee. Plus they're right now carrying Vincent in on a stretcher. Directed towards the Time Out Room is my guess. Will you be okay? Do you feel okay?"

"Maybe I'll just keep that to my own fucking *self*," he said and grinned. "It's a joke you don't know. I'm sorry. I'll explain it to you some other time."

"They don't need me that bad. I'm free to talk," Elise said.

"No, I feel fine. The joke isn't even about me." His index finger traced around and around one of the blue tiles set in the countertop.

"Listen to me a second," she said. "Are you there? This is the last thing I want to say before I have to hang up. Grief is very mysterious, Buddy. It's very personal."

"Bye for now," she said, and Buddy stayed a moment after he'd closed the phone, his hand on the receiver, his arm outstretched.

He stood on the side porch. The night was warm and a full white moon dawdled over Likely Lake.

Across the lane at the Tishman's a car was adjusting behind a line of cars—latecomers for the bridge party Carl and Suzanne hosted every other week. One of them or somebody appeared in the entryway, there to welcome in the tardy guest.

Buddy was thinking about other nights, when he and Elise had sat out here until late, telling each other stories and drinking rum. On his birthday, she had worn a sequined red dress. There were nights with his wife, their last sad year.

How silly, he thought, that Connie's confession had bothered him. He should have absorbed it. He should have taken her hand and held her hand, as a friend, or even clenched it, and said what a very long life it can seem.

Charles Baxter

✠

Westland

Saturday morning at the zoo, facing the lions' cage, overcast sky and a light breeze carrying the smell of peanuts and animal dung, the peacocks making their stilted progress across the sidewalks. I was standing in front of the gorge separating the human viewers from the lions. The lions weren't caged, exactly; they just weren't free to go. One male and one female were slumbering on fake rock ledges. Raw meat was nearby. My hands were in my pockets and I was waiting for a moment of energy so I could leave and do my Saturday morning errands. Then this girl, this teenager, appeared from behind me, hands in *her* pockets, and she stopped a few feet away on my right. In an up-all-night voice, she said, "What would you do if I shot that lion?" She nodded her head: she meant the male, the closer one.

"Shot it?"

"That's right."

"I don't know." Sometimes you have to humor people, pretend as if they're talking about something real. "Do you have a gun?"

"Of course I have a gun." She wore a protective blankness on her thin face. She was fixed on the lion. "I have it here in my pocket."

"I'd report you," I said. "I'd try to stop you. There are guards here. People don't shoot caged animals. You shouldn't even carry a concealed weapon, a girl your age."

"This is Detroit," she explained.

"I know it is," I said. "But people don't shoot caged lions in Detroit or anywhere else."

"It wouldn't be that bad," she said, nodding at the lions again. "You can tell from their faces how much they want to check out."

I said I didn't think so.

She turned to look at me. Her skin was so pale it seemed bleached, and she was wearing a vaudeville-length overcoat and a pair of hightop tennis shoes and jeans with slits at the knees. She looked like a fifteen-year-old bag lady. "It's because you're a disconnected person that you can't see it," she said. She shivered and reached into her pocket and pulled out a crumpled pack of cigarettes. "Lions are so human. Things get to them. They experience everything more than we do. They're romantic." She glanced at her crushed pack of cigarettes, and in a shivering motion she tossed it into the gorge. She swayed back and forth. "They want to kill and feast and feel," she said.

I looked at this girl's bleached skin, that candy bar and cola complexion, and I said, "Are you all right?"

"I slept here last night," she said. She pointed vaguely behind her. "I was sleeping over there. Under those trees. Near the polar bears."

"Why'd you do that?"

"I wasn't alone *all* night." She was answering a question I hadn't asked. "This guy, he came in with me for awhile to be nice and amorous but he couldn't see the point in staying. He split around midnight. He said it was righteous coming in here and being solid with the animal world, but he said you had to know when to stop. I told him I wouldn't defend him to his friends if he left, and he left, so as far as I'm concerned, he is over, he is zippo."

She was really shivering now, and she was huddling inside that long overcoat. I don't like to help strangers, but she needed help. "Are you hungry?" I asked. "You want a hamburger?"

"I'll eat it," she said, "but only if you buy it."

I took her to a fast-food restaurant and sat her down and brought her one of their famous giant cheeseburgers. She held it in her hands familiarly as she watched the cars passing on Woodward Avenue. I let my gaze follow hers, and when I looked back, half the cheeseburger was gone. She wasn't even chewing. She didn't look at the food. She ate like a soldier in a foxhole. What was left of her food she gripped in her skinny fingers decorated with flaking pink nail polish. She was pretty in a raw and sloppy way.

"You're looking at me."

"Yes, I am," I admitted.

"How come?"

"A person can look," I said.

"Maybe." Now she looked back. "Are you one of those creeps?"

"Which kind?"

"The kind of old man creep who picks up girls and drives them places, and, like, terrorizes them for days and then dumps them into fields."

"No," I said. "I'm not like that. And I'm not that old."

"Maybe it's the accent," she said. "You don't sound American."

"I was born in England," I told her, "but I've been in this country for thirty years. I'm an American citizen."

"You've got to be born in this country to sound American," she said, sucking at her chocolate shake through her straw. She was still gazing at the traffic. Looking at traffic seemed to restore her peace of mind. "I guess you're okay," she said distantly, "and I'm not worried anyhow, because, like I told you, I've got a gun."

"Oh yeah," I said.

"You're not a real American because you don't *believe*!" Then this child fumbled in her coat pocket and clunked down a small shiny handgun on the table, next to the plastic containers and the french fries. "So there," she said.

"Put it back," I told her. "Jesus, I hope the safety's on."

"I think so." She wiped her hand on a napkin and dropped the thing back into her pocket. "So tell me your name, Mr. Samaritan."

"Warren," I said. "My name's Warren. What's yours?"

"I'm Jaynee. What do you do, Warren? You must do something. You look like someone who does something."

I explained to her about governmental funding for social work and therapy, but her eyes glazed and she cut me off.

"Oh yeah," she said, chewing her french fries with her mouth open so that you could see inside if you wanted to. "One of those professional friends. I've seen people like you."

I drove her home. She admired the tape machine in the car and the carpeting on the floor. She gave me directions on how to get to her house in Westland, one of the suburbs. Detroit has four shopping centers at its cardinal points: Westland, Eastland, Southland, and Northland. A town grew up around Westland, a blue collar area, and now Westland is the name of both the shopping center and the town.

She took me down fast food alley and then through a series of right and left ninety-degree turns on streets with bungalows covered by aluminum siding. Few trees, not much green except the lawns, and the half-sun dropped onto those perpendicular lines with nothing to stop it or get in its way. The girl, Jaynee, picked at her knees and nodded, as if any one of the houses would do. The houses all looked exposed to me, with a straight shot at the elements out there on that flat grid.

I was going to drop her off at what she said was her driveway, but there was an old chrome-loaded Pontiac in the way, one of those vintage 1950s cars, its front end up on a hoist and some man working on his back on a rolling dolly underneath it. "That's him," the girl said. "You want to meet him?"

I parked the car and got out. The man pulled himself away from underneath the car and looked over at us. He stood up, wiping his hands on a rag, and scowled at his daughter. He wasn't going to look at me right away. I think he was checking Jaynee for signs of damage.

"What's this?" he asked. "What's this about, Jaynee?"

"This is about nothing," she said. "I spent the night in the zoo and this person found me and brought me home."

"At the zoo. Jesus Christ. At the zoo. Is that what happened?" He was asking me.

"That's where I saw her," I told him. "She looked pretty cold."

He dropped a screwdriver I hadn't noticed he was holding. He was standing there in his driveway next to the Pontiac, looking at his daughter and me and then at the sky. I'd had those moments, too, when nothing made any sense and I didn't know where my responsibilities lay. "Go inside," he told his daughter. "Take a shower. I'm not talking to you here on the driveway. I know that."

We both watched her go into the house. She looked like an overcoat with legs. I felt ashamed of myself for thinking of her that way, but there are some ideas you can't prevent.

We were both watching her, and the man said, "You can't go to the public library and find out how to raise a girl like that." He said something else, but an airplane passed so low above us that I couldn't hear him. We were about three miles from the airport. He ended his speech by saying, "I don't know who's right."

"I don't either."

"Earl Lampson." He held out his hand. I shook it and took away a feel of bone and grease and flesh. I could see a fading tattoo on his forearm of a rose run through with a sword.

"Warren Banks," I said. "I guess I'll have to be going."

"Wait a minute, Warren. Let me do two things. First, let me thank you for bringing my daughter home. Unhurt." I nodded to show I understood. "Second. A question. You got any kids?"

"Two," I said. "Both boys."

"Then you know about it. You know what a child can do to you. I was awake last night. I didn't know what had happened to her. I didn't know if she had planned it. That was the worst. She makes plans. Jesus Christ. The zoo. The lions?"

I nodded.

"She'll do anything. And it isn't an act with her." He looked up and down the street, as if he were waiting for something to appear, and I had the wild idea that I was going to see a float coming our way, with beauty queens on it, and little men dressed up in costumes.

I told him I had to leave. He shook his head.

"Stay a minute, Warren," he said. "Come into the backyard. I want to show you something."

He turned around and walked through the garage, past a pile of snow tires and two rusted-out bicycles. I followed him, thinking of my boys this morning at their scout meeting, and of my wife, out shopping or maybe home by now and wondering vaguely where I was. I was supposed to be getting groceries. Here I was in this garage. She would look at the clock, do something else, then look back at the clock.

"Now how about this?" Earl pointed an index finger toward a wooden construction that stood in the middle of his yard, running from one side to another: a play structure, with monkey bars and a swing set, a high perch like a ship's crow's nest, a set of tunnels to crawl through and climb on, and a little rope bridge between two towers. I had never seen anything like it, so much human effort expended on a backyard toy, this huge contraption.

I whistled. "It must have taken you years."

"Eighteen months," he said. "And she hasn't played on it since she was twelve." He shook his head. "I bought the wood and put it together piece by piece. She was only three years old when I did it, weekends when I wasn't doing overtime at Ford's. She was my assistant. She'd bring me nails. I told her to hold the hammer when I wasn't using it, and she'd stand there, real serious, just holding the hammer. Of course now she's too old for it. I have the biggest backyard toy in Michigan and a daughter who goes off to the zoo and spends the night there and that's her idea of a good time."

A light rain had started to fall. "What are you going to do with this thing?" I asked.

"Take it apart, I guess." He glanced at the sky. "Warren, you want a beer?"

It was eleven o'clock in the morning. "Sure," I said.

We sat in silence on his cluttered back porch. We sipped our beers and watched the rain fall over things in our line of sight. Neither of us was saying much. It was better being there than being at home, and my morning gloom was on its way out. It wasn't lifting so much as converting into something else, as it does when you're in someone else's house. I didn't want to move as long as I felt that way.

I had been in the zoo that morning because I had been reading the newspaper again, and this time I had read about a uranium plant here in Michigan whose employees were spraying pastureland with a fertilizer recycled from radioactive wastes. They called it treated raffinate. The paper said that in addition to trace amounts of radium and radioactive thorium, this fertilizer spray had at least eighteen poisonous heavy metals in it, including molybdenum, arsenic, and lead. It had been sprayed out into the pastures and was going into the food supply. I was supposed to get up from the table and go out and get the groceries, but I had gone to the zoo instead to stare at the animals. This had been happening more often lately. I couldn't keep my mind on ordinary, daily things. I had come to believe that depression was the realism of the future, and phobias a sign of sanity. I was supposed to know better, but I didn't.

I had felt crazy and helpless, but there, on Earl Lampson's porch, I was feeling a little better. Calm strangers sometimes have that effect on you.

Jaynee came out just then. She'd been in the shower, and I could see why some kid might want to spend a night in the zoo with her. She was in a tee-shirt and jeans, and the hot water had perked her up. I stood and excused myself. I couldn't stand to see her just then, breaking my mood. Earl went to a standing position and shook my hand and said he appreciated what I had done for his daughter. I said it was nothing and started to leave when Earl, for no reason that I could see, suddenly said he'd be calling me during the week, if that was all right. I told him that I would be happy to hear from him.

Walking away from there, I decided, on the evidence so far, that Earl had a good heart and didn't know what to do with it, just as he didn't know what to do with that thing in his backyard. He just had it, and it was no use to him.

He called my office on Wednesday. I'd given him the number. There was something new in his voice, of someone wanting help. He repeated his daughter's line about how I was a professional friend, and I said, yes, sometimes that was what I was. He asked me if I ever worked with "bad kids"—that was his phrase—and I said that sometimes I did. Then he asked me if I'd help him take apart his daughter's play structure on the following Saturday. He said there'd be plenty of beer. I could see what he was after: a bit of free counseling, but since I hadn't prepared myself for his invitation, I didn't have a good defense ready. I looked around my office cubicle, and I saw myself in Earl's backyard, a screwdriver in one hand and a beer in the other. I said yes.

The day I came over, it was a fair morning, for Michigan. This state is like Holland, and nothing drains out of it, resulting in cold clammy mists mixed with freezing rain in autumn, and hard rains in the spring broken by tropical heat and tornadoes. It's attack weather. The sky covers you over with a metallic blue, watercolor wash over tin foil. But this day was all right. I worked out there with Earl, pulling the wood apart with our crowbars and screwdrivers, and we had an audience, Jaynee and Earl's new woman. That was how she was introduced to me: Jody. She's the new woman. She didn't seem to have more than about eight or nine years on Jaynee, and she was nearsighted. She had those thick corrective lenses. But she was pretty in the details, and when she looked at Earl, the lenses enlarged those eyes, so that the love was large and naked and obvious.

I was pulling down a support bar for the north end of the structure and observing from time to time the neighboring backyards. My boys had gone off to a scout meeting again, and my wife was busy, catching up on some office work. No one missed me. I was pulling at the wood, enjoying myself, talking to Earl and Jaynee and Jody about some of the techniques people in my profession use to resolve bad family quarrels; Jaynee and Jody were working at pulling down some of the wood, too. We already had two piles of scrap lumber.

I had heard a little of how Earl raised Jaynee. Her mother had taken off, the way they sometimes do, when Jaynee was three years old. He'd done the parental work. "You've been the dad, haven't you, Earl?" Jody said, bumping her hip at him. She sat down to watch a sparrow. Her hair was in a ponytail, one of those feminine brooms. "Earl doesn't know the first thing about being a woman, and he had to teach it all to Jaynee here." Jody pointed her cigarette at Jaynee.

"Well, she learned it from somewhere. There's not much left she doesn't know."

"Where's the mystery?" Jaynee asked. She was pounding a hammer absentmindedly into a piece of wood lying flat on the ground. "It's easier being a woman than a girl. Men treat you better 'cause they want you."

Earl stopped turning his wrench. "Only if you don't go to the zoo anytime some punk asks you."

"That was once," she said.

Earl aimed himself at me. "I was strict with her. She knows about the laws I laid down. Fourteen laws. They're framed in her bedroom. Nobody in this country knows what it is to be decent anymore, but I'm trying. It sure to hell isn't easy."

Jody smiled at me. "Earl restrained himself until I came along." She laughed. Earl turned away, so I wouldn't see his face.

"I only spent the night in the zoo *once*," Jaynee repeated, as if no one had been listening. "And besides, I was protected."

"Protected," Earl repeated, staring at her.

"You know." Jaynee pointed her index finger at her father with her thumb in the air and the other fingers pulled back, and she made an explosive sound in her mouth.

"You took that?" her father said. "You took that to the zoo?"

Jaynee shrugged. At this particular moment, Earl turned to me. "Warren, did you see it?"

I assumed he meant the gun. I looked over toward him from the bolt I was unscrewing, and I nodded. I was so involved in the work of this job that I didn't want my peaceful laboring disturbed.

"You shouldn't have said that," Jody said to Jaynee. Earl had disappeared inside the house. "You know your father well enough by now to know that." Jody stood up and walked to the yard's back fence. "Your father thinks that women and guns are a terrible combination."

"He always said I should watch out for myself," Jaynee said, her back to us. She pulled a cookie out of her pocket and began to eat it.

"Not with a gun," Jody said.

"He showed me how to use it," the daughter said loudly. "I'm not ignorant about firearms." She didn't seem especially interested in the way the conversation was going.

"That was just information," Jody said. "It wasn't for you to use." She was standing and waiting for Earl to reappear. I didn't do work like this, and I didn't hear conversations like this during the rest of the week, and so I was the only person still dismantling the play structure when Earl reappeared in the backyard with the revolver in his right hand. He had his shirt sleeve pulled back so anybody could see the tattoo of the rose run through with the sabre on his forearm. Because I didn't know what he was going to do with that gun, I thought I had just better continue to work.

"The ninth law in your bedroom," Earl announced, "says you use violence only in self-defense." He stepped to the fence, then held his arm straight up into the air and fired once. That sound, that shattering, made me drop my wrench. It hit the ground with a clank, three inches from my right foot. Through all the backyards of Westland I heard the blast echoing. The neighborhood dogs set up a barking chain; front and back doors slammed.

Earl was breathing hard and staring at his daughter. We were in a valley, I thought, of distinct silence. "That's all the bullets I own for that weapon," he said. He put the gun on the doorstep. Then he made his way over to where his daughter was sitting. There's a kind of walk, a little stiff, where you know every step has been thought about, every step is a decision. This was like that.

Jaynee was munching the last of her cookie. Her father grabbed her by the shoulders and began to shake her. It was like what you see in movies, someone waking up a sleepwalker. Back and forth, her head tossed. "Never never never never never," he said. I started to laugh, but it was too crazed and despairing to be funny. He stopped. I could see he wanted to make a parental speech: his face was tightening up, his flesh stiff, but he didn't know how to start it, the right choice for the first word, and his daughter pushed him away and ran into the house. In that run, something happened to me, and I knew I had to get out of there.

I glanced at Jody, the new woman. She stood with her hands in her blue jeans. She looked bored. She had lived here all her life. What had just happened was a disturbance in the morning's activities. Meanwhile, Earl had picked up a board and was tentatively beating the ground with it. He was staring at the revolver on the steps. "I got to take that gun and throw it into Ford Lake," he said. "First thing I do this afternoon."

"Have to go, Earl," I said. Everything about me was getting just a little bit out of control, and I thought I had better get home.

"You're going?" Earl said, trying to concentrate on me for a moment. "You're going now? You're sure you don't want another beer?"

I said I was sure. The new woman, Jody, went over to Earl and whispered something to him. I couldn't see why, right now, out loud, she couldn't say what she wanted to say. Christ, we were all adults, after all.

"She wants you to take that .22 and throw it," Earl said. He went over to the steps, picked up the gun, and returned to where I was standing. He dropped it into my hand. The barrel was warm, and the whole apparatus smelled of cordite.

"Okay, Earl," I said. I held this heavy object in my hand, and I had the insane idea that my life was just beginning. "You have any particular preference about where I should dispose of it?"

He looked at me, his right eyebrow going up. This kind of diction he hadn't heard from me before. "Particular preference?" He laughed without smiling. "Last I heard," he said, "when you throw a gun out, it doesn't matter where it goes so long as it's gone."

"Gotcha," I said. I was going around to the front of the house. "Be in touch, right?"

Those two were back to themselves again, talking. They'd be interested in saying goodbye to me about two hours from now, when they would notice that I wasn't there.

In the story that would end here, I go out to Belle Isle in the city of Detroit and drop Earl's revolver off the Belle Isle Bridge at the exact moment when no one is looking. But this story has a way to go. That's not what I did. To start with, I drove around with that gun in my car, underneath the front seat, like half the other residents of this area. I drove to work and at the end of the day I drove home, a model bureaucrat, and each time I sat in the car and turned on the ignition, I felt better than I should have because that gun was on the floor. After about a week, the only problem I had was not that the gun was there but that it wasn't loaded. So I went to the ammo store—it's actually called the Michigan Rod and Gun Club—about two miles away from my house and bought some bullets for it. This was all very easy. In fact, the various details were getting easier and easier. I hadn't foreseen this. I've read Freud and Heinz Kohut and D. W. Winnicott, and I can talk to you about psychotic breaks and object-relations and fixation on oedipal grandiosity characterized by the admixture of strong object cathexes and the implicitly disguised presence of castration fears, and, by virtue of my being able to talk about those conditions, I have had some trouble getting into gear and moving when the occasion called for it. But now, with the magic wand under the front seat, I was getting ready for some kind of adventure.

Around the house my character was improving rather than degenerating. Knowing my little secret, I was able to sit with Gary, my younger son, as he practiced the piano, and I complimented him on the Czerny passages he had mastered, and I helped him through the sections he hadn't learned. I was a fiery angel of patience. With Sam, my older boy, I worked on a model train layout. I cooked a few more dinners than I usually did: from honey-mustard chicken, I went on to varieties of stuffed fish and other dishes with sauces that I had only imagined. I was attentive to Ann. The nature of our intimacies improved. We were whispering to each other again. We hadn't whispered in years.

I was frontloading a little fantasy. After all, I had tried intelligence. Intelligence was not working, not with me, not with the world. So it was time to try the other thing.

My only interruption was that I was getting calls from Earl. He called the house. He had the impression that I understood the mind and could make his ideas feel better. I told him that nobody could make his ideas feel better, ideas either feel good or not, but he didn't believe me.

"Do you mind me calling like this?" he asked. It was just before dinner. I was in the study, and the news was on. I pushed the MUTE button on the remote control. While Earl talked, I watched the silent coverage of mayhem.

"No, I don't mind."

"I shouldn't do this, I know, 'cause you get paid to listen, being a professional friend. But I have to ask your advice."

"Don't call me a professional friend. Earl, what's your question?" The pictures in front of me showed a boy being shot in the streets of Beirut.

"Well, I went into Jaynee's room to clean up. You know how teenage girls are. Messy and everything."

"Yes." More Beirut carnage, then back to Tom Brokaw.

"And I found her diary. How was I to know she had a diary? She never told me."

"They often don't, Earl. Was it locked?"

"What?"

"Locked. Sometimes diaries have locks."

"Well," Earl said, "this one didn't."

"Sounds as though you read it." Shots now on the TV of Ed Koch, the mayor, then shots of bag ladies in the streets of New York.

Earl was silent. I decided not to get ahead of him again. "I thought that maybe I shouldn't read it, but then I did."

"How much?"

"All of it," he said, "I read all of it."

I waited. He had called *me*. I hadn't called him. I watched the pictures of Gorbachev, then pictures of a girl whose face had been slashed by an ex-boyfriend. "It must be hard, reading your daughter's diary," I said. "And not *right*, if you see what I mean."

"Not the way you think." He took a deep breath. "I don't mind the talk about boys. She's growing up, and you can wish it won't happen, but it does. You know what I'm saying?"

"Yes, I do, Earl." A commercial now, for Toyotas.

"I don't even mind the sex, how she thinks about it. Hey, I was no priest myself when I was that age, and now the women, they want to have the freedom we had, so how am I going to stop it, and maybe why should I?"

"I see what you mean."

"She's very aggressive. *Very* aggressive. The things she does. You sort of wonder if you should believe it."

"Diaries are often fantasies. You probably shouldn't be reading your daughter's diary at all. It's *hers*, Earl. She's writing for herself, not for you."

"She writes about me, sometimes."

"You shouldn't read it, Earl."

Tom Brokaw again, and now pictures of a nuclear reactor, and shots of men in white outer space protective suits with lead shielding, cleaning up some new mess. I felt my anger rising, as usual.

"I can't help reading it," Earl said. "A person starts prying, he can't stop."

"You shouldn't be reading it."

"You haven't heard what I'm about to say," Earl told me. "It's why I'm calling you. It's what she says."

"What's that?" I asked him.

"Not what I expected," he said. "She pities me."

"Well," I said. More shots of the nuclear reactor. I was getting an idea.

"Well is right." He took another breath. "First she says she loves me. That was shock number one. Then she says she feels sorry for me. That was shock number two. Because I work on the line at Ford's and I drink beer and I live in Westland. Where does she get off? That's what I'd like to know. She mentions the play structure. She feels *sorry* for me! My God, I always hated pity. I could never stand it. It weakens you. I never wanted anybody on earth pitying me, and now here's my punk daughter doing it."

"Earl, put that diary away."

"I hear you," he said. "By the way, what did you do with that gun?"

"Threw it off the Belle Isle Bridge," I said.

"Sure you did," he said. "Well, anyway, thanks for listening, Warren." Then he hung up. On the screen in front of me, Tom Brokaw was introducing the last news story of the evening.

. . .

Most landscapes, no matter where you are, manage to keep something wild about them, but the land in southern Michigan along the Ohio border has always looked to me as if it had lost its self-respect some time ago. This goes beyond being tamed. This land has been beaten up. The industrial brass knuckles have been applied to wipe out the trees, and the corporate blackjack has stunned the soil, and what grows there—the grasses and brush and scrub pine—grows tentatively. The plant life looks scared and defeated, but all the other earthly powers are busily at work.

Such were my thoughts as I drove down to the nuclear reactor in Holbein, Michigan, on a clear Saturday morning in August, my loaded gun under my seat. I was in a merry mood. Recently activated madcap joy brayed and sang inside my head. I was speeding. My car was trembling because the front end was improperly aligned and I was doing about seventy-five. One false move on the steering wheel and I'd be permanently combined with a telephone pole. I had an eye out for the constables but knew I would not be arrested. A magic shield surrounded my car, and I was so invincible that Martians could not have stopped me.

Although this was therapy rather than political action, I was taking it very seriously, especially at the moment when my car rose over the humble crest of a humiliated grassy hill, and I saw the infernal dome and cooling towers of the Holbein reactor a mile or so behind a clutch of hills and trees ahead and to my left. The power company had surrounded all this land with high cyclone fencing, crowned with barbed wire and that new kind of coiled lacerating razor wire they've invented. I slowed down to see the place better.

There wasn't much to see because they didn't want you to see anything; they'd built the reactor far back from the road, and in this one case they had let the trees grow (the usual demoralized silver maples and willows and jack pines) to hide the view. I drove past the main gate and noted that a sign outside the guards' office regretted that the company could not give tours because of the danger of sabotage. Right. I hadn't expected to get inside. A person doesn't always have to get inside.

About one mile down, the fence took a ninety-degree turn to the left, and a smaller county road angled off from the highway I was on. I turned. I followed this road another half mile until there was a break in the trees and I could get a clear view of the building. I didn't want a window. I wanted a wall. I was sweating like an amateur thief. The back of my shirt was stuck to the car seat, and the car was jerking because my foot was trembling with excited shock on the accelerator.

Through the thin trees, I saw the solid wall of the south building, whatever it held. There's a kind of architecture that makes you ashamed of human beings, and in my generic rage, my secret craziness that felt completely sensible, I took the gun and held my arm out of the window. It felt good to do that. I was John Wayne. I fired four times at that building, once for me, once for Ann, and once for each of my two boys. I don't know what I hit. I don't care. I probably hit that wall. It was the only kind of heroism I could imagine, the Don Quixote kind. But I hadn't fired the gun before and wasn't used to the recoil action, with the result that after the last shot, I lost control of the car, and it went off the road. In any other state my Chevy would have flipped, but this is southern Michigan, where there are shallow ditches and nothing drains away, and I was bumped around—in my excitement I had forgotten to wear my seatbelt—until the engine finally stalled in something that looked like a narrow off-road parking area.

I opened my door, but instead of standing up I fell out. With my head on the ground I opened my eyes, and there in the stones and pebbles in front of me was a shiny penny. I brought myself to a standing position, picked up the penny, a lucky penny, for my purposes, and surveyed the landscape where my car had stopped. I walked around to the other side of the car and saw a small pile of beer cans and a circle of ashes, where some revelers, sometime this summer, had enjoyed their little party of pleasure there in the darkness, close by the inaudible hum of the Holbein reactor. I dropped the penny in my trouser pocket, put the gun underneath the front seat again, and I started the car. After two tries I got it out, and before the constables came to check on the gunshots, I had made my escape.

I felt I had done something in the spirit of Westland. I sang, feeling very good and oddly patriotic. On the way back I found myself behind a car with a green bumpersticker.

CAUTION: THIS VEHICLE
EXPLODES UPON IMPACT!

That's me, I said to myself. I am that vehicle.

There was still the matter of the gun, and what to do with it. Fun is fun, but you have to know when the party's over. Halfway home, I pulled off the road into one of those rest stops, and I was going to discard the gun by leaving it on top of a picnic table or by dropping it into a trash can. What I actually did was to throw it into the high grass. Half an hour later, I walked into our suburban kitchen with a smile on my face. I explained the scratch on my cheek as the result of an accident while playing racquetball at the health club. Ann and the boys were delighted by my mood. That evening we went out to a park, and, sitting on a blanket, ate our picnic dinner until the darkness came on.

Many of the American stories I was assigned to read in college were about anger, a fact that would not have surprised my mother, who was British, from Brighton. "Warren," she used to say to me, "watch your tongue in front of these people." "These people" always meant "these Americans." Among them was my father, who had been born in Omaha and who had married her after the war. "Your father," my mother said, "has the temper of a savage." Although it is true that my mind has retained memories of household shouting, what I now find queer is that my mother thought that anger was peculiar to this country.

Earl called me a few more times, in irate puzzlement over his life. The last time was at the end of the summer, on Labor Day. Usually Ann and I and the boys go out on Labor Day to a Metropark and take the last long swim of the summer, but this particular day was cloudy, with a forecast for rain. Ann and I had decided to pitch a tent on the back lawn for the boys, and to grill some hot dogs and hamburgers.

We were hoping that the weather would hold until evening. What we got was drizzle, off and on, so that you couldn't determine what kind of day it was. I resolved to go out and cook in the rain anyway. I often took the weather personally. I was standing there, grim faced and wet, firing up the coals, when Ann called me to the telephone.

It was Earl. He apologized for bringing me to the phone on Labor Day. I said it was okay, that I didn't mind, although I *did* mind, in fact. We waited. I thought he was going to tell me something new about his daughter, and I was straining for him not to say it.

"So," he said, "have you been watching?"

"Watching what? The weather? Yes, I've been watching that."

"No," he said, "not the sky. The Jerry Lewis telethon."

"Oh, the telethon," I said. "No, I don't watch it."

"It's important, Warren. We need all the money we can get. We're behind this year. You know how it's for Jerry's kids."

"I know it, Earl." Years ago, when I was a bachelor, once or twice I sat inside drinking all weekend and watching the telethon and making drunken pledges of money. I didn't want to remember such entertainment now.

"If we're going to find a cure for this thing, we need for everybody to contribute. It's for the kids."

"Earl," I said, "they won't find a cure. It's a genetic disorder, some scrambling in the genetic code. They might be able to prevent it, but they won't *cure* it."

There was a long silence. "You weren't born in this country, were you?"

"No," I said.

"I didn't think so. You don't sound like it. I can tell you weren't born here. At heart you're still a foreigner. You have a no-can-do attitude. No offense. I'm not criticizing you for it. It's not your fault. You can't help it. I see that now."

"Okay, Earl."

Then his voice brightened up. "What the hell," he said. "Come out anyway. You know where Westland is? Oh, right, you've been here. You know where the shopping center's located?"

"Yes," I said.

"It's the clown races. We're raising money. Even if you don't believe in the cure, you can still come to the clown races. We're giving away balloons, too. Your kids will enjoy it. Bring 'em along. *They'll* love it. It's quite a show. It's all on TV."

"Earl," I said, "this isn't my idea of what a person should be doing on a holiday. I'd rather—"

"—I don't want to hear what you'd rather do. Just come out here and bring your money. All right?" He raised his voice after a quick pause. "Are you listening?"

"Yes, Earl," I said. "I'm listening."

Somehow I put out the charcoal fire and managed to convince my two boys and my wife that they should take a quick jaunt to Westland. I told them about Earl, the clown races, but what finally persuaded the boys was that I claimed there'd be a remote TV unit out there, and they might turn up with their faces on Channel 2. Besides, the rain was coming down a little harder, a cool rain, one of those end-of-summer drizzles that makes your skin feel the onset of autumn. When you feel like that, it helps to be in a crowd.

They had set up a series of highway detours around the shopping center, but we finally discovered how to get into the north parking lot. They'd produced the balloons, tents, and lights, but they hadn't produced much of a crowd. They had a local TV personality dressed in a LOVE NETWORK raincoat trying to get people to cheer. The idea was, you made a bet for your favorite clown and put your money in his fishbowl. If your clown won, you'd get a certificate for a free cola at a local restaurant. It wasn't much of a prize, I thought; maybe it *was* charity, but I felt that they could do better than that.

Earl was clown number three. We'd brought three umbrellas and were standing off to the side when he came up to us and introduced himself to my wife and the boys. He was wearing an orange wig and a clown nose, and he had painted his face white, the way clowns do, and he was wearing Bozo shoes, the size eighteens, but one of his sleeves was rolled up, and you could see the tattoo of that impaled rose. The white paint was running off his face a bit in the rain, streaking, but he didn't seem to mind. He shook hands with my children and Ann and me very formally. He had less natural ability as a clown than anyone else I've ever met. It would never occur to you to laugh at Earl dressed up in that suit. What you felt would be much more complicated. It was like watching a family member descend into a weakness like alcoholism. Earl caught the look on my face.

"What's the matter, Warren?" he asked. "You okay?"

I shrugged. He had his hand in a big clown glove and was shaking my hand.

"It's all for a good cause," he said, waving his other hand at the four lanes they had painted on the parking lot for the races. "We've made a lot of money already. It's all for the kids, kids who aren't as lucky as ours." He looked down at my boys. "You have to believe," he said.

"You sound like Jaynee," I told him. My wife was looking at Earl. I had tried to explain him to her, but I wasn't sure I had succeeded.

"Believe what?" she asked.

"You've been married to this guy for too long," he said, laughing his big clown laugh. "Maybe your kids can explain it to you, about what the world needs now." There was a whistle. Earl turned around. "Gotta go," he said. He flopped off in those big shoes.

"What's he talking about?" my wife asked.

They lined up the four clowns, including Earl, at the chalk, and those of us who were spectators stood under the tent and registered our bets while the LOVE NETWORK announcer from Channel 2 stood in front of the cameras and held up his starter's gun. I stared for a long time at that gun. Then I placed my bet on Earl.

The other three clowns were all fat, middle-aged guys, Shriners or Rotarians, and I thought Earl had a good chance. My gaze went from the gun down to the parking lot, where I saw Jaynee. She was standing in the rain and watching her old man. I heard the gun go off, but instead of watching Earl, I watched her.

Her hair was stuck to the sides of her head in that rain, and her cotton jacket was soaked through. She had her eyes fixed on her father. By God, she looked affectionate. If he wanted his daughter's love, he had it. I watched her clench her fists and start to jump up and down, cheering him on. After twenty seconds I could tell by the way she raised her fist in the air that Earl had clumped his way to victory. Then I saw the new woman, Jody, standing behind Jaynee, her big glasses smeared with rain, grinning.

I looked around the parking lot and thought: everyone here understands what's going on better than I do. But then I remembered that I had fired shots at a nuclear reactor. All the desperate remedies. And I remembered my mother's first sentence to me when we arrived in New York harbor when I was ten years old. She pointed down from the ship at the pier, at the crowds, and she said, "Warren, look at all those Americans." I felt then that if I looked at that crowd for too long, something inside my body would explode, not metaphorically but literally: it would blow a hole through my skin, through my chest cavity. And it came back to me in that shopping center parking lot, full of those LOVE NETWORK people, that feeling of pressure of American crowds and exuberance.

We collected our free cola certificates, and then I hustled my wife and kids back into the car. I'd had enough. We drove out of the Westland parking lot, then were directed by a detour sign into a service drive that circled the entire shopping center and re-entered the lot on the north side, back at the clown races. I saw Jaynee again, still in the rain, hugging her American dad, and Jody holding on to his elbow, looking up at him, pressing her thigh against him. I took another exit out of the lot but somehow made the same mistake I had made before, and, once again, found myself back in Westland. Every service drive seemed designed to bring us back to this same scene of father, daughter, and second wife. I gave them credit for who they were and what they were doing—I give them credit now—but I had to get out of there immediately. I don't know how I managed to get out of that place, but on the fourth try, I succeeded.

Miranda July

❉

Birthmark

On a scale of one to ten, with ten being childbirth, this will be a three.

A three? Really?

Yes. That's what they say.

What other things are a three?

Well, five is supposed to be having your jaw reset.

So it's not as bad as that.

No.

What's two?

Having your foot run over by a car.

Wow, so it's worse than that?

Just a little worse, not much.

Okay, well, I'm ready. No—wait; let me adjust my sweater. Okay, I'm ready.

Alright then.

Here goes a three.

Right. Here we go then.

The laser, which had been described as *pure white light,* was more like a fist slammed against a countertop, and her body was a cup on this counter, jumping with each slam. It turned out three was just a number. It didn't describe the pain any more than money describes the things it buys. Two thousand dollars for a port-wine stain removed. A kind of birthmark that seems messy and accidental, as if this red area covering one whole cheek were the careless result of too much fun. She spoke to her body like an animal at the vet, *Shhh, it's okay, I'm sorry, I'm so sorry we have to do this to you.* This is not unusual; most people feel that their bodies are innocent of their crimes, like animals or plants. Not that this was a crime. She had waited patiently from the time she was fourteen for aesthetic surgery to get cheap, like computers. Nineteen ninety-eight was the year lasers came to the people as good bread, eat and be full, be finally perfect. Oh yes, perfect. She didn't think she would have bothered if she hadn't been what people call "very beautiful except for." This is a special group of citizens living under special laws. Nobody knows what to do with them. We mostly want to stare at them like the optical illusion of a vase made out of the silhouette of two people kissing. Now it is vase . . . now it could only be two people kissing . . . oh but it is so completely a vase. It is both! Can the world sustain such a contradiction. Only this was better, because as the illusion of prettiness and horribleness flipped back and forth, we flipped with it. Now we were uglier than her, now we were lucky not to be her, oh but then again, at this angle she was too lovely to bear. She was both, we were both, and the world continued to spin.

Now began the part of her life where she was just very beautiful. Except for nothing. Only winners will know what this feels like. Have you ever wanted something very badly and then gotten it? Then you know that winning is many things, but it is never the thing you thought it would be. Poor people who win the lottery do not become rich people. They become poor people who won the lottery. She was a very beautiful person who was missing something very ugly. Her winnings were the absence of something, and this quality hung around her. There was so much potential in the imagined removal of the birthmark, any fool on the bus could play the game of guessing how perfect she would look without it. Now there was not this game to play, there was just a spent feeling. And she was not an idiot, she could sense it. In the first few months after the surgery she received many compliments, but they were always coupled with confusion.

Now you can wear your hair up and show off your face more.

Yeah, I'm going to try it that way.

Wait, say that again.

I'm going to try it that way. What?

Your little accent is gone.

What accent?

You know, the little Norwegian thing.

Norwegian?

Isn't your mom Norwegian?

She's from Denver.

But you have that little bit of an accent, that little . . . way of saying things.

I do?

Well, not anymore, it's gone now.

And she felt a real sense of loss. Even though she knew that she had never had an accent. It was just the birthmark, which in its density had lent color to even her voice. She didn't miss the birthmark, but she missed her Norwegian heritage, like learning of new relatives after they have died.

All in all, though, this was minor, less disruptive than insomnia (but more severe than déjà vu). Over time she knew more and more people who had never known her with the birthmark. And you would assume that these people didn't feel any haunting absence, because why should they. Her husband was one of these people. You could tell by looking at him. Not that he wouldn't have married a woman with a port-wine stain. But he wouldn't have. Most people don't and are none the worse for it. Of course sometimes it would happen that she would see a couple and one of them would have a port-wine stain and the other one would clearly be in love with this person, and she would hate her husband a little. Which was ridiculous because he was innocent. But he wasn't an idiot and so he would notice.

Are you being weird?

No.

You are.

Actually I'm not. I'm just eating my salad.

I can see them too, you know. I saw them come in.

Hers is worse than mine was. Mine didn't go down on my neck like that.

Do you want to try this soup?

I bet he's an environmentalist. Doesn't he look like one?

Maybe you should go sit with them.

Maybe I will.

I don't see you moving.

Did you just finish the soup? I thought we were splitting.

I offered it to you.

Well, you can't have any of this salad then.

It was a small thing, but it was a thing, and things have a way of either dying or growing, and it wasn't dying. Years went by. This thing grew, like a child, microscopically, every day. And since they were a team, and all teams want to win, they continuously adjusted their vision to keep its growth invisible. They wordlessly excused each other for not loving each other as much as they had planned. There were empty rooms in the house where they had meant to put their love, and they worked together to fill these rooms with high-end, consumer-grade equipment. It was a tight situation. The next sudden move would have to be through the wall. What happened was this. She was trying to get the lid off a new jar of jam and she was banging it on the counter. This is a well-known tip, a kitchen trick, a bang to loosen the lid. It's not witchery or black magic or anything, it's just a way to release the pressure under the lid. She banged it too hard and the jar broke. She screamed. Her husband came running when he heard the sound. There was red everywhere and in that instant he saw blood. Hallucinatory clarity: you know for sure. But in the next moment your mind relinquishes control, and gives you back to reality; it was jam. Everywhere. She was laughing, picking up the shards of glass out of the strawberry mash. She was laughing at the mess and her face was down, looking at the floor, and her hair was around her face like a curtain and then she looked up at him and said, Can you bring the trash can over here?

And it happened again. For a moment he thought he saw a port-wine stain on her cheek. It was fiercely red and bigger than he had ever imagined. It was bloodier than even blood, like sick blood, animal blood, the blood racist people think beats inside of people of other races: blood that shouldn't touch my own. And the next moment it was just jam and he laughed and rubbed the kitchen towel on her cheek. Her clean cheek. Her port-wine stain.

Honey.
Can you get the trashcan?
Honey.
What?
Go look in the mirror.
What?
Go look in the mirror.
Stop talking like that. Why are you talking like that? What?

He was looking at her cheek and she instinctively put her hand on the mark, and then she ran to bathroom.

She was in there for a long time. Maybe thirty minutes. You've never had thirty minutes like these. She stared at the port-wine stain and she breathed in and she breathed out. It was like being twenty-three again, but she was thirty-eight now. Fifteen years without it, and now, here it was. In exactly the same place. She rubbed her finger around its edges. It came as high as her right eye, over to the edge of her nostril, across her whole cheek to the ear, ending at her jawbone. In purplish-red. She wasn't thinking anything, she wasn't afraid or disappointed or worried. She was just looking at the stain the way you would look at yourself fifteen years after your own death. Oh, you again. Now it was obvious that it had always been there, just around the corner. She had startled it forward, back into sight. She looked into its redness and breathed in and breathed out and found herself in a kind of trance. She thought: I am in a kind of trance. But she didn't try to shake out of it, instead she shallowed her breathing for fear of waking up. In the trance there was one sound and one smell and one sight and one sensation and it was the sound and smell and sight and sensation of her port-wine stain and this stain was her, it was her body. She didn't have to think because plants don't have to think about themselves and weather doesn't have to think about itself, it just blows around. It was this kind of trance, she was just blowing around. It's hard to describe it any more than that, except to say that it lasted about twenty-five minutes. That is a very, very long time just to be blowing around. Mostly you waft for a second or two, a half-second maybe. And then you spend the rest of your life trying to describe it, to regain the perspective. You say: *It was like I was just blowing around*, and you wave your arms in the air. But there were no arms like that and you know it. It's become this long story you tell about this half-second of your life. Only for her it was twenty-five minutes. Do you understand? Twenty. Five. Minutes. If it could have lasted forever, she would have gladly lived there, inside the stain, a red and limbless world. She came back like a plane taking off, she was no longer in the stain, but looking at it from above. It grew smaller and smaller until it was just a tiny region in a larger mass, one which this pilot favored, hovered above, but would not touch down on again. She pulled some toilet paper off the roll and blew her nose.

He found himself kneeling. He was waiting for her on his knees. He was worried she would not let him love her with the stain. He had already decided, long ago, twenty or thirty minutes ago, that the stain was fine. He had only seen it for a moment but he was already used to it. It was good. It somehow allowed them to *have more*. They could have a child now, he thought. There was a loose feeling in the air. The jam was still on the floor and that was okay. He would just kneel here and wait for her to come out and hope he would be able to tell her about the looseness in a loose way. He wanted to keep the feeling. He hoped she wasn't removing it somehow, the stain. She should keep it and they should have a kid. He could hear her blowing her nose, now she was opening the door. He would stay on his knees, just like this. She would see him this way and understand.

Richard Stern

✠

Audit

Constitutionally, temperamentally, against the grain of his better intentions, his background and even many of his actions, Wendell Spear, the film critic and historian, was avaricious.

Well, not quite. *Avarice* didn't do justice to Spear's feelings about money. After his wife Vanessa's death, money became a kind of companion to him, almost a child. The nurturing and growth of his small wealth brought him a profound ease and—though he knew this was absurd—pride.

Every morning, waking, he reached for his bedside phone, pressed its memory button and, successively, the numbers which summoned the electronic voices which reported the status of his accounts. The rare times when there was a glitch in either the reporting system or his account, Spear was gripped by anxiety and anger until he could reach his broker's office and learn what, thank God, had, so far, been a reporting error which, for anxious minutes, appeared to be either a catastrophic decline or an embezzlement.

When, in late August, a letter from the Treasury Department informed him that he was subject to a tax audit, Spear felt a terror unlike anything he'd known since Vanessa's death. Why, after all his placid, solitary years in his Malibu Canyon cabin, had he been singled out? Dismay, astonishment, fear, rage.

The letter was personalized to the extent of specifying the year the IRS was auditing, 1993, and the areas of its concern, his Contributions and Business Expenses. It also indicated the place and time of the audit, the Federal Building on Los Angeles Street, and the auditor's sinister, comic name, G. Whipp.

Spear's longtime accountant, Zack Wool, filed his taxes from Los Angeles, where Spear had lived till his move to Malibu. It accounted for the location of the audit and for another dimension of his anxiety, the hour's drive on the freeways. The freeways were the incarnation, or rather impetrification, of his fears. Until the audit was over, he knew he wouldn't enjoy a single night of peaceful sleep.

He called Wool's office. Frances, the secretary, said, "I'm sorry, Mr. Spear. He's in South America."

"In flight?"

"Vacation. He takes September off."

"It's August."

"He'll be back September 20."

"The audit's September 18."

"I can request a postponement. They're good about granting them."

"I may not last till September 18. I'll go myself."

That afternoon Spear dug out of a closet the manila envelopes which held his 1993 tax forms, checks, receipts, bankbooks, VISA and the Discover bills and went to work.

After two hours' immersion, he went out to the terrace from whose eaves still hung the inverted blue bottles which, so long ago, Vanessa had filled with sugar water for hummingbirds. (The hummingbirds had departed with her.) Now looking over the small lawn bordered with chaparral, palms and cypress, he prepared himself for the actual hearing. He'd wear his oldest decent suit, blue, a frayed blue shirt and a faded blue tie. No, the wrong look. Too much blue. Too much attention to color coordination. The artist disguises his art; the con man also. He needed a shirt that clashed, not enough to agitate a color-sensitive auditor, but enough to suggest an old widower, careful but a bit at sea. Maybe an off-white shirt with black stripes. No, these were prison colors. The lemon-green with a few honorable white threads at the collar. For shoes, the ugly, broad-toed ones with worn-down heels. He'd polish them to show how careful he was of his old, unfashionable things. Whipp would see a decent, even fastidious man, straightforward, plain, a not-quite-with-it man, a bald, sexagenarian widower keeping up as well as he could.

Would the auditor sniff something askew? After all, he knew Spear's income, tiny compared to many in Malibu, but probably three times bigger than Whipp's own. *I'm saving for my granddaughter, Mr. Whipp. I'm not a spender. I skimp, but not on taxes. I pay what I owe. My accountant, Zack Wool, is descended from a Confederate general. He's stricter than a ruler. I'm sure he makes me pay more than I should. I'm hoping to get a refund.*

Spear went back to the checks and receipts, expenses and charities, almost thirty of them, to some of which—thinking to avoid just such an encounter—he'd given $10 or less. The more checks, the more scrupulous the taxpayer and the wearier the auditor. In 1993, however, there were several unusual deductions. The biggest was the gift of part of his film library and filmography to Claremont College. The appraiser—*Deirdre Seale, Mr. Whipp, a respectable professional*—had valued the library at $7,426.00. Was this the nail on which the IRS wanted to hang him? He got out a copy of Ms. Seale's letter, a two page account of her credentials and a detailed description of the gift. Detailed, yes, but impregnable? Perhaps Ms. Seale had left a trail of overassessments which the omniscient Whipp followed?

Omniscient.

Who knew what Whipp knew? The myrmidons of the IRS had immense resources, terrifying power. About money, they might know everything—more than everything! Spear had heard a hundred horror stories: people, companies, studios tied up in decades of litigation, tax penalties mounting at each stage of appeal.

Beyond appeal, beyond litigation, beyond impoverishment, loomed prison.

Spear knew prisons. He'd seen Jimmy Cagney, George Raft, Humphrey Bogart, Wallace Beery and Burt Lancaster behind iron bars; he'd seen brutal wardens, guards with guns ready, willing and eager to shoot prisoners diverting themselves momentarily from sticking cell-made shivs into each others' flanks. Gangs, extortion, rape.

Could a man like himself last a day in such a place? Three years ago, Roger, the grandson of his friend Alice, the cashier at the Mobil station, had been sent away for six months: reckless driving and endangerment. Said Alice, "It turned him around, Mr. S. Fellow in the next cell, a stockbroker, put him onto books. Now he talks of nothing but learning the Latin language. I asked him, 'Does this mean you want to be a priest?' 'Just the opposite,' he tells me. Whatever that means." Roger, an oil-stained giant, had grown up in the service station, not, like Spear, in an English rectory filled with the Latin books Roger apparently craved. (Although he hadn't read one in twenty years, Spear had not given Claremont his father's red and gold Loeb Library Classics.) A minimum-security prison with three square meals a day and stockbroker companions was a step up for him, but for Spear, who lived in the ease of unsupervised, self-pampered solitude, it would be living death.

The IRS district office was on the twelfth floor of the old Federal Office Building. For his 9 A.M. appointment, Spear was on the Santa Monica Freeway at 7:00 and on Los Angeles Street at 8:15. Carrying his schoolboy's briefcase stuffed with rubberbanded papers, he walked around the block to compose himself.

On the twelfth floor, he gave his name to a lovely, already weary black woman who told him to "sit in reception," a bleak beige room with three rows of blue plastic chairs and windows so begrimed Spear did not bother trying to see what could have been a fine view west over the city to the Pacific. Briefcase on his knees, he sat on the blue plastic seat like a penitent.

A small elderly black man sat two seats away. "Morning," he said. He wore bright green slacks and a Hawaiian sport shirt; no blue suit and frayed shirt for him. This was Southern California; not even funeral directors wore blue suits.

"Good morning."

"You being audited?"

"I'm afraid so."

"They wanting twenty-five hundred bucks from me."

"Pretty steep."

"My cousin, he took my social security, went round the Southwest hanging paper." He tapped a vinyl briefcase. "I got copies of two of his checks."

"Looks like you're home free then."

"Think so?"

"I do," said Counselor Spear.

"Mr. McKeeney?" A stout Chinese woman in a lavender pantsuit stood in the doorway.

"That's me," said the man, rising.

Spear watched them disappear round an L-leg of a corridor. The elevator discharged a wheelchair which rolled toward the reception area. Spear looked, then looked away from its occupant, a tiny white man in a brown corduroy workshirt and blue pants from which hung tiny shoes. "Not enough that God has afflicted the poor fellow, the IRS has to pursue him." Then he heard what was surely his name, "Mr. Sthpear," uttered in a sharp, high-pitched voice.

Spear looked at the wheelchair. "Mr. Whipp?"

The man had an almost normal-sized head which was jammed, neckless, onto small corduroyed shoulders. "Pleath follow me."

Spear rose, his seventy inches heavy with normality. He followed the double-wheeled throne of his auditor down the long corridor and into a cubicle. Mr. Whipp's arm pointed him to a wooden chair. He wheeled himself behind the desk. On a table to his left were a telephone, a small American flag on a stand and a six inch plastic Venus de Milo.

"Well, Mr. Sthpear," he said with a pleasant smile, "Thall we begin?"

"I'm ready."

Whipp opened a manila envelope in front of him. "I'm going to wead you your wighth."

The familiar phrase, even in Whipp's infantile phonemes, coiled around Spear's already contracted heart. "You thould have copieth of thith." Spear nodded. "In thwee or four weekth, I'll mail you a weport. If you don't agwee wiv it, you can call me or my thupervithor. If we don't thatithfy you, you can appeal. If—"

"Yes, *I* did read that, Mr. Whipp."

"Have you ever been audited before?"

"No."

Whipp drew a paper from the folder. He said kindly, "It theemth you were—back in 1968."

"Really?" Vanessa had done their taxes, but yes, he remembered something. Hadn't the auditor come to their house in Beverly Glen? "My wife handled our finances. I'm a widower now."

"I thee." This was not an expression of sympathy: Whipp was looking at papers which specified the date of Vanessa's death. "Now I will wead you a litht of thingth. Would you pleath anthwer yeth or no to each? Have you any income from weal ethtate?"

"No."

"Overtheath invethtmenth?"

"Only the royalties described in the return."

"Drug-dealing?"

"No."

"Mining?"

"No."

"Currenthly twanthactionth?"

"I don't speculate. Except for the investments listed."

At each of Spear's answers, Whipp checked off boxes. He put the paper on a pile and pulled out a long pad of yellow paper. "Thall we begin with Contributionths?"

Spear undid the leather thongs on his briefcase and withdrew the envelope in which he'd put charitable checks, receipts and acknowledgments.

Whipp said, "There ith the matter of the car you donated to the half-way houthe." For years, Spear had given his old cars to an exactor who ran a halfway house for ex-prisoners and addicts. The actor tuned up the cars, then sold them to support the house. "I think the appraithal ith too high."

"It's his appraisal, not mine."

"I think it'th too high. Do you know the Blue Book appraithal of an eighty-thwee Buick?"

"No."

"I'll look it up. I think we have to go by that."

"It had an exceptionally good stereo system." An exaggeration.

"It'th hard to appraith thingth. Do you have any retheits for the thound thystem?"

"I probably did," lied Spear, "but I don't know where they are."

Whipp wrote on the lined pad. "I thee. We'd better uthe the Blue Book." He looked up as if awaiting Spear's approval. Spear nodded, and bending low over the pad, Whipp wrote more, his fist encircling the ballpoint pen as if writing required every bit of his strength and concentration. "Now we thould look at the donathon of the film bookth and—thith ith a new word to me—filmogwaphy." His accent was on *gwaph*. "To the college libwary."

Spear said, "I have the appraiser's letters and the college's thank-you note here."

"Your accountant thubmitted them."

"Is there a problem?"

"Ith a filmo-gwaphy movieth?"

"Mine's a detailed, alphabeticized description of films, categorized by genre."

"What is *genre*?"

"Type of film. Comedy, tragedy. Whatever."

"I thee." His neckless head bobbed in appreciative comprehension. "I think we can acthept thith appraithal."

"Fine," said Spear, surprised at the depth of his delight.

Whipp wrote several more lines, then looked up. "Charitieth? You have lotth of thmall oneth, thome under Mithellaneouth. Of courth, people can't document everything. Like you go to church and put in a few dollarth."

"That's right," said Spear who hadn't been to church since he'd listened to his father's tortured sermons forty-odd years ago.

Item by item, the examination continued, Whipp writing away, Spear occasionally contesting, Whipp nodding, agreeing, asking for documentation. "The IREth won't accthept undocumented twan-thacthionth."

"I understand. I wish I'd kept everything."

"I know that'th hard to do."

An hour, two hours, three hours, Whipp and Spear faced each other over the checks, receipts, appraisals and assessments scattered over the desk.

"You mutht be getting hungry. Wouldn't it be better to make another appointment?"

"Lord God no, Mr. Whipp. I'd like to get it over now, if that's all right."

"All right. We're almotht finithed."

The final twenty minutes went by in a blur. Drained, Spear agreed to everything, but he had the impression that most of his claims were being accepted. What a good, decent person Whipp was. How beautifully he handled his deformity and handicaps. He touched Spear's heart. When they discussed the expenses of a trip Spear had made to a film festival in San Francisco, Whipp said, "Than Fwanthithco ith thuch a beautiful thity. I wath there oneth, for four dayth. It wath my happietht perthonal time."

The drive home on the freeway and coast highway was actually pleasant: few cars, much relief. Home, Spear slept, till wakened by the phone. "Mr. Sthpear?"

"Mr. Whipp. Is anything wrong?"

"You left your briefcathe here."

"How careless of me."

"What thall I do with it?"

"Why don't you keep it as a souvenir?" Spear almost said. "I'll have to come get it, unless you could possibly mail it to me. Of course I'd reimburse you."

"I might be able to do that," said Whipp. "Let me athk at our potht offith."

It happened that Jennifer, Spear's granddaughter, had been sent down from San Francisco to do a deposition at the Roybal Building across the street from the Federal Office Building. She was spending the night with Spear, a rare treat for him. She said she'd pick up the briefcase during her lunch break.

That night, she said, "The people in the office here all know him. At least they've seen him in the street being carried into taxis."

"What did he say to you?"

"Not very much. He was embarrassed, I think, a bit gruffer than he might have been with you. All he said was, 'I have it right here.' Strange lisp. Maybe because his throat's constricted."

"I'm sure he was delighted to see you. I don't imagine he gets a chance to talk to attractive girls." For Spear, Jennifer was lovelier than any film star, a solid, pink-cheeked Natalie Wood or Winona Ryder, or like the eighteen-year-old Hannah Arendt as she was spotted in the Freiburg lecture hall by the swinish genius Heidegger. "You made his week," said Spear. "And you probably improved my case." He decided to send Jennifer whatever refund he got. "It makes me feel good about technology. Fifty or sixty years ago, Whipp wouldn't have been able to get a job in a circus; they don't use cripples. He'd have been human junk."

"He makes the case for affirmative action," said Jennifer. "One up for the US of A."

Three and a half weeks later, Whipp's report arrived, six pages long and so ambiguously phrased that Spear couldn't tell whether he owed money or was getting some back. There were also spelling errors and such peculiarities as credit for a safe-deposit box which Spear hadn't listed, let alone claimed. The upshot, though, was that Whipp disagreed with much of what Spear thought he'd agreed to, and Spear owed thirty-four hundred dollars, including two years' interest. It was not a great sum of money for him, and by agreeing to accept the assessment, that would end it, but something held him back. He felt his new friend wasn't such a friend after all, and this made him both angry and sad. It also occurred to him that if he agreed to Whipp's refusal to recognize, say, the tax deductibility of a film festival, then other Whipps could question other returns, past and future. The thirty-four hundred dollars could be the first of many installments.

He called Zack Wool. "How was Machu Picchu?"

"They keep it up very nicely. What can I do you for, Wendell? How was the audit? Sorry I wasn't there, though I'm sure you handled it well. Plus if I'd gone, it would have cost you a bundle."

"I *thought* it went all right, till I got the report just now. The guy went back on everything I assumed he agreed to. I owe them thirty-four hundred dollars. Not a fortune—"

"If you don't owe it, it's thirty-four hundred too much."

"It's the business of questioning my way of life. If I'd been buying hardware instead of watching movies, he would have accepted everything without question. My business is seeing films. If it looks like fun, let him try writing about them. Incidentally, he's a crippled dwarf, in a wheelchair. I actually liked him. I'm hurt he turned his back on me. I don't know what to do."

"Appeal."

"Is it worth it?"

"Is your time so valuable?"

"My leisure's valuable."

"Is it worth seventeen hundred bucks an hour? It'll only take a couple of hours."

"Plus the ride from Malibu."

"If we win, that's deductible."

Wool had spent the weekend in Santa Barbara and said he'd pick Spear up at his cabin.

"Make it the Mobil station down the highway. Then you don't have to drive up the canyon. I leave my car there, they know me."

The appointment with Whipp was at 1 P.M. Wool said he'd pick Spear up at noon, cutting it too close for Spear who liked to be early for appointments. He was down at the station talking to Alice at 11:30. At 11:40 he started looking up the road for Wool's car. At ten of, he began cursing.

"What's up, Mr. Spear," called Roger, who between stints at the gas pump was reading a Latin grammar behind the cash register counter, shoes up on a five gallon oil can.

"I don't like people who aren't on time. It's a phobia."

"When was he supposed to be here?"

"Noon."

"It's ten of."

"Tempus fugit." A week ago, Roger asked Spear if he'd consider giving him Latin lessons. "I haven't read Latin in years. The only thing I'm less qualified to do is train you to be an astronaut." He used the station phone to call Wool's office. "Where's your boss, Frances? We have an appointment at one."

"He said he'd be picking you up, Mr. Spear. I know he'll be there."

"Can you call his car?"

"He won't use cellular phones, says they're carcinogenic."

"I've got a good mind to drive myself."

"I don't blame you Mr. Spear. Mr. Wool is so deliberate it's exasperating. But he is reliable."

"I'll give him five minutes, then I'm taking off. He can meet me there if he likes. G. Whipp, twelfth floor."

"I'll tell him, sir, but please hold just a bit, I'm sure he's on his way."

Spear looked down the road, straining to pick up signs of Wool's Lexus. Nothing. He started to back out his car when he heard something. Shutting off the motor, he looked down the road and saw a black dot.

Wool offered no apology. In fact, he said he wanted to drop by his office to pick up Spear's file.

Suppressing the rage that burst from his anxiety, Spear said coldly, "There's no time for that, Zack. I don't want to be late. I like to have a few minutes to compose myself, and I don't think I'll have them."

"Whatever you say, Wendell. I'll just wing it."

On the coast highway, Spear stewed at Wool's molasses pace and over-caution. Every time a car passed, honking to get Wool over to the right, Spear wanted to strangle him. "He shouldn't be allowed to have a Lexus."

Wool picked up speed on the freeway. Cars still passed them every other second, but the traffic was light, and there was parking space a block from the Federal Building. Spear scrambled along at a pace that caused the much younger Wool to huff and puff.

. . .

In the reception area, Spear, pretending to look through his papers, sat a row away from Wool. When he saw the wheelchair at the end of the corridor, he got up, opened the glass door and greeted Whipp, who today was in tie and shirt. His shoes too, looked new, shiny, tiny black Oxfords which hung from his withered legs. "Mr. Wool. Mr. Whipp."

Wool leaned over and took Whipp's small hand. "I'm the signature at the bottom of the page. You may have seen it at the bottom of other returns."

How tight the blue tie looked on Whipp's necklessness. He was balder than Spear recalled, the remnants of light brown hair like torn curtains on the sides of his head. He did seem more comfortable today, perhaps knowing that there'd be no shocked looks on a strange face. He knew that Spear would have prepared the accountant for his appearance. "Pleathe follow me." He rolled up the corridor, going this time to a door with an alarm system whose buttons he pressed. "Could you pleathe get the door?" Spear opened it, then followed the chair left and right into Whipp's cubicle. "Thame offithe," he said. There was, though, a new ornament, a pumpkin with an unlit candle inside. Had Whipp carved it himself or had some grateful client brought it for Halloween?

"I've done a little wethearch on allowable deductionth for authorth. You are a full-time author, Mr. Sthpear, aren't you?"

"I suppose so. I do sometimes lecture, but basically I am a film critic and historian."

"A hithtorian ith an author?"

"Yes."

"Mr. Spear is modest, Mr. Whipp," said Wool. "He's a very distinguished film critic and historian. His main business is this form of authorship."

"That'th what I thought. Therth a cathe here"—he picked up a xeroxed page—"3/26/71 UTh Dithtrict Court, thentral Dithtrict California. I can make a copy for you. Thith man thpent thwee hundred and thirty-five dayth in New York Thity pwepawing a book on D. W.

Gwiffith. I know you know who he ith. I've theen hith filmth mythelf. *Birth of a Nathon*. I'm not thure it could be thown now." He looked up as if asking for Spear's professional opinion.

"It strains the conscience, but it is shown to film students."

"Gwiffith'th paperth were in New York, thith man lived in California. He claimed twavel and living expentheth for the taxable year. Owiginally, the claimth were dithallowed, but, on appeal, it wath dethided that the expentheth were deductible. They were not nondeductible exthpenditureth for the improvement of a capital athet. If you'd written a book or had wetheived an advanthe for a book about the film fethtival you attended, there would be no quethtion—bathed on thith cathe—that it wath deductible."

"But films are my business," said Spear. "Whether I write about them immediately or not."

Whipp smiled his sweet smile and nodded. "I underthtand. I underthtand that it'th your bithineth to know filmth, but here'th another cathe that applieth. A high thchool teacher of Fwench went to Fwanthe to improve her Fwench. The court dethided that her twavel expentheth could not be deducted thince thhe wath not *wequired* to go to Fwanthe. It wath her choithe, her pleathure. Though thhe wath a Fwench teacher."

"Absurd and unfair," said Spear. "She'd give her pupils the benefit of her new knowledge of the language and the country."

Whipp opened his palms helplessly. "Yeth, I underthtand, but I can only do what the IREth allowth me to do. They would not allow me to deduct your expentheth in Than Fwanthithco unleth you had a contract to write about it."

Spear started to speak, but Wool touched his arm, "Our contention is that Mr. Spear's status as a film critic and historian depends upon his keeping up with what's going on in films around the world. If he doesn't do that, there will be no contracts, no invitations to write articles or books. It's not a question of not being required by an employer to go to such festivals. Mr. Spear is self-employed."

"If I don't keep up, I won't be employed at all. Don't you see, Mr. Whipp, that you're undermining my very way of life?"

Whipp shook his head. "I wethpect your way of life very much,

Mr. Sthpear. I'm thure that you are a very fine and important critic. I underthtand how important it ith for you to keep up with filmth. It'th jutht that I can't thee that your cathe ith ath clothe to the Gwiffith cathe ath it ith to the Fwench teacher'th."

"What would it take to convince you, Mr. Whipp?"

The little shoulders shrugged. "I will do more wethearch and thee if I can find a cathe clother to yourth. I've had only one other author in my time here, and hith cathe wath different."

"Curious. What was his name?"

Wool said, "He can't tell you that, Wendell."

"Let'th thee, you were in Than Fwanthithco from February 11th to the 15th. Do you have thome kind of journal or diary of that time?"

"As a matter of fact, I do. Keeping journals is part of my work."

"Very good." Spear handed over the notebook. Whipp looked it over, turned the pages and handed it back. "It'th a bit hard to wead. Could you pleathe wead the entry for, thay, February 13th?"

Spear took the notebook and began to read a description of his breakfast and said, "I'd better go to what counts."

"Pleathe."

Spear read a section about a new Chinese film, an account of the plot along with speculations about its political and social undercurrents, the quality of the acting and directing, the beauty of the editing and color. He read for two or three minutes till Whipp said, "That'th a very beautiful dethcription of the film. However, there ith no hour by hour account of your activitieth."

"I was watching the film, Mr. Whipp."

"Yeth, I know that. But the quethtion ith what part of your day wath pleathure, what part wath improving your thtudieth ath a cwitic and what part wath actually wemunerated. That ith, bithineth. That'th the difficult quethtion."

"Mr. Whipp, do you enjoy your work?"

"Yeth, I do, Mr. Sthpear."

"I do too. Pleasure, then, isn't the criterion. If I were buying or selling nuts and bolts, there'd be no question about my expenses. Films are my nuts and bolts. They may sound like pleasure—they are pleasure—but they're how I earn a living. I'm not just talking about the money now, Mr. Whipp. I can afford to pay the IRS what it wants, but I can't afford to give it my life. It's my life that it's questioning. That you're questioning. The serious business of my life."

"I'm not quethtioning your bithineth, Mr. Sthpear."

"I agree, Wendell. Mr. Whipp knows that you're a serious critic of films, but," Wool turned to Whipp, "Mr. Spear has put our case well, if more emotionally than I might."

"I underthand that."

"All his experience goes into what he writes, and though we know that some experience, say, taking a drive or a walk is nondeductible, going to a film festival or doing research for an article or book should be."

"I agwee with you."

"I have done the man's taxes for thirty years. I do the taxes of many film people. You've probably seen my signature. I don't let my clients get away with things. With Wendell Spear, I have no worries. He's not a person who tries to get away with anything."

Spear felt himself flushing. Of course he tried to get away with things. He was only less bold than others, more fearful of the consequences. There were drops of sweat in Wool's brow furrows, gray hairs curled out of the inverted crescents of his eyebrows. Wool was worked up. "If he does a review for a local paper and gets twenty-five dollars for it, he notes it down. He is what you call a straight arrow."

"You might thay a weal Sthpear," said Whipp smiling.

Spear smiled too. What a little card he was. A sort of critic, too, observing the actors who performed their evasions in front of him.

"My hope is that we can resolve our problems here and now. If not . . ."

"You can appeal to my thupervithor." Whipp sounded not only sympathetic but encouraging. "And if that doethn't work, the taxth board. They may thee your cathe ath you thee it." Wide went the little palms, wide the smile. Spear surged with affection for him. If things were different, they might be friends, though Whipp's friends—if he had them—would have their hands full lifting his chair and him, helping him dress, helping him in the bathroom.

. . .

Two days later, Whipp's revised examination report was in his mail-box. It was clear that no midnight oil had been burned. The only dif-ference from the first report was that he allowed Spear two per diems at the film festival: sixty-eight dollars. Zack Wool's bill would quadru-ple that. At this rate, the appeal process would cost a fortune.

Disappointed, even angry, still, once again, Spear could not bring himself to dislike the auditor. He debated calling him up to remon-strate or even plead with him to see his side of things. "You're sug-gesting that I don't go to festivals or do archival research since I can review films or lecture about them without going or researching. Don't you—won't you—see that the quality of the reviews and lec-tures will be lower? Is that what you—or the IRS—want to do, lower the quality of a person's work? It almost makes someone like *me*—" Spear was talking out loud to the trees—"an old-fashioned liberal, an admirer of Attlee and Harold Wilson, FDR and Harry Truman, want to side with Republicans." If the green palms, so loftily at home against the blue sky, said anything, it was "pay the two dollars."

Spear took the mail into his study, signed the form which said that he agreed with the assessment and would no longer contest or appeal it and wrote out a check for the full amount. Then he inked a star by the sentence about not contesting or appealing and wrote in the space provided for Other Comments.

I sign this agreement and pay the full amount required but wish to go on record here that I disagree with the Auditor's interpretation of my claim. If I had the energy I used to have, I would pursue the matter and believe that I could substantiate my case in tax court. I say this without any feeling of animus towards the Auditor, Mr. G. Whipp, whom I found to be a person of humanity.

Wendell R. Spear

A week later, Frances, Wool's secretary, called him. "Mr. Wool wants to know if you heard from the auditor yet."

"I should have let him know, Frances. I did. There was no change to speak of. I mailed in the check."

"Do you want to speak to him?"

"I won't bother him, Frances. I followed my instinct. And my fatigue."

"Sounds smart to me."

"One of these days, Frances, I'm going to take you to lunch."

"I can't wait, Mr. Spear. I'll tell Mr. Wool. Not about the lunch."

A delightful little woman, divorced, if he remembered correctly. Maybe she'd be willing to go to lunch with Mr. Whipp. Who knew what that might lead to. The mysteries of companionship, or, for that matter, of solitude. Whipp seemed to be a happy man, as Spear was, perhaps because he too had the best wife of all, life itself.

That evening, after his spaghetti and Napa Valley cabernet, Spear walked the canyon road under the stars. A Pacific wind had blown away the smog, the sky was thick with brightness. At least the audit, thank God, was over. "It was good for you," Spear told himself, almost as if he were his father in the rectory, backed by walls of literate wisdom, offering paternal instruction. "Everyone needs auditing."

Spear himself had been a strict auditor of those around him. His daughter, Jennifer's mother, had early turned from him, and, in a way, so had Vanessa. (Dying was the way.) As a critic too, he was famously strict, weighing every film against not only the greatest films, but the greatest novels. Some producers had stopped giving him passes.

I was harsher than the stars. No wonder everyone turned away from me. I didn't seek solitude, it was my penalty.

The Almighty, that Ultimate Auditor, had raked Whipp's tiny body, legs, torso, tongue, yet also had filled it with honey. Divine Bookkeeping, how bizarre.

Next day, hardly thinking, Spear fetched the twenty-six red and gold Latin volumes of the Loeb Classical Library from his shelves and drove them down to the Mobil station. Roger wasn't there, but his grandmother was. "I promised these books to Roger, Alice. They're Latin. I can't read them anymore."

Another oddity: Spear stopped making his morning calls to the electronic voices. When he finally did realize that he'd stopped, he erased their numbers from the phone's memory bank and substituted Jennifer's, the Mobil station's, and—surprising himself again—his daughter's.

Elizabeth Gilbert

⌖

The Famous Torn and Restored
Lit Cigarette Trick

for Kate

In Hungary, Richard Hoffman's family had been the manufacturers of Hoffman's Rose Water, a product which was used at that time for both cosmetic and medicinal purposes. Hoffman's mother drank the rose water for her indigestion, and his father used it to scent and cool his groin after exercise. The servants rinsed the Hoffman's table linens in a cold bath infused with rose water, such that even the kitchen would be perfumed. The cook mixed a dash of it into her sweetbread batter. For evening events, Budapest ladies wore expensive imported colognes, but Hoffman's Rose Water was a staple product of daytime hygiene for all women, as requisite as soap. Hungarian men could be married for decades without ever realizing that the natural smell of their wives' skin was not, in fact, a refined scent of blooming roses.

Richard Hoffman's father was a perfect gentleman, but his mother slapped the servants. His paternal grandfather had been a drunk and a brawler, and his maternal grandfather had been a Bavarian boar-hunter, trampled to death at the age of ninety by his own horses. After her husband died of consumption, Hoffman's mother transferred the entirety of the family's fortune into the hands of a handsome Russian charlatan named Katanovsky, a common conjurer and a necromancer, who promised Madame Hoffman audiences with the dead. As for Richard Hoffman himself, he moved to America, where he murdered two people.

Hoffman immigrated to Pittsburgh during World War II and worked as a busboy for over a decade. He had a terrible, humiliating way of speaking with customers.

"I am from Hungary!" he would bark. "Are you Hungary, too? If you Hungary, you in the right place!"

For years he spoke such garbage, even after he had learned excellent English, and could be mistaken for a native-born steelworker. With this ritual degradation he was tipped generously, and saved enough money to buy a popular supper club called the Pharaoh's Palace, featuring a nightly magic act, a comic and some showgirls. It was a favorite with gamblers and the newly rich.

When Hoffman was in his late forties, he permitted a young man named Ace Douglas to audition for a role as a supporting magician. Ace had no nightclub experience, no professional photos or references, but he had a beautiful voice over the telephone, and Hoffman permitted him an audience.

On the afternoon of the audition, Ace arrived in a tuxedo. His shoes had a wealthy gleam, and he took his cigarettes from a silver case etched with his clean initials. He was a slim, attractive man with fair brown hair. When he was not smiling, he looked like a matinee idol, and when he was smiling, he looked like a friendly lifeguard. Either way, he seemed altogether too affable to perform good magic (Hoffman's other magicians cultivated an intentional menace) but his act was wonderful and entertaining, and he was unsullied by the often stupid fashions of magic at the time. Ace didn't claim to be descended from a vampire, for instance, or empowered with secrets from the tomb of Ramses, or kidnapped by gypsies as a child, or raised by missionaries in the mysterious Orient. He didn't even have a female assistant, unlike Hoffman's other magicians who knew that some bounce in fishnets could save any sloppy act. What's more, Ace had the good sense and class not to call himself the Great anything, or the Magnificent anybody.

On stage, with his smooth hair and white gloves, Ace Douglas had the sexual ease of Sinatra.

An older waitress named Sandra was setting up the cocktail bar at the Pharaoh's Palace on the afternoon of Ace Douglas's audition. She watched the act for a few minutes, then approached Hoffman and whispered in his ear, "At night, when I'm all alone in my bed, I sometimes think about men."

"I bet you do, Sandra," said Hoffman.

She was always talking like this. She was a fantastic, dirty woman, and he had actually had sex with her a few times.

She whispered, "And when I get to thinking about men, Hoffman, I think about a man exactly like that."

"You like him?" Hoffman asked.

"Oh my."

"You think the ladies will like him?"

"Oh my," said Sandra, fanning herself daintily. "Heavens, yes."

Hoffman fired his other two magicians within the hour.

After that, Ace Douglas worked every night that the Pharaoh's Palace was open. He was the highest-paid performer in Pittsburgh. This was not a decade when nice young women generally came to bars unescorted, but the Pharaoh's Palace became a place where nice women—extremely attractive young single nice women—would arrive without dates, with their best girlfriends and with their best dresses to watch the Ace Douglas magic show. And men would come to the Pharaoh's Palace to watch the nice young women and to buy them expensive cocktails.

Hoffman had his own table at the back of the restaurant, and, after the magic show was over, he and Ace Douglas would entertain young ladies there. The girls would blindfold Ace, and then Hoffman would choose an object on the table for identification.

"It's a fork," Ace would say. "It's a gold cigarette lighter."

The more suspicious girls would open their purses and seek unusual objects—family photographs, prescription medicine, a traffic ticket—all of which Ace would describe easily. The girls would laugh, and doubt his blindfold, and cover his eyes with their damp hands. They had names like Lettie and Pearl and Siggie and Donna. They all loved dancing, and they all liked to keep their nice fur wraps with them at the table, out of pride. Hoffman would introduce them to eligible or otherwise interested businessmen. Ace Douglas would escort the nice young ladies to the parking lot late at night, listening politely as they spoke up to him, resting his hand reassuringly on the smalls of their backs if they wavered.

And at the end of every evening Hoffman would say sadly, "Me and Ace, we see so many girls come and go . . ."

Ace Douglas could turn a pearl necklace into a white glove, and a cigarette lighter into a candle. He could produce a silk scarf from a lady's hairpin. But his finest trick was in 1959, when he produced his little sister from a convent school and offered her to Richard Hoffman in marriage.

Her name was Angela. She had been a volleyball champion in the convent school, and she had legs like a movie star's legs, and a very pretty laugh. She was ten days pregnant on her wedding day, although she and Hoffman had only known each other for two weeks. Shortly thereafter, Angela had a daughter, and they named her Esther. Throughout the early 1960s, they all prospered happily.

Esther turned eight years old, and the Hoffmans celebrated her birthday with a special party at the Pharaoh's Palace. That night, there was a thief sitting in the cocktail lounge.

He didn't look like a thief. He was dressed well enough, and he was served without any trouble. The thief drank a few martinis. Then, in the middle of the magic show, he leapt over the bar, kicked the bartender away, punched the cash register open and ran out of the Pharaoh's Palace with his hands full of tens and twenties.

The customers were screaming, and Hoffman heard it from the kitchen. He chased the thief into the parking lot and caught him by the hair.

"You steal from me?" he yelled. "You fucking steal from me?"

"Back off, pal," the thief said. The thief's name was George Purcell, and he was drunk.

"You fucking steal from me?" Hoffman yelled.

He shoved George Purcell into the side of a yellow Buick. Some of the customers had come outdoors, and they were watching from the atrium of the restaurant. Ace Douglas came out, too. He walked past the customers, into the parking lot, and he lit a cigarette. Ace Douglas watched as Hoffman lifted the thief by his shirt and threw him against the hood of a Cadillac.

"Back off me!" Purcell said.

"You fucking steal from me?"

"You ripped my shirt!" Purcell cried, aghast. He was looking down at his ripped shirt when Hoffman shoved him into the side of the yellow Buick again.

Ace Douglas said, "Richard? Could you take it easy?" (The Buick was his, and it was new. Hoffman was steadily pounding George Purcell's head into the door.) "Richard? Excuse me? Excuse me, Richard. Please don't damage my car, Richard."

Hoffman dropped the thief to the ground, and sat on his chest. He caught his breath and then smiled.

"Don't ever," he explained. "Ever. Don't ever steal from me. Ever."

Still sitting on Purcell's chest, he picked up the tens and twenties that had fallen on the asphalt, and handed them to Ace Douglas. Then he slid his hand into Purcell's back pocket and pulled out a wallet, which he opened. He took nine dollars from the wallet, because that was exactly all the money he found there. Purcell was indignant.

"That's my money!" he shouted. "You can't take my money!"

"*Your* money?" Hoffman slapped Purcell's head. "*Your* money? *Your* fucking money?"

Ace Douglas tapped Hoffman's shoulder lightly and said, "Richard? Excuse me? Let's just wait for the police, okay? How about it, Richard?"

"*Your* money?" Hoffman was slapping Purcell in the face now with the wallet. "You fucking steal from me, you have no money! You fucking steal from me, I own all your money!"

"Aw Jesus," Purcell said. "Quit it, will ya? Leave me alone, will ya?"

"Let him be," Ace Douglas said.

"*Your* money? I own all your money!" Hoffman bellowed. "I own you! You fucking steal from me, I own your fucking *shoes*!"

Hoffman lifted Purcell's leg and pulled off one of his shoes. It was a nice brown leather wing tip. He hit Purcell with it once in the face, then tore off the other shoe. He beat on Purcell a few times with that shoe, until he lost his appetite for it. Then he just sat on Purcell's chest for a while, catching his breath, hugging the shoes and rocking in a very sad way.

"Aw, Jesus," Purcell groaned. His lip was bleeding.

"Let's get up now, Richard," Ace suggested.

After some time, Hoffman jumped up off Purcell and walked back into the Pharaoh's Palace, carrying the thief's shoes. His tuxedo was torn in one knee, and his shirt was hanging loose. The customers backed against the walls of the restaurant and let him pass. He went into the kitchen and threw Purcell's shoes into one of the big garbage cans next to the pot-washing sinks. Then he went into his office and shut the door.

The pot washer was a young Cuban fellow named Manuel. He picked George Purcell's brown wing tips out of the garbage can and held one of them up against the bottom of his own foot. It seemed to be a good match, so he took off his own shoes and put on Purcell's. Manuel's shoes had been plastic sandals, and these he threw away, into the big garbage can. A little later, Manuel watched with satisfaction as the chef dumped a vat of cold gravy on top of the sandals, and then he went back to washing pots. He whistled a little song to himself of good luck.

A policeman arrived. He handcuffed George Purcell and brought him into Hoffman's office. Ace Douglas followed them in.

"You want to press charges?" the cop asked.

"No," Hoffman said. "Forget about it."

"You don't press charges, I have to let him go."

"Let him go."

"This man says you took his shoes."

"He's a criminal. He came in my restaurant with no shoes."

"He took my shoes," Purcell said. His shirt collar was soaked with blood.

"He never had no shoes on. Look at him. No shoes on his feet."

"You took my money and my goddamn shoes, you animal. Twenty-dollar shoes!"

"Get this stealing man out of my restaurant, please," Hoffman said.

"Officer?" Ace Douglas said. "Excuse me, but I was here the whole time, and this man never did have any shoes on. He's a derelict, sir."

"But I'm wearing dress socks!" Purcell shouted. "Look at me! Look at me!"

Hoffman stood up and walked out of his office. The cop followed Hoffman leading George Purcell. Ace Douglas trailed behind. On his way through the restaurant, Hoffman stopped to pick up his daughter, Esther, from her birthday-party table. He carried her out to the parking lot.

"Listen to me now," he told Purcell. "You ever steal from me again, I'll kill you."

"Take it easy," the cop said.

"If I even see you on the street, I'll fucking kill you."

The cop said, "You want to press charges, pal, you press charges. Otherwise you take it easy."

"He doesn't like to be robbed," Ace Douglas explained.

"Animal," Purcell muttered.

"You see this little girl?" Hoffman asked. "My little girl is eight years old today. If I'm walking on the street with my little girl and I see you, then I will leave her on one side of the street, and I will cross the street and I will kill you in front of my little girl."

"That's enough," the cop said. He led George Purcell out of the parking lot and took off his handcuffs.

The cop and the thief walked away together. Hoffman stood on the steps of the Pharaoh's Palace, holding Esther and shouting.

"Right in front of my little girl, you make me kill you? What kind of man are you? Crazy man! You ruin a little girl's life! Terrible man!"

Esther was crying. Ace Douglas took her from Hoffman's arms.

The next week, the thief George Purcell came back to the Pharaoh's Palace. It was noon, and very quiet. The prep cook was making chicken stock, and Manuel the pot washer was cleaning out the dry-goods storage area. Hoffman was in his office ordering vegetables from his wholesaler. Purcell came straight back into the kitchen, sober.

"I want my goddamn shoes!" he yelled, pounding on the office door. "Twenty-dollar shoes!"

Then Richard Hoffman came out of his office and beat George Purcell to death with a meat mallet. Manuel the pot washer tried to hold him back, and Hoffman beat him to death with the meat mallet, too.

Esther Hoffman did not grow up to be a natural magician. Her hands were dull. It was no fault of her own, just an unfortunate birth flaw. Otherwise, she was a bright girl.

Her uncle, Ace Douglas, had been the American National Champion Close-Up Magician for three years running. He'd won his titles using no props or tools at all, except a single silver dollar coin. During one competition, he'd vanished and produced the coin for fifteen dizzying minutes without the expert panel of judges ever noticing that the coin spent a lot of time resting openly on Ace Douglas's own knee. He would put it there, where it lay gleaming to be seen if one of the judges had only glanced away for a moment from Ace's hands. But they would never glance away, convinced that he still held a coin before them in his fingers. They were not fools, but they were dupes for his fake takes, his fake drops, his mock passes and a larger cast of impossible moves so deceptive they went entirely unnoticed. Ace Douglas had motions which he himself had never even named. He was a scholar of misdirection. He proscribed skepticism. His fingers were as loose and quick as thoughts.

But Esther Hoffman's magic was sadly pedestrian. She did the Famous Dancing Cane Trick, the Famous Vanishing Milk Trick, and the Famous Chinese Linking Rings Trick. She produced parakeets from light bulbs, and pulled a dove from a burning pan. She performed at birthday parties, and could float a child. She performed at grammar schools, and could cut and restore the neckties of principals. If the principal was a lady, Esther would borrow a ring from the principal's finger, lose it, and then find it in a child's pocket. If the lady principal wore no jewelry, Esther would simply run a sword through the woman's neck while the children in the audience screamed in spasms of rapture.

Simple, artless tricks.

"You're young," Ace told her. "You'll improve."

But she did not. Esther made more money teaching flute lessons to little girls than performing magic. She was a fine flutist, and this was maddening to her. Why all this worthless musical skill?

"Your fingers are very quick," Ace told her. "There's nothing wrong with your fingers. But it's not about quickness, Esther. You don't have to speed through coins."

"I hate coins."

"You should handle coins as if they amuse you, Esther. Not as if they frighten you."

"With coins, it's like I'm wearing oven mitts."

"Coins are not always easy."

"I never fool anybody. I can't misdirect."

"It's not about misdirection, Esther. It's about *direction.*"

"I don't have hands," Esther complained. "I have paws."

It was true that Esther could only fumble coins and cards, and she would never be a deft magician. She had no gift. Also, she hadn't the poise. Esther had seen photographs of her uncle when he was young at the Pharaoh's Palace, leaning against patrician pillars of marble in his tuxedo and cuff links. No form of magic existed which was close-up enough for him. He could sit on a chair surrounded on all sides by the biggest goons of spectators—people who challenged him or grabbed his arm in midpass—and he would borrow same common object and absolutely vanish it. Some goon's car keys in Ace's hand would turn into absolutely nothing. Absolutely gone.

Ace's nightclub act at the Pharaoh's Palace had been a tribute to the most elegant vices. He used coins, cards, dice, champagne flutes, cigarettes—any item which would suggest and encourage drinking, sin, gamesmanship and money. The fluidity of fortune. He could do a whole act of cigarette effects alone, starting with a single cigarette borrowed from a lady in the audience. He would pass it through a coin, and then give the coin—intact—back to the lady. He would tear the cigarette in half and then restore it, swallow it, cough it back up along with six more, duplicate them and duplicate them again until he ended up with lit cigarettes smoking hot between all his fingers and in his mouth, behind his ears, emerging from every pocket—surprised? he was terrified!—and then, with a nod, all the lit cigarettes would vanish except the original. That one cigarette he would transform into a stately pipe, which he would smoke luxuriously during the applause.

Also, Esther had pictures of her father during the same period, when he owned the Pharaoh's Palace. He was handsome in his tuxedo, but with a heavy posture. She had inherited his thick wrists.

When Richard Hoffman got out of prison, he moved in with Ace and Esther. Ace had a tremendous home in the country by then, a tall, yellow Victorian house with a mile of woods behind it and a lawn like a baron's. He had only one neighbor, an elderly woman with a similarly huge Victorian home, just next door. Ace Douglas had made a tidy fortune from magic. He had operated the Pharaoh's Palace from the time that Hoffman was arrested, and with Hoffman's permission had eventually sold it at great profit to a gourmet restaurateur. Esther had been living with Ace since she'd finished high school, and she had a whole floor to herself. Ace's leggy little sister Angela had divorced Hoffman, also with his permission, and had moved to Florida to live with her new husband.

What Hoffman had never permitted was for Esther to visit him in prison, and so it had been fourteen years since they'd seen each other. In prison he had grown even sturdier. He seemed shorter than Ace and Esther remembered, and some weight gained had made him broader. He had also grown a thick beard with elegant red tones. He was easily moved to tears, or at least seemed to be always on the verge of being moved to tears. The first few weeks of living together again were not altogether comfortable for Esther and Hoffman. They had only the briefest conversations, such as this one:

Hoffman asked Esther, "How old are you now?"

"Twenty-two."

"I've got undershirts older than you."

Or, in another conversation, Hoffman said, "The fellows I met in prison are the nicest fellows in the world."

And Esther said, "Actually, Dad, they probably aren't."

And so on.

In December of that year, Hoffman attended a magic show of Esther's, performed at a local elementary school.

"She's really not very good," he reported later to Ace.

"I really think she's fine," Ace said. "She's fine for the kids, and she enjoys herself."

"She's pretty terrible. Too dramatic."

"Perhaps."

"She says, 'Behold!' It's terrible, Behold this! Behold that!"

"But they're children," Ace said. "With children, you need to explain when you're about to do a trick and when you just did one, because they're so excited they don't realize what's going on. They don't even know what a magician is, Richard. They can't tell the difference between when you're doing magic and when you're just standing there."

"I think she was very nervous."

"Could be."

"She says, 'Behold the Parakeet!'"

"Her parakeet tricks are not bad."

"It's not dignified," Hoffman said. "She convinces nobody."

"It's not meant to be dignified, Richard. It's for the children."

The next week, Hoffman bought Esther a large white rabbit.

"If you do the tricks for the children, you should have a rabbit," he told her.

Esther hugged him. She said, "I never had a rabbit."

Hoffman lifted the rabbit from the cage. It was an unnaturally enormous rabbit.

"Is it pregnant?" Esther asked.

"No, she is not. She is only large."

"That's an extremely large rabbit for any magic trick," Ace observed.

Esther said, "They haven't invented the hat big enough to pull that rabbit out of."

"She actually folds up to a small size," Hoffman said. He held the rabbit between his hands like it was an accordion and squeezed it into a great white ball.

"She seems to like that," Ace said, and Esther laughed.

"She doesn't mind it. Her name is Bonnie." Hoffman held the rabbit forward by the nape of her neck, as though she were a massive kitten. Dangling fully stretched like that, she was bigger than a big raccoon.

"Where'd you get her?" Esther asked.

"From the newspaper!" Hoffman announced, beaming.

Esther liked Bonnie the rabbit more than she liked her trick doves and parakeets, which were attractive enough, but were essentially only pigeons that had been lucky with their looks. Ace liked Bonnie, too. He allowed Bonnie to enjoy the entirety of his large Victorian home, with little regard for Bonnie's pellets, which were small, rocky and inoffensive. She particularly enjoyed sitting in the center of the kitchen table and from that spot would regard Ace, Esther and Hoffman gravely. Bonnie had a feline manner.

"Will she always be this judgmental?" Esther wanted to know.

Bonnie became more canine when she was allowed outdoors. She would sleep on the porch, lying on her side in a patch of sun, and if anyone approached the porch she would look up at that person lazily, in the manner of a bored and trustful dog. At night, she slept with Hoffman. He tended to sleep on his side, curled like a child, and Bonnie would sleep upon him, perched on his highest point, which was generally his hip.

As a performer, however, Bonnie was useless. She was far too large to be handled gracefully on stage, and on the one occasion that Esther did try to produce her from a hat, she hung in the air so sluggishly that the children in the back rows were sure that she was a fake. She appeared to be a huge toy, as typical and store bought as their own stuffed animals.

"Bonnie will never be a star," Hoffman said.

Ace said, "You spoiled her, Richard, the way the magicians have been spoiling their lovely assistants for decades. You spoiled Bonnie by sleeping with her."

That spring, a young lawyer and his wife (who was also a young lawyer) moved into the large Victorian house next door to Ace

Douglas's large Victorian house. It all happened very swiftly. The widow who had lived there for decades died in her sleep, and the place was sold within a few weeks. The new neighbors had great ambitions. The husband, whose name was Ronald Wilson, telephoned Ace and asked if there were any problems he should know about in the area, regarding water-drainage patterns or frost heaves. Ronald had plans for a great garden and was interested in building an arbor to extend from the back of the house. His wife, whose name was Ruth-Ann, was running for probate judge of the county. Ronald and Ruth-Ann were tall and had perfect manners. They had no children.

Three days after the Wilsons moved in next door, Bonnie the rabbit disappeared. She was on the porch, and then she was not.

Hoffman searched all afternoon for Bonnie. On Esther's recommendation, he spent that evening walking up and down the road with a flashlight, looking to see if Bonnie had been hit by a car. The next day, he walked through the woods behind the house, calling the rabbit for hours. He left a bowl of cut vegetables outside on the porch with some fresh water. Several times during the night, Hoffman got up to see if Bonnie was on the porch, eating the food. Eventually, he just wrapped himself in blankets and laid down on the porch swing, keeping a vigil beside the vegetables. He slept out there for a week, changing the food every morning and evening to keep the scent fresh.

Esther made a poster with a drawing of Bonnie (which looked very much like a spaniel in her rendering) and a caption reading LARGE RABBIT MISSING. She stapled copies of the poster on telephone poles throughout town and placed a notice in the newspaper. Ace Douglas called the local ASPCA for daily updates. Hoffman wrote a letter to the neighbors, Ronald and Ruth-Ann Wilson, and slid it under their door. The letter described Bonnie's color and weight, gave the date and time of her disappearance and requested any information on the subject at all. The Wilsons did not call with news, so the next day Hoffman went over to their house and rang the doorbell. Ronald Wilson answered.

"Did you get my letter?" Hoffman asked.

"About the rabbit?" Ronald said. "Have you found him?"

"The rabbit is a girl. And the rabbit belongs to my daughter. She was a gift. Have you seen her?"

"She didn't get in the road, did she?"

"Is Bonnie in your house, Mr. Wilson?"

"Is Bonnie the rabbit's name?"

"Yes."

"How would Bonnie get in our house?"

"Perhaps you have some broken window in the basement?"

"You think she's in our basement?"

"Have you looked for her in your basement?"

"No."

"Can I look for her?"

"You want to look for a rabbit in our basement?"

The two men stared at each other for some time. Ronald Wilson was wearing a baseball cap, and he took it off and rubbed the top of his head, which was balding. He put the baseball cap back on.

"Your rabbit is not in our house, Mr. Hoffman," Wilson said.

"Okay," Hoffman said. "Okay. Sure."

Hoffman walked back home. He sat at the kitchen table and waited until Ace and Esther were both in the room to make his announcement.

"They took her," he said. "The Wilsons took Bonnie."

Hoffman started to build the tower in July. There was a row of oak trees between Ace Douglas's house and the Wilsons' house, and the leaves from these trees blocked Hoffman's view into their home. For several months, he'd been spending his nights watching the Wilson house from the attic window with binoculars, looking for Bonnie inside, but he could not see into the lower-floor rooms for the trees and was frustrated. Ace reassured him that the leaves would be gone by autumn, but Hoffman was afraid that Bonnie would be dead by autumn. This was difficult for him to take. He was no longer allowed to go over to the Wilsons' property and look into the basement windows, since Ruth-Ann Wilson had called the police. He was no longer allowed to write threatening letters. He was no longer allowed to call the Wilsons up on the telephone. He had promised Ace and Esther all of these things.

"He's really harmless," Esther would tell Ruth-Ann Wilson, although she herself was not sure this was the case.

Ronald Wilson found out somehow that Hoffman had been in prison, and he'd contacted the parole officer, who had, in turn, contacted Hoffman, suggesting that he leave the Wilsons alone.

"If you would only let him search your home for the rabbit," Ace Douglas had suggested gently to the Wilsons, "this would be over very quickly. Just give him a half hour to look around. It's just that he's concerned that Bonnie is trapped in your basement."

"Why would we keep his rabbit? Why would we do that?"

Hoffman said to Ace, "Because of the vegetable garden. Think about this. Vegetables, Ace. Naturally, they are against the rabbit."

"If you would just let him look inside once . . ." Ace repeated.

"We did not move here to let murderers into our home," Ronald Wilson said.

"He's not a murderer," Esther protested, somewhat lamely.

"He scares my wife."

"I don't want to scare your wife," Hoffman said.

"He's really harmless," Esther insisted. "Maybe you could buy him a new rabbit."

"I don't want any new rabbit," Hoffman said.

"You scare my wife," Ronald repeated. "We don't owe you any rabbit at all."

In late spring, Hoffman cut down the smallest oak tree between the two houses. He did it on a Monday afternoon, when the Wilsons were at work, and Esther was performing magic for a Girl Scouts party, and Ace was shopping. He'd purchased a chain saw weeks earlier and had been hiding it. The tree wasn't very big, but it fell at a sharp diagonal across the Wilsons' backyard, narrowly missing their arbor and destroying a substantial corner of the garden.

The police came. After a great deal of negotiating, Ace Douglas was able to prove that the oak tree, while between the two houses, was actually on his property, and it was his right to have it cut down. He offered to pay generously for the damages to the Wilsons. Ronald Wilson came over to the house again that night, but he would not speak until Ace sent Hoffman from the room.

"Do you understand our situation?" he asked.

"I do," Ace said. "I honestly do."

The two men sat at the kitchen table across from one another for some time. Ace offered to get Ronald some coffee, which he refused.

"How can you live with him?" Ronald asked.

Ace did not answer this, but got himself some coffee. He opened the refrigerator and pulled out a carton of milk, which he smelled and then poured down the sink. After this, he smelled his cup of coffee, which he poured down the sink as well.

"Is he your boyfriend?" Ronald asked.

"Is Richard my boyfriend? No. He's my very good friend. And he's my brother-in-law."

"Really," Ronald said. He was working his wedding band around his finger as though he were screwing it on tight.

"You thought it was a dream come true to buy that nice old house, didn't you?" Ace Douglas asked. He managed to say this in a friendly, sympathetic way.

"Yes, we did."

"But it's a nightmare, isn't it? Living next to us?"

"Yes, it is."

Ace Douglas laughed. Ronald Wilson laughed, too, and said, "It's a complete fucking nightmare, actually."

"I'm very sorry that your wife is afraid of us, Ronald."

"Well."

"I truly am."

"Thank you. It's difficult. She's a bit paranoid sometimes."

"Well," Ace said, again in a friendly and sympathetic way. "Imagine that. Paranoid! In this neighborhood?"

The two men laughed again. Meanwhile, in the other room, Esther was talking to her father.

"Why'd you do it, Dad?" she asked. "Such a pretty tree."

He had been weeping.

"Because I am so sad," he said, finally. "I wanted them to feel it."

"To feel how sad you were?" she said.

"To feel how sad I am," he told her. "How sad I am."

Anyway, in July he started to build the tower.

Ace had an old pickup truck, and Hoffman used this to drive to the municipal dump every afternoon, so that he could look for wood and scrap materials. He built the base of the tower out of pine, reinforced with parts of an old steel bed frame. By the end of July the tower was over ten feet high. He wasn't planning on building a staircase inside, so it was a solid cube.

The Wilsons called the zoning board, who fined Ace Douglas for erecting an unauthorized structure on his property and insisted that the work stop immediately.

"It's only a tree house," Esther lied to the zoning officer.

"It's a watchtower," Hoffman corrected. "So that I can see into the neighbor's house."

The zoning officer gave Hoffman a long, empty look.

"Yes," Hoffman said. "This truly is a watchtower."

"Take it down," said the zoning officer to Esther. "Take it down immediately."

Ace Douglas owned a significant library of antique magic books, including several volumes that Hoffman himself had brought over from Hungary during the Second World War, and that had been old and valuable even then. Hoffman had purchased these rare books from gypsies and dealers across Eastern Europe with the last of his family's money. In the 1950s, he'd given them over to Ace. Some volumes were written in German, some in Russian, some in English.

The collection revealed the secrets of Parlor Magic, or Drawing Room Magic, a popular pursuit of educated gentlemen at the turn of the century. The books spoke not of tricks, but of "diversions," which were sometimes magical maneuvers but were just as often simple scientific experiments. Often, these diversions involved hypnosis or the appearance of hypnosis. Many tricks required complicated acts of memorization and practice with a trained conspirator hidden among the otherwise susceptible guests. A gentleman might literally use smoke and a mirror to evoke a ghost within the parlor. A gentleman might read a palm or levitate a tea tray. Or, a gentleman might simply demonstrate that an egg could stand on its end, or that magnets could react against one another, or that an electric current could turn a small motorized contrivance.

The books were exquisitely illustrated. Hoffman had given them to Ace Douglas back in the 1950s, because he had hoped for some time to recreate this lost conjury in Pittsburgh. He had hoped to decorate a small area within the Pharaoh's Palace in the manner of a formal upper-middle-class European drawing room, and to dress Ace in spats and kid gloves. Ace did study the books, but he found that there was no way to accurately replicate most of the diversions. The old tricks all called for common household items which were simply not common any more: a box of paraffin, a pinch of snuff, a dab of beeswax, a spittoon, a watch fob, a ball of cork, a sliver of saddle soap, et cetera. Even if such ingredients could be gathered, they would have no meaning to modern spectators. It would be museum magic, resonating to nobody. It would move nobody.

To Hoffman, this was a considerable disappointment. As a very young man he had watched the Russian charlatan and swindling necromancer Katanovsky perform such diversions in his mother's own drawing room. His mother, recently widowed, wore dark gowns dressed with china-blue silk ribbons precisely the same shade as the famous blue vials of Hoffman's Rose Water. Her face was that of a determined regent. His sisters, in childish pinafores, regarded Katanovsky in a pretty stupor of wonder.

Gathered in the drawing room as a family, they had all heard it. Hoffman himself—his eyes stinging from phosphorus smoke—had heard it: the unmistakable voice of his recently dead father, speaking through Katanovksy's own dark mouth. They heard their father's message (in perfectly accentless Hungarian!) of reassurance. A thrilling, intimate call to faith.

And so it was unfortunate for Hoffman that Ace Douglas could not replicate this very diversion. He would've liked to have seen it tried again. It must have been a very simple swindle, although an antique one. Hoffman would've liked to have witnessed the hoax voice of his dead father repeated and explained to him fully and, if necessary, repeated again.

On the first day of September, Hoffman woke at dawn and began preparing his truck. Months later, during the court proceedings, the Wilsons' attorney would attempt to show that Hoffman had stockpiled weapons in the bed of the truck, an allegation that Esther and Ace would contest heatedly. Certainly there were tools in the truck— a few shovels, a sledgehammer and an ax—but if these were threatening, they were not so intentionally.

Hoffman had recently purchased several dozen rolls of wide, silvery electrical duct tape, and at dawn he began winding the tape around the body of the truck. He wound long lengths of the tape, and then more tape over the existing tape, and he did this again and again, as armor.

Esther had an early morning flute class to teach, and she got up to eat her cereal. From the kitchen window, she saw her father taping his pickup. The headlights and taillights were already covered and the doors were sealed shut. She went outside.

"Dad?" she said.

And Hoffman said, almost apologetically, "I'm going over there."

"Not to the Wilsons?"

"I'm going in after Bonnie," he said.

Esther walked back to the house, feeling shaky. She woke Ace Douglas, who looked from his bedroom window down at Hoffman in the driveway, and he called the police.

"Oh, not the police." Esther said. "Not the police . . ."

Ace held her in a hug for some time.

"Are you crying?" he asked.

"No," she lied.

"You're not crying?"

"No, I'm just sad."

When the duct tape ran out, Hoffman circled the truck a few times and noticed that he had no way to enter it now. He took the sledge-hammer from the flatbed and lightly tapped the passenger-side window with it, until the glass was evenly spiderwebbed. Then he gently pushed the window in. The glass crystals landed silently on the seat. He climbed inside, then noticed that he had no keys, so he climbed out of the broken window again and walked into the house where he found his keys on the kitchen table. Esther wanted to go downstairs to talk with him, but Ace Douglas would not let her go. He went down himself, and Esther slid her head under Ace's pillow and cried in a hard, down-low way.

Downstairs, Ace said, "I'm sorry, Richard. But I've called the police."

"The police?" Hoffman repeated, wounded. "Not the police, Ace."

"I'm sorry."

Hoffman was silent for a long time, staring at Ace.

"But I'm going in there after Bonnie," he said, finally.

"I wish you wouldn't do that."

"But they have her," Hoffman said, and he was now crying, as well.

"I don't believe that they do have her, Richard."

"But they *stole* her!"

Hoffman took up his keys and climbed back into his taped-up truck, still weeping. He drove over to the Wilsons' home, and circled their house several times. He drove through the corn in the garden. Forward over the corn, then backwards, then forward over the corn again. Ruth-Ann Wilson came running out, and she pulled up some bricks that were lining her footpath and chased after Hoffman, throwing the bricks at his truck and screaming.

Hoffman pulled the truck up to the metal basement doors of the Wilsons' house. He tried to drive right up on them, but his truck didn't have the power, and the wheels sunk into the wet lawn. He honked in long, forlorn foghorn blasts.

When the police arrived, Hoffman would not come out. He would, however, put his hands on the steering wheel to show that he was not armed.

"He doesn't have a gun," Esther shouted from the porch of Ace Douglas's house.

Two officers circled the truck and examined it. The younger officer tapped on Hoffman's window and asked him to roll it down, but he refused.

"Tell them to bring her outside!" he shouted. "Bring the rabbit and I will come out of the truck! Bring Bonnie! Terrible people!"

The older officer cut through the duct tape on the passenger-side door with a utility knife. He was able, finally, to open the door, and when he did that, he was able to reach in and drag Hoffman out, both of them cutting their arms over the spilled, sparkling glass of the broken window. Once outside the truck, Hoffman lay on the grass in a limp sprawl, face down. He was handcuffed and taken away in a squad car.

Ace and Esther followed the police to the station, where the officers took Hoffman's belt and his fingerprints. Hoffman was wearing only an undershirt and work pants, and his cell was small, empty and chilly.

Esther asked the older police officer, "May I go home and bring my father back a jacket? Or a blanket? May I please just do that?"

"You may," said the older police officer, and he patted her arm with a sort of authoritative sympathy. "You may, indeed."

Back home, Esther washed her face and took some aspirin. She called the mother of her flute student and canceled that morning's class. The mother wanted to reschedule, but Esther could only promise to call later. She noticed the milk on the kitchen counter and returned it to the refrigerator. She brushed her teeth. She changed into warmer autumn boots, and she went to the living room closet and found a light wool blanket for her father. She heard a noise.

Esther followed the noise, which was that of a running automobile engine. She went to the window of the living room and parted the curtain. In the Wilsons' driveway was a sturdy white van with grills on the windows. The side of this van was marked with the emblem of the ASPCA. Esther said aloud, "Oh my."

A man in white coveralls came out of the Wilsons' front door, carrying a large wire cage. Inside the cage was Bonnie.

. . .

Esther had never been inside the local ASPCA building, and she did not go inside it that day. She parked near the van, which she had followed, and watched as the man in the coveralls opened the back doors and pulled out a cage. This cage held three gray kittens, which he carried into the building, leaving the van doors open.

When the man was safely inside, Esther got out of her car and walked to the back of the van. She found the cage with Bonnie, opened it easily and pulled out the rabbit. Bonnie was much thinner than the last time Esther had seen her, and the rabbit eyed her with an absolutely expressionless gaze of nonrecognition. Esther carried Bonnie to her car and drove back to the police station.

She parked her car and got out, tucking the rabbit under her left arm. She wrapped the light wool blanket she'd brought for her father completely around herself, like a cape. Esther walked briskly into the police station. She passed the older police officer, who was talking to Ace Douglas and Ralph Wilson. She raised her right hand as she walked near the men and said solemnly, "How, palefaces."

Ace smiled at her, and the older police officer waved her by.

Hoffman's jail cell was at the end of a hallway, and it was poorly lit. Hoffman had not been sleeping well for several weeks, and he was cold and cut. One frame of his glasses had been cracked, and he had been weeping since that morning. He saw Esther approaching, wrapped in that light gray wool blanket, and he saw in her the figure of his mother, who had worn cloaks against the Budapest winters and who had also walked with a particular dignity.

Esther approached the cell, and she reached her hand between the bars toward her father, who rose with a limp to meet that hand. In a half-mad moment, he half-imagined her to be a warm apparition of his mother, and, as he reached for her, she smiled.

Her smile directed his gaze from her hand to her face, and in that instant, Esther pulled her arm back out of the cell, reached into the folds of the blanket around her and gracefully produced the rabbit. She slid Bonnie—slimmer now, of course—through the iron bars and held the rabbit aloft in the cell, exactly where her empty hand had been only a moment before. Such that Hoffman, when he glanced down from Esther's smile, saw a rabbit where before there had simply been no rabbit at all. Like a true enchantment, something appeared from the common air.

"Behold," said Esther.

Richard Hoffman beheld the silken rabbit and recognized her as Bonnie. He collected her into his square hands. And then, he did also behold his own daughter Esther.

A most gifted young woman.

Frederick Busch

✠

Widow Water

I spent the afternoon driving to New Hartford to the ice cream plant for twenty-five pounds of sliced dry ice. I had them cut the ice into ten-inch long slivers about three-quarters of an inch in width, wrapped the ice in heavy brown paper and drove it back to Brookfield and the widow's jammed drill-point. It's all hard-water country here, and the crimped-pipe points they drive down for wells get sealed with calcium scales if you wait enough years, and the pressure falls, the people call, they worry about having to drill new wells and how much it will cost and when they can flush the toilets again, how long they'll have to wait.

I went in the cellar door without telling her I was there, disconnected the elbow joint, went back out for the ice and, when I had carried the second bundle in, she was standing by her silent well in the damp of her basement, surrounded by furniture draped in plastic sheets, firewood stacked, cardboard boxes of web-crusted Mason jars, the growing heaps of whatever in her life she couldn't use.

She was small and white and dressed in sweaters and a thin green housecoat. She said, "Whatever do you mean to do?" Her hands were folded across her little chest, and she rubbed her gnarled throat. "Is my well dead?"

"No ma'am. I'd like you to go upstairs while I do my small miracle here. Because I'd like you not to worry. Won't you go upstairs?"

She said, "I live alone—"

I said, "You don't have to worry."

"I don't know what to do about—this kind of thing. It gets more and more of a problem—this—all this." She waved her hand at what she lived in and then hung her hands at her sides.

I said, "You go on up and watch the television. I'm going to fix it up. I'll do a little fixing here and come back tonight and hook her up again and you be ready to make me my after-dinner coffee when I come back. You'll have water enough to do it with."

"Just go back upstairs," she said.

"You go on up while I make it good. And I don't want you worrying."

"Alright, then," she said, "I'll go back up. I get awfully upset now. When these—things. These—I don't know what to do anymore." She looked at me like something that was new. Then she said, "I knew your father, I think. Was he big like you?"

"You know it," I said. "Bigger. Didn't he court you one time?"

"I think everybody then must have courted me one time."

"You were frisky," I said.

"Not like now," she said. Her lips were white on her white face, the flesh looked like flower petals: pinch them and they crumble, wet dust.

"Don't you feel so good now?"

"I mean kids now."

"Oh?"

"They have a different notion of frisky now."

"Yes they do," I said. "I guess they do."

"But I don't feel so good," she said. "This. Things like this. I wish they wouldn't happen. Now. I'm very old."

I said, "It keeps on coming, doesn't it?"

"I can hear it come. When the well stopped, I thought it was a sign. When you get like me, you can hear it come."

I said, "Now listen: you go up. You wrap a blanket around you and talk on the telephone or watch the tee-vee. Because I guarantee. You knew my father. You knew my father's word. Take mine. I guarantee."

I said, "That's my girl." She was past politeness so she didn't smile or come back out of herself to say goodbye. She walked to the stairs and when she started to shuffle and haul the long way up, I turned away to the well pipe, calling, "You make sure and have my coffee ready tonight. You wait and make my after-dinner coffee, hear? There'll be water for it." I waited until she went up, and it was something of a wait. She was too tired for stairs. I thought to tell Bella that it looked like the widow hadn't long.

But when she was gone I worked. I put my ear to the pipe and heard the sounds of hollowness, the emptiness under the earth that's not quite silence—like the whisper you hear in the long-distance wires of the telephone before the relays connect. Then I opened the brown paper packages and started forcing the lengths of dry ice down into the pipe. I carried and shoved, drove the ice first with my fingers and then with a piece of copper tube, and I filled the well pipe until nothing more would go. My fingers were red, and the smoke from dry ice misted up until I stood in an underground fog. When nothing more would fit, I capped the pipe, kicked the rest of the ice down into the sump—it steamed as if she lived above a fire, as if always her house was smoldering—and I went out, drove home. I went by the hill roads, and near Excell's farm I turned the motor off, drifted down the dirt road in neutral, watching. The deer had come down from the high hills and they were moving delicately through the fields of last year's cornstumps, grazing like cattle at dusk, too many to count. When the truck stopped I heard the rustle as they pulled the tough silk. Then I started the motor—they jumped, stiffened, watched me for a while, went back to eating: a man could come and kill them, they had so little fear—and I drove home to Bella and a tight house, long dinner, silence for most of the meal, then talk about the children while I washed the dishes and she put them away.

And then I drove back to the house that was dark except for one lighted window. The light was yellow and not strong. I turned the engine off and coasted in. I went downstairs on the tips of my toes because, I told myself, there was a sense of silence there, and I hoped she was having some rest. I uncapped the well pipe and gases blew back, a stink of the deepest cold, and then there was a sound of climbing, filling up, and water banged to her house again. I put the funnel and hose on the mouth of the pipe and filled my jeep can, then capped the check valve, closed the pipe that delivered the water upstairs, poured water from the jeep can through the funnel in to prime the pump, switched it on, watched the pressure needle climb to thirty-eight pounds, opened the faucet to the upstairs pipes and heard it gush. I hurried to get the jeep can and hose and funnel and tools to the truck, and I had closed the cellar door and driven off before she made the porch to call me. I wanted to get back to Bella and tell her what a man she was married to—who could know so well the truths of ice that he could calculate its gases would build up pressure enough to force the scales from a sealed-in pipe and make a dead well live.

Charlie Smith

❅

Crystal River

I

I was on the back porch washing greens when Harold drove around the side of the house with a stolen canoe on top of the truck and a bushel of oysters in back.

"I thought you were down fishing on the flats," I said as he came up the steps with the oysters in a sack over his shoulder. "Your Mama said you'd be down there all week."

"That's right," he said. "I was planning to."

He dropped the sack and pulled half a dozen oyster knives out of his pocket. "Throw that stuff out," he said looking at the greens. "We need to put these babies in the sink."

"Just a minute," I said.

I lifted the sopping greens in a mass and mashed them into a pot. "Let me put them on the stove."

"Just put them in the fridge," he said. "We'll need the pot."

I went into the kitchen, found a couple of ham hocks in the refrigerator and put them with the greens to simmer. When I came back Harold was dumping oysters into the sink.

"Where'd you get the cuties?" I asked.

"Panacea. And they are just delicious."

"Did you try one?"

"Of course. You got horseradish?"

"Sure."

I went inside and got it out of the fridge.

"We got to clean these things off first," he said when I set horse-radish, tabasco, ketchup, saltines, bowls, and forks on the plank be-side the sink. "You remember those oysters we got in Savannah?"

"The muddy ones?"

"Yeah. We had to wash them all afternoon."

"They were good."

"Ugm."

He had poured most of the bushel into the sink. I mixed sauce in a bowl, selected the shortest of the knives and began to open.

"You want one?" I said.

"You crazy?" He speared the biggest one with a fork, dipped it in sauce and ate it without a cracker.

"Christ," he said, "nobody but you can eat your sauce."

"I like it hot."

"You sure do." Gold sand stuck to his wrists and to the back of his hands.

"How come you came back from the flats?" I said.

"Teddy got sick." Teddy was his brother, a pill addict and drunk-ard with a penchant for rifling the medicine cabinets of any house he happened to be in and swallowing whatever he found that might carry a charge. "He was mixing wine and phenobarbs—I had to carry him in this morning to get him pumped out."

"Jesus. Is he okay?"

"Yeah, he's fine, fine as Teddy gets. But it knocked us off the flats. On the way back I stopped for this bushel, and I figured that since I was already primed for a trip I'd come over and see if you wanted to go down Crystal River. You want to?"

"It might be a good idea. Where'd you get the canoe?" It had Fort Benning Rec. Dept. stenciled on the bow. There were a couple of deep dents in the aluminum near the center.

"It's one I relocated from the Army," he said.

"Didn't they miss it?"

"I told them I lost it on the Toccoa. The water was too high and when we went under, it got away from us and we couldn't catch it."

"Sounds like a rough trip."

"Terrible."

He went out to the truck and came back with a bag of ice that he dumped over the cleaned oysters in the sink. "There," he said, tossing the bag on the floor and picking up a knife. "I'm ready to go. Come here you sweet succulents."

"Hold on a second," I said.

I went in the house and got the vodka out of the freezer.

"Now you're talking," he said as I set the bottle on the shelf behind the sink.

We stood at the sink shucking oysters and sipping vodka, looking out through the screen at the warm March sunshine leaning into the garden. The cocker pup from next door came up the steps and scratched at the door and I let him in. He curled up under the sink and went to sleep.

We ate through the end of the afternoon into the evening.

At five the Amtrak train roared by down beyond the garden fence on its way to Miami. From the porch we could see passengers eating supper in the dining car.

Later we drove up to the store for milk and came back and made a stew. We ate the stew, with a side dish of greens, at my work table in the dining room then went back out on the porch and finished the rest of the oysters. They were delicious to the end, cold and salty, full of sea water.

"It's like eating the ocean," Harold said as he banged one of the last, hard-to-open shells on the lip of the sink. "That's what I told Lola."

"She like oysters?"

"Not much. I had to turn them into poetry to get her to try the first one."

"Ugm. Frieda was like that."

"Wouldn't eat them?"

"Not at first. Then she couldn't do without them. The last time I saw her we went down to Appilachicola and she out-ate me by half. Finished sixty-three and eight bottles of Blue Ribbon."

"I guess she got the hang of it. You going to see each other any more?"

"No. The divorce'll be final in two weeks and I don't expect we'll have much to talk about after that. Everything's been settled."

But then I could see her that minute. Leaning over the hoe to pluck a flower from a potato vine. Jelly, jelly, I yell, and her hand swings to cover the backs of her thighs. Jack, is it so? she would say, and I would get up from the steps, cross the garden and take her in my arms, saying, No, it isn't. Your legs are beautiful. And I would drop to the ground and kiss her knees as she threaded the flower into my hair.

"I'll miss her," Harold said.

"Well, you ought to go see her."

"I probably will."

"Give her my love."

"You betcha."

We finished the oysters and dumped the shells into the sack. Harold took the sack out to the garbage. I carried the vodka into the living room, lighted the lantern and when Harold came back we had a final drink sitting in the wicker chairs in front of the empty fireplace.

"It's getting colder," Harold said. "It'll be cold tomorrow."

"You think we'll be all right on the river?"

"I don't see why not. You've got your duck bag, don't you?"

"Yes. What about you?"

"I just got a piece of cotton, but I can wrap up in a poncho."

We finished the drinks, I blew the lantern out and we went into the bedroom and got into my bed.

I woke during the night with Harold's hand in my groin.

"I can't sleep," he said.

"All right."

I turned around, slid down under the quilt and, as I had done so many times since our childhood, took him in my mouth. He smelled just like a woman. I sucked him until he was ready to come then pulled away and let him catch it in his hand.

"Have you got a towel?" he said when he finished.

"In the bathroom."

He got up and got it.

"I was horny," he said when he had crawled across me and slid back under the covers.

"Ugm."

"You want to come?"

"I don't think I can."

"Don't you feel bad?"

"I don't feel much of anything."

We hadn't turned on the lights. I kissed him on the lips, rolled away and went to sleep.

II

I lay in bed in the first gray light thinking, I am a man here, I inhabit this life. I heard Harold rummaging in the kitchen. The morning train came through, bound for Chicago, rattling the window panes. I reached over my head and touched vibrating glass. This hooks me into that run, too, I thought, I'm plucked onto the line, too.

"I think we ought to make this the rule, Harold," I called.

He stuck his head in the door. He had on my old felt hunting hat.

"Make what?" he said.

"Your getting up early to take care of things."

"Jack, my boy," he said, pulling the hat down fore and aft, "I was just getting my turn out of the way. Don't you have any pots?"

"They're under the sink."

I got up, pulled shirt, pants and sweater out of a pile on the dresser and put them on.

He was throwing cans of food into a cardboard box on the dining-room table when I came out.

"Got to get some Viennas," he said. "Can't go into the wilderness without Vienna sausage."

"And saltines," I said. "Jesus, it's cold." I opened the refrigerator and looked in. "Did we drink all the vodka?"

"Don't start that. We got to stay sober until noon at least."

"Okay." I took the pot of greens out. Liquid broke the gray rind of pork grease as I set it on the table.

"You want coffee?" I said.

"I wouldn't mind it."

I fired the percolator and went into the bathroom. Through the window I could see frost in the garden. Broccoli and peas bent over by cold. No Frieda there. Here, only Harold and me, in the oldest of partnerships, still rubbing up the life between us. I collected my kit. When I flushed the toilet I could hear water running onto the ground below the house.

We drank coffee and ate cold greens from the pot. Harold didn't mention last night and I didn't bring it up either; we had long since stopped talking about those things. But when I got up to go into the bedroom for my gear I bent in passing and kissed him, lightly, on the crown of his head. He looked up from his bowl of greens with amused eyes. "Run one out and run another one in," he said. "That's how it works."

"Yeah, boy," I said.

In the bedroom I stuffed clothes into a plastic bag and got my tent and sleeping bag from the closet.

Harold carried the box of food to the truck and put it in the back.

"Anything else?" he said.

"Snackers."

"We can stop at the store."

Behind us the sun was climbing into pines as we pulled out on the road. Davis Kreps, my across-the-street neighbor, pulled himself in his wheelchair one-handed along his front porch toward the day's first warm spot. I waved to him across Harold's lap. His good hand came up and he shouted something I couldn't catch.

"Davis is drunk already," Harold said, throwing a wave.

"He's never undrunk," I said.

We passed the house-that-never-spoke, Willis Faver's old family place that he had let fall back into a ruin of weeds and bamboo after his mother died, and pulled up under a tasseling yellow pine in front of the store.

"Have you ever been in Willis's Mama's place?" I asked.

"No."

"He didn't even take the curtains down after she died. Everything's still there. There's a pump organ in the living room and hand-painted pictures on the walls."

"Hand-painted, huh?"

"And out in the shed bamboo's grown up between the bumper and the fender of his Mama's old Buick."

"I'd like to have that."

"Me too." The gassed-up memory.

We pushed through the door into the store.

Fruit—oranges, apples, tangelos—was piled in bins along the wall, bright as lights. Old potatoes in wire-footed racks, eyes sprouting. Frosty glassed-in drinks. An old red-headed woman, Mrs. Harley Cantrell, was eating cheese and crackers off a newspaper behind the counter.

We want snackers: olives, green and black; pork rinds; canned boiled peanuts; kosher pickles; hot sausages—could we have half a pound of rat cheese, please?

"I got pickled eggs in the truck," Harold said.

"Mrs. Cantrell," I said, "you ever pickle eggs?"

"I wouldn't have them in the house," Mrs. Cantrell said, smiling. "Where you boys off to?"

"Crystal River."

"That down in Florida?" she said, not too enthusiastically.

"Yes'm."

She pushed a wisp of hair out of her eyes with the back of her wrist, stacked a cracker with cheese and stuffed it into her mouth.

"I never ate a pickled egg in my life," she said through the mouthful. "That's drinking trash."

"Kept in a jar in the Ponderosa Sugarhouse," Harold said, "right between the pig's feet and the parched peanuts."

"That I couldn't say. This be all?" she said to the pile on the counter.

"Believe so," I said. We each paid half, pulling bills from front pockets.

"You got enough money?" I said on the way out.

"For what?"

"Beer. Goodies."

"Sure."

Blossoms floated in the branches of a dogwood near the street. Two small boys, shirts flapping, pedaled full speed toward town.

"We can get beer at the Line," I said. "Save cash."

"You betcha."

We slipped south through town out into a country of low pastures and thick horizon-hampering woods. Live oaks and cypress hung over black-water ponds. Cabbage palms dying around a red house. A black man peering from an outhouse door.

Ferns sprung green in fire-blackened woods. They're like blueberries in fired fields up north. Come out of nowhere.

"Harold, have you ever eaten a dog?" I said.

Harold plucked his crotch and said that no, he never had, but he had certainly wanted to.

"It's white meat," I said. "Sweeter than pork."

"I'd like to eat Mama's chihuahua," he said. "You eat a lot of it?"

"Only on my travels."

At the top of a rise we passed a sign that said "Florida State Line." Across the road from a barn yellow with moss. Silver crocus faded among rusted farm implements.

"The very first bar, Harold," I said.

"I got my eyes open."

We flashed down oak-canopied roads, the canoe an aluminum awning shading our eyes.

A blue-shingled store at the edge of a persimmon orchard rose into view.

"Here it is," I said.

Harold pulled up in a flurry of gravel. We broke from the truck tucking in shirttails and striding. What a cold, clear morning, a few clouds like spuds above the trees. Persimmon leaves unfolding big as oranges.

"A case of Blue Ribbon and a furburger," Harold said to the unshaven man in overalls behind the counter.

"And a what?" the man said.

"Nothing," Harold said. "I thought it was a fly."

The man looked at him and stepped into the back and returned with the case. We paid and I lugged it to the truck.

"Where'd you say the pickled eggs were?"

"In a box in the back."

I pulled the gallon jar out and set it on the seat between us. The beer went on the floor under my feet. I ripped the cardboard open, plucked out two, opened them and handed one to Harold.

"Here you go," I said.

He pulled out on the highway and accelerated to sixty before he took a sip.

"Good as springtime," he said.

"Fine with me."

I let my arm out into the air, making signals at empty fields.

III

The river boiled out of a spring just south of a shade tobacco town on the Panhandle. It ran forty miles, clear as tap water, through woods to the Gulf at St. Lukes. You could sit in a boat in the river and watch blunt silver mullet race upstream over grass and white sand beds. The sand looked firm until you stepped out on it. Then you sank halfway to your knees into an underlayer of coffee-colored mud. In high-water season the river flooded the woods so that unless you swung hammocks between the trees there were few places to camp. Pickerel grew in the still water near the banks and hyacinths floated in clumps in the stream.

We pulled up in grass behind the high diving board and got out. Harold jumped out of the truck, ran up the diving ladder and looked down into the water.

"These are the ears of the earth," he said. He hopped one-legged to the end of the board and emptied his beer into the spring. "A little poison, dear," he said, "to help you sleep." He unzipped his pants and pissed into the water, leaning back to make a high arc. The urine splashed and made a froth on the water.

"Did I tell you I once pissed off the flying bridge of a cargo ship?" I said.

"No. Did you hit anybody?"

"Just a crate of chickens."

"This piss," Harold said zipping up, "will mingle with waters that flow untrammeled to the sea. My body is now part of the stream, I am the stream, I am a dream of water running."

"From a tap all night."

"Every time I flushed your fucking toilet," he said, "water ran out on the ground. You must have a lush little cesspool under the house." He climbed down and came over to the truck. I was untying the canoe.

"My mushroom garden," I said.

"I'd like to keep Lola there," he said. "Squatted, naked."

"We could have her duckwalk around the backyard in the nude, eating radishes."

He squatted and quacked, " 'Harold, can I get up now?' No, Lola. Keep walking." He duckwalked to the back of the truck. " 'But darling,' " he squealed, holding onto the tailgate, " 'My knees hurt.' Did you ever get Frieda to duckwalk?"

"Yes I did, duck and crab. I made her do it in pantyhose, wearing a wig. She loved everything I made her do." Where was she—blonde and speaking Italian? "Harold," I said, "do you think there is a time- less quality to rural life?"

"Yeah."

"Timeless and shitless."

We lifted the canoe off the truck, flipped it and carried it to the wa- ter. Minnows darted away from the bank as we slid it in. We loaded our supplies and covered them with a poncho.

"Did you bring paddles?" I said.

"I reckon I must have." He lifted a canvas tarp in the truck bed. "Here they are."

Harold was heavier, but because I was more experienced, I took the stern. He got in and I shoved the bow around into the river. I stepped in and pushed us off, the toe of my boot catching in the wa- ter. When we were out in the stream I shipped the paddle and let the canoe drift. Harold hunched forward in the bow, his collar up around his ears. The sky was clouding over.

"Imagine that you are De Soto," he said without turning around. "This is what you would have seen." He swung his arm toward cat- tails and grasses that grew against the far bank. Behind them leafless hardwoods and evergreens tangled with pines.

"De Soto was going the other way."

"I'm sure he had to turn around somewhere."

I uncovered the case and took out two beers. "Here you go," I said, and when he turned around tossed one to him. I held us steady in the current. The river was shallow. We passed over rusty grasses flowing our way. Up ahead a mullet jumped like a spit seed, landed on its side and disappeared. I turned the cold bottle in my hands and leaned forward into a sip.

I could conjure Frieda spinning into sunlight on this cold day. Weeping at a hotel desk in the Yucatán. Do you want to ride in a carriage? No, no, no. Thick hair on her forearms, her nipples still pink at thirty. Frieda, are you throwing snowballs outside of Denver? Are you traveling by train through the mountains? My stomach turned to think of her. We must be careful today not to splash one another. The sky is almost completely clouded over. High, heavy, light-deceiving clouds.

"What we need is wine," I said.

"Wine?" He turned around.

"Yeah. With beer you have to stop, because it's awkward to paddle with a bottle, but with wine we could just pause for a sip and go on."

"Maybe we can get some."

"There're no stores on this river."

"That's right."

I set the beer between my feet and began to paddle.

IV

We hit Goose Pasture in the afternoon. You round a reedy bend and there it is: a grassy peninsula backed by pines. Two nylon camp tents perched on the bank above the river. A girl stood in front of one of them with her arms stretched above her head. She was naked.

"Jesus Christ," Harold said under his breath. "It's my mother's penis." We shipped the paddles and drifted down toward her. She was tall with black hair to her waist. When she saw us she didn't move.

Don't scare, I thought. Stay where you are. I could take in small breasts and her black pubic hair. We slid up to the bank.

She looked down at us, kicked her leg above her head, whirled and disappeared into the tent.

"What?" Harold said.

She reappeared, still naked, carrying a .410 shotgun. It looked like a BB gun, but it wasn't. She pointed it at us.

"Get out," she said.

I felt my face drain and I thought I was going to faint. Was this going to be some kind of robbery? I put my hands on the thwart in front of me and leaned forward, looking up at her.

"What?" Harold said, this time to the girl.

"Get out," she said. Harold stepped onto the bank. I crawled over the cargo and followed him.

"Is this Tangiers?" Harold said. "We were supposed to be in Tangiers by dark."

"Shut up," the girl said. She had gray streaks in her hair, but she looked to be about twenty. She directed us with the gun into the tent.

The floor was covered with a blue shag carpet and was piled with down sleeping bags in several colors. A heater burned in one corner. Light filtered through green fabric. There were no poles and the ceiling was high enough for the girl to stand upright.

Harold held his hands out. "I can read palms," he said.

"Shut up," the girl said. "Take your clothes off."

Everything focused on my belt buckle. It was large and brass and it came loose and there was my pubic hair, not covered by underwear. I dropped my pants.

I raised my eyes to her belly. Her pubic hair grew onto her thighs; a faint line of it rose to her navel. I straightened up, unbuttoned my shirt and let it fall to the floor. Harold was naked beside me. His body was white as a chicken's.

"Lie down," the girl said. We lay on our backs on the sleeping bags. They were soft, soft. She leaned the gun against the side of the tent and knelt between us. She kissed first Harold's penis, then mine. His hands fluttered up as she kissed him, he half rose and fell back. His penis wavered and rose. "Some dummy," he said weakly.

She stroked him while she sucked me until I was hard.

She sat up. "You first," she said to Harold. She straddled him and slipped him into her.

"You stand over him," she said to me. She fucked him, with a short tight motion that made her breasts jiggle, while she sucked me. I reached between us and took a nipple between my fingers. It was thick and red as roses. Harold came, but I didn't.

"Ah," she said, "Ah." She flushed across her collar bones.

She let me go, got off him and pushed me down. Harold lay with his eyes closed, one hand tracing small circles in the hair on his chest.

"You do me," she said to me.

I got on and we went at it. Her legs locked around my waist.

What I imagined was Frieda fucking her lover. She ran her hands down his sides and took him in her mouth. He stuck a finger in her ass-hole. Thinking of her seemed more dangerous than what I was doing. It made my stomach churn. Frieda spread her ass and let him look.

I came right through both of them, through both of them into the girl. I pressed my palms flat on her temples and rode through, a moan escaping with the fluid. I let my body go loose against her.

"You aren't with me exactly, are you?" was the first thing she said. Where was everybody else? "I like the pattern your hair makes," she said.

"Thank you." I smoothed her hair off her forehead, uncoupled and slid off her. Harold moved up against her other side.

"Do you do this a lot?" he said.

"When I want to."

"Where're the other people?"

"There's no one else."

I pushed up onto my knees and got my shirt. The gun leaned against the wall at the front of the tent, but I didn't reach for it. Harold lay on his side against her, stroking her stomach. Old *ejacula-tio praecox* Harold. She watched me dress.

"You don't wear underwear?" she said.

"Not for years."

"Where are you going?" She had wonderfully delicate hands, long-fingered, the nails bitten back.

"Right now?" Palm moist, soft around me.

"In the canoe."

"To the end of the river."

"The river goes underground in the swamp."

"There's a canal."

"I'll go with you."

"Naked?"

"I have clothes."

I looked at Harold. He was sitting up, pulling on his pants.

"We can ride you with us," he said. "You know how to paddle?"

"Sure."

Harold dressed and we went outside and waited for her. Thin snow had begun to fall.

"My, my," Harold said. "Look at this." He waved his hand at flurrying flakes.

"This is a strange thing," he said. Then he laughed. "It's better than fishing on the flats."

We turned as she came out of the tent. She wore jeans and a green down parka and she carried the gun.

"You're not going to start that again?" Harold said quickly.

"Maybe we'll need it," she said.

"Why don't you get one of the bags," I said.

"Okay." She went back into the tent and came out with one of the sleeping bags wadded under her arm.

We climbed down the bank and got into the canoe. The girl got in the middle, making space for herself between boxes. She laid the gun across her legs. The snow danced in a light wind.

I looked back at the tents. No vehicles, no one around anywhere.

"Did you put out the heater?" I asked.

"It's not mine—I didn't bother with it," she said.

V

We pulled up under a high bank. Roots stuck out of raw black earth. Harold jumped ashore and pulled us around. The girl stepped out and I followed.

We climbed the bank to a grassy field. A board cabin with a screened-in front porch lay back against oak woods.

"Looks all right to me," Harold said. He returned to the boat. The girl and I approached the cabin. Pear and apple trees had been set out in the front yard. They were just head-high. Flower husks and dead tomato vines crawled the ground below the porch. The girl tried the porch door.

"Locked," she said.

"That doesn't matter." Her name was Alene. The door was held by a finger hook. Taped to the screen was a handlettered sign that read: No Firearms or Food Inside. I jerked the door open. High-backed rocking chairs were turned around and leaned against the front of the house, their rockers sticking out like old legs kneeled praying. The house door was bolted from the inside.

"Why don't you try a window?" she said.

"I don't want to break something that'll let the cold in." I kicked the door until it broke open. Raw wood snaggled off the lock. Alene brushed past me into the house.

"Anybody home?" she called.

The room we entered was dark, sparsely furnished. The curled edge of a straw mat on the floor caught light from the door. I found a kerosene lamp on a table under one of the front windows, lighted it and we walked through the rooms. The bedrooms were pine-paneled, small and depressing, like a damp shirt on a cold day, with their iron bedsteads and their stripped mattresses. The kerosene in the lamps on the tables was dark and clotted. In back was a kitchen with a wood stove and a hand pump and behind it a screened porch with a plank counter along the back side. We reentered the living room as Harold pushed through the front door carrying the ax and one of the food boxes. He balanced a beer on top of the box.

"It's good to be home," he said. "Did you tell them we'd be staying for supper?"

"Supper and breakfast—they said come on in."

He set the box and the ax on the floor.

"You folks going to help any?" he said.

"We've been touring the place."

"I'm not touring," Alene said. "I just wanted to see if the bastards left anything I could use. What a shabby hole."

"Now—you'll get used to it," I said.

"Don't play with me." She picked up the ax and went out on the porch.

"Takes your mind off your worries, doesn't she?" Harold said. We followed her out.

"You could gather a little firewood if you wanted to," Harold said to her. "We'll get the rest of the stuff up." She didn't say anything. She stood against the screen looking out. The river curved through snow flurries around a bend into trees. The way her spine curved, deeply like a hook, as she pressed her belly against the screen, made me want to run my hand up her back. She looked at the river, saying nothing.

"Or whatever you want to do," Harold said. We left the house and returned to the canoe.

We unloaded the boxes and pulled the canoe up onto the bank. Our feet sank in mud as we worked.

Coming up the bank we could hear sounds of wood splintering coming from the cabin.

"Looked to *me* like it needed a little trimming," Harold said.

She was hacking up the rockers.

"Bang them to pieces," Harold said. We went into the living room and set the boxes down. Harold pulled two beers out and handed one to me.

"You might save one of them, Alene," he called. "I'll need to sit down after awhile."

"There're chairs in there," she said. I stood in the door watching her. She used the ax awkwardly, not closing the distance between her hands as she brought it down. She broke the rockers up, though. After awhile she let up and stood back, panting a little. I moved in and gathered up the pieces that lay around her, carried them in to the fireplace, doused them with kerosene from the lamp and lighted a fire.

The fire snapped the chill in the place. I pulled an armchair that was covered with green, rose-flowered cloth up to the fire and sat down to think about where I wanted to sleep. A light wind whisked snow against the window panes. We should have gotten Alene to bring the other down bags. They had been deep and soft. It was bad to just go off and leave them. It didn't look, though, as if we were going to be able to get her to do anything she didn't want to. Out on the porch she was still chopping. The floor vibrated faintly with the blows.

Harold pulled a gas stove from a box and began to pump it up. On camping trips he always brought plenty of country goodies to eat, but he didn't like to pioneer. I stretched my legs out and sipped the beer, looking into the fire.

"You got sweet potatoes, Harold?" I said.

"Of course."

"What else we going to have ?"

"Stew. Artichoke hearts."

"Wonderful. This is a night for artichokes." My mind was dancing around, Frieda somewhere in a sheepskin walking in the snow.

"Here, get me some water," he said holding out a pot. I took the pot, went out to the kitchen and cranked the pump handle. Somebody had sown a garden out back, but it was gone now, dog fennel wands nodding among broken corn stalks. Dark was coming on and the snow blew into trees. The well was either dry or the pump needed priming. I came back through the house.

"I'll get some water from the river," I said.

"Okay."

On the porch Alene was gathering up the split chairs.

"I'm going for water," I said.

"Wait," she said. She ran into the house. I heard the wood clatter against the hearth. She came back out.

"I'll go with you," she said.

We walked through descending night to the river. The snow fell so lightly that I couldn't feel it. Flakes caught on our clothes, hung for a moment, then winked out, like little lights, into the cloth.

Three big cedars grew at the edge of the bank. Their riverside roots were exposed and I grasped them to help myself down the steep cut, feeling in my palms the softness of the finest roots that hung like whiskers from the larger stock. Alene came down the trail that we had carried the supplies up.

I made my way carefully across the mushy ground over leaves and broken, river-worn branches to the water, knelt, and filled the pot. I felt her behind me and then she touched my hair. I looked out at the river that flowed smoothly, the color of coffee, undisturbed by the falling snow. She placed her hands on my shoulders and leaned against me. My knee sank deeper in the mud.

"You guys in the army?" she said.

"Harold used to be."

"Where'd you get the canoe?" She indicated with her foot the government stencil.

"Harold relocated it."

"He did what?"

"He took it."

"They won't come after you?"

"Not down here."

Something, a sadness, seemed to gust out of her thin body. I took her hand that stroked my cheek and kissed it in the palm.

"Are you married?" she said.

"Divorcing."

I looked up. Her gray eyes touched mine.

"How come?" she said.

"I didn't love my wife." I felt, as I spoke, something in me subside and fall away. I had a moment of intense exhilaration. But then, behind it, came something else. As Frieda fell suddenly away, fell away, in the vision I had of her, from the window of her new house where she leaned over the kitchen sink to water ferns, I saw something else rise, another shape, larger, darker, deeper in my life—it was that that held me, that shape that had stood gazing at me all along, inevitable and changeless, and in a moment the exhilaration was gone and I felt a panic that nearly threw me sprawling into the river. I emptied the pot to direct her from tears that had come into my eyes, but she saw.

"Are you okay?" she said.

"No. I'm not." I refilled the pot. Particles hung suspended in the drawn-up water.

"Well, you'd better straighten up," she said. "I like you."

"Then I guess I'd better—pull myself together."

"You're damn right." She ruffled my hair, leaned down and kissed me on the back of the neck. "That sure is dirty water," she said.

"It's just tannin—acid from cypress roots. It's not dirty and it keeps the water sweet."

"Maybe you know. Let's get out of this stupid snow."

"All right."

We climbed the bank and returned to the cabin, holding hands as we walked.

VI

The bears have moved farther south, deeper into woods—what bears there are—and no panthers cry at night. The ivory-billed woodpecker has not been spotted for a generation and bald eagles, that once nested in the tops of the tallest cypresses, are not seen anymore, as, for that matter, are the old tall trees. But, in the morning, when I came out at first light, there were raccoon tracks in the snow on the front steps and when I walked to the riverbank I saw, as I shook snow from cedar branches, a flock of ring-neck ducks rise from the water. The ducks flew off south beyond trees under a clear sky. I descended the bank and washed my face in the river. I scooped a handful of snow off the canoe gunwale. It tasted of metal. A snow rug lay in the bottom of the boat. I brushed my teeth in the river water and returned to the cabin.

Harold and Alene were asleep. Harold lay on his back in front of the fireplace, his arms out of the bag, a look of displeasure on his face. I knelt and kissed his open mouth. The saliva rind on his lips tasted of beer. He didn't wake. I looked around and Alene was sitting up with the bag pulled around her shoulders looking at me.

"Are you a queer?" she said.

I held my finger to my lips. "No," I whispered, "but Harold and I are close."

"Close to being queers?"

"He's an awfully fine boy."

"I see." Her eyes sparkled. The way the unzipped halves of the bag hung down her naked chest, like an unbuttoned shirt, excited me. I stood up and stepped over the stove and empty beer case to her. I reached down and touched her graystreaked hair and she pressed her face against my leg.

"Take your clothes off and get in here," she said.

"All right." She lay back.

The zipper stopped just below a crescent of pubic hair. I undressed, peeled the bag back and got in with her.

Her mouth was hot and sleepy and my lips moved from it across her high cheekbones, over her nose that had a depression in one side of it like an old wound, down her face past chin and unlined neck to her breasts. The inverted nipples unfolded, one after the other as I kissed them. I kissed back and forth between them, bringing them up, keeping them hard, as a flush spread across her chest. I kicked my feet in the bottom of the bag, seeking space.

"In high school they called me sunny side up," she said as I licked a nipple. I raised my head.

"Everybody did?"

"Certain ones. Do you think they look like fried eggs?"

"No, they look like hills in Italy."

"Old and green?"

"Covered with olives."

"And a blue sky and sailboats in the harbor?"

"And boys in striped shirts running down the beach."

"You are a queer."

"Must be." The bag was too tight for me to get my face down to her groin. My fingers fluttered through hair and I slipped one inside. "Oh," she said, "oh." She took me in her hand and stroked me upward against her body. I wanted to caress her, to hold out against completion until she was soaked with feeling, until we were drowned, but when she touched me the rhythm broke, I rolled onto her, fumbling for connection, and we came together, my backside freezing in the cold morning air.

The bag was too small—when we finished I pulled my sack over us.

"Where did you go to high school?" I said.

"Different places. What were you doing outside?"

"Brushing my teeth." I told her about the ducks. "There was a whole flock of them," I said, "sleeping on the water. The moment I came up, before I could even get a good look at them, they broke into the air, panicking."

She yawned. "You should have shot one. I wouldn't mind a duck for breakfast."

"You wouldn't want to clean it."

"I'd love to eat it."

I pulled my leg loose, slipped down the bag and punched Harold with my foot.

"Harold, wake up and start the fire."

He opened his eyes and looked down his chest at me.

"You crazy?" he said. "I was lying here waiting to hear the sound of rocker boards crackling and all I'm hearing is whump, whump, whump. I'll take a little coffee with cream and a slab of hot cornbread, please."

"A *little* coffee? Here it comes." I threw the bag off and jumped on him. "I always wanted to get you trussed." I tried to hold him, but his arms were free and it was me, quickly, who got held.

"You want to smell something good?" He laughed and pulled my head down into his armpit.

"Jesus, Harold." I squirmed loose and sat up. He threw his arms back over his head and laughed. The hair in his armpits was redder than the hair on his head. The cold hit me and I snaked off him, scrambled up and got into my clothes. Alene lay on her side watching us, the bag pulled up to her chin, venturing nothing.

With a stick I scraped a place in last night's ashes, piled wood, doused it with kerosene and lighted a fire. I squatted on my heels and held my palms out to the flames. The heat danced on my skin. Alene got up and stood beside me. She warmed herself, making little half turns in front of the fire. Light bustled in her pubic hair. She bent over and with her fingers combed out her hair. A faint, unpleasant odor rose from it.

"You'll catch it on fire," I said.

"Save me the trouble of combing it," she answered, but she moved back a step.

"Where'd the gray come from?"

"Early strain."

"I was wondering," Harold said as he pulled on his pants, "where did those tents at Goose Pasture come from?"

"From somebody," she said twisting her hair into a bun. "You got a pin?"

"No," I said.

"Shit." She let the hair fall loose down her back.

"Well, at least that explains it," Harold said. "Did you get any water when you went down?" he said to me.

"No. I'll go get some now."

I got the coffee pot from the box and went out.

When I returned, as I reached for the house door, I heard inside the sounds of their lovemaking. I retreated down the porch, cleared the top step of snow and sat down. The air was still, the day too cold for birds. I felt completely abandoned, as if, when, last night, I had declared myself free of Frieda (if that was what I had done), I had done so only after another hand seemed offered me, and now, that hand, it turned out, wasn't there. Maybe that is what I had done. Maybe I dreamed Alene as the sweet field I could lay myself down in. "Like that, like that," I heard her say from inside where they rolled. Like that. I dipped my fingers in the cold coffee water, pressed them to my eyelids and rubbed, again, the sleep from my eyes.

VII

I was in the stern, imagining that the ache in my knees was cancer climbing my bones, we were rounding a bend past a sand bar backed by budding black willows, Harold had just reached behind for one of the last beers, when she raised the gun and fired into a low-hanging myrtle across the river.

"Jesus," Harold jumped, "is it Indians?" Then we both saw what she'd hit: a hornet's nest the size of a basketball. She'd shredded the bottom of it.

"Great God Almighty," Harold said. Hornets, blackbodied and big as thumbnails, tumbled from the nest. They didn't fly—it must have been too cold—they spilled like beans into the water. Then a few got their wings and flew sluggishly around the shattered nest. They would have been angry, I guess, if they could.

"They look like dwarfs," Alene said, cracked the breech and tossed the empty shell into the water. "Fly little buggers," she called to them.

"No, you don't want that," Harold said.

She took another shell from the pocket of her parka and reloaded.

"You want to try?" she said to Harold.

"Nah—okay." He set his beer between his feet and took the gun. He smoothed his hair back with one hand, sighted along the barrel and fired. His shot cut the nest loose and it fell into the water among a tangle of branches.

"Now we'll have them with us to the Gulf," I said. "Let me try."

Harold handed the gun to Alene, who reloaded it and passed it to me. Hornets floated on the water, humming.

I fired. The shot cut the top out and the nest sagged, deflated, taking water. White crawling hornet pupae murmured in the mess. Shreds of gray nest paper floated among the bodies. I handed the gun to Alene.

"God's wrath on the hornet world," Harold said.

"Shit—mine," Alene said, reloading. She fired again and the nest went under. "Where's another one," she said, "let's find another one." Her eyes danced with glee.

"They'll show up," I said. "Why don't you keep your eye out for some meat."

"Ah, smothered squirrel," Harold said. He looked back at the floating hornet bodies.

"Dog meat," I said. "A fat pup, white with black spots."

"Not again."

"Yes, again—dog meat."

"Dogs?" Alene said. "I try to hit every one I see in the road."

"Of course you do, darling," Harold said.

"Dogs, guineas and children," I said. "I haven't run over a child in nearly a month."

"You remember that one I got up near Thompson?" Harold said.

"That one on the shoulder? Yeah, I didn't think you'd ever get back on the road. What was he doing?"

"I don't know—digging something. Jesus, did he squeal."

"What?" Alene said. "A kid—a nigger?"

"No," Harold said, "a white boy, about ten years old. It was great. His head busted just like a watermelon. Juice everywhere. We had to stop at a filling station to wash it off the front of the car."

"Did you kill him?"

I trailed my fingers in the water—eee, hornets—and wiped them on my pants. "He wasn't walking when we left."

"I think I'll run over Lola when we get home," Harold said.

"You couldn't hit Lola—she's a dodger."

"Who's Lola?" Alene said.

"That's Harold's young woman," I told her. "Lola's a grounds keeper up at Southwest State."

"The insane asylum?"

"That's right. You should have brought her, Harold. We could have rolled her in meal and fried her."

"Wouldn't she be sweet? The last time I talked to her she said she'd decided to take flying lessons. She wants to be a crop duster."

"Buzz your house on Wednesdays."

"Trip her with telephone wires."

"Poor Lola."

Alene swung the gun in an arc, sighting into treetops.

"Watch for movement," Harold said. "Anything moves, blast away."

We pulled around the bend into a long reach of open water.

"Those hornets," Harold said. "I once dropped a hornet's nest into the boat."

"You did?"

"Yeah. Red Baker and I were doing the Chiporee. I don't know how it happened, but we passed under a nest and Red managed to hit it with his paddle and knock it into the canoe."

"Did you get stung?"

"No. We hit the water at the same time the nest hit the boat."

"How'd you get it out?"

"I reached in with my paddle and flipped it into the water. We stayed submerged until we got out of sight—Jesus, I never moved so fast. I thought we were going to be stung to death."

Sun had burned the snow off; trees dripped water and the ground along the banks was damp and mushy-looking. We paddled around bends where budding willows dragged lank branches in the dark water. The sky was clear, the air thin, sunny and cold.

I swung myself through the rhythm of paddling, my hands chafing, a knot untying in my shoulders, and I thought again of the way paddling a canoe slips you into the heart of things. The first day out is hard, your back aches and your hands hurt, but during the second, aches begin to dissolve and you ease into the flow of the river and after awhile the steady rhythm of paddling, the three-mile-an-hour journey past a landscape that changes as slowly as your heart beats, around bend after bend, each the same in its willows and moss-backed logs, into reaches long as lakes, is the rhythm of a deeper movement, that we slip into, easy as breathing, as we travel, that replaces whatever madness we have come out of and carries us out of time.

That is how I had explained the lure of river travel. Explained it as I lay on living room rugs drinking tequila, my friends on sofas slipping into mescaline dreams. You become a part of the river, I would say, current and cargo. But that seemed to me now an awful fantasy. Here was the world, today, half-frozen and natural as a goat, concussed hornets floating in a stream. Frieda was there still, green-eyed and frightened of bugs, and I stopped paddling for a moment, thinking of her naked body, and of the eyes of her lover looking. I liked him looking. She pulled her knees up, in my mind, her legs fell open, she touched the scar inside her thigh, her hand drifted to her sex and she spread the lips of it with her fingers. She brought the fingers to her mouth and tasted of herself. I didn't mind—I wanted to dream it. I wanted her legs loose for another in my mind. I wanted them loose in fact. As they were, in fact. I wanted to hold the vision of her, locked in her new lover's arms, tease it out slowly into my mind, even if it hurt, even as it hurt. I had loved her too little, then too much and I couldn't find a path between the two. Blocking whatever path there was stood whatever shape I had seen last night. Beyond her supple, Annie Oakley body, stood that other dark form, that I could not embrace.

I reached forward and stroked Alene's hair.

"Don't get it wet," she said.

The river lay flat as a highway, empty and sparkling in the sunlight.

"What is that?" Harold said.

"What?"

"That sound?"

I listened. "It's the Crystal River shoal."

We rounded a bend between high, palmetto-covered banks, and there was the shoal, thrown across the river like a petticoat. I had forgotten it. It was a narrow place where the river lost depth and fell a couple of feet down a limestone ledge. The water, suddenly cinched and dropped, bucked into plumes of spray. Past a front line of heaving waves the river foamed for a hundred yards toward still water as it widened out and calmed before it bent past a headland of bare oaks.

"You want to stop and take a look?" Harold said.

"Yeah, let's do."

We swung over and climbed the bank through the palmettos. Harold ran ahead kicking his legs high through wet fronds. "What snakes there are, stay still," he cried. He reached the highest point and leaned out over the water that had pushed a white edge of foam against the bank, making gestures with his hands.

"Last year in Colombia," he hollered in an English accent, "we ran rivers like this by the dozen." He turned to me as I came up to him, shouting as if I were somewhere else and the river louder. "Do you hear me, Jack? By the dozen. Little river, turn to gin."

"Gin," I yelled, "martini rapids. Vodka collision."

Harold reached down, scooped up sand and bits of plant matter and flung them at the water. "Be calmed, waters," he yelled. "Hornet Harold commands you. I believe we can take it, Jack."

"We have to chance it," I said. "There's no other way. This is an adversarial relationship. Mercy, God's good grace, will get us through."

Alene came up. She had a palmetto frond tied around her hair for a headband.

"Cousin Alene," Harold said, "does the situation smell sweet to you? Do you believe Jesus will carry us through?"

"What jerkoff wouldn't," she said.

I put my arms around both of them. I wanted us all to jump in the water. A fine mist wet our faces. Let's do this every day. Let's not ever do anything else.

"Let's go then," Harold said. He ran down the bank yipping as Alene and I followed.

We tucked the poncho around the boxes and shoved off. Alene sat on the center thwart.

The river flowed sluggishly toward a central chute beyond which reared a six-foot fan of spray; the river, stumbling, had kicked up its own water. We made for that.

"Harold," I called over the noise of water, "stand up."

"What for?"

"In case there's a view."

We all got up. Alene stood on boxes, higher than either of us. Standing, I ruddered us into the center of the channel. The river seemed hardly to move; leaves floating beside the canoe turned lazily in the clear brown current. The bow leaned out over the fall—so slowly—tipped forward, we caught, surged forward the length of the canoe into the high brown wave, Harold striking with his paddle as if the wave were a bear and, as he fell, I felt the bow scrape bottom and then I was in the air, too, grabbing for Alene—wanting her, separately from this, curiously, completely—missing, remembering to hold onto my paddle as I went under, gasping, breath knocked nearly out of me, freezing, fighting up until I surfaced ten yards downstream in waist-deep water, the swamped canoe sagging beside me, empty beer bottles and the gas can floating away out of reach downstream.

We dragged the canoe to shore and tipped it out in the shallows. Everything was soaked except my clothes, which were still dry in their plastic bag. Harold built a fire and we hung the sleeping bags in the trees. We stood around the fire naked, shaking with excitement and the cold.

Alene stood with her back to us, the gun cradled against her hip.

Goose bumps pimpled her buttocks. Harold squatted and cupped his genitals. "What a ride," he said. "What a ride."

"We went straight under," I said.

He laughed. "We didn't make it past the first wave. It was wonderful—it just caught us." He stroked penis and testicles gently upward, looking down at himself. "Unclench, boys," he said.

Alene lay the gun down and went to the canoe. She began to push it back into the water.

"What you doing, babe?" Harold said.

"I want to run it again," she said.

"Let's do," Harold said to me.

So, naked, blue-lipped, chattering, we ran the shoal again.

On the first run Alene took the bow, I sat in the middle and Harold took the stern. Emptied of cargo, we popped through like a cork. After the third run we were too cold to try another. My face felt frozen; I could hardly move my mouth. We pulled the boat ashore and got into dry clothes. The only thing Harold could wear of mine was a sweater. The bags were nearly dry and we spread them out on top of the reloaded cargo. Harold scattered the fire and we pushed off. The sky was clear, the sun white as the moon in the south. Harold began to sing. We passed the bend and put the shoal behind us.

VIII

The sun was going down like a peach into the river and we were still paddling when we heard laughter coming from a cedar grove above a grassy meadow on the right bank. Two red, white and blue striped canoes were pulled up in the yellow grass. We beached in mud and climbed the slope to the cedars. In a needle-floored clearing two couples looked up from a fire on which ribs lay roasting on a grill.

"Hey," one of the men—tall, with a belly—said as we came through trees into the open space. He was drinking something from a white plastic cup.

"All of you stand up," Alene said, raising the gun. The plump woman in padded duck hunting pants jerked half a step forward, her toe kicking coals so that the grate tipped and nearly fell, she looked at the tall man and they both rose.

"What do you want?" the other man—gray chin beard and glasses—said in a hard voice. He moved closer to a woman whose hand had frozen among salad greens on a camp table. The tall man stretched his hand over the fire toward the plump woman, changed his mind and came around and stood beside her.

"What is it?" he said.

"Just get steady and put your hands out in front of you," Harold said. "I've always wanted to talk this way," he added. He held an open pocket knife loosely in his right hand.

"Stay calm," I said to the four of them. I pointed at a cooler under the camp table. "What's in there?" I asked.

"Some beer," the tall man said.

"Jesus, oh, Jesus, fucking robbers," the plump woman said. She looked up into the cedars.

"Shut up," Alene said.

"You got any freckle-face potato chips?" Harold asked.

"What?" the tall man said.

"Or any calico, any red calico?"

"Jesus—what?" he took a step back.

"Stay still," I said, crossed the clearing and got the cooler. I could smell the woman's sweat as I bent down, bitter, like the smell of roaches. I had an impulse to stroke her leg, her thighs were slender in jeans, but I touched only the cooler, picked it up and carried it back to the other side of the fire. Harold speared a sheaf of ribs off the fire with his knife.

"What else have you got that we might need?" he asked over a mouthful. He offered me a hunk of meat, but I didn't want to take it right then.

"Nothing, man," the bearded man said. His army fatigue pants were held up by a white leather belt. A Marine assault knife hung from the belt. "We haven't got any money," he said.

"We don't want money," I said. "We're doing this for love."

"We're doing this to make an impression," Harold said. "We don't want to go down into history only as simple, Christian folk."

"You won't," the tall man said. He scratched under his arm. "Listen, you assholes . . ."

"Shut up," Alene screamed. She raised the gun to her shoulder and aimed directly at his face. "We don't want to hear your side of it."

"Don't!" the woman at the table cried. The tall man blanched. His hands opened and closed—curdled, curdled is the word that came into my mind, but curled is what his fingers did. The woman had screamed the single word 'don't,' but she hadn't moved.

A small breeze slipped vaguely among the cedar branches. Alene lowered the gun.

"Why are you here?" I asked the four of them. "Do you do this often?"

"Nearly every weekend," the tall man said.

"We usually bring retarded children on the outing with us," the woman by the fire said.

"More fucking therapeutic campers," Harold said. "The goddamned woods are being overrun by the afflicted—Jesus. Assholes!" he screamed. "Are you people Americans?"

"We're from Tallahassee," the tall man said. "John and I teach at the university."

"Retardation?"

"Education."

"Well, let this be a lesson to you," I said. "The woods aren't safe."

"Donnez moi un cerveza," Harold said. I handed him one. "We don't want to do anything to humiliate you," he said, "but we want you to keep the special children at home. Behind fences. To whom, by the way, am I addressing my remarks?"

The four of them said nothing.

"Well, all right, you're petrified. It's understandable. Let's see," he said pointing with the beer can, "you'll be Split Silk Capone, you'll be Peewee White and you ladies are their mistresses, Patootie and Miss Marvin."

"Oh, stop it," the plump woman cried. She began to weep. "What do they want?" she said.

"Now, now," Harold said, "now, now." He flicked the knife like there was water on it. "When my brother was little," he continued, "and we had to take him to get a shot he would scream at the doctor, 'Wait, I want to tell you something,' everytime the doc would try to get the needle in. The doctor would hold up and ask him what he wanted to say, but he never wanted to say anything, he just wanted the business to stop." He swigged the beer. "You see, we understand."

"Anything else, Arnold?" he said to me.

"I'm fine," I said.

"Enough, Matilda?"

"Let's go," Alene said.

"Cover the rear," Harold said to her.

We returned down the slope carrying the cooler between us.

"The woods full of the afflicted," Harold said. "It's crazy."

"Keep your asses frozen," I heard Alene say, still in the clearing.

We walked downhill through soggy grass. Daffodils flowered, singly and in clumps along the edges of the meadow. We loaded the cooler into the canoe, got in and waited for Alene. She came running down the slope.

"Wait a minute," she said. She fired from the waist into the bottom of one of the canoes, reloaded and fired into the bottom of the other one.

"You never stop thinking, do you, Alene?" Harold said.

"Come on," she said and jumped in.

We pushed off. The flimsy winter sun was straggling in the river as we paddled into the current.

IX

I just would rather not get up. Where I am is fine with me. It's winter and I'm in the woods tucked in my down bag in this little orange tent.

I watched flames dance against the wall. Alene lay with me, her bag pulled on top of us. She lay on me and her long light weight felt fine. I don't even want supper. I kissed her nipple, rosy as a burn. I held it in my mouth until it hardened. It's like a little scallop, fluttering open. I touched her low down and she squealed.

"Your hands are cold," she said, pushing me away.

"They'll warm up in a minute." I rubbed them rapidly on my thighs. "There, is that better?"

"Noo," she said.

"What?"

"You're just warming your leg."

I rubbed my hand again, hard, on my thigh.

"How's that?"

"That's fine. Touch me there. I like it when you touch my leg there. Your hands are so soft."

"Comes with the territory," I said and chuckled. I wasn't hungry, I wasn't thirsty, I wasn't anything but content. No, I'd like another beer.

"Harold," I called, "toss me a cartridge."

I watched his shadow rise, disappear and then his head came through the flap.

"Here you go, Commander," he said. "You want one, Sugar-shack?" he asked Alene.

"No."

He squatted in the opening.

"What you doing?" I asked. "Come in out of the cold."

He crawled in, pulled a bag around his shoulders and knelt in front of us. "I'm listening to the jeeps," he said.

We had been hearing them for an hour or more, hearing the strain-ing whine of engines far off, coming through rough country. We reck-oned they were jeeps, four-wheel drive something.

"You're dreaming again, Harold," I said.

"I keep listening to them."

There was nowhere for us to go but back on the river. We were camped in the middle of an old raised road that was cut now by the river where a bridge used to cross. Creosoted pilings, bound by steel hoops, leaned in the water; two live oaks, fully-leaved, hung over the stream on either side of the road drop-off. The road itself was grown up in myrtle and alder bushes. From the crown we could look across the tops of young planted pines on both sides of the river to horizons of old woods, wavering bluely in the distance.

"We've got no trouble, Harold," I said and pulled Alene close. I lay on my side; I raised the beer and took a swallow through the corner of my mouth. We could hear the engines working way back in the woods.

"They're miles away," I said. Alene kissed my chest. Her lips were soft. I held her head against me. I wanted to pull her into my body. It was all right, no matter who was coming.

Harold crawled in close. "This is the last time," he said, "that I ever go camping in the winter."

"How come?" With our bags around us we formed a tent within the tent.

"It's too cold—you can't wash the smoke off you."

"Don't stand so close to the fire."

"Ah—Jack, I'm doing the cooking."

"It would be nice to take a dip."

"Yeah. In the summer we could just jump right out of the boat into the water. You remember that school of minnows we jumped into on the Ochlocknee?"

"I remember. We caught them in our hands."

"Pebbles on the bottom shining like mirrors. There were mussels in the water—you remember?"

"We were scared to eat them."

"Have you guys known each other all your lives?" Alene said. Her legs moved against mine.

"Just about." She drew my hand to her and took a sip of my beer.

"Sounds like it," she said. "You're just a couple of crackers."

"Harold's worried about the jeeps," I said. "He thinks they're coming to get us. Maybe they're tanks, Harold."

"I don't know," he said seriously.

"Who gives a shit?" Alene said.

Harold pulled the bag up and leaned forward until his head was between ours. In the darkness he had made he hummed like an engine.

"nnnnnn. NNNNNN," he went, changing gears.

"You'll never get out, Harold," I said. "You can't take a Ferrari into the swamp."

"Ah, Jesus," he said and rolled onto his back. "If it were summer and I were naked."

"You can get naked," Alene said. "Do. I want to see your peter."

"Okay." He stripped, crawled between us and pulled the bag over the top.

"Let me see," Alene said crouching.

"It's too cold for flashing," Harold said.

"Let me look," Harold turned on his back so she could get to him. She bent closer. Her hair swung against his groin. "Your prick's the same color as your skin," she said.

"That's not unusual—it's my prick."

"Jack's is dark—how come it's so dark, Jack?"

"Yeah, Jack," Harold said, "where'd the purple come from?"

"Too much polo, I guess," I touched myself. "I used to worry about it, now I like it."

"Polo?" Alene asked.

"No—a purple dick."

Part of our bodies kept slipping out into the cold. Alene kissed my penis, then Harold's. I stroked the hairs all one way on her arm. She raised her head, listening. With my index finger I traced her profile from her hairline to her chin.

"Quit," she said, "I'm trying to hear." She laughed and fell back. "They're coming to get us," she said.

We were silent.

"I thought the river went underground," Alene said.

"That's some other river," Harold said. "Somewhere else."

I wanted, suddenly, to get out of there. Out of the tent.

"What's there to eat?" I asked.

"Beans and tomatoes," Harold said. "The pot's on the stove."

"You want anything—Alene?"

"No."

I dressed and went out. The sky was crowded with stars. I descended the bank and washed my face in the river. The water stung my cheeks and hands. Chips of light floated in the river. It was too cold to be out, but I didn't want to be in the tent. I stood up and breathed deeply. I felt the cold way down in my chest.

I returned to the fire and spooned a plateful of beans. I could hear them fucking. Fabric, flesh flapping. What could I do about it? She didn't mind which of us she had. Frieda was a thousand miles away. Wearing one of my old sweaters, shaking frost from her hair. There were birds in the live oak by the river. I heard them when I passed under it. I squatted then sat down in front of the fire.

The sound of the laboring vehicles rose and fell. There seemed to be at least two. I couldn't tell that they were getting any closer—they seemed to be straining in one spot, far back. Maybe they are coming for us. I finished the beans and tossed the paper plate into the fire. The edges browned and caught, a brown stain appeared in the center, the whole plate caught, crumpling. Another beer. Green expensive cooler; Red Label, a brand I never drink. No need for a cooler in this weather. How to keep them from freezing was the worry. The beer was cold and bitter. It made my fingers ache to hold it. I wish I had gloves. I had worried about paddling in cold weather, about my hands numbing from dipping in the water, but it was no trouble. I didn't wet them and the action of paddling kept them warm enough.

I dragged the cooler over and sat down on it. I couldn't stop thinking of Frieda. We had been separated a year and now within, at most, two weeks, the divorce decree would appear in my mailbox. I had to let her go. Every day since I had started the stumbling divorce machinery more than six months ago I had been telling myself that I have to let her go. Last night, once again, I thought I had, but here she was, still rising like the moon in my mind. Go on, Frieda, dear, go on. Her hair was blonde, finer than Alene's. She stood, in my mind, in front of the picture window in her cottage at the beach—here, fifty miles from here, in Florida—and kicked her foot higher than her head. It was the one thing she remembered from her college dance class ten years ago. It was a wonderful girlish maneuver—she would do it anywhere; in the grocery store, waiting in line for a movie—and it had been, I thought, the first move I had seen Alene make: one high kick before she whirled into the tent and came out with a gun.

Someone grunted in the tent and I heard the sound of damp flesh slapping damp flesh. I got quickly up and went to the riverbank. The bound pilings leaned in the current like old drunk men in overcoats. A tangle of bushes obscured the road on the other bank. The tops of young pines were silvery.

"Good-bye, good-bye," I called. My voice flew, echoless, into the night. "Good-bye." If she were here I could throw her in the water. Hypothermia, not divorce, would keep her under. "Good-bye," I yelled, and again, "Good-bye."

"What are you hollering?" Harold called from the tent. I turned and saw his head sticking out of the flap. His hair was wild salad. "Be quiet," he said, "you'll let them know where we are."

He crawled out and stood up, fully dressed. He cracked a beer and came over. We looked down the river.

"After these pines it's marshes all the way to the coast," he said. "Who were you saying good-bye to?"

"To Frieda." I held myself in my arms.

"I figured. Is it bothering you?"

"The divorce?"

"Yeah."

"I guess so. I'm trying to let it go."

"You ought to." He took a mouthful of beer and spit a stream of foam into the water. He followed that with a piss.

"Ugm," he said as he arced it. "The simple pleasures."

"You're making a feature of that," I said.

"I like to put myself into the things I do." He zipped up and sat down. I sat down beside him.

"Is there any chance you'll go back with Frieda?" he asked.

"No," I said quickly. The thought scared me. "I can't let myself think about it. She's gone."

"You were together a long time."

"Half our lives."

"It makes me sad," he said. I looked at him. His face was turned away, eyes looking downstream. An ache spread through my chest into my shoulders.

"I'm sorry," I said.

"It's natural. You ought to take a trip."

"I'm on a trip."

"Why don't you do what I did when I quit smoking?"

"What's that?"

"I took my last pack of Luckies out to the garden, dug a hole and buried them, right between the peas and the tomatoes. I said a little funeral service over them. I told them I loved them, but they were dead and good-bye."

"I don't think Frieda would go for that," I said.

"Maybe a photograph. Too bad you didn't marry Lola. I'd help you bury her."

"I'll help *you*."

"First thing when we get back."

"If we do."

He looked at the ground and shook his head. His fair fell forward over his face. He pushed it back.

"I wonder if they're . . . whatever they are, coming this way."

"I don't know. It sounds like they're stuck."

The faraway sound rose, grinding, as if trees were down in front of wheels. We were silent.

"This has certainly turned into something, hasn't it?" he said after awhile.

"I'm kind of liking it—it splits the distance."

"What do you mean?"

"We're off here in the boondocks away from our real lives and we're cutting up in this wild way that we never could at home—at least I thought we never could, then I started thinking this is just the way it was when we were kids, running around free, sneaking through the bushes raising cain. It takes us back."

"Mebbe so," he said.

"You remember when we used to hide out in trees and jump on each other. We're getting to do it again."

" 'Cept we're grown—and it's not each other."

"Adventure has just come along—we do it. Do you mind Alene?"

He chuckled. "I'm enjoying her."

"If that's what it is."

"Something."

He got up and went down to the river where he held his beer can under the water until it filled then threw it out into the stream.

"I'm going to bed," he said when he had climbed back up the bank.

"I'll be along shortly."

He put his hand on my shoulder. "I'm sorry, Jack," he said.

I pressed my cheek against his wrist. The hairs were scratchy against my face.

"It'll be all right," I said. He returned to the tent.

"What you been doing?" I heard Alene ask through a yawn.

"Talking to Jack," he said.

I put the beer down beside me and scratched my thighs with both hands. I wished I itched all over. If it were summer I would throw myself in the water. Where did this restraint come from? I would like to float on my back, in this stream, to the Gulf. Lie on my back listening to the wind in the marshes. Well, well, oh, well. I got up, went down to the river and rinsed my face. There was no way to get around the cold. Except by crawling into my warm down bag where I have been momentarily content. The engines kicked, far off. I waited until no sounds came from the tent. Then I went in, too.

When Harold, fumbling in the dark, woke me, I thought he was getting up to pee. But he sat on his bag pulling on his shoes.

"What are you doing?" I said.

"You hear those fucking jeeps?"

In the woods they were still at it.

"What are you going to do?"

"I'm going outside. I can't stand it."

"Would you guys shut up," Alene said sleepily, but in full command.

"Okay," Harold said. He finished lacing his boots, picked up the gun and went out.

I heard him throw wood on the fire, there was a silence, then a loud whomp and a gust of light that lit up the tent. "Jesus," I heard him say.

"Warmed up, Harold?" I said.

"Damn." Tossed a little gas on the fire.

I chuckled and pulled the bag around my ears. I could hear the engines through the down. Then I thought, well, they can see our signal now. I heard a scrabbling then a shirring, leafy sound and twittering as birds left their roost. I poked my head out.

"What the shit are you doing?" I asked.

"I'm getting up here." His voice came from among branches.

"In the tree?"

"Yes, dammit."

"You going to ambush them?"

"I'm going to get up here."

"Holler if you spot them." He was silent a moment, then he said, "I forgot about the fucking birds. Christ, it's cold."

I drew my knees up and held myself in the bag. Alene had swum up to admonish, now she was snoring lightly again. The engines whined away in the woods. You lie in your camp and wait to be found. It could be anything coming. Robbers or cops. What could be driving this way at midnight? A squeal rose and fell away. Rose and fell again. Like guineas in the bushes, spooked by a dog. The sound came on. Oh, Jesus God, help.

I got up, pulled on clothes and shoes and went out. I crossed the clearing and looked up in the tree. I couldn't see him up there.

"Harold," I whispered, "where are you?" I was shaking from excitement.

"Help, murder, police," he whispered back.

"I'm coming up," I said.

I grasped the lowest branch, swung myself up and climbed to his perch. He was straddling a limb, holding with one hand to the trunk, about halfway up.

"What are we going to do up here?" I asked when I had settled beside him. I swung my legs in the dark.

"I had to get out of the tent," he said. He had the gun propped against the trunk.

We listened to the motors. They seemed to be getting closer, maybe they were, but it was taking a long time.

"Now the birds are stuck in the cold," I said. Blackbirds, I guess they were.

"I forgot they were up here. They almost made me fall—I thought the tree was exploding. Did you like that gas?"

"Ugm."

I thought of the birds huddled on a mud bank, lost in the bushes. Frightening birds seemed a worse error than robbing campers, if error it was.

The vehicles came on. My heart sped up, I could feel it hitting heavily in my chest. Leaves rustled in a light wind, as if the birds were still in the tree. I could see over bushes that the road petered out in the planted pines. If they were coming, they would have to come some other way, else crush trees. Maybe they were driving bulldozers. Maybe there was another road we couldn't see.

"We're as bad off here as in the tent," I said.

"No, we're not." Leaves blocked much of our view. Harold swung back and forth, peering out.

"Don't you remember," I said, "when we played army when we were kids—the guys up in trees always got trapped."

"I just want to see what's coming," he said.

"Well, I'm going down."

"Suit yourself."

I climbed down, threw another stick on the fire in passing and crawled into the tent. Alene woke as I came in.

"What are you crazy people doing?" she said. She spoke through her hair without raising her head.

"We were in the tree."

"What? What tree?"

"The one by the river. Harold's still there. Let me in."

"No. I want to sleep. Why is he in the tree?"

"The jeeps, outlaw buggers after us."

"We're the outlaws."

"We sure are." I got into my bag without taking off clothes or shoes. She turned her face away.

"Go to sleep," she said.

"I don't know if I can." I lay on my back, heart pounding. Cold came through the bag, through the top and bottom.

"Don't lose yourself, boy," she said.

I lay there listening. The engine had hooked to my heartbeat. It must be coming for us. In the night, in this wilderness. I turned over, pulled the bag over my head and pushed myself up on my forearms. In the cave I made I couldn't see, but I could hear. Nothing to think about now: they were coming.

I heard a scrabbling in the tree, then feet running across the clearing and Harold appeared at the flap.

"I see lights," he said. "Let's get out of here."

"Okay." I jumped right up. "Come on, Alene," Harold said shaking her. "Somebody's coming."

"Oh, shit," she said, but she got up and began pulling on her clothes.

Harold collected the supplies while Alene and I wadded up the bags and jerked the tent down. We carried everything to the canoe and threw it in. Alene and Harold got in. I paused on the bank. Harold sat in the bow blowing into his cupped hands.

"Come on," he said.

"Just a minute." I scrambled back up the bank to the clearing and scattered the fire. I stomped the coals into smoke. I could smell the rubber soles of my shoes as I beat the flames down. Vehicles coming through the pines. O, Christ Jesus. I ran to the boat.

"Okay, okay," I cried. I pushed off with the paddle. We glided out into the river. A new moon was up in the west. It held the old moon in its arms. We pulled steadily away from camp, from stalkers drawing closer. Along the banks the reeds were topped with silver. It was a fine, clear night, deep in the heart of winter. This was no time to be on a river. We left the sound of engines behind the third bend but we paddled steadily on into darkness.

"Diminished, I'm diminished," Harold cried.

"Not you, Harold—it's me, goddamn, paddle," I said.

We could follow the course easily past banks darker than the river. Stars shone in the water. I paddled carefully; without entering the rhythm I tried to make each plunge of the paddle into the water as soundless as possible.

Pines gave way to grass; tidal mud stank on the banks. The breeze died. We paddled steadily, as the river, bunched against the sea mouth, twisted on itself.

"Yip, yip," Harold cried, held his empty beer can under until it filled and tossed it ahead of us into darkness. It splashed heavily. "Mullet, jump," he cried, "lost, lost."

"And by the wind grieved," I said, "o mullet, come back again. Alene, hand me a beer."

She threw one back, I cracked it and paddled holding it. The moon had slipped below the horizon. I wanted out of this boat and I placed my hands on the gunwales and rocked it to let them know. Harold lurched and nearly fell in.

"Watch it," he said. I looked back at the thin froth of bubbles trailing. No sounds from the rear but our own wake gurgling.

"Harold, you're not diminished," I called forward, "you're just unsatisfied."

"I am reduced," he replied, "below the level of essentials."

"You people are fools," Alene said. The collar of her parka was turned up around her ears. It pushed her hair up in a dome around her head.

"That's not true," I said. "Harold's upset because we ran out on this cold river."

"Without even snow to obscure us—I can say that. I can tell what I've done."

"What is it, Harold?"

"I've outlawed us," he said.

"You saw lights."

"Maybe it was St. Elmo's fire."

"Swamp gas."

"Farts in the duckweed, quack, quack." He reached behind him into the cooler and drew out another beer.

Tense and angry in the cold, we were little huddling paddling centers of warmth out here in Florida. We wanted to take chances— Harold had run as much because of plain energy as because of marauders—we wanted to frisk, festoon the journey with splashes—I did, at least—but it was cold, the water stung like bees, this was a flimsy boat, it was night and we had to be careful. Alene spit into the water out of a scowl. Harold took his song softly up. It was "Foggy, Foggy Dew," a tune both of us had known since childhood. I joined him, remembering my father singing it when I was little and the fright it gave me to think that the woman of whom he sang—who was clearly not my mother—was the woman he loved.

"You sing like frogs," Alene said.

"But we sing, sugar," Harold answered, "we sing."

He hummed and took it up again. A beautiful woman whom he lost in the foggy, foggy dew.

The tide ran against us. We had to keep paddling or lose ground. My neck ached. When Alene began to curse I shipped my paddle, knelt forward and embraced her. "I am *freezing*," she said.

"Do you want to paddle?"

"No."

"Then there's nothing we can do."

"Let's stop." She held herself tightly under my arms.

"We're near the end of the river—we can stop there. There's nothing along here but mud and grass." Hungry crabs staring out of holes.

"Fuck," she said.

"Why don't you have a beer."

"I don't like beer."

"Okay." I got back on my seat.

We rounded a nearly 180-degree bend. Sticks with strips of cloth tied to the tops marked the channel. I tucked my head and paddled.

The sky lightened in the East. The day came up fair. The river broadened as we approached St. Luke's and a breeze came up, walking the water toward us. Gulls rose from pilings in front of an abandoned marina and wheeled above us crying. An old barge lay half out of the water on the bank, thin waves lapping at the pilothouse. Flour dust floated in patches on the water. A freighter loaded at the mill, its lights faintly gleaming. We passed the city docks. A man in jeans and a blue workshirt swept trash down the public boat ramp. He didn't look up. We slipped past the point where the old Spanish fort slept under live oaks and cedars hung with moss, and headed west along the shore into the refuge. Grass alternated with stretches of gray, seaweed-strewn sand. Grassy islands floated in Oyster Bay, tiny as yards. We reached a beach in the deepest bend of a marshy cove, pulled in and came ashore. Grass grew back from the beach to a sand road and a stand of cedars. A sign on a post in shallow water said: St. Luke's National Wildlife Refuge No Camping No Fires. We spread the poncho on the grass in front of a bank of yaupons, threw the bags down, crawled in and went to sleep under a fair, empty, frozen sky.

X

I woke out of a dream to the sound of geese honking, my heart throbbing like a sting. Harold and Alene were asleep. I got up and walked down to the water. A flock of Canada geese swam out near the point, jostling and talking among themselves. The bay was in a flat calm. Shaggy-headed islands hung low on the horizon far out. One or two had stands of pine rising out of the grass.

In the dream I had been a kind of houseboy for Frieda in a house that I was unfamiliar with. I ran errands and cleaned, I guess. She would smile at me on her way out in the morning. We had been lovers, but we were no longer. I never saw the man she was with now. She teased me, laughing, as she whirled by in a blue dress; I could hear them talking above the sound of a television in the next room. In the morning I would find their empty glasses and rumpled sheets. Even in the dream I felt a pressure to act but could not. Then, for a brief period, the scene shifted and I was walking alone down a sandy road under a canopy of huge live oaks. I was completely at peace. Everything was solved. Later I was at Frieda's again, but I remembered the peace that filled me on the road, and I strained in sleep for the rest of the night, half awake always it seemed, to find my way back there.

I touched my wrist and found the racing pulse. It wasn't going to tell me anything—I knelt and dipped my fingers into the cold water, but I didn't touch myself—better sleep in the eyes than salt. The bay was empty but for the geese, not even oystermen out.

"Good morning," someone said behind me. I turned around. It was an old woman in a long house dress, a gray cardigan sweater and sneakers. She watched me from the road.

"Hello," I said. She crossed the grass, glancing at Harold and Alene, and came up to me.

"Camping?" she asked.

"Yes'm." Her white hair was tied back in a scarf. She was eating a grapefruit half with a spoon.

We looked out at the geese, without saying anything. She spit a seed into the sand. I was glad to see somebody.

"You live here?" I asked.

"For fifty years," she said. She swung her arm toward a green roof among pines. "I live up yonder," she said. "I used to live with my brother, but he died five years ago. Now I'm the only one here."

She spat another seed. "It's a forsaken place," she said.

That was the first time I had heard someone use a word like that in real life. She said it simply, as a fact. There was no emotion in her face or in her voice. I felt a pain in my chest, suddenly, like a heart attack. I filled with something and I wanted to sit down. Things were simpler than I had thought. You just lived quietly and there life was, honking in the bay. In my dream I had walked on the road happy as a ghost. She looked at me.

"You feel all right?" she asked.

"I don't know," I said.

"Well, it'd be terrible if you did—you got a white face."

"I been out of the light," I said.

"Hadn't we all." She looked out at the bay. "When I was a girl this bay was full of geese. We used to scoop feathers off the water for pillows. You could fill a mattress in a morning." The geese bobbed in the water, honking.

"I wish I had one," I said. "Let me sit down here." I sat down on the sand. Cold came through my pants. I felt like things were getting solved whether I wanted them to or not. Frieda was lost to me no matter what I did. I had wanted to hold her even if I had to imagine her naked in her lank-haired lover's arms. I didn't care, didn't care. But there was something else, something else besides watching through a crack in a hall door as my wife fucked another man. Things could be released. I was going to break if I didn't let go of my hold. And here, this woman walks up in sneakers, her freckled hands now holding her sweater around her, a man's sweater with buttons carved from antlers . . . perhaps her brother's sweater. If the place was forsaken she seemed all right. I couldn't say. Perhaps the sweater was her brother's. But what could this sadness be if it wasn't for Frieda?

"Why, you know it snowed here evening before last," she said abruptly. "It was the first snow I've seen in ten years."

"It caught us on the river," I said.

"Which river?"

"Crystal."

"I don't care much for the woods in these kinds of days," she said.

"It didn't do us much good either."

She turned and looked at Harold and Alene who lay close against each other, in separate bags, asleep.

"That looks like a hard way to do it," she said.

"Well, we're not orphans. We're out here for fun." Did she mean fucking?

"I believe indoors is where I'd look for it. But then," she said, "the woods is wide and you can find God's beauty in there."

"It goes both ways."

"I reckon." She squeezed grapefruit juice into her mouth. "If y'all want something hot to eat you can come up here to the house—I'm going to be eating lunch directly."

"We'd like that."

"By myself I get out of the habit of cooking, what with just one person. But y'all are welcome to come. I've got some soup."

"We will then."

She turned to go, then stopped. "I'm out here walking for my doctor," she said. "He says it helps my blood and I have to do it three times a day." She swung her arm as if she might throw the grapefruit husk, but then she let her hand fall still holding it. "I don't mind the walking," she said. "I think I could look out at this bay all day long. I've learned that now." She started away.

"You and your friends come up to the house if you want," she said half turning back.

"All right. We'll be there when I can get them up."

"Good-bye then."

"See you later."

She walked away up the road, bending forward slightly, as if she had walked for a long time with a cane that was no longer there.

I looked out. The geese were too far away to be scared by us. Unless Alene took a notion to bag one for brunch. But a .410 wasn't going to kill from here, not with quail shot in the load.

I ran a few steps down the beach and slowed to a walk. Thin waves, like the remnants of our own light wake, slipped noiselessly up the sand and fell back. Small blue crabs hunkered in the clear water near shore; they scurried away as I passed. The sky was high and white, the sun shone weakly through. There was nothing on the point but grass giving up to water. I turned around and came back.

"O, children," I called when I reached the camp, "time to rise."

Harold looked up.

"Doggie bag," he said. "You, Jack, bring my doggie and my doggie bag. Are the cops out there?"

"In three Mercedes outboards," I said, kneeling on my bag. "They're armed with .12 gauge pumps and they say this time they're not fooling."

"Tell them I'll be with them shortly." He yawned. "Is that geese honking?"

"Sure is."

"My Lord, look at them." The geese had drifted out toward the center of the bay; they were still far out.

"I used to come down here hunting with my daddy and the preacher when I was little," he said. "Must have been down here half a dozen tunes without ever firing a gun."

"Firing one now wouldn't set the table."

He sat up. "Look at them—just talking to themselves. Was somebody here?"

"Yeah. An old woman; she lives up there. She said this was a forsaken place."

"Forsaken by whom?"

"The county commissioners, I guess. She asked us up to lunch."

"I'm for that."

"Well, let's go." I shook my shoulders. I was nervous. I wanted to keep moving and I didn't like the way Harold was sucking his teeth. I wanted to run across the land. I got up and walked down to the water.

Harold had told me a story once of a friend of his in Vietnam who had fallen out of a helicopter. They had been in a field getting picked up, his friend had climbed aboard, the helicopter had taken off, but about fifty feet above the ground it made a sudden lurch and his friend fell out the open door. He landed on his back in the field ("I could have caught him," Harold had said) and immediately tried to get up.

"We had to hold him down," Harold had said. "He kept saying over and over, 'I got to go, I got to go,'—his eyes were wild, no, not wild, just focused on something else; he rolled back and forth in our arms."

"It was strange," he had said, "he was broken up inside and he thought he could run away from it—from his body."

I kicked a clot of seaweed into the water. It seemed, at that moment, all I wanted to do, too—run my ass down the road. I went over to the canoe and got a pickled egg out of the jar. I wonder what the freezing point of vinegar is. Silver fingerling fish played around the stern of the canoe. For yards out I could see the bottom, the sand ridged like muscles.

"You down there martyrizing?" Harold called. "You decided to remain aloof?"

I turned around. "I've decided you don't know how to pickle eggs," I said.

"What?" He came up, pulling my sweater over his head. He spoke through wool. "You say that to the culinary wizard of the country?" His rusty head popped through. "Here, let me have a bite." I gave him the egg.

"They haven't been in long enough," he said chewing. "I just set them up last week."

"And more pepper," I said, "they need more hot pepper."

"That's your affliction," he said, "which reminds me—I was thinking about oysters last night. We ought to stop at Pony's on the way back and get some."

"And some smoked mullet."

"Oh yes—but I heard they don't have it anymore. The town passed an ordinance against burning inside the city limits, so they can't run the smoker."

"Eejits."

Alene had risen and was bent over tying her bag. What a fine ass in jeans. She had on one of my sweaters, too. She came down to us, carrying the bag.

"Which way now?" she said. She threw the bag in the canoe.

"Up there." I pointed at the green roof.

"What for?" She pushed her hair back with both hands.

"An old lady asked us up to lunch."

"Is that who you were talking to?"

"It certainly was." I touched her breast through the sweater. Soft nipple sleeping.

"Are those geese?" she asked. She shaded her eyes with her hand though the sky was not bright.

"Yes," I said.

"Why don't you shoot one?"

"Alene—we can't shoot everything. That woman who was just here told me that when she was a girl they used to gather down off the water and make pillows out of it."

"Isn't that something." She reached into the canoe and pulled out the gun. "Let me see if I can hit one."

"Ah agh," I said. "Don't you do that." I grabbed the gun by the barrel and held it pointed away down the beach.

"Quit it," she cried, trying to jerk loose.

I pulled the gun up, it fired into the sky and I took it away from her. She reached for it, then dropped her hands.

"You shitpiss," she said. Her eyes were cold and murderous. She was willing to shoot me. Something changed in me when I saw that look. I knew how it was for her, how it was going to be.

"There's no reason to kill those birds," I said. "Just cut the shit out."

"You don't do that," she said. "You don't do that." She turned her face away and looked out at the bay. Her eyes could have blasted the whole flock. I felt terrible, and relieved. I had broken the back of my little romance. Then, I nearly reeled away, as the shadow I had called up on the river seemed to move toward me out of the corner of my eye. I touched Alene's rigid shoulder. She snapped my hand away.

"Don't touch me, shit," she said.

"Alene . . . damn, don't."

"You all don't hurt yourselves," Harold said quietly. "Let's go up and get lunch."

He started up the road. We stayed where we were. He stopped.

"Alene," he said, "come on. Aren't you hungry?"

She turned, without looking at me, and followed him, without speaking. I let them get ahead, then followed, too, feeling that I had torn another chance loose and lost it, feeling my penis rise as I watched her ass move in her jeans—not shadows—and I walked along that way, behind them, Harold's hand resting casually on Alene's shoulder, me trailing, touching myself through cloth as I walked.

The house was screened-in across the front and around one side. A galvanized pipe ran off the roof into a wooden water tank. Lank, freeze-burned azaleas grew in the dirt yard. Harold held the porch door open for Alene and waited on the top step for me. I came up adjusting my crotch. He looked at me and smiled but said nothing.

The porch was bare except for a twine seine net folded in a pile next to the front door and a swing hung by chains from a rafter at one end. Alene bent to look through curtained front windows.

"Whose is this?" she asked. "It looks like a funeral parlor."

I knocked on the front door. I heard footsteps and the old woman pulled the curtain back and looked out through the glass panel. She opened the door.

"Come on in the house," she said. She turned her back and was already heading down a dark, carpeted hallway when we got through the door. "Come on to the kitchen," she said. I caught up with her as she banged through a screen door onto another porch that ran along the back ell of the house.

"I just leave that front," she said. "I can't afford to heat it and I don't even turn on the lights." In the backyard a few chickens scratched at dirt. A barbed-wire fence separated the yard from an open lot that was backed by a fallen-in barn and shed. A gourd martin house hung from the top of a pole between the barn and the shed.

"We can eat in the kitchen," she said. Her sneakers squeaked on the bare boards.

She led us into a high-ceilinged kitchen that was bright with light. Geraniums flowered in cans in the windows. We sat down at a table that was covered with a flowered plastic cloth. She crossed the room to a pot steaming on the stove.

"You mind helping me, honey?" she said to Alene as she lifted the pot off the stove.

"No, thank you," Alene said.

"I'll get it," Harold said quickly and took the pot. "Where do you want it?"

"Just put it right over here on the table—wait a minute." She folded a towel and placed it under the pot. I rose.

"I'll get the bowls," I said. Alene stared at the door.

"They're in the cabinet," the old woman said.

I picked four bowls and saucers out of mixed crockery and set them on the table. The woman lay spoons on the cloth.

"Y'all want bread?" she said.

"You betcha," Harold said.

She took a half loaf from the refrigerator. "Milk?"

"Fine," I said. She set the bread and a quart of milk on the table. "There." She sat down and tucked her head in a quick, wordless grace. She looked up. "Y'all eat," she said.

The soup was vegetable. I blew into a spoonful and tasted it. It was just what I needed. Whole tomatoes flaccid as the hornet's nest. Oh, oh. I took another spoonful, closed my eyes and ate.

"I'm Miss Alma Brannen," the old woman said. "I'm glad to have you here."

"I'm Jack Dupree," I said. "This is Harold Johnson."

Alene said nothing. She leaned close to her bowl spooning in soup.

"Who are you, darling?" Miss Brannen asked.

"I'm the one that got shamelessly hauled down here," she said.

"You did? Why is that?"

"Kidnapped," Alene said.

"This is Alene," Harold said. "This cold's got us tired out." Alene gave him a hard look. She took a slice of bread, ripped it in half and dunked it in her soup.

"I'm not too tired," she said.

"Lord, I am," Harold said. "I felt the cold all night long."

"If you hadn't got scared and run," Alene laughed. "Crackers," she said.

"Well, I'm an old cracker woman myself," Miss Brannen said. "Florida cracker. I been down here crackering on this bay all my life."

"I don't see how you stand it," Alene said. "I know I couldn't."

"Be thankful you don't have to, then," Miss Brannen said and laughed through perfect false teeth.

"Don't you worry," Alene said.

I felt like slugging the little maniac. Christ, Alene. The cuffs of her parka were dirty, but the wrist that slipped out as she raised the spoon was clean and white. She held her hair out of her soup and didn't look at anybody. And I wanted to touch her. I wanted to sit on sunny back steps with the scent of her hair in my nostrils as she leaned against me and think about my dream. How peaceful I had felt walking on that road. But, though the trees I could see through the window opposite were green—cabbage palms and pines—it was winter and the sky above branches was that high whooping white, whiter than pearl, that appears in winter only, and what would the dream mean to Alene, and to Frieda flossing in sheets next door? I picked a butter bean off the side of my bowl. This was enough—I was thankful, thankful enough to be in this warm kitchen eating soup. And maybe I didn't need to press my face into Alene's gray-stained hair at all. Wrenching the gun away from her had done me good. The little explosion of action had popped me out of myself. Frieda's grip—someone's—had for a moment weakened.

I looked at Alene as she thrust her fierce face toward her bowl. For a second I saw the thing in her face, her look—brows bunched—the thing that was as different from me and what I knew as I was different from geese cruising in the bay: it was a lie, this easy kitchen relaxation, this warm soup—there was no dream, there was no shadow, there was simply this woman here, simply fine dark hairs on a clean wrist, simply her, now, I wanted, and I reached across the table and with one finger touched a wisp of hair in front of her ear.

"Whatever you do is all right," I said. "I'm sorry about before—I don't expect anything of you."

She flicked my hand away. "I don't worry about that," she said.

Miss Brannen rose. "Let me get you some more soup," she said.

"I wouldn't mind a bit," Harold said getting up, too.

"I'm fine," I said.

Instead of answering, Alene got up, placed her spoon next to her bowl and walked out onto the porch. I watched her wash her hands in the sink, dry them on a towel, then stand looking into the yard. She raised her arms and pressed her open palms against the screen. It was a gesture a man might make, and the way she cocked her knee forward, keeping her weight on the other leg, was a man's attitude, too. I had never seen a woman do that.

At the stove Miss Brannen filled the bowl Harold held.

"I don't usually make this much soup—or make soup at all—" she said, "but I've been collecting leftovers for a week and this morning I decided to go ahead."

"It's delicious," Harold said. "Just a little more."

"Wouldn't you like some more—Jack?" she asked me.

"No, thank you. What day is today?"

"Sunday," she said.

I couldn't keep my eyes off Alene. She stood stiffly, looking out, her palms flat against the screen. As I watched she thrust her hair back smoothly with one hand and turned. Her face was calm though her eyes didn't seem to be seeing us.

"A car just drove into the yard," she said and turned back to the screen.

"It's probably Jimmy Peters," Miss Brannen said, crossing to the door.

"Who is that?" Harold asked.

"The ranger." She paused with her hand on the latch. "He'll probably tell you not to camp here," she said. "They're right touchy about it; and Jimmy is one of the touchiest." She went out.

"Oh, fuck," Harold said looking at me. "The bastard is looking for us."

He jumped up and ran to the back window and came back to the table. "We'd better get out of here," he said.

"You think so?" My heart pounded, but not for fear of capture only.

"Come on," he said, going out the door.

For a moment I couldn't move. My shoulders were heavy as cement though a sharp pain had shot suddenly through them. Four bowls on plastic cloth, three empty, one full; four spoons. Geraniums in the window. Sweet potato roots crawling in a jar. All right. All right. I pushed myself up with both hands. Another slice of bread for the energy that was in it. Thank you, Miss B., but we've got to run.

Harold ran down the back steps ahead of Alene. I followed with the slice of white bread in my mouth.

"We can cut through the woods," Harold said.

We ducked under the fence and ran through the lot scattering chickens. Behind us in the house someone yelled, but no matter, we dashed between barn and shed (my hand slapping the martin house pole for luck), into woods.

The ground was covered with leaves and pine straw. The woods, dark and gummy in summer, rattlesnake and chigger woods, were stiff and odorless. A branch lashed my face. I caught up with Alene and ran beside her. Ahead, Harold fought as he ran, forcing branches back, but Alene ran as if she were the leader of an easy race: upright, head back, hardly bothering with snaps of undergrowth.

We broke out into the marsh and ran through the tough, waist-high grass toward the canoe. Fiddler crabs slipped into holes, quick as roaches. The geese still floated in the bay. Such a high reach of sky I wanted suddenly to tear through. Alene! Alene! I touched her parka, my fingers slid down its nylon skin, but we could not stop for caresses. There ahead the canoe, left dry by tide; it sat, flat as a shoe, in sand.

We reached the beach as the ranger was getting out of his government pickup.

"Hey," he said, "wait a minute," and crossed the grass, holding his gun in its holster.

We walked to the canoe and stopped beside it. Harold touched the bow, brushed off nothing and straightened up.

The ranger came up to us. He was tall and wore a cap.

"I want to speak to you," he said.

"Okay," Harold said, "I got a minute."

"I don't," Alene said, "I'm going."

"Be quiet, Alene," Harold said. It was the first time he had spoken harshly to her. He reached for her but she pulled her arm away.

"No, thank you," she said.

"Come up here to the truck," the ranger said. He unsnapped his gun and ran his hand along the butt. The pain in my shoulders had moved into my chest. Wait, wait just a minute—we're all right.

"I'm not going with *you*," Alene said to the ranger. He started to speak as she whirled on us. "And I'm not going with *you*," she said. She began to drag the canoe by the stern into the water.

"You wait right there," the ranger said. He took a step forward.

"No," Alene said. She waded into the water pulling the canoe. We didn't move.

"I can't let you go," the ranger said and grabbed the canoe by the bow.

"You can't do anything about it, squirt," Alene said. She got in the canoe. It rocked, barely afloat, in the shallow water.

"Stop it right there," the ranger cried.

"Shit." She laughed and reached for the gun that lay across the boxes in front of her. The ranger reached for his gun, too, but he wasn't as fast as Alene. From the waist she had the .410 leveled at him before his pistol was halfway out of the holster. "You dummy," she said.

The ranger's face went white. For a second I thought she was going to shoot him. But she didn't. She didn't back down on it though, she just had other plans.

She made him ease his gun out and throw it into the bay. Then, with a cargo rope, she made Harold tie the ranger up. She didn't bother with us.

"What now?" Harold said, trying to joke. He was smiling hard.

"I don't care what happens to you," she said, crossed the grass and got in the truck.

"Easy come, easy go," Harold said.

I touched my face; there were tears. I had an impulse to follow her, to go where she was going, to see one more time how she banged past whatever was trying to stop her, to learn whatever lesson I hadn't learned from Frieda, but I stayed where I was.

She leaned out of the window. "You'll just have to learn to live with it, sport," she said, I guess to me. Then she wrenched the truck into gear and gunned it out of there.

Nobody ever saw her again, nobody I ever heard about. They found the truck two days later on a street in Mobile. Alene was wanted before she pulled the gun on the ranger and we had a lot of talking to do, but in the end, after a nonjury trial in Tallahassee, we got off with a couple years probation.

She said I'd have to learn to live with it, whatever it was. That is what I am doing.

Issue 88, 1983

Contributors

Rick Bass is the author of several books of fiction and nonfiction, including a novel, *Where the Sea Used to Be*. His most recent book is *The Hermit's Story*, a collection of short stories.

Charles Baxter is the author of several novels and story collections, including *The Feast of Love*. His most recent book is *Saul and Patsy: A Novel*.

Frederick Busch is the author of numerous novels and story collections, including *The Night Inspector*. His most recent book is *A Memory of War*.

Elizabeth Gilbert is the author of several books, including the novel *Stern Men*. Her most recent work is *The Last American Man*.

Denis Johnson is the author of several novels and story collections, including *Jesus' Son*. His most recent work is *Shoppers: Two Plays*.

Miranda July is a performer, filmmaker, and writer. Her fiction has been published in *The Harvard Review, The Mississippi Review,* and *Tin House*.

James Lasdun received the Sundance Film Festival's best dramatic feature and screenplay awards in 1997 for *Sunday*. His most recent book is *Walking and Eating in Tuscany and Umbria*.

Malinda McCollum's stories have appeared in *The Pushcart Prize XXVII, McSweeney's, EPOCH,* and *Zyzzyva*.

Ben Okri has published many books of fiction and nonfiction, including *The Famished Road,* for which he received the Booker Prize. His most recent work is the novel *Astonishing the Gods*.

Julie Orringer is the author of *How to Breathe Underwater: Stories*.

Annie Proulx is the author of numerous novels and story collections, including *The Shipping News,* for which she won the Pulitzer Prize. Her most recent work is *Bad Dirt: Wyoming Stories 2*.

Mary Robison is the author of numerous novels and story collections, including *Tell Me: Thirty Stories*. Her most recent work is *Why Did I Ever,* a novel.

Norman Rush received the National Book Award for his novel *Mating*. His most recent work is *Mortals*.

Joanna Scott received a Guggenheim and MacArthur Foundation Fellowship in 1993. The author of several novels and a story collection, her most recent book is *Tourmaline*.

Charlie Smith, a Guggenheim Fellow, has published numerous books of fiction and poetry. His most recent work is *Women of America,* a collection of poems.

Richard Stern is the author of numerous novels and story collections, including *Noble Rot: Stories 1949–1988*. His most recent work is *Pacific Tremors,* a novel.

Wells Tower's work has appeared in *The Believer, Fence,* and *The Anchor Book of New American Short Stories*.

Acknowledgments

Rick Bass, "The Hermit's Story" © 1998 by Rick Bass.

Charles Baxter, "Westland" © 1986 by Charles Baxter.

Frederick Busch, "Widow Water" © 1974 by Frederick Busch.

Elizabeth Gilbert, "The Famous Torn and Restored Lit Cigarette Trick" © 1996 by Elizabeth Gilbert. Reprinted with the permission of The Wylie Agency, Inc.

Denis Johnson, "Train Dreams" © 2002 by Denis Johnson.

James Lasdun, "Snow" © 1987 by James Lasdun.

Ben Okri, "The Dream-Vendor's August" © 1987 by Ben Okri.

Julie Orringer, "When She Is Old and I Am Famous" © 1998 by Julie Orringer.

Annie Proulx, "The Wamsutter Wolf" © 2004 by Dead Line Ltd. Reprinted with the permission of Scribner, an imprint of Simon & Schuster Adult Publishing Group. From *Bad Dirt: Wyoming Stories 2* by Annie Proulx.

Mary Robison, "Likely Lake" © 2002 by Mary Robison. Reprinted with the permission of The Wylie Agency, Inc.

Norman Rush, "Instruments of Seduction" © 1984 by Norman Rush. Reprinted with the permission of The Wylie Agency, Inc.

Joanna Scott, "A Borderline Case" © 1992 by Joanna Scott.

Charlie Smith, "Crystal River" © 1983 by Charlie Smith.

Richard Stern, "Audit" © 1974 by TriQuarterly Books.